Praise for Elle Croft

'An original and thrilling page-turner with an end I didn't see coming'   **Victoria Selman**

'I couldn't put this down. Pacy and gripping'   **Cass Green**

'A relentless and intense pace that kept me completely rapt and eager to find out answers. I loved the final twist'
KL Slater

'A gripping psychological thriller. Skilfully plotted – I just couldn't put it down. And the ending! You just have to read it. I am looking forward to more from Elle Croft'
Patricia Gibney

'A gripping tale of betrayal, deceit, and duplicity. The ending will stay with you long after you've finished the last page. Fabulous'   **Jenny Blackhurst**

'*The Guilty Wife* will make you question those closest to you as the plot unfolds at pace, with an ending that pulls the rug from under your feet'   **Phoebe Morgan**

'Twisty and fast-moving, *The Guilty Wife* kept me guessing until the very end! A great read'   **Isabel Ashdown**

'What a clever idea! This kept me reading through the night...'   **Jane Corry**

Elle Croft was born in South Africa, grew up in Australia and moved to the UK in 2010 after travelling around the world with her husband. She works as a freelance social media specialist and also blogs about travel, food and life in London.

Follow Elle on Twitter @elle_croft to find out more.

Also by Elle Croft

The Guilty Wife
The Other Sister

Like Mother Like Daughter

ELLE CROFT

ORION

An Orion paperback

First published in Great Britain in 2020
by Orion Fiction,
This paperback edition published in 2020
by Orion Fiction,
an imprint of The Orion Publishing Group Ltd,
Carmelite House, 50 Victoria Embankment
London EC4Y 0DZ

An Hachette UK Company

1 3 5 7 9 10 8 6 4 2

A CIP catalogue record for this book
is available from the British Library.

ISBN (Paperback) 978 1 4091 8723 3

Typeset at The Spartan Press Ltd,
Lymington, Hants

Printed and bound in Great Britain by Clays Ltd,
Elcograf S.p.A.

www.orionbooks.co.uk

This one's for Adelaide, the city where I fell in love with books, beaches and Brendan.

Prologue

SALLY

Serial killer.

It has a ring to it, don't you think? A certain... prestige. A little thrill that runs up the spine and ignites the imagination at the utterance of those two words.

I know, I know; I shouldn't revel in it. I'm well aware of that, and yet... well, I suppose you could say that my macabre title is more than I could ever have hoped to achieve in this life. It's my legacy. My name will be written into history books and talked about well after I die. People – smart, successful, well-respected people – will study me, will talk about me, will spend years wishing they could somehow get inside my brain. Wishing that they could understand.

If I hadn't done what I did, I'd be forgotten. I'd die unknown, except to a handful of people, who themselves would be unheard of. I'd have no achievements to my name, no one would even notice that I was gone. It's not why I did it; I didn't crave the notoriety. I never planned this. But I can't pretend it isn't a bonus.

My honesty is surprising to some, but it shouldn't be. So many people out there would kill – only figuratively, of course – to have what I have. To be immortalised the way I have been.

They'd deny it, acting outraged at the mere suggestion

1

that they envy me. People are so precious about distancing themselves from the darkness inside of them. Everyone wants to pretend that they don't have it, that they are free from demons, untethered from their basest impulses. But depravity is there, lurking inside each and every one of us. For some, like myself, it's a deeper shade of darkness, a shadow filling my lungs like oxygen and pulsing through my bloodstream. Feeding me, nurturing me. For others, perhaps, it's tamer, a creature that occasionally wends its way around their conscience, reminding them of its presence. But whether loud and raging or timid and mewling, it's there. In everyone.

If only the others could throw off the burden of expectation. If only, like me, they could allow themselves to surrender completely to their true nature. But they won't. They can't. They care too deeply about 'Doing the Right Thing', even if 'Doing the Right Thing' is little more than a social construct, designed to subdue the masses, to control the behaviour of the many.

If everyone was brave like me, I suppose the label 'serial killer' would hold less power. It would be the ordinary, not the exceptional.

So, no. I shouldn't take pride in it. Logic tells me that. Society tells me that. But it's who I am. And, in the end, everyone in this country knows my name. I'll just take a stab in the dark here (pun obviously intended) and say that that's a hell of a lot more than you can claim.

So tell me: who's the real success here?

PART ONE

Chapter 1

KAT

My hands grip the steering wheel, my knuckles leached of their colour. I glance distractedly in the rear-view mirror, catching a glimpse of my paler-than-usual face as I check for traffic. Indicating, I turn the wheel, steering onto the side road and then into the already full parking lot, my heart thudding, my mouth dry.

Taking a deep, shaking breath, I tap the screen in front of me and select 'Redial'. As it rings, I lean forward and stare through the windscreen at the giant Australian flag sailing above the building's entrance, white stars flapping against the backdrop of a cloudless blue sky.

'Hey, Kat, what's up?' My husband's voice, usually an instant injection of calm, isn't enough to stop the bubble of anxiety from ballooning in my chest.

'Hi, um, can you come home please?'

'I'm right in the middle of getting this frame up, so it's not a great time. Everything OK?'

Of course it's not a good time. But, then again, is there ever a convenient moment for something like this? Dylan needs this job, and needs to do it well; the house he's building in that new suburb down south is the first big contract he's had in months. If he impresses this client, the referrals could keep his business booming for years, so he's been working flat out for weeks, regardless of the weather. I don't know how he does it – lugging timber and climbing scaffolding and driving forklifts in the scalding sun – but he says he's used to it after so many years.

'No, not really,' I say. 'I just got to the school. Apparently, Imogen . . . well, they're saying she punched someone.'

Saying the words out loud sounds like a betrayal. Of our daughter, of everything we've worked so hard for, of our secrets.

A rush of air fills the car from my speakers. Dylan's quick intake of breath. Shock, to match mine.

'That's my girl.'

I catch his words, despite them being muttered almost under his breath.

'Dylan!'

It was never a secret that Dylan dreamed of having a son. He had visions of kicking a football around in the backyard with a brown-haired little boy who would take over his business after transforming into a man, who he could have a beer with and light bonfires with and whatever else it is that men imagine doing with their sons. I wonder, not for the first time, if he wishes things had been different. If he regrets the decision we made all those years ago. If he'd prefer to have tonight's stern talk about peaceful conflict resolution with a boy.

'What?' he says, interrupting my thoughts. 'I'm not allowed to be proud of my daughter for standing up for herself?'

'We don't know what happened yet. We don't know if she *was* standing up for herself.'

'Well, I choose to believe the best in people. Especially my own children. So, unless I'm presented with proof that suggests otherwise, I'll be assuming that Imogen was doing the right thing.'

He doesn't need to say the words *unlike you*. They fill the car, swelling around me.

'Please don't tell her that punching someone is the right thing,' I groan, my anxiety gradually dissipating. Maybe I was blowing this out of proportion. Perhaps Dylan is right, and it's just a misunderstanding. I nod, even though he can't see me. 'You're right. I'm not going to jump to conclusions.'

'Exactly,' he says. 'Wait till you have all the facts.'

'Just get home as soon as you can, please. I don't want to deal with this on my own.'

'OK,' he agrees. 'Just let me get the guys started on this roof, and I'll head home as soon as I can.'

He hangs up and I let the silence wash over me. Talking with Dylan temporarily calmed my nerves, but now I'm left to walk into the school office alone, to complete the parental version of a walk of shame without any backup.

The heat of the day blasts me as I step out of my air-conditioned cocoon and follow the line of gum trees to the school office.

I'm met with unconcealed contempt when I introduce myself to the receptionist, stepping aside so the bunch of pink roses in the vase on her desk is shielded from view.

'Oh, hello Mrs Braidwood,' the silver-haired woman says, looking me up and down judgementally, as though my daughter punching someone is somehow my fault. I suppose, indirectly, it is. It's always the mother's fault, isn't it?

After a thoroughly disapproving look-over, I'm led down a corridor with small rooms on the left-hand side. Sick bays, presumably, although I've never been to this part of the school before. The door to the first room is open, and I peer inside. Sitting on the bed, sobbing quietly, is a girl with dark hair and features, an enormous bruise blooming across her left eye and blood smeared underneath her nose. My veins turn icy. Did my daughter really do that?

Somewhere in the dark recesses of my mind, an old, nagging fear begins to rise. I force it back down, knowing it won't do anyone any good for me to dwell on those thoughts. It didn't help me then, and it won't help me now. And revisiting those anxieties certainly won't help Imogen. She's my focus now.

Breathing deeply in an attempt to slow my heartbeat, I continue following the receptionist down the corridor. She gestures into the next room. There's my daughter, blonde and lithe, tall and poised. The complete opposite of the distraught young woman I saw in the room next door.

'Imogen!' I say, rushing towards her. 'Are you OK? What happened?'

I'm desperate for her to tell me that she was defending some younger girl's honour, or that she was stopping a bully, that she had no other choice, that she knows it was wrong but she didn't know what else she could possibly do in the moment.

She stares at the floor and says nothing.

'Immy?'

'She hasn't said anything since the fight,' says a voice from behind me.

I turn to find a nurse, young and stern – and clearly unimpressed – standing in the corner.

'OK, but what happened?'

'The students won't say,' she replies, her lips drawn into a tight, thin line. 'Emerald – the girl who was assaulted – says it was unprovoked. There weren't any witnesses, so it seems like it's your daughter's word against hers.'

Dylan's declaration from our phone conversation echoes

in my mind: *Unless I'm presented with proof that suggests otherwise, I'll be assuming that Imogen was doing the right thing.* I should be making the same assumption. She's my daughter. I should trust her over anyone else.

But there it is again: that fear, like a creature in hibernation, long-forgotten but still alive. Curled up in some dark corner, strengthening and growing and waiting for the opportune moment to strike.

'Well, I stand by whatever my daughter says happened,' I say, hoping my voice doesn't betray my doubts.

Imogen looks up at me in sharp surprise.

'As I mentioned, she hasn't said,' the nurse points out sarcastically.

I narrow my eyes at her and pick up Imogen's school bag.

'Come on,' I say to my daughter. Then, turning to the nurse, 'I'm taking her home.'

'That's fine, Mrs Braidwood, but you will need to speak to the principal to discuss next steps and potential disciplinary action.'

'Fine. I'll call her,' I snap. 'Right now, my main concern is my daughter and making sure she's OK.'

She begins protesting, but I tune her out.

Imogen follows me out of the head office, past the receptionist who's calling my name and into the car park, where I let out a long, trembling breath. We get into the car without a word, and I start the engine, driving away from the school with my heart in my throat.

It's only when we're halfway home that I risk glancing at my daughter. She's staring straight ahead, looking younger than her sixteen years in her blue and green striped polo shirt. Her hair is poker-straight and unruffled, her clothing intact, only a tiny smear of blood on her chest that indicates anything is amiss. She must have cleaned herself up.

9

She's calm, no trace of a violent incident to be found in her posture, on her face. A thrill of fear ripples down my spine.

Focusing on the road again, I use the distraction of changing lanes as a chance to compose myself, to dispel the image of Emerald, blood pooling under her nose, tears coursing down her cheeks.

I clear my throat, unsure how to broach the subject, how to ask the questions burning in my chest without starting a fight. She's difficult to talk to at the best of times, and this certainly doesn't count as one of those.

'Mum,' she says.

Out of the corner of my eye, I glimpse her head swivelling to face me. I keep my focus on the road.

'Yes?'

I can barely breathe while I wait for her to speak again. I have no idea what she's going to say, but I desperately want her to tell me she didn't do it, that it was all a big misunderstanding. Or at least that it wasn't her fault, that she's the victim in this. Not the poor girl with the crushed nose and black eye.

'Thanks,' she says.

I wait for more, but nothing else comes. I whip my head around, but she's focused on something ahead of us again, her arms crossed over her chest.

'That's it?' I'm incredulous. 'That's all I get, just, "thanks"?'

'Mum—'

'Imogen, I didn't stand up for you in there so you could just carry on and pretend nothing happened. I need to hear from you exactly what made you assault that poor girl—'

'*Assault* her?!' Imogen yells. 'So much for believing whatever I tell you. You've clearly just jumped to your own conclusion, as always. So what was that back there, were you just acting the part? Did Dad tell you to stand up for me?'

'I saw her face, Imogen,' I say through clenched teeth, struggling to control my emotions. I wish Dylan were here; he'd know how to speak to our daughter without starting a war. He'd believe the best in her. He'd know how to trust her.

'Yeah? Well, did you see what happened, too?'

'No, but—'

'But nothing, Mum,' she says, flipping her hair over her shoulder. 'If you didn't see it, maybe you should keep a lid on your opinion. Otherwise you're just as bad as that bitch of a nurse.'

'Imogen!'

'What? She *is* a bitch, everyone knows it.'

My blood is pounding behind my eyes, a mix of rage and panic. Panic that I can't get through to her. That my fears aren't just deep-seated paranoia. I take a breath and try to imagine what Dylan would say.

'I'm sorry I jumped to conclusions,' I say, forcing the words past the lump in my throat. 'I should have waited for you to explain what happened.'

Silence.

'So . . . what happened?'

I keep my eyes ahead as I turn off the main road, too nervous to look at my daughter in case my fragile calm is shattered.

'I can't tell you,' she says quietly.

'What do you mean, you can't tell me?'

'I just . . . I really need you to trust me, Mum. I can't tell you what happened, but I can say that I didn't *assault* Emerald. I was . . . helping someone.'

Relief washes over me, but it's only temporary. I want to

11

believe that Imogen was doing the right thing, but what she's saying doesn't make sense. My relief is replaced almost immediately by more questions, more doubt. 'Was Emerald bullying someone?'

'Mum, I just told you, I can't say.'

'Why not?' I ask as I pull the car into our driveway. I turn the engine off, and as Imogen reaches to grab the door handle, I grip her arm lightly. 'Imogen. Answer me, please.'

'God, Mum,' she huffs, wrenching her arm away from me and opening the door with as much force as she can muster. 'What part of "I can't say" don't you understand? Why can't you ever just take my word for it? I thought you were on my side, but you're not. You never are.'

She climbs out and slams the door, stalking towards the house as the car reverberates. I stay buckled in, my body trembling, my mind whirring, wondering what happened to my sweet little girl. But I don't need to wonder; I know what happened. She grew up. This is just normal, hormonal teenage behaviour.

Isn't it?

That voice, the one that's been nagging at me since I received the phone call from the school, is growing louder and more insistent, gnawing away at me, eroding any confidence I might have had in my daughter's version of events.

I close my eyes.

'No,' I whisper out loud. 'She's just a teenager. That's all this is. It's just a phase.'

And an inner voice comes echoing back, loud and clear, sending a chill down my spine, despite the baking heat.

But what if it's not a phase? it taunts. *What if that's exactly who she is?*

Chapter 2

IMOGEN

Slowly, methodically, Imogen rubbed the sudsy plate with a damp tea towel, going over the same spot again and again, smearing the water around rather than drying it. She could hear her parents whispering in the living room, discussing her. Well, not so much her as *the incident*. She tried to imagine their conversation. Her dad, level-headed and determined to avoid conflict, would be telling her mum to give their daughter a chance, to listen to her point of view. And her mum, who seemed to believe that there wasn't a single good bone in Imogen's body, would be coming up with every excuse not to trust her.

Imogen closed her eyes tightly, letting resentment take over. But then a memory surfaced – her mum's dismissal of the school nurse, the way she had marched Imogen out of the office – twisting around the edges of her carefully arranged rage. She felt a surge of . . . what was that? Pride? Affection, maybe. It wasn't anger, anyway. And that made things complicated, which was the last thing she needed. She'd had enough of complicated.

It seemed that, over and over, Imogen was learning that life wasn't fair, no matter how desperately she wanted it to be. She'd done the only thing she could have done earlier that day at school with Emerald. She didn't have any other choice, she was certain of it. But she couldn't explain herself without making everything so much worse, so she just had to let everyone assume the worst about her. Imogen knew that wasn't who she was – who she *really* was.

She almost let out a bark of laughter. What would her mum know about who she really was, anyway? She couldn't see what was right in front of her.

'Imogen?' Her dad's raised voice cut through the whispers.

Imogen finished wiping the plate, placing it carefully in the cupboard above her before walking through to the living room, tea towel hanging limply by her side.

She stood in the doorway and absorbed the scene: her dad sitting on the sofa, his hands clasped awkwardly in his lap – his serious pose. And her mum standing with her arms crossed, her face stony, like she was suppressing rage. Which, Imogen guessed, she probably was. They hadn't spoken since arriving home, when Imogen had stormed to her room, slamming the door with a satisfying *wham*. She'd expected her mum to march after her, to continue their battle and insist on knowing everything. But she hadn't come.

The silence in the house had been suffocating, even when her dad had arrived home an hour or so later, much earlier than usual. He'd picked Jemima up from school, and every so often her cheery voice had filtered through Imogen's door, setting her teeth on edge. They'd all remained down the hall, not summoning her until dinner was ready. The meal had been torturous for Imogen, the storm that brewed in the kitchen crackling with tension and impending disappointment. Only Jemima seemed unaware, chattering away about an upcoming science excursion her class was taking and doing over-the-top impressions of her maths teacher until she was sent reluctantly away to brush her teeth and get ready for bed.

'Imogen, love,' her dad said warmly, patting the sofa next to him.

Imogen paused for a second, then sighed and crossed the room to sit down, focusing on the damp tea towel in her hands, refusing to meet either of her parents' eyes.

'Your mum and I are worried about you.'

He was so transparent, Imogen thought bitterly. She knew that what he really meant was, 'your mum can't get the truth out of you, so she's getting me to have a go', but he was too loyal to say it.

Imogen's heart squeezed at his complete refusal to betray his wife, even when she was being a total control freak. He was different. He trusted her; saw the best in her. But should she trust him? Should she trust either of them?

She didn't like the way she was feeling, all of her emotions conflicting and jumbled and flip-flopping from one moment to the next. She didn't want to think about it any more. She wanted the burden taken from her. She just wanted to know for certain.

'Imogen,' he said again, his tone sharper this time.

Imogen rolled her eyes, no longer concerned with gaining anyone's trust. She wasn't going to get it, so she didn't see why she should try. What she wanted now was brevity – a quick exit from this charade so she could go back to her room and check for new messages.

'Dad,' she said curtly, 'I told Mum that I couldn't say what happened today. I asked her to trust me. She obviously doesn't, but it would be nice if *you* did.'

'That's not fair, love,' he said softly.

Guilt pinched at Imogen's guts, but she pushed the feeling aside. This wasn't her fault.

'It's true,' she argued. 'If Jemima was in the same situation, you'd trust her, wouldn't you?'

Jemima, her baby sister, the child who could do no wrong. The one who was innocent until proven guilty, and even then sometimes long *after* being proven guilty.

'This has nothing to do with your sister,' her mum snapped. 'Leave her out of this.'

'Kat,' her dad said gently, his palms out, pleading with her, with both of them.

Her mum threw her hands up and sighed, relenting.

'It's not that we don't trust you,' her dad said, turning to Imogen. 'It's just that the school is going to want answers. I spoke to your principal this afternoon, and she said that if you don't offer an explanation, they'll have no choice but to take Emerald's word for it and suspend you.'

Imogen shrugged.

'That's not really what you want, is it?' he asked.

'No,' Imogen said lightly. 'But I don't really have another choice, do I?'

'Of course you do,' her mum's words burst out of her. She couldn't seem to help herself. 'Just tell us what happened – *that's* the other choice.'

Imogen stared at her, attempting to convey her utter contempt with just a gaze.

Tears wobbled in her mum's eyes, which only made Imogen's anger burn more brightly. Her mum wasn't the victim here. She didn't deserve to act like one.

'You can ask me as many times, and in as many different ways as you want,' Imogen said coldly. 'But I can't tell you.'

'Honey.' Her dad took her hand. She considered snatching it away, but his was strong and tanned and rough from all those years of building. His were safe hands, and for a second she was tempted to forget the last few months, forget

16

the events of that day, and curl up against his chest like she used to. But she couldn't do that. Not without knowing. She squeezed his hand in response, and he looked into her eyes, the words that followed gentle and brimming with concern. 'Are you being threatened by someone? Is that why you can't tell us? Are you in danger, Immy?'

He didn't look mad. He looked ... heartbroken.

Imogen could feel her resolve, so carefully and purposefully crystallised, dissolving in his protectiveness. She couldn't let that happen. She needed to get away, to be alone.

'No,' she said firmly, taking her hand back. 'I'm not being threatened. There is nothing wrong. I'm not some kind of awful person, OK? I did what I did for a reason, and I know you want to know what that reason is, but I really can't tell you, and I can't tell you why I can't tell you, and whether you believe me or not doesn't actually matter because it doesn't change anything. So I'll take the suspension, and I'll deal with the consequences, OK?'

'No, Imogen, it's not OK,' her mum said, her voice raised, her cheeks blooming pink. 'This is serious, you know. Suspension? We didn't raise you to be like this!'

'And what *did* you raise me to be?' Imogen's anger flared as she stood to face her mum. 'A liar? Want me to make something up? Fine, I beat up that girl because she called me ugly, is that good enough for you? Or what if I said it was because she was picking on a girl who always gets teased? Would you leave me alone then, would that make me acceptable to you?'

Imogen was crying now, which only made her more angry. At herself, at her parents, at the whole damn situation. She was sick of it; sick of dealing with the mess she was in; sick of feeling the tight ball of anger inside her.

She spun around and stomped out of the living room, throwing the tea towel on the ground as she went. Her mum's shouts followed her down the hallway, but she ignored them. Her parents' confusion wasn't her problem.

As she passed Jemima's room, she spotted her sister's brown eyes in the space where the door had been left slightly ajar. Her anger surged, and she slammed her bedroom door as hard as she could, satisfied when the noise reverberated down the hall. She knew that she was being the perfect stereotype of a moody teenager, but she didn't care.

She crouched down, fumbling on the ground for a second. Then, checking her door was properly closed, she reached down the back of her desk, her fingers scrabbling against the wood until she retrieved the device that had been on her mind all day, every day, for the past few weeks. Hope swelled in her chest as she pressed the home button. It deflated just as quickly: no new messages. The disappointment was physical, a hollowing out that made the tears stream more forcefully down her cheeks.

And then the device buzzed in her hand, as though the person on the other end could read her thoughts, and her heart leapt. She smiled as she read the words on the screen. She didn't need her parents to believe her; to trust her, because there was someone else who always did.

Imogen typed a reply, wiping the tears from her wet cheeks, her anger gone. What did it matter if her mum thought she was a terrible person? Her parents' opinions didn't matter. What happened at school today didn't matter. Her punishment didn't matter.

She'd take the suspension. She'd let her mum and dad believe what they wanted. They always had, anyway. As long as things stayed the way they always had been, they'd see her as someone to be suspected, someone who couldn't quite be trusted.

Which was why, Imogen knew, something had to change. She crossed her fingers, and opened her inbox.

Chapter 3

KAT

Imogen's door slams, the force of it making me blink. I did my best to stay impassive in the face of her anger – I even managed to refrain from crying in front of her. But still, her words stung, and the tears have started now that she can't see me. I'm completely thrown, and totally unsure of how to parent our teenage daughter.

I wipe my eyes. Dylan will know what to do. Of the two of us, my husband has always been the sturdy, logical one, whereas I've always reacted emotionally. While I lead with my heart, he looks at a problem from every angle, working through all potential scenarios before arriving at a decision. He'll be able to reach Imogen, to make her see that she can trust us enough to tell us what really happened. I want to believe the best in her, like Dylan does. I really do. But she's not making it easy for me. What could be so important that she can't just let us know the truth? And is it really that she can't say, or does she just want to avoid us hearing that she was needlessly violent? Is this her way of appearing innocent, or at least maintaining enough doubt so that we can't officially lay the blame on her?

I turn to face Dylan, needing him to reassure me, to tell me that I'm being ridiculous and that this isn't a crisis that I need to obsess over. But he's not even looking at me. He's stretched out on the sofa, one arm over the back of the headrest, the other wrapped around the remote control.

'Dylan!'

'What?'

'Are you kidding me right now?' I seethe. 'Our daughter punched someone, she won't tell us or anyone else why, she just screamed at us and stormed out of here, and all you can think to do is watch the bloody cricket highlights?'

'I know you're upset,' he says, putting the remote control down on the coffee table. 'But I think you're blowing this out of proportion. She's a teenager. Not a criminal.'

I stare at him for a second, rage building and threatening to explode. When I speak, it's with all of the restraint that I can muster.

'I didn't say she was a criminal.'

'Well, sometimes you treat her like she is one. You make her feel like she's a bad person.'

'She told you this?'

'She doesn't need to. I can see it.'

He's wrong. Isn't he?

I press my hands against my face, then sink onto the sofa next to my husband. He switches the television off and puts his arm around me. I lean into his chest and listen to his heartbeat. Slow. Steady. Predictable.

'You know I'm not trying to see the worst in her . . . right?'

'Of course I know that,' Dylan says, kissing the top of my head. 'But she doesn't. And at some point you have to make a decision. Either you choose to believe the best, or you let fear get the best of you, and you keep obsessing over a worst-case scenario that'll probably never happen.'

I nod slowly, trying to understand how I can make that choice, how to live with the risk, how to turn a blind eye to the facts.

'Don't you think that ignoring it – that burying our heads in the sand about the truth – could be dangerous?'

Dylan pulls away from me, twisting his torso to look me in the eye.

'I know you find it hard, but you need to trust her. You need to trust all of us.'

I open my mouth to argue, then snap it closed again. I want to disagree with him, want to hide from the accusations he's making, but I'm weary. We've travelled this path before, so many times that the way ahead has been smoothed over with use. And so I don't fight.

Instead, I put into words the thoughts that I normally don't dare say.

'You know why I'm worried about Imogen,' I say tentatively. 'Don't make me spell it out.'

'You're wrong,' Dylan says immediately. 'I know why you're worried – of course I understand why. You think I've never thought about it myself? But she's fine. You can trust her, you know. We've been through this. We've done everything we can.' He pauses. 'And you don't have to worry about her finding out.'

'That's not what I'm worried about.'

'Isn't it?' he asks, one eyebrow raised. 'I know you're trying your best, but I think you need to take a look at yourself. Because while you're pretending that you're protecting her, you're smothering her. Imagine how that feels.'

Imagine how it feels, I think, to be waging constant battle with your daughter. But he can't imagine. Of course he can't. He's the good cop, the one who always has her back, the one who's always meant to have my back.

But I don't say any of this. I nod and turn away, letting my husband get back to his sport. I'm not going to win this argument.

I suppose I just have to accept my role as the bad cop. It's not what I want – it's not what any of us want – but this isn't just about Imogen. She's not the only one in this family. And no matter what Dylan believes, no matter how much he wants to look at the world through rose-tinted glasses, I have to do what I can to protect us.

Even if what I'm protecting us from is inside our own home.

Chapter 4

KAT

I grimace as a blast of hot, dry air hits me full in the face. It's like I've stepped into an oven. Balancing a bowl of potato salad on my hip, I pull the door closed quickly behind me to keep the cold air trapped inside.

'Kat!'

I turn my head towards the voice. Bill, one of the neighbours we invited over, is waving flamboyantly as he walks through our side gate and into the garden. I smile and tip my head back, a half-nod greeting in lieu of a wave, one arm wrapped firmly around the cold bowl, the other hand clutching the bottle of wine I just retrieved from the freezer.

'You picked a scorcher of a day,' he says, walking over and kissing me on the cheek. 'Where do you want this?' He brandishes a tray of sausages and a six-pack of beer in my direction and I flick my head towards the sizzling, smoking barbecue.

'Dylan's over there,' I say to him. I can't actually see my husband through the haze that's wafting from the grill, but whenever we have a barbecue, that's undoubtedly where he'll be found. Men do meat. Women do salads. And the shopping. And the prep. And the cleaning up. But, of course, the guys get the glory. 'He'll put those snags on for you. And

24

I'm sure he'll take one of those cold beers off your hands, too.'

As Bill walks away, I stretch my neck to wipe the sweat that's building along my top lip onto the shoulder of my T-shirt. There's a pause between the songs that are playing from the overpriced speaker Jemima begged us to get her for Christmas, and in the few seconds of transition, I take in the noises of our summertime revelry. Meat hissing and popping above the flames. The little ones squealing as they run from one another's water guns. Adults laughing. Beer bottles clinking. And the kids a few doors down whose cricket game is providing the odd crack as the ball connects with the bat. But the birds, I notice, have retreated. Their usual warbling has been silenced by the heat. They've headed for shade, I suppose, finding respite somewhere that isn't this baking-hot garden. I envy them.

'It's like a furnace out here,' Linda says, sipping a glass of wine and holding out another towards me.

'Tell me about it. I wish we'd cancelled, but Dylan insisted this heatwave would have ended by now,' I say, placing the potato salad on the picnic table I set up earlier, which now displays an assortment of random salads, breads, dressings and sliced veggies: offerings from our guests.

I bend down and put the rapidly warming bottle of wine into the Esky, the ice now little more than a cold pool of water, a few stubborn cubes floating at the top. I keep my hand submerged for a second longer than necessary, savouring the sharp contrast from the midday air, then replace the lid and take the extra glass from Linda's hand gratefully. It's already tepid. I grimace as the liquid hits the back of my throat.

'Sorry,' she says. 'It's impossible to keep anything cold

out here. Ridiculous. Trick is just to down it while it's still lukewarm instead of boiling.'

I laugh and take another gulp.

'I reckon we should go for a dip in a bit,' she suggests.

'Yeah,' I say. 'Although the sea's probably like bathwater by now, I doubt it'll be very refreshing.'

'Mum,' calls a high-pitched voice from behind us.

Linda and I both turn around. It's Kailah, her eldest. She's twelve: the same age as Jemima, although their age is where their similarities end. My daughter is confident and extroverted, more likely to be leading than trailing along behind. Kailah is timid and easily influenced. Still, somehow, they get along in spite of – or perhaps because of – their differences, just like their mothers. I've often wondered if our friendships can simply be chalked up to physical proximity: Linda and her kids live three doors down from us, and we're at each other's houses as much as we are our own.

'What is it, love?' Linda asks.

'It's too hot, can I go home?'

Linda grimaces at me.

I smile at Kailah. 'How about you go inside and keep Jemima company? She's hiding out in her room, but maybe you can convince her to come out and enjoy herself.'

Kailah hesitates, looking at Linda for approval. I resist the urge to roll my eyes.

'The air conditioning is on full blast in there,' I add, hoping to tempt her into making a decision for herself. 'And there are some Magnums in the freezer. Just don't tell anyone.' I wink at her and she looks at Linda again, who nods encouragingly.

Kailah looks like she might say something, but then her shoulders drop and she slowly turns around, dragging her feet as she shuffles towards the sliding doors.

Linda laughs and takes another sip.

'She must get that from my ex,' she says, 'because I'm certainly not indecisive.'

Someone calls my name from across the backyard.

'Back in a sec,' I say to Linda, walking over to the barbecue, where the voice came from. When I emerge on the other side of the cloud of beefy smoke, Dylan's brandishing a sausage with a pair of tongs.

'Kat, where are the trays for the meat?'

I walk two steps back to the salads table, rolling my eyes at Linda, and fetch one of the trays I left there earlier. I hand it to my husband with a raised eyebrow.

'Probably could have got that one myself, hey?'

'I'd say you could have managed.'

'Sorry. Thanks, darl.'

Relief washes over me, cool and refreshing. His smile, the way his eyes crinkle at the sides, they mean that we're OK. They mean that the walls we've had up since Thursday, when I called him from the school car park, are coming down. They're not falling, though; I've been disassembling them, brick by brick. I'm not finished yet, I know that, but Dylan can see that I'm working on trusting my daughter, the way he does. The way every parent should.

And maybe it's just the wine and the sunshine and the laughter, but today I feel like maybe he's right. Maybe I was just overreacting, letting old paranoia surface when it should stay buried, hidden. Forgotten.

Maybe everything is going to be OK.

Chapter 5

IMOGEN

The girl standing in the small scrap of shade under the blue gum tree was so still that no one in the crowd around her even noticed her presence. The only sign of her existence was the occasional stirring of a wisp of fine blonde hair as she exhaled shallowly.

Her stillness concealed the frenetic bubbling of emotion that was building beneath her skin. Ignoring the laughter and squeals of the small children running around the garden, she focused all of her energy on remaining statue-like, and waiting for the anger to subside. She knew it would, eventually. It always did.

She didn't notice Tyson, one of the neighbours' kids, until he ran right into her, forcing a soft *oof* from her lungs.

He looked up at her in shock, the appearance of a girl seemingly out of thin air at first confusing and then delighting him. He grinned, the gaps between his teeth making him look crazed, unhinged. He pointed his water gun right at her expressionless face.

'Stick 'em up, Immy,' he shrieked, laughing maniacally, and before she had a chance to react, he'd sprayed tepid water all over her.

She gasped in shock, mentally hovering between outrage and laughter, but before she could decide which of these emotions to cling to, Tyson had run off to find another victim. She laughed, then; anger evaporating as quickly as the water on her skin.

It was too hot to bother being upset, she decided. She plucked her phone from the back pocket of her shorts and pressed her thumb onto the home button, hoping that when it lit up she'd see a reply from Paige.

There was nothing. She knew her best friend was at work, a weekend job at a chicken shop near her house. But her shift would be finished soon, and then she could come over and rescue Imogen from this awful barbie. She wasn't allowed to leave – her mum had made that clear – but there was no rule against inviting her friends around.

'Imogen,' a voice called from across the garden.

'Yeah,' she yelled back, making no move to walk over. She waited, motionless once again, forcing her mum to cross the space between them, over the parched grass that was now littered with plastic toys and paper plates, the debris of a successful barbecue.

'Ready to go to the beach? Got your towel? And sunscreen?'

Imogen let out a small sigh, rolling her eyes in frustration. She'd been so careful to stay within the tiny scribble of shade that the tired leaves of the gum tree had created, and the SPF fifty sunscreen she'd slathered over every inch of her skin earlier was now sliding, along with rivulets of sweat, into her eyes. She blinked away the burning sensation, knowing that wiping her face would only make it worse.

'Immy!'

'Yes,' Imogen snapped, seething. 'I have my sunscreen and towel, OK? God, I'm sixteen, I know how to go to the beach.'

Her mum blinked and jerked her head back as though she'd been slapped. Her words had stung, Imogen realised with a mean spark of satisfaction.

'OK. Good,' her mum said tersely. 'Please can you look after your sister until we get down there?'

'Why should I have to look—'

'Immy, does everything have to be an argument?'

She looked down at the parched grass, but said nothing.

'You'll all be in the water before we're halfway down the street,' her mum said. 'I'm not asking you to hold her hand, but I need you to keep an eye on her. Just make sure she's safe, OK? Please?'

Imogen nodded in resignation.

Her mum squeezed her shoulder.

'Thanks,' she said, walking off towards the cluster of adults.

Imogen silently counted to ten, then scooped up an old volleyball and her beach bag from the deckchair beside her.

'Hurry up, Paige,' she muttered to the sky, hoping her best friend would somehow hear her from the chicken shop.

She found Jemima doing a handstand against the side of the house, Kailah watching nervously from a distance.

'Come on, Jems, Kailah,' Imogen called out. 'We're going to the beach. Last one there's a rotten egg.'

Before they could respond, Imogen took off, running through the side gate, the younger girls' laughs and shouts chasing her through the front garden, along their street and down the small road that led directly to the beach. Imogen relished the sensation of her muscles working hard, the strain providing a release from her turmoil. She increased her pace, the fire in her lungs soothing her, only slowing when she reached the main road that separated them from the water.

She waited for the younger girls, and the three of them stood together, watching for a gap in the traffic, Jemima panting like she had just run a marathon rather than a few hundred metres. When it was safe to cross, they ran down the soft sand path lined with spindly seagrass, ditching their belongings as soon as they reached the wide expanse of beach, dodging other beachgoers and flicking sand up into the air as they ran. Imogen held back to let the other two reach the water first. Everything in her wanted to win, but she knew better.

Splashing awkwardly, Imogen kept her knees high as she leapt over the small waves until the water was deep enough to dive in. Her head plunged under the bath-like water and, when she surfaced, her arms sliced powerfully, propelling her away from the beach, away from her home, away from her family.

When her lungs screamed, she stopped and turned around, treading water to survey the beach from a distance. She watched as Kailah and Jemima took turns doing somersaults underwater, whooping as they surfaced, then splashing one another with squeals of delight. Imogen felt the tight ball of emotion that had been building up behind her ribs slowly unfurling, giving way to a sort of calm she rarely experienced.

A small plane puttered overhead, a sobering reminder that sharks were close enough to require monitoring. Spooked by her own imagination, Imogen headed for shore, scaring Kailah on her way back by diving underwater behind her and grabbing her ankle. Laughing along with Jemima as she left the shaken girl behind, Imogen stopped a short distance from the adults, who had now arrived, armed with umbrellas and Eskies.

'Mum,' she shouted.

Multiple women turned around, including her own mum.

'I'm just going to lie down over here, so I won't have my eye on Jems.'

'That's OK,' her mum called back. 'I've got it from here, thanks.'

Imogen retrieved her bag from the scalding sand and spread her towel out a safe distance from everyone else. She watched them laughing and drinking for a few minutes before the heat overwhelmed her, and she dozed lazily, her hat shielding her face from the baking sunshine.

A scream pulled her from her drowsy reverie and she scrambled to sit upright, her heart in her throat. There was a commotion down by the water. Imogen stood and ran towards the shouting, her mind only on one thing: Jemima.

As she got closer, she could see her little sister standing on the wet sand with Kailah by her side. She felt a rush of relief, until she noticed that the neighbour's girl was crying.

'She held me underwater,' she gasped, pointing her finger at Jemima. 'She wouldn't let me come up for air.' She coughed and spluttered, and Linda pulled her daughter close to her body, looking at Jemima for an explanation.

'We were just playing,' Jemima whined. 'She's such a baby; I can't help it if she can't take a joke.'

'Jemima,' Kat said sternly. 'Apologise to Kailah right now.'

'But I didn't do—'

'Now, please, young lady.'

'Fine,' Jemima said reluctantly. 'Sorry.'

She turned away and stormed off, heading straight towards Imogen and leaving her mum, who seemed satisfied enough with the insincere apology, to placate the neighbours.

Typical, Imogen thought bitterly. If it had been her, her mum wouldn't have settled for anything less than a gushing, sugary-sweet, down-on-her-knees plea for forgiveness.

But, of course, it must have all been a misunderstanding with Jemima. It was true that Kailah was a sensitive kid, prone to crying and finger-pointing and sitting out any kind of fun activity for fear of being hurt. But still.

'Jems,' she called out as her sister stomped past.

The younger girl looked at Imogen, who raised an eyebrow in question.

Jemima held her gaze for a few seconds, something unspoken passing between the two of them. Then she nodded.

Imogen relaxed. 'Good. OK. Well, I need someone to reapply the sunscreen on my back. Think you could help?'

They walked back to Imogen's spot further up the beach, and Jemima flopped down on the towel, spraying Imogen with sand.

'Ugh, Jemima!'

'What? Do you want me to help you or not?'

Imogen sighed and handed her sister the bottle, crying out with the shock of the cool cream hitting her scalding-hot back. Jemima giggled.

'You have to be careful,' she warned. 'Kailah's sensitive. You know she gets upset easily.'

'She's a wuss,' Jemima said matter-of-factly.

'Well, maybe, but that doesn't mean you can do what you want.'

She turned around to face her sister.

'I mean it, Jems.'

The younger girl flapped her hand, dismissing her concern.

'Yeah. OK.' She handed the bottle back to Imogen and stood up. 'Awesome, Dad's got the cricket bat out! Come and play!'

Imogen glanced at the phone lying on top of her bag. There was still no word from Paige.

'How about some volleyball?' Imogen asked, already knowing what her sister's answer would be, but hoping for the unexpected.

'No way,' Jemima said, screwing up her face. 'Volleyball's boring. Come on.'

Jemima tugged her hand until she stood up, and dragged her over to where their dad was sorting people into teams.

'Awesome, my girls are playing. OK, Jems, Kailah and me against Tyson, Immy and Linda.'

Kailah pouted and refused to look at Jemima, but she didn't complain. She was too passive to say that she didn't want to play with the girl who had just made her cry, who had deprived her of a proper apology.

Jemima was right, Imogen thought meanly. Kailah *was* weak.

They arranged themselves into their respective positions along an empty stretch of beach. Imogen lost the hasty rock-paper-scissors tournament and dutifully took her place in front of the wicket, bat in hand, patience already wearing thin. She wanted this day to be over.

She struck the end of the bat into the sand once, twice, keeping her eyes on the tennis ball that Kailah was ineptly hurling towards her from beyond the other wicket. The ball went wide. Her dad, who was crouched behind Imogen, taking his wicketkeeping duties seriously, called out for her to try again. Imogen made a *tsk* noise, already regretting her decision to play.

'Try to remember this is just a game of beach cricket, OK, love?' her dad said from over her shoulder.

She looked at him, pursing her lips.

'That doesn't mean I have to suck, does it?'

'That's not what I'm saying, Immy, and you know it,' he said, stepping back behind the wicket.

The ball sailed towards her, and Imogen reached over to smack it with the bat, but it was wide again and the plastic bat caught the very edge, sending it glancing behind her. She knew the instant it connected that she'd made a mistake. Her dad reached out and caught the ball easily with one hand, his team members whooping in jubilation at their early success.

'Come on!' Imogen yelled, throwing the bat into the sand in frustration.

'You're out, you're out,' Jemima chanted in a sing-song voice. Kailah joined in the taunting, and tears sprung to Imogen's eyes.

'Whatever,' she snapped, spinning on her heel in the sand. If she didn't get away, she'd do something stupid, something rash. She couldn't risk it. 'I didn't want to play this dumb game anyway.'

'Imogen!'

She tried to get away, but her mum, who had been standing nearby watching the game, caught her arm, halting her flight.

'Imogen, what's going on?'

'Nothing, I just don't want to play any more. I hate cricket.'

'Don't be a bad sport, Immy. The younger kids are just trying to have some fun. You should be setting an example...'

As her mum launched into a lecture about her attitude, Imogen clamped her jaw closed so firmly that she was sure a molar would crack. She couldn't concentrate on her mum's words; her focus was on the flames of fury that licked at her chest, her tightening muscles and the clenching of her stomach. She tried to tell herself that it wasn't a big deal, that soon her mum would run out of steam and let her walk away. When she was alone, she could vent her frustrations on someone who wouldn't tell her she was blowing things out of proportion.

But as she stood in the sand, being berated in front of everyone, Imogen couldn't stop the vision that formed in her imagination, taking shape and looming brighter and larger until it was all she could see. She pictured herself launching herself at her mum, resorting to the kind of bad behaviour – the violence – that was so clearly expected from her. It would feel so good to release the rage that was building up; a pressure she knew she couldn't keep locked away forever. She allowed herself to indulge the fantasy, her heartbeat quickening and her breath becoming shallower as she imagined the satisfaction of shutting her mum up.

And then, slowly, she let out a long breath and released her fists so her hands hung loosely by her side. She didn't want to hurt anyone, not really. That wasn't who she was. She just wanted some peace and quiet. She just wanted to be left alone.

'Sorry,' she mumbled, and walked away with her head down, ignoring her mum's protests.

She hated herself for being so pathetic. After all, it *was* just a game of beach cricket, for crying out loud, not a bloody state volleyball championship. But that wasn't the source of her bitterness, and she knew it, even if no one else understood. Her anger was just a symptom of something hidden and malignant, like blood oozing from a wound, dark and full of poison. She could feel it festering inside her, growing and morphing and filling up the dark spaces between her organs. It pushed on her lungs when she breathed, tugged at her heart when she thought she was happy, reminding her of the truth.

She wanted to get rid of it; she desperately wanted to be free from the anger and fear and confusion, but she didn't know how. She wanted a cure, but maybe there wasn't one.

And then the small voice in the back of her head, the one that she tried so hard to ignore, spoke the questions she fought never to ask, because she couldn't bear to know the answers.

What if there is no cure because this is just who you are? it taunted her. *What if this darkness is in your blood?*

Chapter 6

IMOGEN

Imogen stared at her screen, the words blurring as she tried to make sense of them, her stomach in chaos.

She'd pictured this moment hundreds of times in the past few weeks, and yet, now that it was happening, despair swelled, rushing through her veins and reaching parts of her she didn't know existed.

Overwhelmed, she sat heavily on her bed, new emotions crashing over her, one after another: confusion, anger, helplessness and, threaded through them all, hope. Gasping for breath, she let herself be battered by these waves, powerless to stop them, or even slow them down. She didn't know how long she sat there before the world began to come back into focus. Laughter trickled through her window, along with clinking and chatter.

She clenched her fists.

Here she was, being crushed by the weight of their bare, ugly truths, while they were giggling and joking with their friends, completely oblivious. Rage built up inside her, the emotion so strong, she wasn't sure she could control it, wasn't sure she could restrain herself. Her overwhelming compulsion was to run outside and let it all out, let them know exactly what she thought of them, let their friends know exactly who they were.

But in the midst of her blinding fury there was a pinprick of logic. If she followed her instincts, there would be consequences. And, worse than that, she would lose control of the situation.

She needed to stay calm so she could manage how this all played out. The last thing she wanted was to relinquish her future to them. They already had her past, and that was all she would allow them to have.

Forcing the anger down, she blinked her tears away and furiously typed a message on the phone that had been resting by her side. She hit send and waited, her heart in her mouth, her hand trembling. Within seconds there was a reply. Despite herself, her mouth stretched into a wobbly smile. At least she didn't have to go through this alone. There was someone who understood. Who would help her find a way forward.

She typed another message, a reply lighting up her screen almost instantly. Texts flew back and forth between them, and before long she was faced with a single question: *Are you sure? If you say yes, you can't breathe a word of this. To anyone.*

Imogen stared at the message, feeling like she was on the edge of a precipice, her toes curled over the rim, staring down into the gaping unknown.

She took a deep breath, giving herself over to her anger again. She needed its intensity to drown out her doubts and fears. She'd known that this might happen, she reminded herself. Since that very first message, there had been a place at the back of her mind that had always suspected this was a possibility. As the weeks went on, the idea had begun to consume her, until it was all she could think about, until she daydreamed that it was true, that this moment would come. But now that it was happening, now that it was real . . . she couldn't concentrate on anything other than the hundreds of reasons why she shouldn't go through with it.

Imogen pressed the heels of her hands into her eyes, hoping for a bolt of clarity, for a sign that pointed her in the right direction. But she was old enough to know that she wouldn't get one.

Sighing, she stood and walked to her door, opening it just a crack. If she was going to do this, she'd have to find a way to get past the adults, whose voices still drifted in from the back deck, brash and confident, the sounds of people who weren't weighed down by things like honesty and integrity. And she couldn't wake the tangle of kids in the living room or they'd alert their parents. If she couldn't get away, then maybe that was her answer. Maybe it was as simple and as practical as that. Maybe that would be the universe's way of saying no.

As she tiptoed down the hallway, a loud *whoosh* filtered through the air from the kitchen, the sound of the back door sliding open. Two female voices rang through the house, loud and clear.

'She's just a nightmare at the moment,' the first voice said. Imogen thought it might be coming from Jo, the wife of one of her dad's work friends.

'Oh yeah, you think that's bad?' her mum said dramatically. 'You should hear what Imogen did on Thursday.'

Imogen stiffened, her jaw clenching in instant indignation.

'What happened?'

'She punched someone. Just . . . just punched her, right in the face. And then wouldn't tell us why, just refuses to speak to us about it.'

Imogen noticed that her mum's words were tripping over

one another. She was drunk, or at least tipsy, her speech loud and sloppy.

'Oh my God! That's awful. That's not like her, is it? I thought she was a pretty well-behaved kid.'

'No, that's Jemima,' her mum replied, and Imogen's stomach lurched. 'Imogen is... well, she's just more complicated.'

'Has she done anything like this before?'

'Well... not exactly,' her mum said slowly. 'Nothing like this. But she's just... All I'm saying is that it didn't exactly surprise me. It's who she is.'

Imogen whirled around and tiptoe-ran back down the hallway, back into her bedroom, and resisted the urge to slam her door, closing it carefully, quietly, instead. The tears came when there was a solid barrier between her and the traitorous woman in the kitchen.

She picked up her phone again and stared at the message that had turned her world upside down just minutes earlier. There it was: proof. As the words sank in again, betrayal and resentment settled over her, heavy; an anchor that focused her thoughts until they honed in on the only thing that mattered.

Then she let her fingers type the message she'd been too scared to send before: *Yes*.

She tapped the send button. She didn't hesitate. She didn't need to. Her mum thought she knew who Imogen was, but she had no idea. If that's what she thought of her, that was fine. That worked perfectly, in fact.

It was time to show her mum who she really, truly was.

Chapter 7

KAT

The sun is climbing, higher and brighter by the minute, the birds are warbling outside, and the other side of the bed is empty. I roll over and groan, letting my body adjust to being awake.

Last night's barbecue went on much later than we'd anticipated. A few people trickled away in the afternoon, and the rest came back to our place after a few hours at the beach to continue the revelry on our back patio. I don't know how many bottles of wine we got through, but judging by the pounding behind my eyes, it must have been a few.

I squint at the clock, blink in disbelief and shoot upright. I can't remember the last time I slept this late on a Sunday. Imogen rarely surfaces before midday unless she's dragged from her bed, but Dylan and Jemima are usually up; Dylan rising early to blend spinach and protein powder into a green sludge, the noise never failing to haul me out of bed, grumbling, while Jemima slouches on the sofa and watches cartoons. But this morning the house is eerily quiet.

Stepping out of bed, I cautiously test my body for more signs of a hangover. As well as my throbbing head, my mouth feels like I've been sucking on towels all night, and my stomach is ropey. I throw on a robe and make my way groggily towards the kitchen in search of coffee and toast.

There's a hastily written note on the kitchen table from Dylan.

Thought you might need a sleep-in, his childlike scrawl reads. *So I took Jems for breakfast.*

I smile at the attempt to sound fatherly, when I'm pretty sure he's doing it for purely selfish reasons: he wants bacon. And hash browns. My mouth waters at the thought.

I send him a text asking him to bring something greasy home for me – toast suddenly seems completely unappealing. He replies with a winking emoji.

Smiling, I turn on the coffee machine and stare at it blankly while it heats up. I steam the milk and pour myself an extra shot of espresso to make the strongest cappuccino I can stomach. Adding extra chocolate sprinkles, I sip it as I sit at the kitchen table, half-heartedly spooning the passion fruit off a chunk of leftover pavlova and nibbling tentatively at the seeds.

My stomach turns as the fruit hits my tender stomach, and I groan. I'm far too old to drink like that, and I should know better. I *do* know better. It's never worth it the next day; it hasn't been since my twenties.

As I slowly regain some strength, I try to gather my thoughts and plan for the day ahead. Hangover or not, I need to get on with things. Imogen's volleyball practice isn't going to be magically cancelled because I'd like to nurse a headache in peace. I get up, brushing meringue crumbs from my satin robe and swig the dregs of my coffee.

With a burst of energy – thank goodness for caffeine – I go back to my room and take a shower, the steam filling my lungs and making me feel vaguely human again. I step out and sit on the edge of the bed, sending texts to Linda, seeking comfort in knowing I'm not the only one feeling wretched today. She asks if I can look after her kids later while she meets an old friend for dinner. The last thing I want to deal with today is extra kids, but as I owe her way more than one babysitting favour, I agree, then get dressed and dry my hair, listening for any indication that Imogen is up.

The house is still silent. I have to wake her, get her ready and drop her at volleyball practice across town. Then I need to drop Jemima at Carly's birthday party, stop at the butcher's to get lamb chops for tonight, collect Imogen, collect Jemima and bring everyone home in time for Linda to drop her kids off for the evening.

Standing outside Imogen's door, I take a deep breath to prepare myself and then knock softly. Whatever she decides to throw at me today, I'm too fragile to face it head-on. I cross my fingers that she'll be in a good mood.

'Imogen? Are you awake? It's eleven . . . we need to leave in forty-five minutes if you're going to get to practice in time.'

I wait. There's no sound. She must have stayed up late if my knock hasn't woken her, but that's no surprise. I don't recall her going to bed, although I certainly wasn't paying attention to what she was doing once we got back from the beach. We weren't making an effort to be quiet, though, and her window is right next to the back deck, so if she was trying to sleep, we probably kept her up pretty late. I almost feel guilty, but then I let the feeling slide. Keeping her up past her bedtime really is the least of my parenting failures.

'Imogen?'

I knock again, louder this time. Still nothing.

Frustrated, I turn the handle. She'll be mad at me for intruding, but if she doesn't wake up soon she won't get to practice in time, and she's bound to blame me if she's late. Her coach takes their practice seriously, which is understandable, given that it's the state under-eighteens squad and not some social league. I open the door to rouse my daughter, to get her going.

'Imogen, we really don't have time for this,' I'm saying as the door swings open. 'You're going to be late, and you know how Coach Cresswell feels about that. It's after—' I stop, mid-sentence, my eyes struggling to register what I'm seeing, what it means.

Imogen's room is in perfect order: no dirty clothes on the floor, no schoolbooks strewn across her desk, no backpack explosion in the corner. That's not so unusual, but my eyes have settled on her bed, and confusion leaves me momentarily paralysed.

Imogen's bed is made, the covers pulled tightly, the gold patterned cushions we got her for Christmas artfully arranged at the top. But my daughter isn't in it.

She's not here. Imogen is gone.

Chapter 8

SALLY

I miss him.

I like to remind people of this when they suggest that I'm a psychopath. Psychopaths, you see, don't feel emotions in the same way that you and I do. Oh, I can see you shrinking away as you consider me throwing us in the same category together, as though we could never be considered equals. Perhaps we're not the same in terms of the way we think, or how we choose to raise a family, but in terms of brain chemistry, you and I, we feel things. We feel remorse. Pain. Regret. Love.

You probably don't believe me; probably don't see how it's possible that I could have done all of the things that they say I did if I could feel love. But it shouldn't surprise you. Some of the worst things in this world have been committed in the name of love. Love of another person, love of a nation, love of a god, love of an ideal, love of power.

People throw around platitudes like *love conquers all* as though *all* doesn't really mean all. As though its meaning is selective, encompassing nothing but hardship and obstacles and doubt, and leaving out goodness and innocence and justice. No, love really does conquer all. It's a powerful weapon. Believe me.

So, yes, I feel love. I know because I love Tim. He's my

soulmate, was the one for me ever since I first clapped eyes on him. In my trial, my lawyer tried to claim that he'd forced me to do the things I was being tried for, that he manipulated and groomed me. Coercive control, he called it. But my lawyer didn't understand, won't ever understand. Neither would the jury members, or the witnesses, or the judge.

Because, you see, Tim saved me. He rescued me from an impossible situation, a home so unbearable that no human should have to endure it, let alone a young girl. Mum wasn't around, then. When I was just ten years old, Dad told me that she had run away, abandoned me, and for the longest time I believed him. But then there was the rose bush out the back, the one he lovingly tended while everything else around us went to hell. The backyard was a barren scrap heap, apart from that one flourishing rose bush; buttery yellow blooms of Sweet Memories. And on the rare occasion when he was in that precarious drunken state, still able to stand but not aware enough of his surroundings to have his guard up, he'd be out there, talking to that bush, calling it Pat. Mum's name.

So I don't know what really happened – never will, I suspect – but either way, she wasn't around to see what was going on. Wasn't there to stop it. No one could stop it. I was totally helpless, at the mercy of a monster.

And then Tim walked in the front door one Friday afternoon. He was new, not one of the regulars Dad brought around night after night to, as he described it, 'blow off some steam'. I never understood what drove him to do it, that first time. What tipped him over the edge from neglectful and angry to downright abusive. Maybe he was desperate to get his workmates to like him. Maybe he needed the money. Maybe he just hated me. Me, and Pat.

47

Tim wasn't like all of the others. I knew that the first time I met him. He was gentle with me. He asked questions. And he always brought me a treat: a piece of bubblegum, sometimes. Or a chocolate bar. Once, a set of sparkly pink hair clips that made me beam from ear to ear until Dad took them away and told me they made me look like a common whore. But to Tim, I was special. He saw me. He loved me. And, eventually, he rescued me.

The day he took me away from that place was the happiest day of my life. It was a Sunday, a bright and clear April afternoon with fluffy white clouds hovering above the horizon, like they were taken straight from a picture book.

As we drove away, Dad standing in the driveway with a wad of cash in his hand, I looked back expectantly. I don't know what I was hoping for. A wave, maybe. A smile. A remorseful tear sliding down his face.

But he wasn't looking. His head was down, his focus directed at the pile of blue notes resting on his palm. He was too busy counting his profits to bid farewell to his only child, the only family he had left in this world.

Years later, I found out the truth about what was in his hand, what was so important that he didn't care to offer me a parting gesture. Two hundred dollars.

It's what he sold his thirteen-year-old daughter for.

It wouldn't have lasted him a week.

Chapter 9

KAT

Don't panic, I tell myself, as fear rises.

'Imogen?' I call out, walking quickly from her room and down the hallway. She's probably just having breakfast, or watching TV, or any number of activities that mean she's fine and definitely not missing. 'IMOGEN!'

I dart between rooms, my chest tightening as every door I open reveals nothing but an empty space. She's not here. She's not in the house. I wrench the back door open and check every corner of the garden, knowing even as I do that she won't be here. Why would she be? I run back inside, through the kitchen and the living room, and swing open the front door. She's not out here, either.

Forcing the panic down, I try to think clearly. Did she tell me she was going out somewhere before volleyball today? Did she leave before I woke up?

I stride back to the kitchen to check the family calendar on the fridge. In the square that marks today's date, my small handwriting reads *Volleyball 12:30, J at Carly's, 2–5 p.m.* I double-check Dylan's note on the table, but he definitely only mentioned taking Jemima out for breakfast.

I rush back to the bedroom, where I left my phone. Imogen's number is in my favourites, so I dial, and get straight through to voicemail.

'Damnit!' I mutter to myself as Imogen's recorded voice instructs me to leave a message. Then, after the beep, 'Immy, it's Mum. Where are you? I don't remember you telling me about going out this morning and I'm worried. Do you still need a lift to practice? Please call me right away, OK? Love you.'

I hang up, then dial Dylan's number.

'Pickuppickuppickup,' I chant as it rings.

'Hello?'

He sounds like he's mid-laugh. I resist the urge to scream at him for being so oblivious.

'Dylan, where are you? Do you know where Imogen is?'

There's a slight pause while he processes my question.

'What do you mean?'

'I just went to wake her up for practice and she's not here. Do you know where she is? Is she with you?'

For a hopeful second I allow myself to imagine the three of them sitting in a cafe together somewhere. She just woke up early, I think, and decided to go out for breakfast with the others, and Dylan didn't think to amend his note before they left.

'No, she's not with me,' Dylan says, shattering the illusion.

Silence fills the phone line as we both scramble for an explanation that makes sense. Finding none, Dylan speaks.

'I'm coming home,' he says, more serious now. 'Have you tried calling her?'

'Of course I've bloody tried,' I snap. 'I'm not an idiot!'

He ignores my reaction. 'OK, I'll try her now, and I'll give Paige and Esther's mums a call. Why don't you go and check with Linda, just in case she's popped over there for something, and maybe try Maddie's mum too. I'll see you in twenty minutes, but call me if you hear from her, OK?'

'OK,' I say dumbly, relieved that he's taken charge. 'You too, call me if you hear.'

I hang up and grab my house keys from the hook in the entryway, pulling on some sandals and slamming the front door behind me. I run past two houses and then down the driveway of Linda's home. I knock hard and twist the front door handle. The house is unlocked. I open the door, shouting Imogen's name.

Linda appears at the end of the hallway, her mouth open in surprise and indignation at my uninvited entrance. Her children are shouting in the living room, arguing over something, but I'm not listening to what they're yelling about. I run towards the sound, hoping my daughter will be in there with them.

'Have you seen Imogen? Is she here?' I ask, breathless.

I reach the living room and look inside, my chest deflating with disappointment. It's just Kailah and Brayden, tussling on the sofa.

'Kat, what's going on?'

'Is Imogen here?' I yell, wishing I could stop the dread from building, wishing I could keep my voice down. But I'm suddenly terrified, worst-case scenarios running through my mind. What if she hates me so much that she ran away? What if she's been kidnapped? What if the reason she couldn't talk about the fight at school was that she really was being threatened and now someone has harmed her?'

'Kat!' Linda has grabbed my arms and is shouting my name.

I blink and focus on her blonde curls, her bright green eyes.

'What's going on?' she asks again calmly, kindly.

'Imogen's gone,' I say. 'She's not at home. She's not answering her phone. I don't know where she is.'

51

'OK, come with me.' Linda guides me by the arm into the kitchen and puts the kettle on. I try to protest, but she sits me down firmly and says, 'I'm going to help, but you're not going to find her while you're in this state. Hang on.'

As the kettle boils, she takes my phone from my clenched fist.

'Who do you want me to call?'

I look at her blankly.

'Any of her friends? Her friends' mums?'

I remember Dylan's instructions. 'Maddie,' I say. 'Maddie's mum. Um, Caroline Lee.'

She scrolls through my phone and fills a French press with water from the kettle. As she opens and closes cupboard doors, she speaks to Maddie's mum.

'Hi, Mrs Lee, this is Kathryn Braidwood's friend Linda . . . yes, Imogen's mum. Listen, is Imogen there with you? OK, could you ask your daughter please? No, she's not at home, we don't know where . . . Yes, OK, thanks. Please call if you hear anything.'

My heart sinks. Linda places a steaming-hot cup of coffee in front of me, and I stare into the black liquid in disbelief. A hand appears over mine. I look up.

'Is Dylan at home?' Linda asks.

My eyes fill with tears.

'No, he's on his way. He's calling some of her other friends.'

'I'll just give him a call,' she says, and I nod.

I'm only half listening to her, and barely hear what she's saying as she speaks to Dylan. I'm trying to make sense of what's happening. My daughter is missing. Is that really true? Or has she just popped out without telling us, gone for a run or down to the beach, or—

'I'm going to check the beach,' I say, standing up. 'What if she's at the beach?'

My daughter never goes to the beach. Not alone, anyway. I love going for walks by myself, feeling the sand between my toes and watching the ever-changing water, the dolphins, the birds diving into the waves. But not my daughter. She'll go, as long as there's someone else with her. But what if someone *is* with her?

Linda runs after me, catching me at the front door.

'Your phone, Kat,' she says, pressing it into my palm. 'Call me as soon as you hear. Let me know what I can do, OK?'

I nod, then turn around and run, more convinced with every step that my daughter will be there, on the sand, laughing with her friends, calling me stupid for overreacting. My feet slam into the pavement in time with my heart, and before I know it, I'm there, on the pavement above the sand, looking out at the blue water and matching sky.

My stomach churns, last night's alcohol protesting against the physical activity, but I ignore it and scramble down the dune, sharp blades of wiry grass stinging the tops of my feet as I go. I scan the beach, which is scattered with dog walkers, children making sandcastles, runners, couples taking strolls and teens kicking footballs. But there's no sign of Imogen.

Determined to keep looking, although I know I won't find her here, I run a short way along the soft sand, my calf muscles screaming and sand scraping the skin between my toes. I only stop when I hear my name.

I can't see him, but I know it's Dylan. Panting, I look up towards where the voice came from and spot him standing at the top of a small dune. I scramble up the soft sand, ignoring the sign that warns me about snakes in the area, more concerned about reaching Dylan than what could be lurking in the grass.

When I get to the top, I look at him for any indication of news. The worry in his face must mirror my own, and I know instantly that he hasn't found our daughter, either.

'Paige and Esther haven't heard from her,' he says, and I stand with my hands on my hips, helpless and unsure what to do next, what to say, how to find her.

'Where's Jemima?'

'I left her with Linda.'

I glance at my phone. It's only been forty-five minutes since I noticed Imogen was gone. But how long since I really knew where she was? Hours? Or worse – since last night?

'I think we should call the police,' I say.

'Whoa.'

Dylan grips the tops of my arms, as though that will somehow steady me. It only makes me more agitated. I shrug him off.

'I think it's too soon for that.'

'But, Dylan—'

'Think about it. What if she *has* just gone out with a friend and forgotten to tell us? After everything that's happened lately, the stuff about you trusting her . . . maybe this is the time to actually prove that you do.'

I pause. He might be right. My head can see the logic in what he's saying, but my heart, my gut . . . This doesn't feel OK. My maternal instinct has kicked in, and I know something is wrong. But I've known that before, been convinced that my children have been in mortal danger, and they've been fine. I take a breath as both of these thoughts battle each other for dominance. I look up at Dylan's face. He's concerned, I can tell by the hunch of his shoulders and the slight sloping of his eyebrows, but he's calm, as always.

'Why don't we go back to the house,' he suggests gently. 'And call her coach? If she doesn't turn up for practice, that's when we can worry, OK?'

'And if she doesn't show up,' I swallow firmly to dislodge the lump in my throat, 'then we call the police?'

Dylan pauses.

'OK,' he says after a beat. 'But I'm sure she'll be there. I'm sure it won't come to that.'

I nod. I want to feel the same solid certainty as Dylan, want to believe she'll come home before we have to face the possibility that she's really missing. But something inside me knows that this is no misunderstanding, no miscommunication.

My daughter is gone. And all I can think – the awful, horrible thought that keeps running through my head – is that I knew this was coming.

I knew it all along.

Chapter 10

KAT

'Thank you for letting me know,' I whisper into the phone, feeling anything but grateful. 'Please call me if she shows up.'

I end the call and look across the table to meet Dylan's gaze. He's staring at me, waiting for me to tell him what he already knows.

I avoid looking at Jemima, who we picked up on our way back to the house. She's sitting next to Dylan, looking between the two of us. I don't want to worry her, but there's no way of hiding the truth, either.

We've been sitting like this for an hour, making phone calls, dividing and conquering, speaking to anyone who we can remember Imogen ever mentioning. Old friends, new friends, teachers. Even during most of the calls, I knew I was clutching at straws, but that didn't stop me from feeling more and more panicked with every 'sorry, I haven't seen her' I heard.

'That was Martin,' I say woodenly to Dylan. 'She didn't show up.'

I'd called Martin Cresswell when we'd got home, as soon as I'd run through every room again to check for any sign of my daughter. The house had been empty. I'd sat heavily at the kitchen table and had dialled Imogen's volleyball coach.

'Martin,' I'd said when he'd picked up. 'Are you at the courts yet? Have you seen Imogen today?'

'I'm here, but I haven't seen her yet. Still a while till practice. Everything OK?'

Tears had welled in my eyes and I'd forced them back down. Crying wouldn't find Imogen. I'd rearranged my face, which had begun to crumple automatically, and had taken a breath.

'We don't know where she is,' I'd said, the same combination of words I'd end up giving dozens of times over the next hour. I avoided using the word 'missing'. That seemed too dangerous. She was somewhere safe, I told myself; I just didn't know where that was. Yet.

'Well, I'm sure she'll be here. She's never skipped a practice,' Martin had reassured me.

'OK, but if she's not there when it starts, please will you call me right away?'

Despite his confidence, despite my belief that Imogen would never miss her Sunday practice, Martin's call has confirmed my fear that something is seriously wrong.

When Imogen was small, I'd spend hours looking at her squishy cheeks and rounded belly and wonder what she was going to be when she was older. I imagined a high-powered lawyer who fought for the rights of the oppressed, or a surgeon, skilled enough to save lives, or a politician, but one who would actually do some good.

I didn't imagine a professional sports player, which is a short-lived career at best, or non-existent at worst. But, despite my best efforts, she won't be talked out of it, and in the end, I've had to accept that she might not have the career I once dreamed of for her.

Which is why, if she's not turned up today, we know that she's not just off with a friend somewhere. Imogen knows the rules: no practice, no game. And skipping one game could seriously hinder her chances of being selected for the national team. If she's not there, it's not because she's chosen not to be.

'I'll call the police,' Dylan says now, standing suddenly, his face pale, his calm demeanour gone.

I nod, unsure what to do. I sit, both palms planted on the table, frozen by shock and indecision. Dread sits like lead in my stomach, heavy and solid, contaminating my bloodstream.

When the doorbell rings, I gasp and launch myself from the kitchen table, knocking over my chair with a crash that I barely hear. It's only when I throw the front door open and see two policemen in uniforms standing there that I realise it would make no sense for it to have been Imogen. She has keys. She wouldn't need to ring the doorbell.

The realisation deflates me, and it's like my world has been pulled out from beneath my feet. I sway slightly, and lean on the side table for support. Jemima appears by my side.

'Mum?'

'Mrs Braidwood?' one of the policemen asks.

I nod. I take a breath, open my mouth. Close it again. Then I say, 'How did you get here so fast? Dylan only just called.'

Dylan's hand lands on my shoulder for just a second. Then he reaches over and grabs Jemima gently by the shoulders.

'Jems, love, Mum's fine, but can you go and wait in the living room for us? We'll just be a sec.'

She hesitates, but moves away, making room for Dylan to shake the officers' hands and invite them inside. I'm not listening to their names. I'm trying to make sense of this.

'Why are they here already?' I whisper. I'm suddenly hit

by an awful thought: what if they're not the police that Dylan called? What if they're here to deliver some kind of horrifying, terrible news? My vision blurs and I double over, gasping for breath.

'Come on,' Dylan says, steering me with a hand in the small of my back.

'But Imogen,' I say thickly, trying to understand what's going on.

'These policemen are here to help us find her, OK? They're here to help, but you need to answer some questions for them. Imogen needs you. All right, love?'

'But how did they get here so fast?'

'They didn't. It's been half an hour since I called them. You're just in shock. It's going to be OK, just come and sit on the sofa.'

He puts me down gently, carefully, as though I might break, and then offers the cops a drink. They follow him into the kitchen and Jemima crawls into my lap like she's a toddler again. I put my arms around her, whispering words of reassurance that I don't think I believe. As we wait for the three men to return, I try to pull myself together. I glance at the clock on the wall. It's after one, which means Dylan's right – I've somehow lost half an hour. I shake my head in an attempt to snap into the present.

For a second there, I truly believed that the police were here to tell me the worst news imaginable. Dylan always tells me that I catastrophise, but I can't seem to help it. It's a coping strategy: if I consider the worst-case scenario, maybe I'll be a little bit prepared if ever it actually happens. Of course, I was completely unprepared now, when these police officers showed up at my door.

They walk back in, ice cubes clinking melodically in their glasses. The policemen sit opposite me, and Dylan takes a seat beside Jemima and me, placing three cold glasses of water on the coffee table. I reach for one with shaking hands and take a long sip.

'Sorry to give you a fright, Mrs Braidwood,' says the man with the deep tan and sandy golden hair. He looks like a surfer, not like someone who can help me find my daughter. I force myself to smile.

'Sorry I reacted like that,' I say. 'I'm just so worried.'

'I understand,' he replies. 'Can I take a few details first, before we get into the specifics of your daughter's disappearance? Could you please tell me her full name and date of birth?'

'Her full name is Imogen Rae Braidwood, she was born on 12 January 2003, so she's just turned sixteen,' I say.

Dylan reaches over and taps my knee. I didn't realise I'd been jiggling it up and down, but I force myself to keep it still. To breathe. I pull my arms more tightly around Jemima.

'OK,' says the other policeman, an older guy with a bushy salt-and-pepper moustache. 'And can you tell us when you last saw Imogen?'

Dylan and I look at each other.

'Last night,' we say in unison.

'What time would that have been?'

'Uh ... maybe eight thirty?' Dylan guesses. 'We had some friends over yesterday, and people stayed till quite late. Imogen's grounded, so she was in her room sulking, you know, typical teenager ...'

'Why was she grounded?'

I frown at the shift in the policeman's tone. He's still friendly enough, but there's something underneath his smile. Something that sounds a bit like suspicion.

'That's not really relevant, is it?' Dylan asks sharply.

'We don't know what's relevant yet,' the cop answers

patiently. 'So we'd rather get a full picture right off the bat. It's better for us to have more information than not enough. Letting us know everything, no matter how small you think it is, could be the difference between us finding your daughter or not.'

My temples throb. I open my mouth, then snap it closed, my teeth making a clicking sound. Then I shake my head. Finding Imogen is too important.

'Well, then there's something you should know about Imogen,' I say, my voice trembling.

Dylan's hand lands on my leg, making me jump. I look over at him, and he tilts his head, ever so slightly – *don't*.

I narrow my eyes.

'What is it, Mrs Braidwood?' the older cop asks.

'Uhhhh . . .' I keep looking at Dylan, who is frantically trying to communicate without words. He glances at Jemima, then back to me. I can't think quickly enough.

'She's allergic to shellfish,' Dylan says, his eyes still firmly on me.

After a second, I nod.

'That's right,' I agree. 'Severely allergic.'

'OK,' the younger officer says, scribbling in his notepad. 'We'll keep that in mind, and we'll check the hospitals, just in case. Now if we could go back to the reason she was grounded . . . ?'

'She got into some trouble at school,' I explain.

'What sort of trouble?'

Dylan shifts awkwardly next to me.

'She punched another student,' I say quietly.

Jemima tenses in my lap, and I stroke her hair gently.

I glance up to see the officers' reaction to this news. They exchange a knowing look.

'Mr and Mrs Braidwood,' the older cop says, his voice

quiet and calm, 'I know this is difficult to accept, but it's not uncommon for teenagers to run away, especially after arguments with their family, or when they're in some kind of trouble with the law or at school—'

'No,' Dylan interrupts firmly.

The policemen exchange another glance, one that says *here we go again*.

My husband ignores it and carries on, his tone even and steady. 'I understand that you've probably seen a lot of runaways in your time, and I do know that teenagers can be difficult. I could accept that Imogen might have run away from *us*, but she would never, ever run away from volleyball. Not for anything. That's why we know there's something wrong here, OK? She's never missed a practice before, not even when she was sick. She'd sit on the bench, shivering under a blanket, sweating and coughing and spluttering. But she didn't turn up today. Something, or someone, is keeping her away, and we need you, please, to find her for us. If she's being kept from volleyball, something is wrong.'

There's a silence as the older cop considers Dylan's plea. Then he sighs wearily, and nods. Pulls out a notepad.

'OK. Do you have a recent photograph of Imogen?'

Chapter 11

IMOGEN

Imogen blinked her eyes open, her pale lashes glowing in the golden sunlight. For a moment she lay frozen in fear, her surroundings unfamiliar. She was looking at a grimy, textured ceiling. It wasn't her bedroom at home; that one was smooth and bright white, not covered in strange stains, the presence of which, when she thought about it later, she struggled to understand.

But she wasn't thinking about that just yet. Cautiously, she slid her eyes to her left, to try to piece together the puzzle of where she was and what was happening. As her eyeballs moved in their sockets, a red-hot pain seared through her skull, slicing along the nerves behind her eyes. She clamped them closed and scrunched her face until the sharp, piercing agony was reduced to a dull ache. She pressed her fingers to her head, probing to see if she was injured. There was nothing – no bruising – and when she hovered her fingertips above her face and gingerly opened her eyes again, there was no blood.

Confused, she tentatively rolled onto her side so she could assess her surroundings without having to move her eyes. As soon as she heaved her body around, the nausea hit, enveloping her. She leaned over the side of the bed and threw up, her chest aching and her head throbbing.

Imogen stared at the sticky mess on the grubby green carpet, too weak and sick to feel bad about it. She closed her eyes and rolled onto her back again, urging herself to pull a coherent thought together. Her brain felt like it was at sea, sloshing back and forth, constantly moving, swaying. Drowning. She lay perfectly still and closed her eyes to concentrate.

Where was she?

She forced herself to claw her way past the panic, to wait for everything to make sense. There had to be an explanation for why she was here, in this strange, squalid room, rather than in her own bed, in her own room. There had to be a reason for her to be feeling this sick, this battered.

Gradually, like a camera coming into focus, snippets of memory sharpened in her mind: salty air, bright headlights, a pastel pink ocean, roaring anger, a white car, a blue stripe, a gravelly voice. Bubbling nerves. A bottle of clear liquid. Fire. A laugh. A strange pram. A glaring, naked light bulb. Her head spinning.

She waited for each of the memories to slot together, puzzle pieces that would fit perfectly to form a clear recollection, but they just floated, suspended and jumbled together, unwilling to fall into place. Her stomach lurched again. She rolled over and retched, but this time it was only bile, thin, bitter strands of it, that dangled from her lower lip. Tears stung her eyes, but she blinked them away and wiped her mouth with the back of her hand.

Imogen squeezed her eyes closed again, willing her brain to play along, to spit out the information she wanted. But there was nothing. Blackness. She gave up after a few seconds, too tired and weak to fight the mental battle.

Exhausted and in pain, she tentatively rolled onto her side, more cautiously this time, and curled up into a ball. Closing her eyes, she let oblivion claim her once again.

Chapter 12

KAT

'Any news?' Dylan asks breathlessly, rushing towards me as soon as I open the door.

After the policemen left our house, armed with a recent photo of Imogen and names and contact details of her best friends, her school and her volleyball team members, I'd paced up and down the hallway, nervous tension eating away at me until I couldn't take it any more.

'I'm going out to look for her,' I'd exploded, and before Dylan could argue or Jemima could insist on joining me, I was out the door, in the car and reversing off our driveway. I didn't know where I was going or how I was going to find Imogen. All I knew was that I couldn't just sit in the house and wait.

I'd driven aimlessly at first, the windows wound all the way down, the hot air whipping my face, the stinging of my skin somehow soothing the anxiety inside. Eventually I'd calmed down enough to think more strategically. In my daze I'd driven along the coast, past the conservation park, onto the main road until I'd found myself in Port Noarlunga, staring at the sapphire water, the reef jutting out at the end of the jetty and the seagulls lazily swooping down to snatch any fish swimming too close to the surface. I couldn't imagine any reason why Imogen would be there, but it seemed silly not to at least try.

I wasn't sure how to begin, so I stopped the car outside a beachside cafe and went inside.

'Can I help you?' A young woman with a lip ring and bright blue hair had turned around as the bell above the door jingled. She started. 'Are you OK?'

I must have looked disastrous. I'd been crying, and dishevelled probably didn't begin to cover my appearance.

'I'm OK,' I'd said to her automatically. Then, 'Actually, my daughter is missing. Have you seen her? Here, I have a photo.'

I'd tapped my phone with trembling fingers to find a picture where Imogen's face was clear. I didn't have to search for long. I'd taken a photo of her yesterday – although how could it possibly have only been yesterday? – at the barbecue. It had been snapped when she wasn't looking, which is the only way I can capture her these days. Imogen was standing behind Jemima, teasing her, probably. In the photo, the two girls are staring right at one another, a silent conversation no one else was privy to. My throat had closed over at the sight of the two of them, but I swallowed firmly, zoomed in on Imogen's face and turned the screen of my phone towards the waitress.

She peered at the photo, her forehead scrunched in concentration. My whole body tensed in anticipation. She pressed her lips tightly together and shook her head slowly.

'Nnnnooo, sorry,' she said, drawing out the no and looking me in the eye. She tipped her head slightly to the side, presumably an attempt to seem apologetic, or sympathetic. It only made her look dim-witted. 'I don't think I've ever seen her before. Sorry I can't help.'

I mumbled a thank you at her and hurried out of the

door, disappointment wafting after me like the girl's cheap perfume. I got back into my car and drove north, stopping in every cafe, restaurant and shop I saw along the way. It was the same every time. That exaggerated squinting at Imogen's photo, the look of intense concentration, the slow, apologetic nod. The sympathetic head-tip.

I wanted to scream. I wanted to shake them and yell 'I don't need your sympathy. I need my daughter,' but, of course, I smiled and said thank you and tried to walk out upright, the weight of despair growing heavier with each failed attempt.

When I got to the shopping mall, one of Imogen's favourite places to hang out with her friends, I stood at the bottom of the escalators that lead up to the cinema and spun in a slow circle, my eyes greedily scanning the crowds for any sign of my daughter.

'Kat?'

I turned my head sharply, unable to recognise the woman in front of me for a couple of seconds.

'Kat? Are you OK?'

'Oh. Tammy,' I'd said eventually, the face and name of one of the mums I see regularly at the school gates coming into focus all at once. 'Hi.'

'Is everything OK?'

It had struck me as strange, in that moment, that she didn't know. How could she not know? How was anyone oblivious to the earth-stopping emergency that was happening? But of course she didn't know. Why would she?

'I— No,' I'd stammered. 'No. Imogen's missing. Have you seen her?'

'Oh my God, I'm so sorry. When did she go missing?'

'Last night,' I said, my eyes flicking back and forth to scour the faces of the shoppers passing by.

'Can I do anything to help?'

'Thanks, but I don't think—'

My heart had stopped. The noise had disappeared.

'Imogen!'

I took off at a run, ignoring Tammy's startled questions. Imogen was there. It was just a glimpse, a split second, a flash of blonde hair in the crowd, but I knew it was her. I just knew. My lungs burned as I pushed through huddles of teenagers and families with prams. A few people protested, but I didn't bother apologising. I was oblivious to anything but the blonde hair bobbing in and out of sight towards the food court. I dodged and weaved, hope bursting in my chest.

'Imogen!'

She didn't turn around. I almost tripped over a trolley, and stumbled for a few steps, regaining my balance just before hitting the polished floor. I looked up as I steadied myself, and scanned the people ahead of me.

'Imogen? IMOGEN!'

I took off again, looking around desperately as I ran. People stopped to stare, the crowds parting for the deranged woman hurtling towards them. I didn't care. As I reached the food court, I caught sight of the blonde hair again, and the relief pushed me onwards, knocking chairs to the floor with a clatter as the distance between us closed in.

I was a few metres away, then a metre, and then she was within my grasp and I grabbed the top of her arm with a cry of relief.

'Whoa, watch it!' The girl tore her arm from my grip, and as soon as she began to turn around, I knew it wasn't Imogen. Of course it wasn't. She looked nothing like her. She was too short, too tanned, too curvy to be Imogen. How could I have mistaken a random girl for my daughter? The only thing they had in common was their light blonde hair.

'I'm sorry,' I'd muttered, all of the energy drained from my body in an instant.

'What the hell is wrong with you? Crazy bitch,' the girl said, and her friends burst into high-pitched cackles.

I wanted to collapse, right there on the food court floor, to just give in to the disappointment and fear and desperation. But I told myself to keep walking, to keep moving, to keep looking. I wandered the mall for a while longer, my heart skipping at every blonde head, then sinking again as I looked, properly, and saw a stranger each time. In the end, dehydrated and defeated, there was nowhere to go but back home.

Now, faced with Dylan's hopeful tone, the pleading look in his eyes, I want to run away again, to not have to let him down.

I shake my head. 'No. I searched all over. I don't know where she could be.'

'Where did you look?'

I explain to him my route down south, up to the mall and back home. He chews his bottom lip.

'I'm going to keep looking,' Dylan says, and I nod. I understand the compulsion to move, to act. And the more ground we cover, the more people we speak to, the more likely we'll find her.

Part of me doesn't want to ask, but I need reassurance, so I whisper the words I've been thinking. 'Do you think we should have told them . . . ?' I don't finish. I don't need to.

Dylan stops and turns, looking at me intently. He runs his hand through his tawny hair.

'No,' he says, looking down. 'It wouldn't help us find her. It doesn't have anything to do with this.'

I press my lips together and sigh. He's right. Of course he

is. But I can't seem to stop the pinpricks of doubt that are needling at my conscience.

Dylan kisses me on the top of my head, but, I notice, he doesn't meet my eyes.

'Trust me,' he says. 'We did the right thing.'

I nod, unconvinced, as he jangles his keys in his hand and walks away.

'Wait!' I cry out, and he stops. 'Jemima?'

'India's mum came and picked her up to go to that party,' he says. 'I thought it would be good for her to be away from all of this for a while. She'll get dropped off again a bit later.'

'OK,' I say as he turns again. 'Call me with any news.'

The sound of the front door closing echoes down the hall, and then I'm alone in resounding silence. Dylan is so confident that we've made the right decision, that there's no way the truth we're hiding could be relevant to Imogen's disappearance. Logic tells me he's right. I'm just being paranoid; there's nothing to suggest that the two things are linked.

So why do I feel like the past is lurking behind me, ready to pounce?

Chapter 13

KAT

I'm rummaging through Imogen's closet, trying to work out whether any clothes are missing, when a small, quiet voice breaks the silence.

'Mum?'

My heart stops for a second. I whirl around, expectation exploding behind my ribs.

It's Jemima. My stomach twists in disappointment, and then again with guilt for being disappointed. But it's only momentary; relief floods over me as I realise that my youngest child, at least, is safe and accounted for. It's exactly why I made her stay home from school today.

'Jemima,' I say, stepping across the room to pull her to me. I hold her tightly, and tears gather behind my eyes again. I blink them away, pressing my emotions into a hidden part of me that I'll deal with later. When Imogen is home.

In the past twenty-four hours, I've become a pro at crushing my feelings, a skill borne out of necessity and practicality. Dylan came back yesterday after visiting the homes of each of Imogen's best friends, no closer to knowing where she is than I was after my erratic drive around Adelaide's suburbs, and we both just stood in the hallway, facing one another, paralysed by our helplessness.

We'd waited all evening, trying not to stare at the front

door, at our phones, as Linda – who had cancelled her plans to wait with us – cooked us food we didn't touch. The hands on the clock in the hallway kept sliding onward, forward, signalling the unthinkable. Midnight came and went and still we waited and watched, unsure what to do or think or feel. Imogen wasn't home. She was out there, somewhere, and we didn't know where or with whom or how to reach her. We tried to remind each other that the police were doing their job, that they were out there looking. And when the sun finally crept up over the horizon, Dylan reached for his keys and drove away to continue the search. He's not home yet. I've been messaging him constantly for updates, but so far his search has been as fruitless as mine was yesterday. While I wait – for news, for Imogen to walk through the front door, for *something* – I've been trying to keep busy, keep doing, keep searching, but I feel helpless, and it's excruciating.

It's been tempting to crumble, to give in and collapse into my panic and fear, but I won't find Imogen if I'm immobilised by my feelings. I have to stay composed until we find her. Then I can acknowledge the terror and guilt and anger. Then I can mull over the what-ifs that got us here. Now's not the time.

'Mum, did Imogen run away?' Jemima mutters into my torso.

I kiss the top of my daughter's head and stroke her hair. Tilting her head so her eyes meet mine, I sigh. She's barely spoken, barely reacted, since she got home from the party yesterday, when we told her that her sister still wasn't home.

'We don't know yet. Her window was open, so it looks likely. But the important thing is that there are lots of people looking for her, and we'll find her very soon, I'm sure of it. Jemima, are you sure she didn't say anything to you? Did she ask you to keep a secret for her, because it's OK if you tell us now. It could help.'

I hold her out at arm's length, and Jemima shakes her head, looking down at her feet. I pull her into another hug, feeling the tension in her small frame. I wish I could absorb it all, take on everything that she's going through, make her anxieties my own.

'Do you want to help me look through Immy's room?' I ask. 'The police think that if she did run away, then she might have taken some clothes with her, so we need to see if anything is missing. Then we might know more about where she's gone, and for how long. Does that make sense?'

Jemima nods.

'OK,' she says. 'But I don't think she ran away. She knows that she belongs here.'

Her innocence makes my heart contract, as though squeezed by an invisible hand. I don't know how to tell Jemima that her sister's phone – her lifeblood – isn't in her room. Or that the flowers under her window were crushed as she slipped out in the night.

The police agree that she left voluntarily. But what happened next – where she went, and who she's with – that's what we can't figure out. None of her friends have seen her, at least none that we know of. Does she have secret friendships? A boyfriend we've never heard about? The thought sends a trickle of dread down my spine.

We rummage through Imogen's clothes and her desk drawers. I thought the police might have wanted to search through her belongings, but when I asked them, they looked at me like I was crazy.

'This isn't some TV show, Mrs Braidwood,' the younger one had said. 'There's no reason to suspect foul play, and running away isn't a crime. Talking to her friends is a much better use of our time.'

I'd been too dazed at the time to feel embarrassed by my naivety, but now, replaying the exchange in my mind, my cheeks burn.

I sigh, taking another sweeping look around Imogen's room. For her sixteenth birthday, we gave the space a makeover, and in one weekend we removed any evidence of a little girl – the pink bed frame, the Disney posters and the stuffed animals – and replaced them with the markings of a young woman – lots of white and grey and gold, at Imogen's request. There's a wall hanging that looks to me like it's straight out of my grandma's front room, but which my daughter assures me is cool. There's a grey throw at the end of her pristine white bed, and black-and-white photos in gold frames of various sizes. The whole effect is trendy and grown-up, and whenever I come inside, I get a pang of nostalgia for the cotton-candy pink of days gone by.

I sit heavily on the bed, waiting for some kind of answer to come to me. Nothing appears. My strength wavers, the lump in my chest moving rapidly to the surface, on the verge of spilling over in an uncontrollable tide.

'Mum,' Jemima says, stopping her search and looking squarely at me, 'Imogen's not a little girl, you know. She's pretty smart. She can look after herself.'

My darling Jemima, so rational and calm, even when it would be perfectly natural for her to be the one breaking down. She's inherited her dad's steady nature, and right now I couldn't be more grateful that she's not driven by her emotions, like I am.

'Can I go make a sandwich?' she asks. 'I'm hungry.'

'Of course, baby,' I say, giving her another hug. 'I'll be there in a sec.'

She leaves Imogen's room and I stay where I am, the white bedcover soft beneath my fingers. I stare for a second at a photo on her bedside table: Imogen and her best friend, Paige. Laughing, happy. Innocent. I open the top drawer. It's filled with charging cables, pens, a notepad emblazoned with the words 'Good Vibes Only' in gold. I flip through it, but there's nothing. A few pages have been torn from the middle, but it's otherwise blank. I place it back and close the drawer, moving methodically to the next one, and then back to her desk. I've already searched it, but I know I have to be missing something.

After looking through her entire desk, I run my hand under her mattress, peer beneath her bed, and then pull her wardrobe apart. I find schoolbooks filled with her neat handwriting, a stack of old *Girlfriend* magazines, and a secret stash of Picnics at the back of her wardrobe. I sit at her desk, tear the wrapper off one of the chocolate bars and tuck in, smiling at my daughter's act of rebellion. Well, not so much rebellion as possession. She knows that with Jemima and me in the house, any easily accessible chocolate will be sniffed out and eaten immediately. She's smart enough to keep her own stock, away from her sweet-toothed family.

Feeling sick from the sugar in my otherwise empty stomach, I open her laptop and stare at the password screen for a few seconds. Then I type *RoaringTigers*, the name of Imogen's beloved volleyball team. It doesn't work. I try again, in various upper and lower case combinations. When that doesn't let me in, I try her friends' names, her favourite band, combinations of Dylan's, Jemima's and my names. Nothing works. Frustrated, I stand up.

I glance at my phone. There are messages from friends and fellow parents offering to help, but nothing telling me where my daughter is. Sighing, I throw the chocolate wrapper at the gold waste-paper basket beside Imogen's desk, cursing when I miss. I bend over to collect it, but it's just out of my reach. Stretching over her desk chair, my fingertips brush the wrapper, failing to grip it, and I lose my balance, tipping the empty basket over.

Swearing, I steady myself on the edge of the bed, then kneel down to reach the chocolate wrapper. As my fingers curl around it, I notice a scrap of paper stuck to the bottom of the wire basket. I dislodge it from the rim and tip the waste-paper bin back upright. I throw the wrapper in and move to do the same with the scrap paper, when three letters catch my eye.

It's a logo, the bright blue shape sparking a memory from high school. A helix, I think it's called. Two parallel strands, twisted around, with rung-like lines between them. The small piece of paper is the top corner of what looks like a letterhead, but the rest of the page is gone, presumably in another week's recycling.

But this scrap I'm holding, with the blue helix, and the company name underneath, sets every nerve in my body on high alert. The hairs on the back of my neck prickle and stand to attention, and my mind is wiped clear of everything but the words I'm reading, black and bold against the pure white, glossy paper.

SureDNA, it reads.

My hand shakes.

She knows. Imogen knows.

And that changes everything.

Chapter 14

IMOGEN

Imogen strained her ears, but all she could hear was booming silence.

The absence of noise.

An abyss.

She thought that maybe she was plunging through time, through space, infinite falling, spinning, weightless; her stomach lurching and twisting. Then a jolt, her limbs forcing her back into fleeting consciousness, her eyes flinging open, only to snap closed against the light.

Was she alone?

She couldn't tell. There was so much she didn't know: how long she'd been in the same tiny bed, on that lumpy mattress, staring at the stained ceiling. How she got there. Who brought her. What was making her feel so disconnected, so weightless and yet so leaden at exactly the same time.

All she knew for certain was that every time she rolled towards the wall, a spring in the bed frame squealed, triggering a slicing pain behind her eyes that left her moaning and writhing. But movement meant nausea, and she'd emptied her stomach long ago. Now, her ribs screamed and her throat burned, and she was too tired to expend any unnecessary energy.

So she'd learned not to move. Instead, she'd laid there,

still as a corpse, her eyes firmly closed as the colour behind her eyelids morphed from bruised purple to angry red to bright white and all the way to black, when the silence fell on her like a blanket, comforting her. Suffocating her.

A magpie warbled, its melody echoing and building, coiling around her, finding her ear, a thread of silver that wound its way into her brain, tighter and tighter, a nightmare of minor notes she couldn't stop, couldn't control. Moving slowly, cautiously, her muscles protesting with every millimetre, she drew her hands up towards her face, pressing them against her ears, pushing harder, wincing as the melody turned into a cacophony of screams inside her head.

She needed it to stop. She had to find a way to stop herself from hearing it. She was spinning again, spiralling into blackness, but she didn't want the magpie's taunts to follow her to that place where time stretched and snapped. She opened her lips and screamed, the pain that she forced from her lungs drowning out the mayhem in her mind. It poured out of her, a battle cry, and as she squeezed every last drop of volume from her lungs and gasped to fill them once again, she heaved where she lay, her battered ribs howling, her throat clawed by invisible nails.

Blinded by the pain, by the fear, by the onslaught on her senses, she didn't see the long, silver point of the needle. She didn't hear the soothing voice, the one she couldn't place but which was oh-so familiar. She didn't feel the pinprick of pain in the crook of her arm, right beside the tiny day-old wound, insignificant against the agonising symphony she was drowning in.

And, all at once, the hateful music playing around her was snipped mid-bar, the notes falling to the ground in a pile of black shapes, a pitiful patter against the carpet, and Imogen's body slumped into the mattress, sensation melting into nothingness, silence enveloping her, beckoning her back to obscurity.

And so she fell, once again, her lungs emitting a small, surprised breath of surrender.

Chapter 15

KAT

My hand is shaking as I search for the company on my phone. I try to come up with any other explanation that could make sense. Maybe she doesn't know and this tiny scrap of paper doesn't mean what I think it means. Maybe it's for school – a biology project, perhaps.

I click the first link that appears in the search results. It loads in the blink of an eye.

Discreet DNA testing, the website reads. *Paternity, maternity, ancestry and more. No blood required. Private, fast and reliable. Send an enquiry today or read our frequently asked questions here.*

My head spins. I blink back the darkness that hovers in my peripheral vision. Is it really possible that she found out?

I navigate through to the contact information page and tap the call button. I will them to answer the phone, will them to have real people, not voice-activated robots, at the other end of the line.

'SureDNA customer service, how can I help?' an overly cheery woman answers.

I take a breath.

'Hi, I think my daughter used your services, and I'd like to find out if she's a customer please.'

'I'm afraid I can't give out details of our customers. We take privacy very seriously.'

'My daughter is sixteen, and she's missing. This could help find her. Please.'

'I'm very sorry to hear that, but I'm afraid I still can't help you,' she says. 'Not without a police warrant.'

I hang up and redial the same number right away, tapping my screen furiously.

'SureDNA customer services, how can I help?'

It's the same voice. I hang up again and swear loudly, hitting redial once more. I close my eyes and mutter 'Be someone else, be someone else' as the phone rings.

'SureDNA customer services, how can I help?'

My shoulders drop in relief at the deep voice.

'Hi, my name is Imogen Braidwood,' I say, affecting a higher-pitched, girlier tone. I sound nothing like my daughter, but I don't need to. 'I lost the information you sent me and I was wondering if you could email it over please?'

'Sure,' he says brightly. 'I just need a few details from you first.'

My stomach clenches. I think I know my daughter, but the next few moments will prove whether I really do, or if she's a complete stranger.

'OK,' I say, my mouth claggy, like I've gargled glue. I clear my throat.

'Could you confirm your date of birth, please?'

I almost laugh. Easy. I offer the date confidently.

'Thank you. And your mother's maiden name?'

I open my mouth, the name Crouch on my lips. I stop and clamp my mouth shut. They don't want *my* mother's maiden name. They want Imogen's mother's maiden name. My maiden name. I mentally pinch myself. I need to concentrate.

'Heppner,' I say.

I hold my breath as I wait for confirmation that I've passed this test.

'Great, thanks. Just a couple more,' he says, and I silently empty my lungs.

I breeze through the remaining security questions. Address, phone number, first pet. No problem.

'OK, what email address shall I send this to?' the man asks.

I rattle it off, grateful that he doesn't question the fact that it's Kathryn, not Imogen, in the email address. I thank him and rush down the hallway to the living room, where my laptop is sitting on the small desk in the corner.

I open the lid, my heart pounding, and type in my password. The screen springs to life. I open a browser window and click on the tab that's displaying my inbox. There's nothing new. I click refresh. And then again. I keep clicking furiously, until, finally, a bold message appears at the top of the list. I hold my breath as I wait for the email to load.

Dear Imogen, it reads. *Thank you for choosing SureDNA. Please find attached the results of your recent DNA test. If you have any questions . . .*

I stop reading and scroll to the bottom of the message, where a PDF file is attached. As I click on it, and a new window pops open, my throat closes over, stopping me from taking the breath I need. My world, once wide and full, has now been narrowed down to a tiny pinpoint, my vision laser-focused. Nothing else matters. Nothing else exists. I wheeze, trying to fill my lungs, blinking back tears.

A document appears on my screen, and for a second my brain struggles to unpack the information I'm seeing. There are four columns, all filled with numbers that mean nothing to me. The first column, the header of which I don't understand, is also filled with codes. I suddenly wish I'd paid more attention in school all those years ago. Panic washes over me. I need to understand. I need to know.

I close my eyes for a second and tell myself to concentrate. I open them again and focus.

I ignore the first column and keep reading. The second column has the title CHILD. The next, Alleged MOTHER.

The word 'Alleged' is like a punch in the stomach, but I resist the urge to dwell on it, and read on frantically, desperate to get to the part where I understand. Where I know what Imogen knows.

The last heading reads, Alleged FATHER.

Underneath all of the columns are the words that make the walls of the living room feel like they're closing in, imprisoning me, smothering me. I take a shaky breath and read the two simple lines again, just to be sure. But there's no mistaking what they say.

Probability of paternity: 0%

Probability of maternity: 0%

It was all for nothing, I realise as my heart tumbles behind my ribs, tearing itself free and plummeting towards the ground. All these years of well-intentioned lies, all that time spent worrying and watching, looking for signs, imagining I've seen a likeness, a resemblance in behaviour, and telling myself that of course I haven't, that she doesn't know, that it's not in her DNA.

All of the heartache and lying awake at night desperately hoping we've done enough to change her future, to rewrite her fate. All of the energy we spent to protect her from the truth. It was all for nothing.

She knows. And she's gone. And even if we find her, we might have lost Imogen forever.

Chapter 16

SALLY

It doesn't happen often, but on the rare occasion when it does, there's nothing I hate more than being pitied. I can handle being hated. But pity is intolerable.

Sure, I had a terrible childhood. My dad didn't love me, he passed me around like a cigarette, he sold me to his colleague, he might have killed my mum. I know it's tragic. But *I* am not tragic. I made my own choices, and I stand by them.

Well, most of them. I don't regret what I did – I was doing my best – but suppose I regret what happened as a result of some of my actions. Or maybe I regret what could have been, if things had been different. I loved those kids. I love all of my kids. And I'm proud of the fact that I'm nothing like my waste of space of a father. He used me. He opened his home and let just anyone come in and use me, too.

When I found out that I was pregnant with my first, with my beloved Tim's child, I was scared. I was only fifteen. I didn't know anything about taking care of a baby. The only thing I knew for certain was that I'd never do anything like what my dad did to me, to any of my own kids. And I never did.

I didn't let anyone near them. Didn't allow anyone into our home, didn't expose my children to others, didn't put them in that awful, vulnerable position that I knew all too well. I protected them.

I did the best I could. I was so young when I had Jared. I didn't know what I was doing; didn't have anyone to teach me. I loved that boy so much that my heart hurt when I looked into his big golden eyes. My eyes. My mum's eyes.

Those first few years were brimming with joy. The day Tim saved me was the happiest I've ever been, but the year after Jared arrived, and then the first couple of years of his brother Anthony's life, came pretty close. I couldn't believe how perfect they were, my little ones. So innocent, unblemished by life and all that it could throw at them. They were completely pure.

And then, slowly, gradually, things changed. Well, the children changed. Jared became stubborn and wilful. He'd try to get out of the house, wouldn't listen when I told him it was dangerous outside of our four walls. I had to teach him, had to make him understand. Home was the only safe place for him, the only place in the world where I could protect him. But he didn't listen, wouldn't respond to my pleas, my shouts. I had to resort to methods that couldn't be ignored. But it was for him. For his safety.

It was hard, at first, to watch my little angel crying, screaming, begging. But it got easier every time. And then – there's no point denying it, at this stage – I realised that it wasn't so hard after all. I loved when my children behaved themselves, when we could all sit around together in the evening playing board games or poring over a puzzle. But I also felt a pull inside me, a yearning to continue what I'd started. It became necessary, a way to keep my children the way I loved them the most: pure, innocent, unsullied by the world.

I know that things went too far. At least by the world's

standards. I was overcome with grief when Jared left us. We buried his little seven-year-old body in the back garden, and I planted a rose bush above him, a bright and cheerful Love Always. I tended to him every day, watered him. Kept him safe. Cared for him. At first I didn't want to go on. I'd lost my precious child. My firstborn. But Tim helped me to see. He helped me to remember how much I loved having babies, how much I enjoyed it when they were pure and blameless. And malleable. He reminded me that I was still young, that we could have as many babies as we wanted. That's when I saw. That's when I understood. I could have everything I wanted. I could have my babies, and I could enjoy every moment of their first few years. I could protect and teach them when they became unruly and stubborn. And then, when they couldn't be controlled, I could take care of them forever. I could prune them and fertilise them and water them.

Tim helped me to understand that I hadn't lost anything at all. Not really.

I'd gained a spectacular rose garden.

Chapter 17

KAT

I'd always believed that if Imogen so much as suspected the truth, I'd know about it right away. I thought there would be a confrontation. Or at least a sign.

My shoulders go slack and I hang my head as I realise how stupid I've been. Of course there were signs; I just misread them. Imogen's violence, her refusal to let us in, her anger towards us; towards me. Suddenly, in the light of the document on my screen, they now seem, so clearly, to be the emotional outpouring of a girl who is no longer certain of her identity.

'Mum? What's wrong?'

My head whips around. Jemima's standing in the doorway holding two plates, a frown plastered on her face.

'Oh, honey,' I say, desperate to reassure her. 'I just want Immy to come home.'

'Me too,' she says, not meeting my eye. 'I want things to go back to normal.'

I rush over to her and gently grab the plates from her hands. She's made two chicken sandwiches, one for each of us. She looks at me, her eyes clear but full of emotion, and my heart melts for her.

'Imogen is going to be fine,' I tell her, putting the plates down. I think the words might be to convince myself as much as Jemima. She nods slowly. I wish I could believe it, but with this new information, I'm not so sure. I can only imagine Imogen's state of mind right now, the anger she feels towards Dylan and I, the sense of betrayal. No wonder she ran. But how far? And to whom?

'Is it OK if I watch TV for a bit, Mum?'

Jemima looks guilty, as though she should be sitting in sombre silence until Imogen returns.

'Of course, baby. I have to go make some calls, I'll just be in my room, OK? Call me if you need anything.'

'I made you a sandwich,' she says, and I give her one more squeeze.

'Thank you.' I force myself to smile, taking the plate from the coffee table, along with my laptop. I leave her curled up on the sofa, hugging a cushion and munching her sandwich as some vapid teenage drama blares from the speakers.

As I walk down the hallway, glancing back to make sure Jemima is really OK, I'm hit with another thought. Imogen knows that she's not our daughter. But how much more does she know? What has she discovered? Terror crawls up my throat. How did she find out? Who told her?

Adrenaline shoots through me like electricity, and I rush to close the door of our bedroom, spurred on by the knowledge that our daughter could be in much greater danger than any of us had suspected. I unlock my phone and call Dylan.

He doesn't bother with pleasantries when he answers. 'Any news?'

'She knows.'

'What?'

'She knows, Dylan. She had a DNA test done. She knows. Where are you?'

There's a moment of stunned silence over the line, and

then my husband's voice is in my ear again, strained and distant, his mind probably going to the same dark destination that mine has parked itself in, where all of the awful things that this could mean for our daughter dwell.

'I'm just in Unley, but I'm turning around now. Be there as soon as I can.'

While I'm waiting for him to arrive, I make four frantic, tense phone calls, while frantically clicking through the SureDNA website, trying to understand how our daughter arranged a DNA test without us providing samples for her. I always thought you had to use one of those cotton buds they show on cop shows on TV, swiping the inside of your mouth with it. But, as I learn from the FAQ section of the slick, reassuring website, a DNA test can be done using hairs, or even toenail clippings.

The front door opens and I leap up. As I run down the hallway, Dylan's standing at the entrance to the living room with a finger pressed to his lips. Jemima is asleep, her mouth hanging slightly open, the drama unfolding on the TV screen lost on her. I motion for Dylan to follow me to our room, and when the door is firmly closed, I hand him my laptop, my jaw clenched.

He sinks onto the bed as his eyes flick over the report, his eyebrows moving closer and closer together.

'But how did she even know to look into this?' he whispers. 'How would she know to check?'

'I don't know,' I admit. 'But we need to tell the police.'

Dylan stares at me for a long moment, weighing up my words.

'I don't know.'

'This is important. It could be the piece of the puzzle that could help them find Imogen and to get her home safely.'

'Or it could be her downfall,' he says sharply. 'We've kept

this secret for a good reason. If it gets out, if the press get hold of it . . .'

'But if she already knows—'

'How could she possibly know?' he interrupts. 'OK, so maybe she knows that we're not her parents, but she can't know the rest. There's no way. Barely anyone in the world knows the truth . . .' His eyes widen. 'You don't think . . . ?'

I shake my head.

'I called everyone. Your mum, my parents, Sarah, Byron. They all swear they've never said anything to anyone. And they haven't heard from her.'

'OK,' Dylan says. 'So Immy doesn't know. She can't possibly know, and she doesn't need to know. What if this is totally unrelated to her disappearance? What if all of this gets out, and we put her in danger, or we put Jemima in danger, for nothing?'

I weigh up his words. He's right; it is a risk. But I need Imogen home more than this secret needs to remain locked away, and I don't see how this could be unrelated to her disappearance. Besides, she's almost an adult now, and if she's already worked out that she's not ours, she'll eventually piece the rest together. I need the chance to explain to her why we've been lying to her for so many years. I want her to find out the truth from me. She deserves that much.

'I want Imogen back,' I say slowly, 'I want her back safely. And maybe this is unrelated to that test, but I seriously doubt it. It would explain a lot. We need to give the police all of the information we have in case it's related, and we'll just tell them how important it is that no one finds out. They'll understand. We need to protect her. From . . . from them. Because what if she's trying to find them? Or worse – what if they've been trying to find her? Oh my God, what if they've succeeded?' My hands fly to my face, as the horror of all of the possibilities hit me.

My husband jumps up and grabs my wrists, peeling my palms from my face.

'OK,' he says. 'You're right. We've got to risk it. We've got to tell them. I'll give them a call.'

We stare at each other, terrified by the thought of having to dig back into the past, nervous of what this means, of what it could bring up. But I can see it in his eyes. He knows it's time. He knows it's right.

So why does it feel like our life is about to go up in flames?

Chapter 18

KAT

'Cops are here!'

Dylan's been keeping watch since he called them, anxiously pacing up and down the rug in the living room, not letting his eyes wander from the front window. After just a few minutes, his restlessness became too much for me to cope with. Besides, I was twitchy myself. I needed to stay busy, to feel like I was playing my part in the effort to find Imogen.

'I'm going to get the paperwork,' I'd announced, more to myself than to Dylan, who barely glanced my way before resuming his back and forth sentry duty. As I'd left, I'd scooped Jemima up from the sofa and carried her to her room, where I'd left her to sleep with the door closed. She didn't need to hear the revelations we were about to make.

Since then, I've been on my hands and knees in the study, shuffling through papers, the contents of which we've tried desperately to remove from our memories over the years. It's easier to keep a secret when you've convinced yourself it doesn't exist. Only, I never did manage to forget. How could I?

I opened the safe without hesitation. Even after all these years without opening it, without even needing to think about it, the lock's combination is still etched into my

92

memory: the date Imogen came into our lives. The day when everything changed.

Inside was a stack of paperwork, concealed behind an inch of reinforced steel and a locked cupboard door, the key to which has been hidden in a small, locked jewellery box in the top drawer of my bedside table. The key to that is on a chain around my neck, hidden among a cluster of mismatched keys in varying colours and sizes. Getting to this paperwork is like a treasure hunt, only the prize is a dossier of nightmares.

But for me, the keeper of the keys, it was easy to access this stash of secrets. Physically, anyway. I've spent fifteen years burying the information we keep here, trying to erase the past, wishing it didn't exist, wishing that our family was exactly the way we've always said it was. I was stupid to believe it ever could be.

As I skim-read each document, each record of the past, fear loomed larger and larger, impossible to ignore, too enormous to shut out. The past was chasing us down, the way we always feared it would.

Now I sigh and grab the pile of papers from the carpet, tapping it against the floor a couple of times to try to neaten the edges. I make a silent wish that the information in my hands won't have anything to do with Imogen's disappearance, that the police won't let anyone else get hold of it, and then I roll my shoulders back, lift my chin and walk out into the hallway.

Dylan's standing at the front door, welcoming the same two policemen who were here yesterday. They move inside and close the door behind them, commenting on the heat, on how nice it is to be in air conditioning.

'Hi,' I say, reaching the front door. 'Come in. I'm Kat. I

know we met yesterday, but I was in a bit of a state and I'm afraid I can't remember your names.'

'Troy,' says the older one, whose face is open and kind. He has laughter lines at the edges of his eyes, and as he smiles at me now, they scrunch together. I feel safe with this man. Confident that he wants the best for Imogen, too. I shake his hand, then turn my body to face the other one, the surfer.

'And I'm Ruben,' he says, offering his hand and taking mine firmly, shaking it once, like we've just made an important deal.

'Hi. Thank you for coming. Please, come through,' I say, waving them towards the living room.

Dylan walks in from the kitchen as we're sitting down, holding a tray of glasses as well as a jug of water straight out of the fridge. The ice in the glasses cracks as he pours us each a glass, and when we're settled back in our seats, Ruben clears his throat.

'Mr Braidwood, you said on the phone you have some important information regarding your daughter's disappearance?'

His glass is already empty, so I move to refill it, my stomach bubbling with nerves.

'Yes,' Dylan begins. 'Well, yes, we have information. But we don't know for sure if it's relevant to Imogen's disappearance. We just don't want to take any risks by not telling you, in case it's important.'

'Well,' says Troy quietly, 'why don't you let us know what it is, and we'll be sure to follow up on it, so we don't miss anything. We're committed to finding Imogen, Mr and Mrs Braidwood.'

'Please, call us Kat and Dylan,' I insist with a nervous laugh. My voice is shrill and unnatural. I'm trying to put off saying the words that need to be said, but it's time.

I glance at Dylan and he nods at me, reassuringly. I clear my throat.

'Have you heard of Satan's Ranch?' I ask Troy. I deliberately direct my question at him. He's old enough to have been around back then. Maybe he was even on the force when it happened.

His eyes widen. 'Do you mean that case from Victoria back in the day? Must have been, what, twenty years ago?'

'Fifteen,' I correct him.

'Yeah, course I remember,' he breathes. 'Bloody awful affair, that. Why do you ask?'

'Well, do you also remember that there were some children who survived?'

He nods, his face paling. I don't know if he's already there, if he's pieced the information together, or if he just knows that whatever is coming – whatever I'm about to say that's connected to Satan's Ranch – it can't possibly be good. Either way, his eyes are locked on mine. He's waiting for the bombshell.

I take a deep breath. I can't believe I'm about to say this. I'm certain my chest will explode.

'Those kids were rescued and fostered, put into homes, given new identities, adopted. There was a boy and a girl. And the girl ... well, the girl is Imogen.'

Chapter 19

SALLY

They say that my kids were 'rescued' from our home. But I know the truth: they were torn from safety and security and love, and thrown into the unknown, into the scary, messy world I worked so hard to shield them from.

I'm not sure which one broke my heart more: Kimmy or Amy. Kimberley was my fifth child, the eldest of my living babies. She'd always been a happy one, with big golden eyes, the most perfect nose and pretty rosebud lips. I'd been transfixed when she was born, soaking up every detail of those newborn days, the old feelings of elation and pure love returning again. Tash had been six when Kimberley was born, and Ashley eight.

Ashley had been a bad egg, rebellious from the start, determined to pave the way to his own destruction. He ran away from home once, a short-lived adventure he'd taken when he was five. I'd been furious, perhaps the angriest I've ever been. My children couldn't be exposed to the world, to the evil that lived beyond the safety of our sanctuary. The only way to cool the red-hot rage bubbling within me was to show Ashley how irresponsible he'd been, how unacceptable his behaviour was.

He'd been with us for another three years, but I'd known on the night of his failed escape that he wasn't meant for this world for long. Some children make better rose bushes, that's all there is to it. So Kimmy never really knew her older brother, except as the burst of white Little Pet blooms, which was just as well, as he probably would have tainted her, found a way to turn her against me. She was my perfect little girl, so docile and compliant, always understanding of my rules, of my moods.

She comforted me when I had a miscarriage, and then another. I knew that they were punishment for what I'd done. The rose bushes in the back garden were finding a way to haunt me, after all. But, once again, Tim helped me to see that I was wrong. He reminded me that I had nothing to feel guilty about, that I'd done nothing but protect my babies, keep them from people like my father. He explained that the babies I lost were rotten, like Ashley had been. He said they had bad blood, that they would have brought me more pain than joy.

I'd understood, in the end. And all the way through those hard days, Kimmy had told me she loved me, had put her fat little arms around my neck and pressed her soft, perfect cheek against mine, and my heart had melted.

It had taken some time after the miscarriages, but we'd had two more, a few years later. First came Brad, and then Amy. Brad's greatest downfall was that he was a boy. Girls, I'd discovered, were so much easier to raise. For a time, at least. Boys were wild and unmanageable from much earlier on, and I was forced to be much more harsh with them to make sure they didn't do anything dangerous. Of course, by that time I was an expert in disciplining my children. I knew exactly how to make them behave. But, as I got older, it took less and less for them to push my buttons.

The only one who never did was my Kimmy. Oh, she wasn't perfect. No one is. But she was a joy to raise, and as we celebrated birthday after birthday, we began putting more candles into her birthday cake than we ever had before. By then, Tash was fertilising a lovely bright orange Fearless rose, the perfect variety to suit her stubborn personality. For Kimberley, I'd have selected a blush and gold Bright Spirit. But I never needed to visit the garden centre for her. She remained pure and innocent, long after the rest of them had.

Too bad then that she stabbed me in the back and broke my heart at my trial. Turns out she's no Bright Spirit. She is The Dark Lady. I thought I'd raised someone who couldn't be spoiled, but I should have known, should have learned, that after a while, all kids lose that. They all become rotten. They're all bad apples.

My Amy was still just an innocent, perfect baby when she was torn from my arms. They literally pulled her from my embrace one Tuesday afternoon as she was gulping greedily at my breast. She was so small, so helpless. Brad was young, too, but he'd already started showing signs of insurgency. I loved him – of course I did – but he was developing a mind of his own, and that was a dangerous thing.

I'd screamed as they carried Amy out of the front door, out into the evils of the world, the very thing I'd fought so hard to protect all of my children from. I couldn't keep her safe out there. I couldn't stop terrible people from doing terrible things to her.

She was on her own.

And my heart had splintered into fragments.

Chapter 20

KAT

'Wait,' says Ruben, one palm held out towards me, his body shifting to face his partner. 'What are you guys talking about?'

I raise my eyebrows at Troy, indicating that he can take this one.

'It's a case from, well, fifteen years ago,' he says. 'Horrible stuff. A woman moved into a new place, out in country Victoria. Closest neighbours weren't for over a kilometre. But this woman was a runner, training for triathlons or something, so she went past this house every day, this ranch where a family lived. Only she kept noticing strange things happening. Screams, and kids staring out of the windows at weird hours, looking dirty and malnourished. She reckons she just had a gut feeling, one of those instinct things I guess, so she reported it. Cops paid the family a visit and discovered that none of the little ones had ever set foot outside. Those poor kids—'

He swallows hard. I do the same. Loathing for those parents builds and increases, the same feeling I get every time I acknowledge the truth of what happened all those years ago, but I push it down. I'm well rehearsed in keeping this particular truth at arm's length.

Ruben shifts uncomfortably in his seat and looks at his shoes.

'Yeah, OK,' he says quietly. 'I remember now. We learned about it in training.'

'So your Imogen is a Sanders kid,' Troy confirms, clearing his throat. 'And you just thought to tell us now?'

'Look,' I say, anger clawing its way up my chest. 'We've spent her whole life trying to protect her from the truth. And, more than that, we need to protect her from her biological parents. We can't risk them knowing where she is. And, honestly, we just didn't think it was relevant to her disappearance.'

My voice cracks, and I clamp my hand over my mouth.

Dylan moves closer to me and rubs my back in slow, calming circles. I focus on the warmth of his hand, on the way my skin feels when my T-shirt moves across my back. I remind myself to keep my mind on the small, real details. Not the what-ifs.

'So,' Ruben says hesitantly, 'what changed? Why are you coming to us with this now?'

'Kat found this today,' Dylan tells the two policemen, offering them a printout of the attachment I was emailed, while continuing to stroke my back with his other hand.

The two men lean in towards each other so they can both read the document at once.

Troy whistles. 'She got a DNA test?'

'Looks that way,' Dylan replies. 'Which means she knows she's not our biological daughter. We have no idea what made her think to do the test, or how much she knows about who her real parents are. I honestly don't know how she'd have found anything out – her name was legally changed when she was about eighteen months old, and we've only told a few of our closest family members, who would never breathe a word. We've checked in with them, and they assure us they haven't said anything to anyone. So we don't know if it's relevant, but we thought it'd be better to let you know in case it's connected, somehow.'

'We appreciate that,' Troy says. 'Do you know when she got the results?'

I shake my head. 'I got them to email it to me, but I had to pretend to be Imogen. And I can't get into her computer to check.'

'That's OK. It would be helpful if we could take her laptop back to the station with us. We might be able to get a better idea of what she knows about her past. And don't worry, we'll look into this thoroughly.'

'Please don't tell anyone you don't have to,' I say, my tone pleading. 'If she doesn't know, we want to keep it that way, at least for now. It could put her in danger if anyone else found out. Especially the media.'

'Of course,' Ruben promises, his tone reassuring. 'We'll make sure this information is need-to-know only.'

I fetch Imogen's laptop from her desk, and we spend a few minutes showing the cops the pile of paperwork that sits on the coffee table between us. They tell us that they need to take it with them, that they'll make copies and return the originals to us later. I'm relieved that they're shouldering the burden of this information, that they'll know what to do with it. That they'll know how best to use it to find Imogen.

I'm waiting for the police officers to get up and leave, but they remain seated. The two men exchange a look, and Troy clears his throat uncomfortably.

'We, uh . . . we'd like to talk to you some more about this fight Imogen had at school.'

I look at Dylan, not understanding the sharp change in direction. He doesn't return my look.

'OK,' he says, frowning. 'What about it?'

'Well, we've spoken to a few of Imogen's fellow students today. And it seems this wasn't the first time she's been involved in an incident of this nature.'

'What are you talking about?' I ask. 'She's never been in trouble like that at school before. The odd detention, maybe. But for stuff like not handing in her homework. Not violence.'

I don't want to bring up the times when Jemima has come to me, tears streaming down her face, telling me that her sister had hit her, slapped her, tripped her. Every single time, I'd spiral into panic. And every single time, Dylan would talk me down. Sibling rivalry, he'd say. It was totally normal, not a sign that Imogen was turning into her parents. I'd desperately wanted to believe him. But still, I'd watched her like a hawk.

'The school didn't know about the other incidents,' Ruben explains. 'But a number of students have repeated the same stories about alleged aggressive and violent behaviour in the past.'

'Rumours?' I scoff. 'Your investigations are based on high-school rumours?'

'Kat,' Troy says, 'we're fully aware that the information we're working with isn't backed up by evidence. But multiple students have mentioned the same stories again and again, and we believe it's worth following up. We haven't been able to get the victims to talk—'

'Victims?' Dylan interrupts. 'Victims? You make her sound like a tyrant! What is it she's allegedly done?'

'There was an incident with the contents of a child's water bottle being laced with a laxative. And another with a young man's finger being broken, quite deliberately, in multiple places.'

102

'And you have absolutely no proof that Imogen was involved in any of this?' Dylan asks, his tone measured.

'Well, no, but they all said—'

'I don't care what anyone said,' Dylan is standing now, his arms crossed. 'I know my daughter, and I know she would never do anything to hurt someone else intentionally. And you wonder why we didn't bloody tell you about Imogen's birth parents? This is why. You're supposed to be professionals, and here you are acting like she's some kind of monster as soon as you found out.'

I'm glad he can muster the conviction to say the words I can't. I think he genuinely believes it, too. Me, I'm not so certain, but, of course, I can't say so. Not to them. Not when my daughter is missing. What kind of mother would that make me?

'I assure you, Mr Braidwood, this has nothing to do with Imogen's biological family.'

'Yeah, and I was born yesterday. I think it's time you gentlemen stopped wasting time on hearsay and started looking for my daughter.'

There's a heavy silence as the two police officers assess Dylan. I remain seated, incapable of moving or speaking, watching the ice cubes in my water shrinking into oblivion.

'I guess we'll leave you alone,' Troy says eventually.

Dylan just nods.

I can't look them in the eye as they leave the room without another word.

They see themselves out, and when the door closes behind them, I'm hit with a blinding tiredness. My bones ache, and my head feels like it's filled with lead. My vision blurs and the idea of talking, or moving, or thinking, makes me want to cry.

'I'm going to lie down,' I finally manage to murmur, and

with monumental effort, I pull myself up from the sofa and walk like a woman twice my age, slowly and carefully, as though I could spontaneously shatter at any moment, to Imogen's room. I crack open the door and peek inside.

It's empty. Of course it's empty. But, for just a second, I half expected to see her lying there, rolling her eyes at me, yelling at me for not knocking. I wish we could go back to that, to the time when I thought life was complicated, but it was actually so perfectly simple.

I step inside and crawl onto the bed, where I curl up and hug her pillow, breathing in the smell of her, the grown-up patchouli notes of her shampoo and the sweet perfume she loves so much, a bottle adorned with plastic flowers that her friends got her for her sixteenth birthday. I close my eyes and silently beg God to bring me my daughter. To let her come back home to her family.

To give me one more chance of being the parent she deserves, the parent I've desperately wanted – and completely failed – to be.

Chapter 21

IMOGEN

She groaned again, clutching her stomach, wishing she was dead.

Dying was all she could think about now, during those brief interludes when she wasn't trapped in endless, spiralling nightmares. She didn't think she wanted to die, not this young, anyway. But she didn't want to feel the way she did any more, all dizzy and detached, her mind a swampy, soupy muddle of thoughts and visions and memories. She couldn't stand it.

She was sick, that was obvious. Maybe this was what dying felt like. Maybe it was only a matter of time before whatever it was that was devouring her from the inside took over her whole body, kicking her out and leaving nowhere for her to go but wherever it was that homeless spirits went.

Imogen tried to call out for help, but her mouth was stuck closed. She needed water, but she didn't know how to ask, or if anyone was even there to attend to her. She thought she'd seen someone – a shadow, a vision – coming into her room, and the idea of a voice pressed at the edges of her memory, blurred and distorted, but definitely there. Had it been a hallucination? Was all of this a figment of her imagination?

The low, pulsing throb in her head gathered in intensity,

and she dropped the thought. Thinking hurt almost as much as moving did, so she'd mostly given up on both. She closed her eyes and willed death to just hurry up. She had no idea how long she'd been sick for. Time didn't move the same way as it used to. It had become elastic, sometimes stretching eternally, and other times fast-forwarding at breakneck speed. She measured time by daylight, but she hadn't remembered to count, so she could have been in that lumpy, sweaty bed for hours or months. It didn't seem to matter any more.

A noise cut through the fog in her brain. It took a few seconds for Imogen to understand that the door to her room had been opened. She lifted one eyelid, just a sliver, preparing for the pain that she knew the light would bring. It wasn't as bright as she had expected; a milky glow shrouded the room, and standing in the doorway was a man. Somewhere at the back of her mind, Imogen knew she should probably scream, or at least be wary of this stranger.

Instead, she tore her dry, cracked lips apart and whispered one word: *help*.

Time seemed to skip again, because without warning the room was completely dark, and there was a weight on the side of the bed that was causing her body to sag. Her eyelids fluttered open and she tried to focus, but all she could make out was shapes and shadows, shifting and shrinking against the dark.

'Shhhh, little one, it's OK,' a voice, low and gravelly and medicine to her soul, cut through the void.

'Help,' she whispered again. She knew he would. She could sense it.

'I've got you. I've been taking care of you. Don't worry, I won't let anything bad happen to you.'

A hand reached under her head, warm and dry and sturdy.

She nestled into it, desperate suddenly for human contact. The hand lifted, and her head tilted upwards, Imogen's view changing from the ceiling to her feet, which swayed and swirled. Lights popped in her vision and she blinked until they disappeared.

'Here,' the voice said, and something warm and smooth touched her lip. Instinctively, she reached her tongue out. It made contact with liquid, salty and hot. She licked her lips, then slurped the rest of the liquid on the spoon. She didn't know what it was. All she knew was that suddenly she was ravenous, her stomach growling, her body crying out for nutrition.

Another spoonful was lifted to her lips, and she gulped that down, and the next, and the one after that, and then they stopped. She whimpered.

'That's enough for now,' the voice said.

She tried to shake her head, but he gently lowered her back onto the pillow.

'You'll get sick if you have too much, too quickly. I'll be back, little one. Rest for now. I'll take care of you. Don't worry about anything. Just rest.'

She wanted to argue, but she was too weak for words, and her vision was getting blurry again. He had told her to rest. He had told her he would take care of her.

And so she let her eyelids fall, and sleep stole her away, a smile playing on her cracked and broken lips.

PART TWO

PART TWO

Chapter 22

KAT

Fifteen Years Ago

I can sense it: the hope that keeps trying to force its way to the surface like a child's helium balloon. No matter how hard I try to press it down, stifle its enthusiasm, there it goes again, floating up, rising to the top, making me beam from ear to ear at the very idea of what is possible.

I'm late.

Only by a week, but it's enough to erode the edges of my stoic cynicism. I should know better. I *do* know better. But I can't stop the excitement from welling up and taking me with it, drifting higher and higher, high enough for the impact to destroy me, if I should fall.

I close my eyes and count slowly, taking small sips of air so that I don't hyperventilate. The packaging said two to four minutes, but when I've counted to two hundred and forty I keep going until I reach three hundred. That should do it.

I'm desperate to open my eyes, to look at the stick, to see the tiny plus sign I've been hoping for every time I've done this. But I also can't bear to know. Because if it's the little minus symbol, the one I'm already so familiar with, I'd rather just stay in this moment of possibility for as long as I can.

In the end, though, hope wins, and I open one eye, just a sliver, to peek at the white stick balancing on the sink.

Finding out shouldn't be this dramatic any more. I shouldn't be emotionally invested in the result, not after all of the absences of pluses that have devastated me over the past two years. I should be resigned to it, the taking of a test just another expected disappointment, another failure, another reminder that I don't get my dreams, when everyone around me does.

I should know better than to even do a test by now. I should know that it won't be positive, should be so achingly aware of that fact that I don't need a stupid white stick to taunt me with its scientific proof of my biological shortcomings. I read somewhere that the definition of insanity is doing the same thing over and over again and expecting a different result. So I suppose the only explanation for the fact that I traipsed off to the chemist today in search of this test is that I'm crazy.

Because here I am, stupid enough to let hope fool me into peeing onto that stick again. Stupid enough to let my chest swell with plans and names and the idea of finally painting the room that we've set aside as the nursery, the one with the firmly closed door and the thick layer of dust. The one I can't bear to even peek inside, because the dark, unused room only serves to remind me of the unoccupied space in my own body.

It's anger that wells up first when I see the straight little line on the end of the stick. Anger at the injustice of it, when that ditz Susie down the road got pregnant without even trying, when Melissa at work just had her fifth, when it's all I've ever wanted but I'm not allowed to have it. Grief bubbles up next; a mourning for something I couldn't lose because I never had it. And yet still it feels like a loss, the emotion stronger with each negative test.

I grip the porcelain edge of the sink for support as my body doubles over, the sobs forcing my chest and shoulders inwards, the tears leaving me breathless. I wish Dylan could be here to comfort me, but I'm also glad he's not. I didn't tell him I was late this month, or two months ago when the last result blindsided me, or even the time before that, five months ago now, when I thought the disappointment might actually crush me.

And the months in between, when the bleeding started right when it was supposed to, when my body betrayed me again and again, I hid my tears from him. In the end, the pressure isn't on him to bring forth new life. He does his part, but after that there's nothing more he can do, no input from his body while we wait for mine to perform. I can't bear to tell him, month after month, that I've let us down again, that our dream is slipping further and further from our reach. That I've failed, and that my body is broken.

So he doesn't know what to do when he arrives home early from work, his hand covered in a thick white bandage – something about a nail gun and an apprentice, he explains later – and finds me sobbing uncontrollably in our en suite bathroom.

'Kat? Kat, what's wrong? What happened?'

He's by my side in an instant, his strong arm around my shoulders, the smell of sweat and sawdust filling my nostrils. I'm crying too much to speak, but he spots the test, now discarded at my feet, and folds me into his chest, lifting me easily and laying me gently on our bed. We lay side by side until my gulping cries peter into whimpers and sniffs.

'You know,' he says, hesitantly, 'I heard they're not always accurate.'

I love him for trying. But he's wrong. I know it. I know my own body, and I'm not pregnant. There have been none of the symptoms that I've heard go hand in hand with the early weeks: no nausea, no sensitivity to smell, no exhaustion, no sore boobs. I knew it before I took the test. I feel the same as I always have. Except now I feel worse. I feel barren.

'I'm not pregnant,' I say weakly. 'I don't think I can get pregnant.'

He squeezes my hand.

'We'll keep trying,' he says, but I shake my head.

'We've been trying for two years, Dyl. That's not normal. We should have been pregnant by now; you know we should have. I just . . . I don't know what to do any more. We've tried everything.'

And we have. I borrowed books from the library that explained how to increase our chances of conceiving. I bought a thermometer so I can measure when I'm ovulating. I haven't had anything to drink for well over a year. I've taken vitamins, I've exercised, I've lain for hours with my legs pressed against the headboard of our bed. There's only one thing left.

'I think we should get tested,' I say to the ceiling, my heart pounding as the words leave my lips, because what if he doesn't want to? Or worse: what if he does, and we get the results and they tell us something we don't want to hear?

'OK,' Dylan says immediately, surprising me. I expected at least some resistance, some hesitation at the idea of his virility being called into question. But he sounds sincere.

I turn to face him, my vision blurred with fresh tears.

He lifts my hand to his lips and kisses it.

'I want a family, too,' he says. 'I want this. Whatever

114

it takes, all right? Let's go get tested. We'll work it out, I promise.'

For the second time that day, I let hope soar.

And for the second time that day, I should know better.

Chapter 23

KAT

'Kat. Dylan.'

Troy, the same cop who sat here yesterday and the day before nods at us from the exact same position on the opposite sofa. He's joined by Ruben again. They called earlier, wanting to tell us something, and I've been on the edge of a panic attack ever since, the corners of my vision closing in around me.

'Have you found her?' I ask breathlessly.

'No, no, nothing like that, I'm afraid,' Troy says, 'but in light of what you told us yesterday, we believe Imogen is at greater risk than we originally suspected. She's clearly emotionally unstable and likely to be very angry. We got in touch with the DNA company, and they confirmed that the results were first sent to Imogen on Saturday evening, which explains the timing of her disappearance. But it doesn't tell us anything about where she's gone, so we'd like to hold a press conference tomorrow to appeal to the public for more information about her whereabouts. And we'd like you to make a statement.'

'A press conference?' Dylan asks. 'What does that mean? I mean, I know what a press conference is, but why?'

'We still believe she ran away,' Ruben says gently. 'But none of her friends or teachers have heard from her, which is concerning, as she's not reaching out to her regular network. And this is clearly out of character for her. But even if she has run away, we believe that this could be the best way to appeal to her to come home...' He pauses. 'Or at least tell us where she is, and let us know that she's safe.'

It's a sharp slap, the shock of the police officer's words. So home is no longer the end goal. They're judging us, thinking that we're bad parents for letting her find out the truth the way she did. I try to ignore it, but the shame rises up, flooding my cheeks. Of course she shouldn't have found out like this. Of course she'll feel angry and betrayed and alone. But that doesn't mean she shouldn't come home. We're her family. Whether she knows it or not, this is where she belongs. This is where she's loved.

'We said from the start that her leaving was out of character,' I say bitingly, trying to keep the conversation on getting Imogen back, and not on where she'll go when she's found. 'Why have you been wasting all of this time? You have no idea where she is, and she's been gone since Saturday night. She could be in serious danger!'

I want to blame someone for what's happening, for the lack of progress in Imogen's case. I *need* to blame someone, because if I don't, there will be no one to point the finger at but myself.

'We understand how concerned you are,' Troy says. 'And I know you can't see what's happening behind the scenes, so it might not look like we're doing a lot, but I can assure you we're doing all we can to make contact with Imogen.'

I nod, gritting my teeth. I don't know what to say, what to do. I'm completely helpless. And, above all else, I'm terrified for Imogen. We have no clue where she is, what she's doing, who she's with, or if she's even OK. I've seen the stories on the news, the crime dramas. I know that after seventy-two

117

hours, the chances of finding Imogen grow rapidly slimmer. We reported her missing on Sunday morning, over forty-eight hours ago. But she might have been missing for way longer than that, if she left right after we got home from the beach on Saturday evening. Which means that seventy-two hours is closing in on us aggressively.

'So what do you want us to say at the press conference?'

Dylan, ever practical, just wants to know what he can do, how he can get involved. This is where he excels, and I'm grateful to have him here, asking the right questions, absorbing all of the information for both of us. I'm too dazed to take any of this in.

'We need you to appeal to Imogen, to ask her to come home. You mentioned you'd had an argument a few days before she disappeared, so maybe you could tell her that you're not angry, and that you love her no matter what—'

'Of course we love her no matter what,' I snap.

'We're not suggesting you don't. All we're saying is that Imogen might need to hear that from you, especially given what she discovered when she got the results of that test.'

'How do we know she's even going to be watching?' Dylan asks.

'We don't,' Troy says. 'But this is a public appeal for information, too. It might jog someone's memory, if they've seen her, or something that could be relevant. That's why we want to do this now, while people's memories are still reliable.'

I listen numbly as the police officers explain how the press conference will work, who we need to speak to when we arrive at the police headquarters in the city the next morning. We'll be provided with a media specialist who's experienced in meeting with families of missing persons, who can help us to refine and practise our statement.

'It's their job to make you feel comfortable in front of the cameras,' Ruben explains.

I resist screaming at the men in front of me: *I don't want to be more comfortable. I want my daughter back, safe and sound.*

When the officers stand to leave, I shake both their hands and thank them for their time, even though I'd rather they were out looking for Imogen than checking in on us. I watch their car as it backs out of our driveway, and I remain where I am, staring blankly out of the window long after they've disappeared. I try to imagine what I would say to my daughter if she were standing in front of me now, how I'd convince her that I love her, how I'd regain her trust, how I'd explain the truth of how she ended up with us.

But she's not in front of me. She's nowhere near me. She's somewhere I can't reach, somewhere beyond my understanding. Beyond my control.

Dylan's voice cuts through my thoughts.

'Do you know what you're going to wear tomorrow?'

I shake my head. 'I don't care what I wear.'

'I know, I'm not . . . but listen. Troy said that this public appeal could help find Immy. I know that your appearance isn't your priority, that Imogen is the only thing that matters, but if we come across well, it could help. Troy said—'

'I know what Troy said,' I shout. 'I was right here, too. I'll go find a bloody dress, OK? Happy?'

'Kat,' Dylan starts, but I ignore him and storm down the hallway to our bedroom, where I start pulling dresses and tops from the wardrobe as though I'm late for a flight and haven't packed.

In truth, I don't know what to wear to the press conference tomorrow. Which outfit says everything I need to say to Imogen? What style of dress can possibly convince her to come home, to face the people who she knows have lied to her for her whole life?

The police have agreed to keep Imogen's real identity, and her past, hidden. For now. They'll show her photo, and ask for anyone who's seen her to come forward with information. I'm praying that her resemblance to her infamous family will go unnoticed, but I know that's unlikely. She's the spitting image of her biological mother. I'm only surprised that no one's noticed it before now, but I suppose no one's ever thinking about Sally Sanders when they meet Imogen Braidwood. Maybe they've just never made the connection.

I snatch a dress from its hanger so violently that the plastic snaps and I'm pulled off balance, falling onto the bed, where I dissolve into sobs. Within seconds, Dylan's sitting on the edge of the bed, stroking my back, telling me it'll be OK.

'We don't know that. We don't know anything at all.'

'I know. I know. And I'm scared too, of course I am, but Imogen needs us to be strong. She needs us to do all that we can. And we need to show her how much we want her back, we need to prove that we trust her, and that the only place she needs to be is right here with us, OK?'

I nod, sniffing, wiping my eyes.

'I just...' I pause, trying to collect my thoughts. 'What if she doesn't see? What if it doesn't help?'

'You heard the officers. Even if Immy isn't watching, someone who could help might be. We have to try, don't we? We have to give it everything we can. Imogen deserves that.'

He's right. I feel like there's nothing I can do, but maybe that's not true. Maybe what I say in tomorrow's press conference will get through to Imogen. Maybe it could actually make a difference.

'I'm sorry,' I say. 'I'm just over-tired.'

'Don't be sorry,' Dylan says. 'How about you take something to help you sleep tonight?'

He holds up his hand when I start to protest.

'Just so you're fresh for tomorrow. It's a big day, OK? We need all the energy we can get. And it's an early start.'

I agree miserably. I want to stay awake, to keep watch for Imogen's return, to make sure I don't miss anything. But I need some rest. I can't keep running on fear alone. I take the pill Dylan offers me, pull my clothes off and crawl into bed. For a second, I worry about what will fill my mind when sleep does take me, but then I shake off the thought.

I'm already in a nightmare. It can't possibly get any worse.

Chapter 24

IMOGEN

The cracking of her spine sounded like a volley of gunshots to Imogen's sensitive ears, and the pain was almost blinding. She stared triumphantly at the wall, doing cartwheels in her imagination. She had done it – she had rolled over onto her side without the movement making her sick.

It had taken most of the day for her to work herself up to such a huge achievement. And it had been a good day, Imogen thought – what little of it she'd been conscious for. She didn't think she wanted to die any more. And that was something.

The stranger with the voice she could have sworn she'd heard before had woken her by stroking her hair, consciousness arriving slowly, luxuriously. She'd felt better, she realised when her eyes had fully opened. Not good. Not well. Definitely not herself. But better. She'd moved her head ever so slightly to try to catch a glimpse of the man who was nursing her back to life, but his hat was pulled down low over his face, and when she tried to speak, to ask him who he was and what she was doing there – wherever *there* was – he would stroke her head and murmur, 'Ssshhh, little one. I'll take care of you. Everything is going to be OK.'

She thought maybe she believed him. She wanted to ask questions, to make sense of what was going on, but she found she couldn't speak, couldn't articulate the half-sentences that whirled in her mind and then vanished. And so she'd silently accepted his assurances and let him feed her another mug full of the hearty, sodium-rich liquid, lifting it to her lips teaspoon by teaspoon. She'd slurped hungrily, the heat travelling down her chest and hitting her empty stomach, fuelling her, igniting the embers of her being.

When he'd gone, his absence left an ache of emptiness. But as the soup thrummed through her, nourishing her bones and filling her blood with life, she'd felt her energy returning, flooding the hollowness inside her. It was slow, nothing like the intensity the old Imogen had carried, but it was enough.

Enough to focus for a few seconds at a time before her vision had liquefied again. Enough to breathe steadily, to hold her eyes open, even when they tried to drag themselves closed. Enough to hold a few words in her mind before they dissolved again, impossible to grasp, scattered to the wind.

And so she'd tried to wiggle her fingers. They'd become stiff from lying dormant by her side for so long, like the rest of her body, but slowly, painfully, she moved her fingertips, tapping them against the sheets, convinced that she'd shatter if she wasn't careful. But she didn't shatter. She was OK, just like he said she would be. Emboldened, she bent her knuckles, which took all of the strength she had left. Satisfied, but drained from the exertion, she'd let her eyes fall closed and passed out again.

When she'd woken, the daylight was bright, garish. She struggled against it, but eventually she won, her eyes straining to stay open; alert.

'Hi, little one,' the man on the bed had said. She'd moved her head further around, trying to take in more of him. His face was still hidden, but she could see his arms, muscular and tanned. His hands were calloused and rough, the nails short and neat. They were safe hands, Imogen decided, although she couldn't think why. He was wearing a tattered grey T-shirt and faded blue jeans, as well as the hat, black and unbranded, pulled down so that the peak concealed his face.

'Hi,' she'd croaked, the sound scratching her throat and making her recoil.

'Relax,' he said gently, stroking her head. 'There's no hurry. Just heal, and don't worry. I'll take care of you.'

She'd sipped another mug of soup, this one with tiny chunks of vegetables floating on the top, and immediately slept.

It must have been hours before she came to, but when she did, her energy had swelled again, filling her chest with hope. She had wanted to move, to talk. To find out who the stranger was, and why she was here, and where her family was.

Her family.

The words were like a slap in her face. She had been so completely disconnected from reality that she hadn't even, for one moment, thought about her family. Where were they? Why wasn't she with them?

Fear and adrenaline and confusion and determination rose up in her, and she'd heaved her body over, an effort so monumental that she thought she might pass out right then. The crunching noise reverberated down her spine, and the scream of her muscles reached all the way to her toes. She panted into the wall she knew was in front of her face, knowing that she was coming back to life again.

She wasn't dead. She was OK.

And she needed answers.

Chapter 25

KAT

'You need to look right into the camera,' the media specialist reminds me as a microphone is clipped onto the neckline of my dress.

I nod at her, trying to remember everything I have to say, trying to keep calm amidst this madness.

On my right is Jemima, nervously holding my hand. I give hers a squeeze and look down to offer her a tight smile. It's meant to be reassuring, but I can tell that she's scared and uncertain. My heart tugs as I think about her bravery in agreeing to do this with us.

'It'll be more impactful if all of you are together as a team. As a family,' Troy had said before he left yesterday. I'd barely needed to ask before Jemima said she'd do it. Although now, surrounded by strangers and cameras, she's less sure of herself.

To my left, Dylan's microphone is being attached by Troy, who's standing by his side, ready to start the press conference. He clears his throat and the murmurs of polite chit-chat die away instantly. A few people sit down, others hold cameras or microphones our way.

'Thank you for attending today,' Troy begins, but I can't focus on the rest of his words. I'm too busy wondering whether this could possibly work, whether Imogen will be watching, whether she'll want to hear what I have to say. The index card in my hand is damp from the sweat that's building on my palms. I wipe my hand on my dress, the black one that Imogen always says makes me look like I'm going for a job interview. Linda came over this morning to help us get ready. She curled my hair, although it's already dropped in the heat and just looks dishevelled.

Jemima tugs my hand. I look down at her, my vision blurred with tears.

'Mum,' she urges me. 'You're up.'

I look at Dylan and he nods. I didn't even hear him speaking. I straighten my shoulders and clear my throat. I don't need the prompts in my hand, I know what I need to say.

'Imogen, darling. If you're watching this, we want you to know that we miss you, and we want you to come home to us. To your family. We just want to know that you're safe, so please, if you're able to get in touch, please, darling, just let us know that you're OK. We all miss you so much and our family's not the same without you.'

My voice cracks, and I swallow hard to keep my emotions from swelling and erupting out of me.

'And if anyone has any information about Imogen's disappearance, anything at all, please get in touch with the police. No detail is too small, or too insignificant. Please, just help us get our daughter home safely.'

Cameras flash, and Troy reminds viewers of the phone number they can call if they have information, then thanks the small cluster of journalists for attending. Then Dylan's hand is on my back and we're being led out of the room and into another, smaller space, where someone hands me a bottle of ice-cold water. I sip it nervously.

'Do you think it helped?' I whisper to Troy.

'We won't know for a while,' he says kindly, 'but we do

know from past experience that appeals like this can be really effective.'

'What do we do now?'

'I know it's difficult, but the best thing you can do is go home, get some rest, look after young Jemima and wait to hear from us. And, of course, let us know if you think of anything new.'

I stare at him. 'There has to be something we can do. I can't just sit around waiting.'

'I'm sorry, but the best way for you to help us is to let us get on with what we do best. You have to trust us; we're doing everything we can to get Imogen back.'

Trust us. His words echo in my mind as I sit on the sofa a few hours later, cradling an iced coffee and staring at the wall opposite me. The curtains are closed to block the glaring midday sun, so the house is cool and dark. And so quiet. When we got home from the press conference, Jemima begged us to let her go back to school. I suppose I can't blame her. The house isn't a fun place to be, and distraction is probably the best thing for her. Distraction, and friends. Dylan offered to drop her off. He had to go back to work, said there was some kind of staff problem at his site that he needed to be there to fix. I wonder if he's looking for a distraction, too. Or just a way to avoid being around the constant reminders of our missing daughter, of the decisions we made all those years ago.

I'm restless. My skin itches from the inside, like there are ants crawling under the surface. I try to sit still, but I need to do something, to take charge, to get my daughter back. I know the police want me to trust them, but it's not their daughter who's missing.

I'm standing up now, pacing, and chewing my nails, pulling them away from the flesh on my fingers.

Where is Imogen? It's the only question that matters, the only words my brain can conjure. Only the answer is completely beyond my reach. I can't think my way out of this one, can't magically make Imogen come home. I have to trust.

Trust that she'll be OK. That she's alive. That she'll come home.

Chapter 26

SALLY

I suppose, for a while, I allowed myself the indulgence of forgetting. Of pretending.

I like to think of myself as an intelligent woman, strong-willed. Logical. But I'm susceptible to the same temptations as you are: the pull of ignorance, the bliss of letting your brain travel in a completely roundabout path, avoiding the truth so that it doesn't have to be conquered.

The upshot of having been here for so long is that I'm afforded the luxury of peace and quiet, which means I can think about – or ignore – whatever I want. Some of the inmates complain that it's too loud to hear yourself think in here, but compared with when I first arrived, this is positively tranquil.

I'm not like most of the women in prison. They're usually beaten down by the system, victims of their circumstances, acting like they're tough, when actually they're the kind of pushovers who let themselves be taken advantage of. No, I'm not like them. I *mean* something. People know me. Guards, fellow inmates, outsiders visiting loved ones, whose eyes constantly flick my way in a kind of thrilled horror.

It was knowing that I was better than the others, knowing my life had amounted to something, while they would be forgotten and overlooked, without legacy or achievement, that got me through those first few years. It had begun as soon as I was transferred, as soon as my sentence had been handed down and I was brought here to start the rest of my life. I'd been shown to my cell, which looked exactly as you might expect it to, complete with a tough-looking cellmate who growled at me when I entered. I'd rolled my eyes at the cliché of it all, which, looking back, probably wasn't my smartest move.

As soon as the guard had left, locking the door behind me, my cellmate, a dark-haired woman with a hook nose and bad breath, had slammed me up against the wall. She'd leaned close, her hand pressing against my windpipe, her breath warm and acrid in my nostrils.

'I know who you are,' she'd hissed, and I resisted the urge to point out that everyone knew who I was. It wasn't worthy of congratulation. 'I know what you did.' Her hand pressed further into my throat, and I'd squeezed the tiniest bit of air into my lungs. 'You're a monster. I may be a criminal, but I have kids of my own, and I'd rather die than do what you did to those poor babies.'

I'd wanted to ask her where her precious kids were then, while she was locked away, but I couldn't breathe. If I'd had to guess, though, I'd have said they were probably in care somewhere. Maybe with relatives, if they were lucky. Either way, they weren't with their mother, where they belonged. She couldn't protect them from within the walls of our cell. I'd struggled to see the difference between her parenting skills and my own, ultimately.

'I'm going to do to you,' she'd whispered, 'exactly what you did to them. That's a promise.'

She'd let me go, and I'd fallen to the floor, gasping for air.

'I'm Tracey, by the way,' she'd said, then. Sweet as pie.

I had to admire my cellmate, as much as I detested her.

She had a masochistic streak, an ability to make people trust her before stabbing them in the back, at least metaphorically. And she was true to her word, too.

Over the first few months, she stole my meals. Three times a day, she'd find me in the dining hall, swipe my tray from under my nose and throw the whole lot in the bin. If I was lucky, I'd get a couple of mouthfuls in before she found me. I'd try scoffing it down in the line-up, but she was usually right behind me, hovering, waiting to take it away. The guards did nothing. They knew who I was, too, and they revelled in my starvation. I was weak, too malnourished to muster any energy to fight.

Next came the burns. There weren't any curling irons in the prison, but Tracey made do with her cigarette butts. I was her personal ashtray for weeks, until I was put into solitary confinement, 'for my own safety'. Which, looking back, I understand was just another phase of Tracey's plan. She was keeping her promise, making sure I experienced everything my children did, isolation included.

Once I was back in the general prison population, she broke seven of my bones over the course of just a few months: three fingers, my wrist, my ankle and two ribs. She laced my water with sleeping pills and shaved my hair and eyebrows off in my sleep. For two weeks straight, she didn't let me sleep at all. She'd keep me up all night, sleeping in the day while one of her friends would make sure I couldn't get back to my cell or fall asleep.

But I survived. I didn't cry, and I didn't report her.

On the morning of her release, I woke her up with a screwdriver to the eye, a bit of contraband I'd procured after threatening a new inmate who had the right connections. When she screamed, I made her look at me with the eye that was still working, and then I skewered that one, too. I was the last thing she ever saw; I'd say that made us even.

There wasn't much they could do to punish me. I was put into solitary again for a few months, but I'd survived worse. And when I came out, Tracey's cronies knew better than to come near me. I had a reputation, and finally, after a year inside, I was left alone.

Actually, left alone is a bit of an understatement. For about five years, the women who had known Tracey pretended I didn't exist. I was a ghost, invisible. I wasn't bothered by anyone, but I didn't have any interactions, either. When you spend long enough not existing, you begin to act like a ghost, too. My life, and everyone in it, faded from my memory. What I'd done, it just evaporated, for a time.

Tracey's bitches were slowly replaced by new blood, people who had only heard rumours about me, kids too young or too dumb to have been watching the news during my trial. I was part of the furniture by then. I was seen as harmless – a convicted murderer, yes – but not wont to strike out, unless provoked. Which is how I've always been. I never hurt anyone who hadn't done something to warrant punishment. It's not in my nature to attack.

By that time, though, I'd let myself fade, the colour bleeding from me like an old photograph. The story I told myself was one of half-formed memories and greyed-out scenes, diluted and powerless. I'd shrunk, turned into a husk of the person I'd always known I was.

And then the letter arrived. And my world was splashed in technicolour once again. My past slammed right back into me. Reminding me. Urging me.

I'd spent too much of my life lounging around in a state

of half-living. But after that letter, I couldn't do that any more.

I was back. I knew who I was. And I knew that it was time to get to work.

Chapter 27

KAT

Fifteen Years Ago

'So what does that mean?' Dylan asks as I grip his hand, absorbing everything the doctor just told us.

'Well,' Doctor Parker says, folding her hands in her lap, 'it means that, although not impossible, the chances of you conceiving naturally are very, very slim.'

Finally, after years of overwhelming disappointments, I'm not crushed by this revelation. I've known it for some time, although I didn't have a doctor to confirm it. And so, as she says the words and Dylan's shoulders hunch over, I set my jaw and take a deep breath, readying myself.

'So what are our options at this point?'

My voice is calm and steady. Dylan looks up at me in surprise. His eyes are glistening with tears, the corners of his mouth turned down. He's expecting me to fall apart, like I have so many times before. But, if anything, I'm relieved. Relieved that my instinct was right. Relieved that I don't have to keep allowing hope in, month after month, only to have it taken away again. Relieved that now we can start moving forward, start taking action.

'You can keep trying, of course,' the doctor says, as though it's all just so easy, and just a matter of trying more, trying better. I try not to roll my eyes. 'There are obstacles – for both of you – to conceiving naturally, but it's absolutely not impossible.'

Except that, for the past two years, it has been impossible.

'Or?' I prompt.

'Or you could try IVF,' she continues. 'Although I should point out it's not some magic formula to conceiving. There's a lot of cost involved, not to mention the emotional strain it tends to have on couples. It can take a long time, it's not guaranteed, and there are some risks involved.'

'So what's the bad news?' I joke.

Her lips form a thin line.

My cheeks heat up. I wasn't trying to be inappropriate, but I'm nervous, and uncomfortable, and it just came out. I look to Dylan for help. He offers a wobbly smile, his tears gone.

'Well, OK,' he says. 'Are there any other options aside from just keeping on trying, or IVF?'

We talked about IVF before coming here today. The conversation was inevitable, knowing that the results of our fertility tests were looming. We'd tried to carry on as normal, had tried to avoid the elephant in the room, but in the end I caved. I couldn't cope with pretending any more. I did enough of that outside of our home: with my friends who have kids, with our families, with the nosy strangers who ask when we're going to start a family.

'I just want to talk about what happens if the results come back and they're . . .' I'd struggled to find words that didn't scare me '. . . not good?'

'Well, there's really no point talking about a hypothetical situation, is there? Because we might get there and they say that things are fine.'

I didn't bother pointing out that when things are fine it doesn't take over two years to fall pregnant.

'OK, and if that happens, great, but if that's not what the doctor says, I don't want to be blindsided in there. I want to at least know what you're thinking.'

Dylan was silent for a few seconds.

'Here's the thing,' he'd said eventually, and I'd felt my stomach clenching. This didn't feel like a conversation I was going to enjoy. 'I want a family, I really do. But I can see how hard all of this is on you already. And you know Chris at work? Him and his wife went through IVF, and it looked bloody awful. They fought all the time, they had to remortgage their house, and it still didn't work. I feel for them, but I just ... I don't know, Kat. It doesn't sound like something I want us to go through.'

I'd been deflated. Not because I disagreed with him, but because I felt the same way. Paula at work had IVF last year, and she's now divorced. She's also got a three-month-old, so it wasn't a total disaster, but still. She'd warned me, when I'd tentatively asked, that it wasn't an easy path. If Dylan had been keen, if he'd had no reservations, I probably could have pushed my own fears aside. But if we were both nervous about the risks ...

'There have to be other options,' Dylan had said, interrupting my thoughts. 'It can't just be IVF or nothing.'

I'd nodded, unconvinced.

'This is why I didn't want to talk about this,' he'd sighed. 'You're all upset now and we don't even know what our test results say.'

But now we do know our results.

'I'm afraid with your specific conditions,' the doctor says, 'there aren't any other treatments available to you at this stage.'

And now we have all of the facts.

Facts like: my womb is hostile. Or: we can't afford IVF. Or: we're running out of options.

When we get home, I head straight for the kitchen and reach for the bottle of wine we bought on our first anniversary, with the intention of drinking it together on our fifth. The date of that particular milestone passed us by in March last year, but as I wasn't drinking, it had remained unopened, taunting me and my body's failings from the pantry cupboard.

'Whoa,' Dylan says. 'You sure?'

'Absolutely,' I say, twisting the corkscrew aggressively. 'Now that I know there's nothing I can do – or not do – to change my inhospitable womb, I'm planning on getting good and bloody drunk. Finally.'

He knows better than to argue, reaching for two glasses and placing them in front of me.

I pour generously and hold my full glass up to meet his.

'To bad news and no options,' I say with mock cheer.

'Kat . . .'

'Don't,' I say, holding my free hand out. 'I don't want sympathy. I want to forget about all of this for a bit, and get drunk and eat junk food for dinner, and have sex because you're hot and not because my body temperature is up by half a degree. Can I do that, just for tonight? Please?'

I take a huge swig, not waiting for my husband to reply. He mirrors me, and before long we're giggling, throwing M&Ms into each other's open mouths and acting like the irresponsible, child-free couple we are, but wish we weren't.

We're both so drunk – thanks to another opened bottle, and the fact that I haven't touched a drop since January last year – that I don't know who actually says the word first. All I know is that once the idea lands, it settles and sprouts and grows with a speed that takes my breath away. It's the most obvious solution; I can hardly believe we haven't thought of it before.

Any other idea, formed under extreme stress, grief and alcohol consumption, would have fizzled and died, drowned out by the next morning's hangover. But this wasn't just any idea. It was *the* idea, the one that would save us, the one that would give us hope again, and bring us more joy and struggle and heartache and love than we could ever have imagined. But we didn't know that just yet. All we knew was the whispered idea, the sentence one of us uttered, that set our hearts on fire.

'What about adoption?'

Chapter 28

KAT

I wake with a start, pulled from a deep, dreamless sleep by a heavy hand coming to rest on my shoulder. My eyes fly open and I gasp as I sit upright.

'It's just me,' Dylan says, as my head spins and blackness threatens my vision.

I press the heels of my hands into my eyes to stop my head spinning, staying perfectly still for a few seconds until the sensation passes. Dylan sits heavily on the bed next to me.

'What time is it?' I ask groggily.

'It's seven in the morning,' he says. 'You were out cold. I didn't want to disturb you.'

I look at him sharply. How could I have slept for so long, wasted so many hours, when I should have been looking for Imogen?

'The police just called,' he says, and hope explodes inside me. 'They haven't found her,' he adds quickly, apologetically.

The weight of fear and loss, temporarily lifted for just a couple of seconds, settles again heavily, landing in the pit of my stomach, the mass of it forcing the breath from my lungs.

'They do have some news, though. I thought you'd want me to wake you up to talk about it.'

I look at him for more information. My husband, I realise, has aged what seems like a decade in just a couple of days. His usually solid frame seems frail, somehow. There are new grey hairs playing at the edge of his temples, and the corners of his eyes are creased with far more lines than I've ever noticed before.

'Come into the kitchen,' he says softly. 'I have some coffee for you. And Linda brought around some pastries. She says we should eat something. She's probably right.'

I nod, wanting him to just spit out whatever information he has, but terrified of what it might be. If he's stalling me like this, it can't be good. I follow him out of our room and past the living room, where Jemima is sitting on the sofa, eating a blueberry Danish as a rerun of *Pretty Little Liars* plays in the background. I give her a kiss on the top of her head as I walk past.

'Morning, Mum.'

Dylan guides me, one hand on the small of my back, into the kitchen, where I obediently sit at the table and sip a fresh cup of coffee while he slides a couple of pastries onto a plate. He places the plate in front of me, then serves his own and sits at the opposite side of the table. I stare at him, then at the croissants.

'We really should eat,' he says, tearing off a corner of a crescent.

I do the same, then pull it apart, breaking the pastry into tiny pieces. After a few seconds, I drop the crumbs onto my plate in frustration and wipe my hands on my shorts.

'I'm not hungry. I just need to know what the police said.'

He sighs and pushes his plate away, then leans back in his chair. He crosses his arms over his chest.

'They said they looked into the records from the Satan's Ranch case,' he says, his voice low and strained. 'And they found the file for one of the other children who survived. A five-year-old boy, at the time he was rescued. Brad.'

I nod impatiently. When we adopted Imogen, we knew everything there was to know about the case. This might be news to the police, but it's far from fresh information for us.

'He's been living in Perth, in and out of homes, in and out of trouble as a teenager. He never really settled anywhere and ended up in some group homes, by the sound of it, then working on the mines. His name was changed to Tristan.'

My stomach twists. I picture the little boy, broken and alone, and something inside me tugs as I think about his agony.

'He's an adult now, but about three months ago he went missing. Didn't show up for work, hasn't been seen by neighbours or anything, just disappeared. The police over in Perth didn't treat it as suspicious, though. He's a grown man, and there was nothing to suggest foul play. He didn't have much of a community, so they figured he was just something of a drifter.'

I narrow my eyes.

'So . . . what? They think their disappearances are linked?'

A muscle in Dylan's jaw pulses. He looks at me, as though weighing up whether I can cope with what he's about to say.

'Oh, just spit it out,' I plead. 'I can handle it.'

'They found a bunch of information at his house in Perth about Adelaide. Looks like he was planning to come over here, although there was no information as to why.'

I keep staring, waiting for Dylan's words to sink in, for their weight to crush me.

'They think he might have been looking for Imogen. They think he might have taken her.'

Chapter 29

IMOGEN

The first time she'd tried to sit upright, she'd fainted and had woken up all twisted on the bed, her arm completely numb from having been squashed under her ribcage. The effort to straighten herself out again had sapped all of her energy, and she'd given up on moving for the rest of the morning.

But the stranger had come, with his kind hands and his nourishing words and his delicious soup – this time with thin strands of chicken bobbing at the top along with the vegetables – and she'd wanted to try again. As he'd walked into the room, she'd clenched her jaw and heaved herself into a sitting position, breathing deeply to retain consciousness as darkness pressed in around her.

'Look at you, little one,' he'd exclaimed, and she'd smiled broadly, her first smile since . . . well, she didn't know how long it had been. She could see his mouth beneath the shadow of his hat, the corners twitching upwards, a shy smile of his own. She studied the curves of his lips, the smattering of blond stubble across his square chin, the way his jaw moved when he spoke, desperate for clues, greedy for information.

He sat on the edge of the bed, a mug in one hand, a spoon in the other.

'You strong enough to feed yourself?' he asked, waving the spoon in her direction.

She shook her head slowly, careful to avoid sudden movements. Sitting up had been so strenuous that she couldn't achieve much more than simply not collapsing. She knew that trying to lift something – even a spoon – would require more energy than she had.

He nodded, and as he fed her the soup, she focused on collecting her thoughts, on completing a sentence. Her heart pounded as she mustered the courage to ask. She realised, as the words were on the tip of her tongue, hot like the liquid that he was feeding her, that she was scared to hear the answer.

When she'd thought she was going to die, when her days were nothing more than snippets of agonising consciousness, barely awake, halfway lucid, nightmares wrapping themselves around her aching, confused mind, she hadn't thought to question what was happening.

Then, when she first saw the stranger, when the shadow had appeared at the door and whispered that he'd take care of her, she'd been too relieved by the human contact, by his kindness, to wonder who he was or what she was doing with him instead of at home, with her family.

It had only begun to dawn on her the previous night that she could be in some kind of danger. Except... she couldn't be in danger, because he was looking after her. He had told her, over and over again, that he'd take care of her, that she'd be OK. And he'd nursed her back to health, back to life. But then an image of her family would pop into her mind again and the confusion would cloud her head, bringing her all the way back to the beginning: was she in danger?

'Who are you?' Imogen croaked.

He paused, the spoon hovering just below her chin.

'You don't remember?'

She shook her head.

'I'm Brad.'

She frowned. Brad. Yes, that rang a bell. But why couldn't she remember who he was, or how she knew him? She strained against the fog in her brain, thinner than it had been in days, but still swirling and obscuring access to her memories. She fought through it, battled to see beyond the silvery mist, and gasped.

'Brad!'

The phone. The messages. The one person who seemed to understand. How had she found him? And where was she?

'You've been through a lot, little one,' he said. Why did he keep calling her that? 'I promise I'll give you all the answers you're looking for. But you're still weak. You need to rest.'

'No,' she said, forcing herself to remain alert. She'd had enough oblivion. She needed to know. 'I'm fine. I need to know what's going on. Why can't I remember?'

'You've been really sick,' Brad said. 'Like, really, really sick. I was worried there for a while. I'm sure your memories will come back, you just have to be patient. But you're safe with me. And I'll help you fill in the gaps. What do you want to know?'

'Where are we?'

'That's easy,' Brad said. 'We're at my place. Well, my temporary place until . . . well, it's just for the time being. It's no palace, I know that. But it's starting to feel more like home.'

'Why aren't I home? Where is my family?'

'Ah,' he said. 'I wondered if you'd remember this part. You remember talking to me, right? Our text conversations?'

'Yes,' Imogen said. 'Well, I remember that there *were* text conversations. I remember a feeling more than what we actually said. I felt—' She stopped, embarrassed. Her cheeks warmed as she realised what she had been about to say to this stranger, this man who she barely knew, barely remembered knowing. She had felt safe, she was going to say. And like he was the one person in the world who truly saw her for who she was.

'You felt what, little one?'

'Why do you keep calling me that?'

'What else do you remember?' he asked, ignoring her question. 'Do you remember the first time I contacted you, what I asked?'

Imogen squeezed her eyes closed and strained to remember, to not give up, her memories slowly getting closer until she could almost reach out and touch them. They danced and shimmered like a mirage, ever-moving, disappearing when she looked directly at them, but the more she focused, the clearer they became.

There had been a Facebook message. From a stranger. She remembered that much. He'd asked her to do something. What was it? Something about her family.

'The DNA test!' she shouted, adrenaline surging through her as the rest fell into place. 'How could I forget that? My family . . .' She trailed off, a fresh wave of despair and betrayal washing over her, overwhelming her.

'They're not your family,' Brad said gently.

She looked up at him, at the shadow over his face. He hadn't told her how he'd known she should do the test. He hadn't said why he had been willing to pick her up in the middle of the night when she fled the home that had been a lie.

But now she understood.

'*You* are,' she whispered. 'Aren't you? You're my family.'

His lips twitched upwards again, and she felt her heart

growing, expanding. Her stomach exploded with butterflies as he reached up and tugged on the peak of his cap, his face coming into view. Despite her nausea, her exhaustion, the ache she felt deep in her bones, despite the anguish at the memory of the people she had believed were her family, despite the many questions still swirling in her head, Imogen felt like she might burst with joy.

The man in front of her was no stranger. Looking at him was like peering into a mirror. The light blond hair, the caramel eyes, the dimple – just one – marking his left cheek.

'Are you my brother?' she whispered, almost too scared to hear the answer in case it was no. If she was wrong about this, she thought she might break.

'I knew you'd get it, little one,' he said. 'I *am* your brother. Your big brother. And I promise you, you're safe with me.'

Chapter 30

KAT

I press my back against the cool metal of the fridge and close my eyes as a blast of cold air envelops me, the bead of sweat that slides between my breasts making my skin tingle. When I told Linda that the police were coming to update us on the case, she offered to take Jemima, who I'd just picked up from school when the phone rang, for as long as we needed.

I walked my daughter the few doors down, despite her insistence that she could find it herself. I didn't let go of her hand until she was safely inside the front door. Even now I can't help but worry. The meaning of safety has changed for me. I once thought that if my children were under my roof, nothing bad could happen to them. How stupid I'd been.

I text Linda to check that Jemima is OK. She texts back immediately and assures me that she won't let my daughter out of her sight. I sigh and let my arm drop to the floor. I'm aware of how much Linda is doing for me, and I'm grateful for it. When all of this is over, when Imogen is safely home, I'll do something nice to thank her. But right now I have more important things to think about.

The short walk along our street has drained me. The heat isn't showing any signs of abating, and it's sapped what little energy I have to offer. Even the light breeze is hot, like the devil is breathing down my neck. I know I need to get up soon, to prepare for the police to arrive, but I need a moment to cool down, to stop the panic that sits inside me, hotter than the air outside. As I focus on the sensation of the tiles against my legs, the back of my neck prickles. Not from the sudden change in temperature. There's something else.

Opening my eyes warily, I look up, instinctively knowing what I'll see before I lift my gaze. And there it is: a huntsman spider, its body thick and black, its thin, hairy legs spread menacingly.

It's out of reach, up high in the corner of the ceiling, probably basking in the electric chill that envelops our house, just like I am. I shudder. Usually, I'd leap straight for the vacuum cleaner and chase the swift, unpredictable thing around until I sucked it up with a satisfying *whomp*. But, right now, I'm too drained to react.

I watch lethargically as it creeps slowly towards a fly that's settled above the sliding doors, and as it edges closer, I try not to think about the little boy with hate in his eyes. It's a memory that's haunted me for years, the knowledge of what our decision meant taking my breath away whenever I've thought about it.

The spider edges closer to its victim, its legs stretching carefully, its hairy body propelling hungrily forward. I hold my breath. In a movement so swift and accurate that even the fly couldn't have seen it coming, the huntsman leaps onto its prey, capturing it with a scuttle of skinny legs. Emotion rises in me so forcefully that before I know what's happening, I'm standing, energised by rage, coiled for action.

I reach for the spray under the sink. Moving carefully so I don't scare off my victim, I hold the can high and press the button, waving the can with abandon, following the predator as it sprints for safety. Unwilling to let go of its meal, it's slower than usual, although still lightning-fast. I leap over a chair, my finger pressing down on the aerosol release button, the toxic stench surrounding me in a deadly cloud.

After a few seconds, the huntsman falls from the wall, and I know I've won. It lies on the cold tiles, its body convulsing, until it gives up with a shiver. I step on it for good measure, my stomach churning as the crunch reverberates through the soles of my shoes and into the tiny bones in my foot.

'Kat?'

I look over my shoulder and burst into tears.

In three short strides, Dylan has his arms around me, protecting me, holding me together so I don't crumble into pieces here on the kitchen floor.

'There was a huntsman,' I sob into his chest. I let him hold me, taking comfort in his broad chest, knowing that with his arms around me, I'm safe. 'Would you mind getting rid of it for me, please?' I sniff. 'I can't bear to touch it.'

Dylan reaches for the paper towel and mops up the sticky remains of the spider. Stepping back into the kitchen, he disposes of it just as the doorbell rings.

'I'll get it,' I say, and I stride out of the kitchen to answer the door.

Troy and Ruben are standing on the front porch uncomfortably, so I usher them in and hand them glasses of ice water, which they accept gratefully. It's beginning to feel like a routine, now: they call, our hearts leap in hope and fear, they tell us they haven't found Imogen but they have new information, or more questions, for us. We wait, fragile with nerves until they arrive at the door, sweaty and weary.

'You said you have an update?' Dylan asks them as he sits next to me on the sofa.

'We do,' Ruben says, draining his water in one long gulp.

I watch a droplet of condensation slide slowly down the glass, pooling on the coaster. The officer clears his throat.

Troy straightens and takes over from his partner.

'We managed to gain access to Imogen's social media accounts,' he says. 'And we found some messages from someone calling themselves Brad S.'

I sit up straight, my nerves humming with fear.

'It seems that the account was used solely for contacting your daughter, as we haven't found any additional information yet, but right now we're working on the assumption that this Brad S is the Sanders boy, Imogen's brother.'

'What kind of messages?' Dylan asks, the same words ready on my lips.

'The first contact we can see was about two months ago,' Troy says gently. 'Brad sent a link to that DNA testing company Imogen ended up using and asked her if she wanted to know the reason why she felt like she didn't belong.'

He lets the last part of his sentence hang in the air before the weight of it crashes over us.

'Did she ever talk about that, about feeling like she didn't belong?'

Dylan and I look at each other. I look away again instantly. I focus on my hands, on keeping them in my lap, on twisting my wedding ring around and around my finger. I don't look up when I speak.

'No,' I say, my voice small, my tongue catching on the letters. I clear my throat. 'She never told us.'

Ruben coughs, and Troy gives him a sharp look. It's too late, though. I already know what his cough meant, and I've thought the same thing myself. She shouldn't have had to tell me. I should have known. She's a teenager, and she's adopted. I should have done everything I could to make sure she never felt isolated. Instead of worrying about her nature, looking for signs of violence, I should have been looking for signs that she was unhappy. That she felt like she didn't belong in her own family.

No wonder she left. No wonder she listened to the words of a stranger, someone who validated her secret fear. No wonder she listened to him when he said he could explain why she felt something that she'd never spoken out loud, should never have had to.

I let her feel like an outsider. I pushed her away, into the hands of someone dangerous; unstable. I did this.

It's my fault.

Chapter 31

KAT

The night is stagnant; the heat like a blanket that muffles movement and dulls the rhythmic *tick tick tick tick hiss* of the neighbour's sprinkler and the *chirrup* of nearby crickets. Overhead, the Milky Way smudges the sky, a painter's stroke of light that lends a ghostly glow to the trees below. There's no hint of wind, not a whisper of a breeze, so the leaves that usually sway back and forth are eerily still, as though they've given up, exhausted.

There's a smell to the heat, too; it's sharp and bitter, a dusty kind of decay. The scents of dead grass, melting bitumen and overchlorinated pools sit low and heavy in the night, adding to the suffocating temperatures.

I sip the air in slow, shallow breaths; anything too sudden burns the back of my throat and scorches my lungs. Even at this time, even without the sun, there's no relief. I drain a glass of water, now tepid after only a few minutes outside, and wipe the sweat from my top lip with a damp forearm. I don't want to be out here, but I can't bear being inside, either. After the constables left, I was certain that the walls were pressing in on me, moving closer and closer, threatening to trap me in the world I'd so carefully and deliberately built. I had to escape, had to get outside so I could think.

I should have known that Imogen would find out eventually. I should have planned for it, prepared myself.

No, that's not it – I just should have been the one to tell her; it never should have come down to this. But I've been so scared of what it would mean – her being in possession of the truth – that I took the coward's way out. I kept her in the dark, telling myself that it was for her own good, for her safety.

Of course she ordered the test. Of course she replied to the mysterious message that Brad S had sent her. He offered what I didn't: answers. Even if she'd never asked the questions, she deserved to know.

My hand shakes, and the paper I'm holding rustles gently, reminding me of the words I've read over and over again since the police left. I lift up the printout that Troy handed me on his way out the door and read the messages they found on Imogen's Facebook Messenger account.

Hi Imogen, you don't know me, but I think you'll want to hear what I have to say. Because I bet you're wondering why you feel different from your family, like an outsider...? If you are, if I'm right, then get this test done. I'm not some creep, I can explain everything, but only if you want to know. Only if you're looking for answers. I'll be here if you want to talk.

Under his message was a link to the maternity and paternity test that Imogen had ordered from the DNA website. According to the date on this message, and the date of the test, she waited a month before deciding to find out. What made her want to do it then? I've been racking my brain for hours, reaching for memories, for an explanation. Did we have a fight? Did I make her so angry that she was convinced she couldn't possibly be mine?

I don't know the answer. All I know is that she did the test and received the results the night she left.

Between sending the test and getting the results, Imogen had replied to Brad's message.

Who are you? And what do you know? I sent the test...
I have so many questions. Please tell me who you are!!

His reply is time-stamped as just a few hours later.

I will tell you absolutely everything, I promise. And I promise that if the test results come back and tell you what I think they will, there's a place where you fit in perfectly, where you belong. A new family, who will love you exactly the way you are. But if anyone finds out about this, they'll keep us apart. We need a way to talk that's not traceable. Don't message me, but keep an eye on your mail. I promise I'll give you a way to contact me soon.

The police think that he sent her a phone so they could communicate without anyone knowing. The idea of it makes me dizzy – the thought that my daughter was holding such an enormous secret, that she didn't come to me with it, that she carried the weight of it alone. Not alone, I remind myself. With Brad.

My stomach clenches as questions fly through my mind. How much does she know? Does she understand what we took her away from, what we shielded her from? Is she safe? Did she go with Brad willingly, or did he have to trick her into leaving us?

The paper flutters from my hand. My head is pounding, in part from the endless stream of the unknown that's running through my mind, and in part from the heat. I stand up wearily, feeling ten years older than I did just a few days ago. My body aches and groans with the effort of being alive, of moving forward when all I want to do is press rewind.

I step back into the sterile chill of our home and refill my glass. As I chug the water in the kitchen, I think about what I've just read, about the man who sent those messages. What does he want with my daughter? What does he think stealing her away from us is going to achieve? He promised Imogen something in his messages, something about belonging. What was it?

I dart over to the sliding door and heave it open, flinching as the hot air hits my face again. I lift the paper from the ground, feeling it crinkle between my fingers, and read Brad's words again: *There's a place where you fit in perfectly, where you belong. A new family, who will love you exactly the way you are.*

He's offering her what we can't: a genetic family, verified by science.

Despite the red-hot temperatures, my blood chills inside my veins. He can't mean that. Maybe he's just talking about himself. Maybe he wants the two of them to be a family. He can't mean anything else by it. But now the idea has emerged, and it's taken hold, making my nerves sing with fear.

I run back inside and open my laptop, navigating to Google and typing *Tim and Sally Sanders*. The results load, and I shudder involuntarily. There at the top is a series of photos showing Tim, with his lank blond hair, intense blue eyes and lopsided smile, and Sally with her instantly recognisable pixie cut and dark-rimmed glasses, features that made her seem fragile and innocent. It was the thing that the whole nation was fixated on; the fact that she looked so sweet, and yet was capable of such evil. My stomach churns, and nausea threatens to overwhelm me. I close my eyes for a second, take a deep breath, and swallow the bile that's rising up.

When I open my eyes again, I stare hard at the photo, as I've done so many times before, wondering whether my parents were right, if we were reckless to take on a child who had had such horror branded on her life. I try to shake the thought aside, the way I've always done, never allowing the doubt to linger, never entertaining the possibility. But this time it sticks, clinging to my skin like sweat.

For a few moments a battle rages inside my head, the habit of resistance struggling with the need to explore my deepest fears. They've been repressed for so long, pushed down deeper, further away from my consciousness as time passed, threatening to bubble to the surface occasionally, but never like this. Never with so much vehemence. Maybe it's the tiredness. Maybe it was just bound to happen one day, but whatever it is, I give up. I let go of the struggle, and the thoughts and fears I've denied for so long bob to my consciousness with an alarming ease, like they've been straining to be released for all these years, knowing their time would come.

I turn each thought over, inspect it and lay it carefully to the side to come back to later. Imogen was born to pure evil. No one really knows what made Tim and Sally into the monsters they are – was it their upbringings, undoubtedly tumultuous and cruel, that made them turn to violence and torture? Was it the combination of the two of them, the perfect recipe for malevolence, a kind of destruction that would never have thrived had they not met one another?

156

Or were they both simply born that way? Does it run in their blood?

If it's the latter, then that means it runs in Imogen's blood, too. It means that the vile, hateful things of Satan's Ranch live somewhere deep inside my daughter, at a cellular level, ingrained in every single part of her. That's what my parents believe. They made that clear when we broke the news to them all those years ago. A child had been matched with us! A baby girl! We had been overjoyed, choosing to see the positive in the situation, choosing to believe in nurture over nature.

And we'd been right. Imogen is a good girl. Maybe I've watched her a bit too closely, maybe I've panicked when she's lashed out in anger, or had a tantrum, or, well, punched someone at school. I don't know what to make of the rumours the police mentioned, but even if they're right, even if she has acted cruelly before, does that mean that she is capable of what her parents did? I want to believe she doesn't have it in her, that, violent streak or not, she's nothing like those monsters. I want to believe that we nurtured that out of her, that the strength of our love drove out any darkness. I have to choose to believe that.

Her brother, though . . . I don't know him. I don't know his nature. I do know he wasn't nurtured. And that frightens me.

I stare at Brad in the only family photo that was ever released to the press, the one taken a few months before the couple was arrested, before their surviving children were assessed, before the kids were placed into care and, in the case of fourteen-year-old Kimberley, into a psychiatric facility. The five of them are in the back garden of Satan's Ranch, all facing the camera, which must have been set to self-timer mode, and all except Brad smiling widely. Peeking out from behind them are colourful bursts of pink, white, yellow and red, the cheery rose bushes concealing secrets so dark and tragic that when I think about them – about the tiny, broken bodies lying beneath those delicate flowers – I can't seem to fill my lungs with enough oxygen.

I try to focus, to keep my eyes on the faces in the photograph, to breathe. Imogen – Amy, as she was known then – is being held by Brad, who has a soft toy stuffed into the waistband of his jeans. Beside him is Kimberley, the girl who testified against her parents at the trial before being taken into psychiatric care, and behind her are the murderers who were found guilty on every count. Proud, smiling, looking for all the world like a happy, normal family.

After the adoption was finalised, I had done my best to forget about them, for Imogen's sake – she was a Braidwood, not a Sanders, and I wanted nothing more than to free her from her past – and perhaps, if I'm honest, a little bit for my own sake, too. To appease the guilt, the sadness, that I felt for the other children. They'd endured so much in their short lives, and although being taken from their parents was the right thing, the best thing, for them, it was just another trauma for them to live through. It was too painful for me to dwell on, and so I'd trained myself to not remember, to not be curious for information.

But now, I need to know.

I ignore the criminal Wiki entry and click the 'News' category. I select a year-old article titled 'Satan's Ranch – Tim and Sally Sanders: Where are they now?' with a ball of dread growing in the pit of my stomach. I scroll through the information as quickly as I can, past the festive family portrait and chilling images of the couple in their early years until I find what I'm looking for.

Tim Sanders, now 72, is serving a life sentence without parole in Port Phillip maximum security prison in Victoria, and his wife, Sally Sanders, 55, is one of only five women in Australia serving life without parole. She is incarcerated in Dame Phyllis Frost Centre in Deer Park, Victoria. The identities of their three surviving children were changed at the time of the couple's sentencing.

I slam the laptop shut, sickened by the memories that have emerged thanks to the images and headlines on my screen, and relieved that the couple are still in prison with no hope of being released.

But that doesn't stop the prickling on the back of my neck. Brad promised my daughter a place where she belongs, a new family. I don't know where Kimberley ended up, but if Brad is somehow trying to get the Sanders children together again – and if he's managed to get hold of Imogen, there's no reason to believe he couldn't find Kimberley, too – then there's someone I might be able to speak to who might just know what he's got planned.

I clench my jaw.

The police told me to stay put, to trust them. They'd never agree to this plan. They'd never help me. Even Dylan would tell me I'm crazy. But I need answers. I need to find my daughter.

And I know someone who can help me.

Chapter 32

IMOGEN

The slow *drip, drip, drip* that marked the passing of time had become hypnotic, mesmerising. Imogen let her body relax completely and her arms floated to the surface, her hair fanning out like a halo around her head. With her ears submerged, she could hear her own heartbeat between the soft *plink* sound of the water droplets that leaked from the ancient tap at her feet.

Plink, whump, plink, whump, plink, whump. You're adopted, Amy.

Imogen's eyes flew open, her focus settling on the cobweb-encrusted bulb that hung from the ceiling. She had a new name, and along with it a whole new existence to unearth.

Amy. She rolled the word around in her mouth, getting to know it, tasting the letters. It was so short, so open-ended. Nothing like Imogen, all pointy sounds, with a finality to it. She liked it, she decided. She could get used to Amy. Adopted Amy.

Every time her mind drifted from the stark facts of her new-found life, the word *adopted* would come hurtling towards her, colliding with her chest and taking her breath away. The truth echoed in her mind, haunting her, filling up the spaces between her thoughts.

And it had become so much more than just a word, in the few hours since she had remembered that those seven letters applied to her. It was her identity now, as much a part of her as her blood type, or her fingerprint, or her DNA. The DNA that was a zero per cent match to Kat and Dylan's. Now that the fog in her brain was clearing, she could remember more about the night she'd run. She remembered the feeling of total isolation, when she realised that the one place where she should automatically belong had never really been hers.

It shouldn't have shocked her as much as it did. After all, she'd been the one to order the test, hurrying to check the mailbox every day after school before Kat or Jemima could get to it, sneaking into Kat and Dylan's en suite bathroom to collect hairs, telling them she was going to meet Paige when really she was going to the post office with her completed kit and all the accompanying paperwork.

She had known it was possible, or she never would have ordered the test, never would have gone through with it. When Brad had first asked her if she felt like she fitted in, if she ever felt like an outsider, it was like he had been reading her mind. It wasn't just the physical differences: their dark hair versus her blonde locks, her lean physique versus their curves, their hazel eyes versus her golden ones, their tanned skin versus her pale complexion. It was the other things that made her stand out. Her complete inability to hold a tune. Her raspy laugh. The way she scrunched her nose when she was concentrating.

The truth really shouldn't have shocked her. And yet it had completely turned her inside out, her entire life changing in the split second when she read the words on her screen:

Probability of paternity: 0%

Probability of maternity: 0%

Imogen slowly sat up, water splashing over the side of the tub and onto the tiles below. She reached for the bottle of shampoo on the side of the bath and squeezed, too hard, the liquid in her hand spilling over and into the water. She rubbed her hands together and lathered the shampoo into her sweaty, greasy hair, relief flooding her.

After her memory had returned the previous day, she'd wanted Brad to stay with her, telling her everything, until her entire history had been unfolded, nothing left hidden within its creases. But her body had betrayed her, and her eyes had grown heavy once again, her thoughts muddling until she passed out, her energy sapped.

She'd woken up again with bright light streaming onto her, something sharp and pungent making her nose wrinkle up. It had only taken a few seconds to realise that the smell was coming from her sweaty, fevered body. Appalled, she'd sat up, momentarily delighted by the return of her strength, until another realisation filled her with burning shame. Since she'd arrived at Brad's place, she hadn't been to the bathroom. Or at least, she couldn't remember having been. Which meant . . .

She'd buried her face in her hands, and wished once again for death to claim her. She was mortified, but she needed to go, and she knew she didn't have the strength to walk.

'Brad!' she'd called.

He'd been by her side within seconds.

'What do you need, little one?' he'd asked.

She'd felt her cheeks flushing.

'Could you show me where the bathroom is, please? I don't think I can walk.'

Gently – so, so gently – her big brother had lifted her from the bed and carried her, like a child slung across his arms, down the corridor. She looked around as they moved together, taking in her new surroundings, hungry for anything that might betray a piece of information about her brother, about her family. The hallway was dimly lit, with dark, floral wallpaper peeling off the walls in thick strips, like a bad sunburn. The bathroom was only a few steps from the bedroom, a grimy space with mould growing in the grout and a thick layer of dust and dead flies on the small windowsill.

She scrunched her nose up at the filth, but immediately felt ashamed of herself for her reaction. Brad was looking after her without a word of complaint, and here she was, worrying about a bit of mould. Besides, she told herself, she'd dealt with worse. The only difference was, the Braidwood brand of dirt was invisible. She knew which one she'd rather live with.

Brad had carefully lowered her legs, still supporting her body, and she'd gripped the sink for balance.

'I've got it from here,' she said, uncertain, but far too embarrassed to ask for help.

'OK,' he said. 'I'll be just outside, so shout if you need me.'

A simple task, usually completed without any kind of thought or effort, was suddenly a monumental hurdle to overcome. But slowly, painfully, she'd managed it.

As she washed her hands, sitting on the lid of the toilet and reaching across to the sink, Brad knocked and, when she answered, peered around the door.

'I can run you a bath if you'd like?'

She'd almost wept with gratitude. The smell coming from her skin was putrid, and she could hardly bear to face him, knowing he'd cared for her while she was in such a terrible state, knowing how kind he'd been not to mention it, not to turn away from the smell or sight of her.

The bath was cold – not because she'd been in it for too long, but because it was so hot outside that she'd requested it be run that way – and a film of dirt had floated to the top of the water, creating an oily sheen.

As Imogen rinsed her hair, slowly and methodically massaging her scalp, she wondered how her parents – no, Kat and Dylan – had kept the truth from her for so long. Maybe in some countries people could be adopted without knowing, but in Australia, people knew. It wasn't hidden from them. She'd read up on the policies, when Brad had first sent her the test, when she'd been trying to convince herself that it was impossible. She'd discovered that once an adopted child turned eighteen they could request all of the information on their biological parents. According to the government, they were entitled to find out the whole truth. Imogen also read about how rare it was for adoptions to even happen; something like three in a busy year, in the whole state. So how had she been so spectacularly unlucky to end up with adoptive parents who were willing to throw policy to the wind to keep her in the dark? How had they lied to her for so long, about something so huge? And, more importantly, why? She'd had a brother this whole time, and they'd kept him a secret. They'd stolen that from her.

As their betrayal settled over her and became a solid reality, anger rumbled, a dark storm visible only on the horizon, brewing inside her, ready to burst.

Chapter 33

KAT

Fifteen Years Ago

'I have to warn you, though, it's extremely rare for an adoption to happen in South Australia. I don't want you to get your hopes up.'

It's too late. Our hopes are already through the roof.

Since we first uttered the 'A' word all those months ago, giggling on the kitchen floor to mask our grief, our hopes have inflated and risen, far beyond our expectations.

I'd woken up the morning after with my head and heart still tender from the previous day, but with a single thought running on a loop in my mind: we could adopt. I'd been nervous to bring it up in the stark daylight, in case Dylan thought it was just a fleeting, drunken idea, like the time a few years ago, before trying to start a family, when we made the wine-fuelled decision to sell our house and go travelling. We were adamant about it at the time, had written a to-do list and everything. But after that night, we never spoke of it again. The list disappeared, along with our temporary enthusiasm for upheaval.

I knew this idea wasn't like that for me. But I couldn't be sure how Dylan felt. I half expected him to argue the necessity of passing on his family name, or keeping his genes alive, or whatever macho platitudes men tend to default to when thinking about reproducing. I'd tiptoed out of our bedroom and to the kitchen, where I'd made a French press of strong, black coffee. I'd brought two steaming mugs into our room and kissed Dylan on the forehead, placing a mug on his bedside table.

'Morning, handsome.' I'd smiled.

He'd groaned in response. 'My head.'

'I know. Me too. There's coffee.'

'Thank you. You're my hero.'

We'd sat up in the bed, sipping our coffees to clear away the cobwebs, my mouth filled with words I was too nervous to speak, in case my hopes were, like so many times before, shot out of the sky, landing with a dull thud on the ground at my feet.

'Honey,' Dylan had said quietly, tentatively. My stomach clenched in preparation. He was going to let me down gently. 'Remember what we talked about last night?'

I'd paused to make it seem like I was dredging up the memories; a ruse, a kind of self-protection. After a couple of seconds, I'd nodded. I couldn't trust myself to speak.

'I don't know about you, but . . . I can't stop thinking about it. I think I want to do it.'

I'd stared at him, unable to stop my smile from spreading. 'Really?'

He'd nodded. 'I want to adopt a baby. I really, really do.'

I'd burst into tears, then. Elated, I'd flung my arms around him, spilling hot coffee across our white bedcovers. I didn't care. Nor did he. He'd been worried to bring it up again, he told me, because he thought I'd want the experience of being pregnant, of childbirth, of that natural, instant connection. But all I ever wanted was a family. I didn't care how it happened.

We'd started making calls that same day, and for the past six months we've been meeting with organisations, filling

166

in paperwork, taking training courses, asking friends and colleagues for references. And, miraculously, we're both still just as excited about the idea as we were on our kitchen floor all those months ago.

'As you know,' the support worker says, 'you're a great match, and you've ticked all of the right boxes, so to speak. So, if we are seeking a permanent family for a child, you stand a very good chance of being matched. It's just that foster care is the primary route.'

We've been told all of this before. A child's reunification with their birth family is always prioritised, which I can understand, especially given the government's appalling history with forcibly separating children from their parents. During the majority of the 20th century, countless indigenous Australian children, now known as the Stolen Generations, were removed from their families and communities without cause. And between the 1950s and the 1980s, babies born to unmarried mothers were taken away and forced into closed adoptions. The consequences of these practices were devastating and far-reaching, and although this wasn't the only reason why adoptions had become so rare, it was the one I most understood.

We've talked about fostering. We've discussed and debated it for hours at a time. We've considered all of the pros and cons. But, in the end, I don't think I'm strong enough to love a child and let them go. It would break me.

And so we're going to go home and wait and hope, and try to manage our expectations.

'We'll be in touch,' the woman says as we leave her office, and I cross the fingers on both of my hands as we walk to our car, and all the way home just for good measure.

'Right,' Dylan announces when we get home. 'So now what?'

I flop onto the sofa and frown.

'I don't know,' I say, genuinely unsure. For so long – two and a half years, now – we've been trying to fulfil our dream of starting a family. First we were trying to get pregnant, doing all of the right things, monitoring and abstaining and testing and supplementing. Then we were undergoing tests and making decisions. And since we decided on the path we wanted to take, we've been filing and interviewing and learning and researching and applying. It's been all up to us. Until now.

Now we wait. Now we get on with our lives and try not to obsess over the phone call that might never come. We hope. But beyond that, there's no action we can take that can hurry this along, that can change the outcome. It's a strange feeling. I'm not the most patient person generally, but when it's something this enormous and overwhelming, I don't know how long I can cope with the constant butterflies in my stomach before I explode.

I turn the TV on as a distraction. I'll have to take up a hobby, I think. Something so that I don't spend all of my free time fantasising about bringing a baby home with us, our own little bundle of joy who we'll love with everything we've got.

I'm not really concentrating as the news headlines are announced. I'm immersed in my daydream starring a little boy – we said we'd adopt either gender, of course, but I can't help picturing a boy – whose room we've painted blue, with little elephants painted along the wall. I'm picturing the crib, the little animal mobile we'll hang over it, and the tiny outfits all folded up, ready for day after day of adventures together.

'Kat!'

I snap out of my imaginary parenting. 'Huh?'

'I said, could you please change the channel? I'm done with hearing about these sickos. I don't understand why they give them all this airtime. They don't deserve a second of it.'

I bring my focus back to the TV. It's a clip of Sally Sanders, the sweetest-looking devil the world's ever seen, walking towards the courthouse in Melbourne. I make a hiss of disgust and hand the remote to Dylan. He's right: they shouldn't be getting this kind of notoriety, not after what they've done.

It makes me so mad, the fact that there are people out there who can reproduce without having to consult anyone, who then abuse and torture and murder their helpless children, while Dylan and I, who want nothing more than to love and protect and cherish a child, have to go through months of rigorous and invasive questioning.

I get it. I know that children can't be given to just anyone. But surely, by that same logic, not just anyone should be allowed to have their own children? At least not twisted, vile humans like Sally and Tim Sanders. Their deeds have shocked the country, but more than what they did, it's the fact that they got away with it for so long that has left everyone reeling. How many others are out there, committing unspeakable crimes without consequences?

Dylan flicks the channel over to a footy match, and I sit in silence, stewing on the injustice that Sally Sanders could have children without trying, and here I am, waiting for a phone call that I've been told is highly unlikely, desperately wanting the same thing she was happy to throw away like garbage.

And for just a moment – one shameful, secret moment – I'm actually jealous of the monster whose crimes make my stomach turn. I want what she has.

And, more importantly, I deserve it.

169

Chapter 34

SALLY

They made me sign my children away, as though they were used cars I was handing over to new owners. That day is still seared into my memory, every detail as vivid now as it was when it happened.

The woman who came to extract my signature was a timid, weak little thing. She had mousy hair pulled into a bun, rectangular glasses that were far too wide for her face, and a single dark hair protruding from her chin. Even in prison, I pay more attention to my appearance than she did, but then again, she was one of those do-gooder types, more concerned with saving the world than looking presentable.

A whole lot of good she was doing that day, legally separating a baby from her mother.

'We have to look at the facts,' she'd said quietly, her trembling voice confirming my suspicion that she was terrified of me. She wouldn't look me in the eye. Perhaps she was worried that evil was contagious. Or maybe she was nervous that she'd see a little of herself in me, if she looked hard enough. 'You've been sentenced to life without possibility of parole.'

'Yes, but there's an appeal process,' I'd said slowly, as though explaining something to a small, slightly stupid child.

'That may be so,' she'd replied, distaste for me dripping from her words, 'but that could take years. And even if you did manage to win an appeal, the government would never allow you to look after your own children.'

'They're mine,' I'd snarled. 'I'll see them if I want to.'

Her eyes had widened in alarm, and I'd felt the reassuring warmth of satisfaction. I'd scared her. She'd scurry away and leave me in peace.

Except she didn't.

To my surprise, she looked me directly in the eye. Her own were hazel, sort of bland and nondescript, but they were full of emotion. She'd tensed her jaw and a muscle in her cheek had pulsed.

'Sally,' she'd said, the tremor gone from her voice. 'Do you have any idea what it's like for children in care?'

I didn't say anything.

'Well, I do. I grew up in care. I never knew my dad, but my mum was an addict, and the government decided that she couldn't care for me. I was angry, and scared, and I was placed in home after home, because every new placement unsettled me and I acted out and pushed away anyone who tried to look after me. I had no stability. I didn't make any friends because I moved so much. Sometimes I'd go into group homes because they couldn't even find an emergency foster carer. This is what will happen to your children if you don't sign these papers. There's no way you're getting them back, so the best way you can protect them now is to make sure they have some stability. I know you must care, somewhere deep down, about what happens to those babies of yours. And if you have any concern for their futures, I urge you to sign these papers. This has nothing to do with you any more. It's about them.'

Them. My little flowers. Out in the world, exposed to the

dangers that lurk around every corner. It hurt to breathe when I thought about it, when I considered what could happen to them.

I hated to admit it, but the bland social worker had a point. I didn't care about her sob story. But I did want to protect my babies.

My biggest wish was that I'd had some warning that they were going to be taken from me, so that I could have prepared, so that I could have kept them safe. If I'd known, they would have been resting with their other brothers and sisters, free from danger, released from the burden of growing up in the hands of strangers.

But I hadn't known. And I was going to be locked up for the rest of my life, with Tim behind his own bars, while my innocent children were passed around, exposed to dangers I couldn't bear to think about. I knew what I *should* do. But still. The idea of signing them over to strangers, of relinquishing ownership of what was rightfully mine ... it was unbearable.

'If I sign this,' I'd said, and the woman had straightened, surprised even by the hypothetical, 'I want to still see my children.'

'I'm afraid that can't happen,' she'd said immediately. 'There's a clause in the child protection act about protecting the physical and mental well-being of a child, which trumps just about everything else in the act. You having access to your children is too dangerous, I'm afraid. We can't allow it. This is going to be a closed adoption. No access. No records.'

I'd pressed my lips together and shaken my head.

'Then I can't sign them.'

'You know,' she'd snapped, 'this isn't actually a negotiation. You don't get to dictate the terms of this. It's either sign the documents and give your poor children a chance of having a normal, stable upbringing, or don't sign them and practically guarantee a life of turmoil and chaos and not having a family to call their own.'

I'd folded my arms across my chest and leaned back in my chair.

'It might be too late for Kimberley and Brad,' she'd continued talking, as if my body language wasn't screaming that I was finished with her. 'But what about Amy?'

I didn't react.

'She's too young to remember you,' she said. 'So whatever happens, you've lost her. She's not yours, and she never will be. What can you possibly gain by not signing these papers?'

Out of nowhere, my ribs felt like they were shrinking, compressing my heart. Amy wouldn't remember me. I didn't know if that was true or not, but she *was* just a baby. I don't remember anything before I was three or four, so in all likelihood what that woman was saying was right. And even if, by some miracle, I got out of prison, that wouldn't be for years; long enough for her to have formed a new identity, have a new life.

She was right. Amy *was* lost to me.

I'd wanted to wail, but I knew that wouldn't achieve anything. Instead, I'd slumped, defeated, my shoulders hunching forward and my chin dropping. And, just like that, the fight just left my body. My stubbornness evaporated. Pride dissolved. It didn't matter any more; I'd lost my baby, my perfect little girl. And none of what had once been so important to me mattered any longer. I'd be imprisoned till the day I died, I knew that. I acted like I was going to appeal, but it was just something to do; something to keep me busy. It was delusion to believe I could fight to keep Amy close to me. Her best chance at having a childhood as different to mine as possible was for me to sign the papers, and let her be taken to a set of strangers. It was my greatest nightmare, and yet they were asking for my permission to make it come true. I hated myself for giving it to them, but I couldn't see another way.

'Fine,' I'd snapped. 'Where do you want me to sign?'

I'd lost Tim. I'd lost my freedom. I'd lost my rose bushes. I'd lost the trust of my Kimmy. And, although I didn't realise it till then, I'd lost my babies, too. They'd been taken from me. Stolen by strangers. And I knew that one day, somehow, I'd find a way to make them pay.

Chapter 35

KAT

'Bye,' I call as Dylan and Jemima walk out the door. 'See you later.'

My conscience whispers at me to come clean, but I ignore it. Dylan's car roars into life and makes that familiar whining noise as he reverses down the driveway. I'm still in my dressing gown, my hair dishevelled, bed unmade. Dylan asked me, in that calming, concerned voice he's taken to using with me now, what I'm planning to do today. I assured him I'd be OK without him here. He insisted that his crew needs him at work again, and Jemima is going to school. I pretended to argue, but eventually conceded that they needed to carry on because – and only because – when Imogen comes back, I want her to return to life as normal.

I wait for thirty seconds to make sure they're safely off our road and then rush around the house like a whirlwind, showering and dressing in record time, pouring my coffee into a travel mug and packing a few snacks and other essentials into a backpack. Within ten minutes I'm in my car, breathing heavily, trying to remember why I thought this was a good idea.

'It's for Imogen,' I whisper at my reflection in the rear-view mirror. Then I nod once, firmly, and reverse out of the

175

driveway, tapping my destination into the satnav as I edge the car onto the road.

As I drive through Brighton, I peer at every face I pass, hoping, against logic, that one of them will be Imogen. Or Brad, assuming that I'd even recognise him, having nothing but the photo of him as a child to go by. But it's just stranger after stranger, disappointment after disappointment, until I'm safely in the hills where there are no more pedestrians to pin my hopes on.

Everything up here is dead. Even the gum trees, usually a greyish green in the middle of summer, are brown and sparse, like languid skeletons, exhausted with the effort of staying alive. The grass is scorched and dusty, the golf course a small green oasis in a world of brown.

I make it onto the highway and breathe a sigh of relief, flipping the car into cruise control and pulling a bottle of cold water from my backpack.

With shaking hands, I reach for my phone, resting in its Bluetooth cradle. I select the number I saved in my contacts last night and tap the call symbol.

The phone rings a couple of times and is answered by a bright-sounding woman.

'Good Morning, Peltzer, Griffin and Associates, how can I help?'

'Hi, could I speak with Owen Griffin, please?'

'May I ask who's speaking?'

'Just tell him it's about Sally Sanders.'

There's a pause, then a sharp intake of breath. Another pause, longer this time.

'One moment.'

Hold music fills the air as I overtake a couple of cars, and then there's a click.

'Owen Griffin?'

The deep voice at the other end of the line offers his name as a kind of question.

'Mr Griffin,' I say, concentrating on making my own voice sound assertive, 'I need you to get in touch with your client, Sally Sanders, and ask her to put my name on her approved visitor list.'

There's a noise that falls somewhere between a cough and a laugh. 'I'm sorry. Who are you?'

'My name is Kathryn Braidwood. Kat. My daughter is Imogen Braidwood.'

There's another pause. I wait for the penny to drop.

'Oh, you mean the teenager who's missing over in Adelaide?'

'Yes,' I say, unable to add any more. Hearing it from someone else is startling.

'I'm so sorry, Mrs Braidwood,' he says, genuine warmth in his voice. 'How can I help?'

'I'm assuming what I say here will be kept confidential?'

'You're not a client, so I can't legally guarantee it, but unless you're about to confess to a crime, I'm sure your secret will be safe with me.'

I hesitate, staring at the line in the middle of the road. This is my last chance to back out, my last opportunity to turn around, go home and pretend I'd never even considered this ridiculous and dangerous plan. It's the final opportunity for me to do as the police instructed: trust their expertise, trust that they are doing everything they can to find my daughter. Then I think about the days that have passed since Imogen disappeared, the lack of anything resembling a lead. I grip the steering wheel and take a breath.

'Well, the reason I'm calling you is ... Imogen is actually Amy. Amy Sanders. We adopted her around fifteen years ago.'

I let the revelation settle on Sally's defence lawyer before I speak again.

'I need access to Sally Sanders.'

'I'm afraid I can't—'

'I've looked it up,' I interrupt him, my resolve strengthening now that the weight of my confession is off my shoulders. 'I need to be on her approved visitor list, which means Sally needs to add me to it. But I don't have time to go via the regular routes. And I can't call her as I'm not on the approved call list. But I'm guessing you are. So I need you to call her, convince her to put me on that list and get me an appointment with her today.'

'Where are you?'

'On the road,' I say. 'Driving to the prison.'

There's a whooshing sound, a deep sigh from the lawyer. 'Look. Mrs Braidwood. I'm really sorry about your daughter, I honestly am. And I'd love to help, but I don't know how speaking to my client is going to change anything. She doesn't have your daughter.'

'Yeah, I know that,' I say impatiently. 'But Brad, Sally's son, has been in touch with Imogen, and possibly other members of the family. I don't know how, but I need to know if he's been in touch with Sally, if she knows *anything* about his plans that could help.'

'Shouldn't the police be looking into this?'

'Probably,' I admit. 'But I don't know if they are. They keep telling me to just sit at home and wait, and I can't do that. Look, I know it's a long shot, and I know it might not help me find Imogen, but I have to do something, why is that so hard for people to understand? I can't just sit around. I have to find my daughter. Please help me.'

There's a tapping sound, as though he's drumming his fingers on a desk, contemplating my plea.

'I can't promise anything,' he says eventually. 'But I will try to call Sally, and I will ask the question. I must warn you though, I haven't spoken to her for some time, so I don't know how willing she will be to speak to me. And I doubt all of this can happen as quickly as you want it to. But I'll try. I'll do my best.'

I thank him and give him my number and then hang up, hurtling towards my daughter's past and the woman who's been giving me nightmares for fifteen years.

Chapter 36

KAT

Five hours later, I'm exhausted and running out of fuel. I groan, frustrated. The air conditioning is chewing through my petrol, but it's far too hot to be stingy with the air. My dashboard tells me it's forty-eight degrees outside, and judging by the liquid silver shimmering along the horizon, I'm certain it's hot enough for the roads to be melting.

I spot a sign for a petrol station in twenty kilometres and glance nervously at the gauge. It tells me I have forty-three left in the tank. I hope it's clever enough to account for the air con. Once I get there, I'll text Dylan and tell him he needs to pick Jemima up from school today.

A fresh wave of anxiety washes over me as I consider what lies ahead; the convict I might soon be meeting. I keep picturing the moment I'll come face to face with her, the words I'll choose, the things I'll have to leave unsaid if I want her to help me.

My phone rings, and I'm grateful for the interruption. It's Griffin.

'Kat speaking,' I answer.

'Hi, Mrs Braidwood, it's Owen Griffin.'

'How did you go?' I ask, bracing myself. I need this to be good news; I have no plan B.

'Well,' he sighs heavily, 'she agreed to see you. But she couldn't get visitation before tomorrow.'

'Damn it. OK. Thank you,' I say, fear and relief coursing through my blood.

Dylan's going to be furious with me. If I tell him where I am, or what I'm planning, he'll make me come home, or he'll tell the police and they'll stop me. Or, even worse, he'll drive over here to convince me to come back. I'll have to invent a lie believable enough to keep him from meddling, just until tomorrow. I'll face his wrath once I'm done, when I have what I need. At least, I hope I'll have what I need. I hope this won't be for nothing.

'You have an appointment at ten o'clock in the morning. You'll need photo ID, and don't bring anything inside that you don't need. And just ... be careful, OK? I know this woman, and I wish I didn't. She's evil, Mrs Braidwood. There's no other word for it.'

'Thank you,' I breathe. 'I'm really grateful.'

'I hope I don't regret this,' he says. 'Let me know how you go tomorrow. And best of luck with finding your daughter.'

I thank him again and hang up, a strange mixture of fear and hope brewing inside me. What if this is the answer? What if she knows something that will lead me to Imogen? I try to put a lid on my imagination. I don't want to set my expectations too high only to be disappointed tomorrow, but if Brad really is trying to get his family back together, then it's not completely implausible to think that he's been in touch with his mother, or that she's somehow behind this, encouraging him to bring them all back together again. My stomach heaves, and I breathe deeply, in through my nose and out through my mouth, until the nausea subsides and my light-headedness abates.

I try to prepare myself for looking into the eyes of a killer, of facing someone who I've only ever seen in a few photos that were released to the media, the same ones I saw when I searched for her online yesterday. Whenever I think of her – and I really, really try not to – I am confronted by my own conflicting emotions. Boiling-hot rage at the things she did to those children – to my daughter – comes first and foremost. But, inevitably, another emotion comes creeping in, making me wonder what kind of person I truly am: gratitude.

Of course I wish she'd never done those heinous things. Of *course*. But if she hadn't, I'd never have met Imogen. I'd never have my beautiful daughter. The day I met Imogen – still Amy, then; her new name wasn't chosen until a few weeks later – I felt it, deep within me. It was a stirring, an ache of instinct, from somewhere in a place hidden from me until then, a part of myself I'd never accessed before. I recognised her. She was mine. I knew then and there that I'd do anything to protect her. I loved her, fiercely and wholly, in a way I couldn't explain.

The only other time I've felt that way was the day Jemima was born. She was our surprise, our miracle. The doctor told us that it wasn't so uncommon, that couples who had previously struggled to conceive would later fall pregnant when they weren't trying.

When I looked into Jemima's eyes, I felt the exact same emotions that I'd experienced when I met Imogen. Impossible as it may seem, my maternal instinct was visceral, even with my adopted daughter. It was real. She was mine and I would give her the life she deserved. I would protect her, even if it meant putting my life on the line.

I grit my teeth as I hurtle towards the devil who brought my daughter into this world. She might be a psychopath, but she doesn't have what I have. She doesn't have a family; not any more.

I took it from her.

I've already won.

Chapter 37

IMOGEN

It had taken, Imogen guessed, about forty-five minutes for her to get dressed. She'd had to stop for frequent breaks to sit – or even lie – down for minutes at a time, while her head swirled and her vision narrowed to a tiny point of light. Her muscles ached like they did the day after a volleyball tournament, screaming with every movement.

But despite her uncooperative body, Imogen knew that she was getting stronger, and she revelled in the small victories. Like being able to stand, and talk, and string an entire thought together without passing out or slipping into that strange middle ground between waking and nightmares, the place filled with snippets of reality, too fast and slippery for her to catch them.

Slowly, cautiously, holding onto the walls for support, she shuffled down the hallway and walked through an archway into what she presumed was some kind of living room. It wasn't much bigger – or more appealing – than the room she'd been confined to. The floor was covered in sticky green linoleum, and the furniture looked as though it had been picked up off the side of the road on hard rubbish day. There was an olive-green armchair, with dark stains dotting the arms and seat. The sofa beside it, which Brad was sitting on, looked like it came from a grandma's house, the delicate floral pattern faded, the fabric torn here and there to reveal cheap spongy stuffing.

'Hey, little one, you're walking! Here, let me help you.'

He crossed the room in two strides and was at her side, gently guiding her by the elbow towards the armchair. Imogen leaned into him, grateful for his strength, his solidity. She landed heavily on the lumpy armchair with a sigh of relief.

'Are you feeling any better?' Brad asked.

She nodded, licked her dry lips.

'I think so.'

'And were the clothes OK? Sorry, I did my best, I didn't know what size you were, so I just had to guess.'

After her bath, Imogen had wrapped herself in the towel that had been hanging from the rail on the opposite wall and had sat on the edge of the bathtub staring at the pile of filthy, sweaty clothes she'd been wearing for ... well, too long. She could smell them from where she sat, the stench making her stomach turn. She hadn't wanted to put them back on, but she didn't have the energy to walk to the bedroom to see whether there was anything there she could wear. She'd wracked her brain, but she couldn't remember whether she'd brought clothes with her when she left home. Her memory of that night was still a little fuzzy.

There had been a small knock on the bathroom door.

'Amy?'

'Yes?' she'd called out, falsely bright. It was so strange being called by someone else's name, only it wasn't anyone else's. It was hers.

'I don't know if you want ... I have some clothes here ...'

Brad had sounded shy, apologetic, but at that moment, if she'd had the energy to move, she'd have leapt up, wrenched the door open and hugged him. She'd told him he could

185

come in, and he'd appeared, holding out a plastic Target bag. She'd thanked him profusely, and when he'd closed the door again, she'd looked inside and found three T-shirts, all too small, a pair of denim shorts, far too tight, and a skirt with some pink floral pattern that she was pretty sure must have been found in the kids' department. There was also some underwear, which was, to her relief, the correct size. Imogen's heart swelled as she imagined her brother browsing Target for clothes, completely unsure of himself, but wanting her to be comfortable.

A tear found its way down her cheek. She didn't even remember him until yesterday, didn't know he was her brother, and he'd looked after her when she was at her absolute worst. She couldn't help but think about Kat and Dylan, and their notable absence. Yes, she'd run away, but where were they? Weren't they supposed to want to look after her? But then again, she wasn't their daughter, was she? Not like Jemima.

'The clothes are great,' she said as she shifted her weight. 'Perfect size.'

It was a lie, but Brad's face lit up like it was Christmas morning, and she knew in that moment that she'd do whatever she had to so that he always looked so pleased.

'Awesome, sis. OK, now how about some food? Real food, not just soup?'

Imogen nodded. 'Food would be great.'

'I should warn you, it won't be fancy. Does an omelette sound all right?'

'Sounds incredible,' she said, watching as he turned his back to her and busied himself in the small nook that could generously be called a kitchenette.

While he cooked, she looked around, familiarising herself with the strange house. There was a coffee table, chipped and rickety, and, strangely, an empty pram pushed against the wall opposite her. It made her uncomfortable to look at, although she couldn't say why, so she focused instead on the small window to her left, beside what she assumed was the front door. It was covered by a dusty mesh curtain, the kind she saw in her friend's nanna's house once, but through the flimsy fabric she could see lush green gum trees and thick scrub. She frowned.

'Are we still in Adelaide?'

'Yep,' Brad said above the sizzle of eggs in a pan. 'Just up in the hills. I like the peace and quiet out here.'

'Have you always lived here?'

The idea that he'd been so close, and yet completely out of her reach, was too awful to consider.

'Nah, I grew up over in Perth. Been there till just recently.'

'So what made you come here?'

He turned around and looked directly at her.

'You.'

He'd pulled his hat off to cook, and when his eyes met hers, she felt a thrill of recognition, of connection. Imogen's face grew hot and her insides warmed. Had he really moved across the country just to find her?

'Why?'

'Why? Because family is everything, Amy. I'd finally got my life together, but it just didn't feel right, because I wasn't sharing it with the most important people.'

'So who is our family? Where are our parents?'

Brad laughed and turned back to the stove to flip the omelette. 'I'll answer all of your questions in a minute, but unless you like burned eggs, you're going to have to give me a second.'

Imogen wondered if it was possible to explode from having too many questions sitting unanswered inside her.

All she wanted to do was fire every single query – about her past, about her present, about him, about who she really was – at Brad, and get all of the answers in one neat package. She had been in the dark for sixteen years. She didn't want to wait another second.

Brad walked across the room holding a plate out for her. She took it gratefully, and instantly began cutting up the first solid food she'd had since . . .

'What day is it?' she blurted out. She couldn't have even guessed how long she'd been there. It could have been days, weeks, or even months. The idea of it having been so long sent a cold trickle down her spine, although she wasn't sure why. In the end, she was right where she belonged, with her brother. She'd stay forever if she could.

'It's Thursday afternoon. You've been here for five days. Sorry, I should have told you. You must be so confused.'

She shrugged, but she wanted to cry. She *was* confused. She was scared – not of Brad, or of his house – but just because she couldn't understand what had happened, or what might come next. She felt untethered, like there was nothing stopping her from floating away, higher and higher until she reached the atmosphere, and further still, into nothingness.

'Little one,' he said, walking over with his own plate and gently putting his hand on her shoulder. 'It's OK if you're feeling overwhelmed. You've been through a lot.'

He sat down and shoved a forkful of omelette in his mouth. Imogen did the same, making a *mmmm, that's delicious face*, even though it was rubbery and definitely needed salt.

'I'm going to tell you everything,' Brad said to her from his place on the floral sofa. 'But there's something I need to talk to you about first.'

She swallowed. 'OK.'

'This is really hard,' he said, not meeting her eye. 'I really didn't want it to be like this, and I was hoping for better news, but ...'

'What?' she asked, her stomach now a solid tangle of knots. She put her fork down.

'When we got here, and you got so sick, I was so busy taking care of you that I kind of forgot about the fact that you'd run away from home. There's no signal or Wi-Fi here, so I wasn't seeing any news, but on Tuesday, when you were out of the woods, I decided to go get some supplies and check the news. I figured you'd have been reported missing, that there was probably some kind of search going down.'

Imogen's heart dropped. She hadn't thought about that when she'd left – she hadn't been thinking about anything, other than just getting away from the people who were holding her captive in a lie. She'd never considered that her escape from her bedroom window could end up on the news. She chewed the side of her thumbnail, her stomach squirming at the thought of all that attention.

'But when I finally got into a spot with signal, I looked and ... I'm so sorry, little one. There was nothing.'

Imogen felt like she'd been slapped.

'They're not looking for me?' she whispered, hoping he couldn't hear the devastation in her words.

'I'm sorry,' her brother said, looking at his toes. 'I really am. You deserve better.'

'No,' Imogen said, shaking her head. 'No, they would be. They might be liars, but they wouldn't just let me run away from home without trying to find me.'

Would they?

'That's what I thought,' Brad said. 'So I got in touch with Kat. I found her on Facebook, sent her a message to let her know that you're with me, and that you're OK. She replied, and ... well, I really hate to be the one telling you this, but she ... she said that you shouldn't come back.'

'What?' Imogen whispered.

He had to be mistaken. Imogen had once gone to the beach with some friends without telling their mums, and Kat had found out and been beside herself, flying across the sand and screaming Imogen's name at the top of her lungs. It had been social suicide, but it had taught her not to go out without saying anything. Surely Kat would be losing her mind right now?

Could Brad be lying? She couldn't think of a reason why he would. He'd been so kind, so gentle, putting up with her throwing up on his carpet and sweating on his sheets and not being able to take herself to the toilet. He'd been nothing but generous and sweet to her. And, Imogen reminded herself, he'd moved across the country to find her. That wasn't the sort of thing someone would do unless they had your best interests at heart.

Kat, on the other hand, was already a proven liar. She'd been hiding the truth for Imogen's entire life. She'd kept her from knowing her brother, her own flesh and blood. Maybe she didn't care. Maybe she didn't really want Imogen, anyway. Maybe the fact that she wasn't Kat's real daughter meant that she was disposable, somehow.

'You don't have to believe me,' Brad said quietly. 'I probably wouldn't believe me.'

'No,' she hurried to reassure him. 'It's not that, I believe you, I just ...' She couldn't finish the sentence, didn't know where to go from there.

'You can see if you want,' he said earnestly. 'I mean, I can't show you on Facebook because I can't get online here, but I took a screenshot.'

He dug in his back pocket for his phone and stretched out to pass it to Imogen. Her hand shook as she accepted it, the blue glare from the screen causing her tender eyes to ache. She blinked a few times until the screen came into focus.

There she was, in the tiny circle at the top next to the name Kat Braidwood. The picture was one that Jemima had taken of her on their last family holiday to the Gold Coast. Kat was smiling, the ocean in the background, her hair flying over her shoulder. She didn't look like the kind of person who was living a lie. But then again, Imogen thought, lying was second nature after all these years.

She couldn't scroll through the full message, but she could see the end of Brad's in the block of blue text at the top:

. . . making a good recovery and she should be up for visitors in the next couple of days. I'm sure she'd love to see you, and I'm sure you have a lot to talk about. Let me know if you want to talk on the phone in the meantime, or I can come and meet you? I just want what's best for my sister. Brad.

Kat's reply was below, and as Imogen read, her eyes stung and the words blurred together.

We've always known that Amy was an ungrateful, wilful child. We did our best – we really did try – but Amy is damaged, and we can't have her rubbing off on our daughter. Jemima's our priority, and now that we know that Amy is safe with her real family, we can all move on and live our lives where we belong.

Imogen's heart cracked wide open, and as the sobs burst from her, deep and raw and heavy with grief, she let herself be held by the only person who understood.

The only person who cared.

Chapter 38

KAT

Fifteen Years Ago

I'm blow-drying my hair when the phone rings. I tut.

'Dylan! Can you get that please?' I yell in no particular direction. I have no idea where he is – as usual he's ready ages before I am, and he's been banished from our room so I can preen in peace without him hurrying me along. We're due at the restaurant in half an hour, and it takes almost that long to get there. I'm worried we'll lose our reservation, although I suppose if we do, we can always rebook for another night.

It's been months since we were approved to adopt a child, and we're learning to be patient. We're doing our best to enjoy the time we have left without responsibilities, without being constantly tired, without having to find a babysitter. We can't wait to be parents, to have all of the complications that come along with it, but we made a pact to make the most of this time; to see it as something to be enjoyed rather than endured.

That had been Dylan's idea, obviously. He'd had enough of me anxiously waiting around for the phone to ring, and one evening a few months ago, he stepped through the door after work and ordered me to put on a nice dress. I'd argued at first, but eventually he'd got me out the door and we'd spent the evening sipping wine in a fancy bar with a

192

view of flapping sails and glassy water. I'd been tense in the beginning, unable to stop myself from picturing the phone at home ringing out, until the adoption agency got tired of trying and moved on to another, more available, couple. But it didn't take me long to realise that I was being silly, that we had an answering machine, that I wasn't hurrying our adoption process along by becoming a hermit, that having fun wouldn't ruin our chances of being matched with a baby.

And so we've made our date night a regular tradition, an evening each week where we don't talk about adoption or children, where we just focus on being Kat and Dylan. Until we arrive home and I practically dive for the answering machine to check for messages.

'Dyl?' I yell, turning off the hair dryer to hear his response. There isn't one.

Frustrated, I stomp down the hallway to pick up the land-line, too distracted by Dylan's unresponsiveness to consider that this could be *the* call.

'Hello?'

'Hello,' says a pleasant female voice. 'Is this Mrs Kathryn Braidwood?'

'Yes. Speaking.'

'Hi there, this is Monica from Adoption South Australia.'

My mouth drops open in surprise. I'm so taken aback that I have no idea how to react, or what to say.

'Oh. Hi,' I say, completely incapable of coming up with anything more sophisticated.

'We have some great news for you,' she continues. 'A child has provisionally been matched with you and your husband, Mrs Braidwood.'

I lean on the side table for support and hear myself making a noise that's somewhere between a gurgle and a squeak.

'Are you OK? I know this is significant news, but before you get too excited, there are some details about the child's situation that we need to discuss with you and your husband before you make a decision. As I said, the match is just provisional at this stage.'

Dylan strolls in from the back garden a few minutes later to find me still standing in the hallway, staring at the phone, now back in its cradle, with my hand over my mouth.

'You're not ready yet? Kat, we need to leave or we'll miss our booking.'

I look up, still lost for words, but I don't need them. I don't know what's written across my face, but whatever it is, it stops my husband in his tracks.

'What is it? What happened?'

I'm almost too scared to say the words out loud, in case I scare the truth away.

'It was the adoption agency,' I whisper. 'We've been matched.'

'Are you serious?' Dylan's eyes have grown wide, and his mouth is open in a silent scream.

I nod.

'But they said...' I pause. I can't actually remember what they said. 'Something about it being provisional. We have to go and see them tomorrow morning.'

Dylan lets out a shout of joy and runs at me, grabbing me around my waist and lifting me over his shoulder. I squeal and laugh as he runs up the hallway, whooping and laughing until we reach the living room, where he throws me onto the sofa and shoots his arms in the air like he's just won an Olympic medal.

I'm still laughing, until somehow I'm crying – great, shaking sobs that come from somewhere deep inside me, and then Dylan's beside me, propping me up, arms around me, laughing and crying and every few seconds saying, 'Oh my God.'

We stay like that until I'm all cried out, and then the giggles begin again. We're smiling so hard that our cheeks ache, and we completely forget about our reservation, about our fancy dinner, because none of that matters any more. We're going to be parents.

The next morning, we're trying to contain our elation when we arrive at the adoption agency, exhausted from lack of sleep but buoyed by what's to come. After the initial pleasantries, we're ushered into Monica's office.

'Thanks for coming in,' she says, and we nod gleefully. 'The reason I wanted to meet with you is because the circumstances surrounding this particular adoption are extremely complicated, and totally unprecedented. There are certain things you learned in your training that we'd have to revise if you do decide to go ahead.'

I frown, as nervousness creeps along the edges of my joy. 'Why wouldn't we go ahead? This is what we've been wanting for so long.'

'Well,' she says, 'the other four couples ahead of you on the list have been waiting for much longer and they all chose not to proceed. In fact, we couldn't find anyone who was willing to adopt in the state the child is from, which is why we're trying our list here in South Australia.'

My chest burns with anger. What kind of people, desperate for a child, would turn a baby away?

'You've already signed non-disclosure agreements as part of your application,' Monica says, 'but I'd like to remind you that what we discuss today is highly sensitive and should not be discussed with anyone at this point.'

I can't imagine what she's about to tell us, but it's obvious that this is serious. What have we got ourselves into? I squeeze Dylan's hand. His palm is sweaty.

'I'm sure you've seen the news surrounding Tim and Sally Sanders, and the Satan's Ranch case?'

My mind doesn't grasp what she's saying in time to understand, in time to prepare myself.

'The children we're looking to have adopted . . . they're the Sanders kids.'

It's like I've been punched in the stomach. My breath whooshes out of me, and I struggle to fill my lungs again. There's no time to get my head around it though, as Monica keeps talking. I try to catch her words.

'Now, we understand that you have applied for a single child, an infant. One of the children removed from the Sanders home is a baby girl; she's eleven months old. She's our priority at this stage, so if we can find a placement for her that's our main goal for now.'

A baby girl. The child of a killer. Even in my shock, I can't escape the irony of the fact that, just a few months ago, I was sitting on my sofa thinking that I deserved children, while Sally Sanders didn't. Now I'm being offered her child, her flesh and blood, a baby whose parents live and breathe evil.

'As I mentioned already, some of our regular procedures won't apply in this case. As an example, our policy is to always be honest with a child about their birth family and to make sure they know that they're adopted. In this case, however, we believe that any contact with her family could be harmful to her, mentally, and maybe even physically. We also don't believe it's in her best interest to be identified by the public, given the general feelings towards her parents. So we'd need to meet to discuss in detail how to handle this. And, of course, there would be therapy and counselling required. She is still a baby, but that doesn't mean that she hasn't been affected by the trauma she's experienced.'

I sit in silence as the gravity of what Monica is telling us gradually sinks in. I take a deep, shaking breath.

'Of course, this is a lot to process, and it's not a decision to be taken lightly. So we'll give you some time to think this over, and you can come back to us with whatever questions you may have. Then we can work through the details before you make a final decision.'

My body knows my response before the words come out. My heart begins pounding, faster, more insistently, and a sense of inevitability is building inside me, growing larger and larger until I'm certain I might burst.

I glance over at Dylan. He's looking straight at me, his eyes meeting mine, the connection sparking like an electric shock. When Dylan and I met, it wasn't love at first sight. We were friends first, and so by the time we started dating we had that easy familiarity, which meant that we didn't feel the fireworks that some people describe when they fall in love. But here, in this room, I'm completely in tune with him in a way I never have been before. I know, with just one look, that we're perfectly aligned. It's better than any romance I could dream up.

'We'd like to adopt her,' I blurt out, the words spilling out of me before I've properly thought them through. But I've never meant anything more in my life, and I know that we'll work through any complications that come our way.

'Are you sure you don't want more time to consider this?'

'No,' Dylan says firmly. 'We know it's a complicated adoption, but we want to go ahead. We're sure.'

'OK,' Monica says, nodding at us. 'We'll get some meetings set up to go through the particulars, and once those details are ironed out, we'll have some paperwork for you. There is just one more thing, though.'

She swallows, presses her lips together, then takes a deep breath.

'She has a brother. Would you consider adopting a second child as well?'

Chapter 39

KAT

My phone buzzes violently in my pocket. I take it out and look at the screen. It's Dylan. I reject the call and switch the device to airplane mode before shoving it into the glovebox and stepping out of the car.

He's frantic. I messaged him from the petrol station yesterday afternoon, telling him I wouldn't be able to pick Jemima up, and could he please do it for me? He replied that he could, but I ignored the part where he asked what I was up to. I decided it was better to avoid him than lie to him. Later, when I had reached the motel closest to the prison, paid for a room for the night and appeased my growling stomach with leftover Tim Tams I'd packed for the trip and Pringles from the vending machine, I'd messaged him again.

I won't be home tonight, sorry. I am trying to find Immy, but can't say any more. Will explain tomorrow.

He'd tried to call me again. I'd rejected each one of his calls, too much of a coward to answer. If I spoke to him, I knew he'd get the truth out of me. And I couldn't risk that. He'd call the police. They'd intervene. And I'm fairly sure Sally won't tell the cops if she knows something. She has no reason to give them what they want. But maybe – and I know it's a very big maybe, but still – I can appeal to her as a mother. Not just any mother: Imogen's mother. We have something in common, and that's the best chance I have.

Dylan sent me a text after about seven rejected calls.

Where are you, Kat? Please don't do anything stupid. Please tell me where you are.

My reply had been short and sweet.

You always ask me to trust you more. Now I need you to trust me. Please.

I knew it was hypocritical. If the shoe were on the other foot, I'd be climbing the walls. I want to trust my family, I really do. But if I don't know where they are, then how can I protect them? I could see the irony in it even as I sent the message, and I knew I was being emotionally manipulative, but I'd deal with the consequences later. This was more important.

Dylan had tried to get through to me all night, but I'd turned my phone off. When I turned it on again this morning after a night of fitful sleep, I had three voicemails, seventeen text messages and a voice note. I ignored all of them. He's still trying now. I know he'll be a wreck not knowing what I'm doing, but I have bigger things to worry about than his feelings.

I stand in the car park and inhale deeply, trying to muster the courage to walk towards the dull white building across the burning bitumen. Trees and shrubs are dotted around the parking lot, as though someone made a half-hearted effort to make the place look welcoming, but they're neglected and scorched, so instead the space has an air of desolation. It's isolated, too; its only neighbour a men's correctional centre next door.

Steeling myself, I walk towards the bright blue sign that reads Dame Phyllis Frost Centre, dread growing like a tumour beneath my skin as I step towards the unknown.

The interior is no more inspiring. The word *institutional* screams at me when I walk nervously through the doors. The walls are painted grey, with a ring of smudges at toddler height all the way around, and signage is plastered at eye level explaining security procedures and visiting hours. A couple of children are running around, screaming and whingeing, while an exhausted-looking mother watches on, unmotivated to stop the disruption. I wonder what it's like to be familiar with these grim surroundings as a child. And then I think, with a shudder, how close Imogen could have been to living a life like that. If things had only been slightly different, if the trial hadn't gone the way it did, she'd have known her parents through weekly visits, where physical contact was monitored, and where she had to live with the knowledge of what they did, of who they are.

Shaking the thought away – imagining how Imogen's life could have been isn't going to help find her – I step towards the reception window, which is covered in – presumably – bulletproof glass.

I lean into the microphone. 'Kathryn Braidwood, here to visit Sally Sanders.'

I'm certain that the temperature in the room drops a couple of degrees. Even over the noise of the children, I can make out a sharp intake of breath from someone behind me. I ignore it, but my shoulders tense and my back straightens in defence.

I fill in some paperwork, and then I'm told to sit and wait until my name is called. I scan the room for a spare seat. Everyone is staring at me, eyes narrowed, as though I'm a monster myself, simply by association. I keep my focus fixed on the grimy carpet as I walk to the seat furthest from anyone else, avoiding eye contact as I sit.

The minutes tick by, and doubt begins to trickle into my

thoughts. When I decided to come here, I was so convinced that Sally would hold the answers, that she'd be able to tell me where to find Imogen. But now I can't remember any of the reasons why I believed that. For a second, I consider getting up, walking out, getting back into my car and driving home, forgetting this whole insane idea. But I know I can't. If there's even the tiniest chance that Sally knows something that can help, it'll be worthwhile. And if not... well, at least I'll know. At least I will have tried.

I wish I'd brought a magazine – or something to distract me from what I'm about to do. Instead, I watch the second hand on the clock as it journeys around the face, and I think about Imogen. About how tiny she was when she came home with us. Malnourishment, they had explained. But soon she was guzzling milk by the cupful, devouring whatever we put in front of her as though it was her last meal. While other children her age threw tantrums over vegetables, demanding sweeter substitutes like stewed apple or pureed carrots, Imogen was licking smears of steamed broccoli off the plastic tray of her high chair. When she spoke her first word, it wasn't Mamma or Dadda, or even no, like Jemima. It was *more*. That one syllable, which spoke volumes about her unmentionable beginnings in life, had broken our hearts.

But while we'd silently grieved for her, she'd smiled, banged her spoon against the side of the table and brightly demanded *more*. She was a marvel. What she'd been through in her short time on earth had been unthinkable, and yet she'd carried on as though life was a magical thing to be devoured with gusto. She doesn't know it, but Imogen is, without a doubt, the most incredible person I've ever met. I wish I could tell her that. I wish I'd trusted her with the truth, that I'd ignored the potential dangers and just explained how brave and amazing she is.

It suddenly dawns on me that I might never have the chance to tell her these things, and the anguish that washes over me is physical, a hollowing out that threatens to scrape away everything inside me. I close my eyes and beg myself to think positively, to refuse to give in to the fear. But all I can focus on is the fact that she could be in the hands of a man who doesn't know the truth, who doesn't know who Imogen really is. She's so much more than her DNA, than her early experiences. She's not a victim. And she's not the sum of her birth parents' failures. She's a fighter, a survivor. She's my daughter.

'Kathryn Braidwood?'

I look up nervously. A woman in a brown uniform and a bright blue lanyard is standing at the door marked *SECURITY*. I stand up, and she gestures for me to follow her. My heart is pounding in my ears, my legs shaking as I complete the security procedures. I'm hardly able to follow the instructions I'm given, as every cell in my body is willing me to run away, to forget this idea, to call Dylan and confess how reckless I've been, how stupid.

But, instead, I let myself be led further and further into the prison, closer and closer to the woman who gave me my daughter. The phrase 'lamb to the slaughter' flits through my mind. I dismiss it and lift my chin in defiance of my own thoughts. My fears don't matter. I'm here for Imogen, not for myself.

And then I'm in a room filled with tables and chairs, with guards dotted along the walls, watching the conversations that are already taking place. And at a table in the middle is a lone woman in a brown tracksuit, with blonde hair, her arms chained in front of her, attached to the ring that's welded to the tabletop. I'm almost upon her when she looks up, and my blood sizzles, as though electricity has been shot directly into my veins.

I'd know this woman anywhere. Anyone in the country would. I've seen her face a thousand times, on the front page of countless newspapers, on the evening news, in articles about criminals, in documentaries. This innocent-looking woman with a childlike face and delicate features is synonymous with evil. She's a kind of bogeyman, a symbol of the darkness we all wish didn't exist in the world.

It's surreal, seeing her in the flesh like this. Like seeing a celebrity, except instead of wanting to lean in and memorise every detail for future anecdotes, I want to recoil, to stay as far away as possible, to erase this encounter from my memory. I don't want to be around that perfectly formed nose, those rosebud lips.

And those eyes. They're amber, like my daughter's; warm pools of caramel flecked with small brown dots around the pupils.

She smiles, and an intense hatred that I've never felt before fills me from head to toe.

'Hello,' she says. Her voice is like thousands of tiny knives being dragged slowly across my skin. 'You must be Kathryn. I've been waiting a long time to meet you.'

Chapter 40

SALLY

She's scared. I can sense it.

I have that effect on people and, quite frankly, I like it. My whole life, I was the one who was scared. First, of my father. Then anyone in the world who could hurt my children. So... everyone.

Now, though, the tables have turned. At this particular table, we have me on one side, chained like a dog, in a deeply unattractive tracksuit, watched over by guards. And opposite me, a free woman, here of her own volition, trembling with fear. It's perverse. It's delicious.

It's clear that I hold the power. More than she knows. As soon as I saw the press conference on the news, as soon as they flashed up the photo of my Amy, spitting image of her older sister Tash – lovely, unruly, Fearless Tash – I knew. I knew who Kathryn Braidwood was, before I demanded that the other girls turned the volume up and the news presenter confirmed it. I knew what had happened to the girl she claimed was her daughter. My chest had swelled with triumph. I guessed it'd only be a matter of days before she turned up here, wanting to see me.

She thinks she's the one who got the wheels of bureaucracy turning yesterday, but, in fact, I'd already filled in the required forms to add Kathryn Braidwood to my visitor list.

I know she's curious about me, and I'd be lying if I said I didn't want to look into the eyes of the woman who stole my precious little girl.

I can tell she's rich, from the clothing she wore at the press conference and her posh Adelaide accent, to those manicured nails, now chipped and ragged, but still showing signs of lifelong care. She's a city chick, comes from money I expect, and has always had the whole world handed to her on a silver platter. If she adopted, I'm guessing that means she couldn't have kids of her own. Must have come as a shock to someone who always got what they wanted. Must have been a tough pill to swallow. I bet they spent ages umming and ahhing about taking someone else's offspring, about not carrying on their precious family name.

And somehow, by some twist of fate or government intervention or whatever you want to call it, my baby girl ended up calling this posh bitch Mum instead of me. It was my breast she latched onto, me she cried for in the middle of the night, my DNA that built every cell in her body, my blood that runs through her veins. She's mine. A Sanders. Not a Braidwood.

I try not to think of the horrors my girl has had to endure since she left me all those years ago, the things she's been exposed to and the people I haven't been able to protect her from. I wonder if she turned out like Kimberley, a traitor who was only after what she could get for herself, or if she remained as flawless as she was when she left me. It's not important, in the end. It doesn't change anything.

I've been thinking, since I saw that news report, since my Amy's face flashed in front of me – that unmistakable Sanders face with the small mouth and the golden eyes and Tim's perfect jawline – I've been wondering what kind of rose I would have picked out for my Amy, if I'd been given the chance. I've decided that she might just be a Soaring Spirits. A shock of cheery colour, climbing, reaching for the sun, escaping the darkness, growing into the light. That's my girl. That's my Amy.

The chair scrapes as Kathryn shifts, her small hands twitchy, flitting between her lap and the table. Every time they land on the hard metal surface, she remembers where she is, who she's with, and they lift again as though the table is electrified. Or maybe it's because there are only a few centimetres between her hands and the hands of a killer. Everyone seems to think I'm infectious, like if they come too close, they might suddenly go on a killing spree against their will. That suits me just fine; it keeps the fear coursing through their veins.

Kathryn's perfectly cut, expensive-salon-dyed chestnut bob is dishevelled, the roots only just betraying her age. She's probably missed a regular appointment by just a couple of days. Losing a child will do that to you, make you forget things that were once important, cause you to lose focus. I'd know.

Her skin is smooth, good for her age, but she's wearing no make-up and the stress is showing in the dullness of her cheeks, the sagging grey hammocks that her chocolate eyes are resting in. They dart from the guard whose presence I sense behind me to my hands to any other prisoner in this room. She doesn't want to look at me.

She despises herself for being here, for even acknowledging my presence.

I smile. I'm going to enjoy this.

Chapter 41

KAT

'So,' Sally says with a prim smile as I perch tentatively on the seat across from her, careful not to touch anything, careful to keep my distance, 'you're the woman who stole my baby girl.'

My blood is pulsing so violently through my body that I'm scared the force of it will rupture my skin. I blink a few times to fight the black spots that are dancing across my vision. I breathe. And I look into the face of the woman who would have killed my daughter if she hadn't been caught when she was.

Time may have lost its meaning for her in here, but Sally's ageing process seems to have been accelerated. Her hair, once perfectly styled and finished with a curling iron – the same one that was used to administer punishments on her children – is lank and sparse, the shine gone, switched off, along with the spotlight she adored so much. Her skin is dull, the dark circles under her eyes suggesting that her life perhaps isn't as cushy as the papers make it out to be. My eyes trace a constellation of marks that dot her once-perfect skin. There's a livid red slash above her left eyebrow and a series of small, round scars, puckered and shiny with age, smattered across her cheeks. At a guess, I'd say they were cigarette burns. Triumph flares up inside me at the thought of the vigilante justice she's being served in here.

'Do you actually have something to say, or are you just here to stare, because I can just give you a photo if you like? I'll even sign it for you.'

Her voice is sweet; childlike, almost. She's well spoken, giving her an air of affluence, despite the surroundings. It's unnerving.

I shake my head slightly in an attempt to focus on what I came here for. I clear my throat.

'Imogen's missing,' I say simply. Then, 'Amy. Amy's missing.'

Sally's mouth curls up a little in one corner. She sits back in her chair, completely relaxed, in perfect contrast to me. Her eyes – Imogen's eyes – slide from the top of my head to the point where the table conceals the rest of my body. My skin bristles as I force myself to keep still. I will myself to stare back at this woman, to not be cowed by her. Every muscle in my body is tensed as I wait for her to speak. When she does, her voice is calm, and perfectly pleasant.

'Why is it that you expect I should care?'

'You should care,' I seethe instantly, without weighing up my words, 'because she's your daughter, you selfish bitch!'

I sit back with a small gasp, unsure of what kind of damage I may have just caused with my outburst. Sweat forms in my armpits, making me sticky and hot. I risk a look at Sally. She hasn't moved. She's calm, unflinching. Her mouth is still curled in a little half-smile.

'Ah, so I'm the selfish one, am I?'

Her eyes are gleaming with mischief. She doesn't quite wink, although it wouldn't surprise me if she did.

I keep my jaw clamped shut. Pressure builds behind my eyes, the self-control it's taking not to launch myself across the table and strangle her exerting far more energy than it should.

'Tell me,' she says lazily, her words drawn out and song-like. 'Why is it that you think I'm selfish, but you think you're selfless? No, let me finish.' She spreads her fingers out, imploring, as I open my mouth to answer her apparently rhetorical question. 'Correct me if I'm wrong,' she continues, raising her left eyebrow and drawing attention to the vivid red scar. 'But children don't *ask* to be born. It's got absolutely nothing to do with them. It's the parents who are desperate to see a little clone of Mummy and Daddy toddling around the house to satisfy their narcissism, isn't it? Seems to me, and I'll readily admit that I'm hardly a shining example of motherhood, but it looks as though everyone – myself included – has kids because *they* want them. Look at you. You took a convicted murderer's child, because you were so desperate for one yourself. If that isn't selfish, I don't know what is!'

'How is it selfish,' I spit, 'to take in a child that would otherwise be tortured, beaten, unloved and probably m— murdered?' I can hardly bring myself to squeeze out that last word. Imogen's alternative reality is so horrifying that most of the time, I can't bear to acknowledge that it was ever possible. Bile rises in my throat, hot and fast. I swallow it back down.

'It's selfish,' Sally replies lightly, as though we were talk-ing about nothing more serious than how best to keep plants alive in a heatwave, 'because you wanted her for *you*. People don't get pregnant out of selflessness, although they like to think they do. People have babies because of their own wants and needs. They're scared of being lonely. They want the things they've accumulated to end up in the hands of someone they know, as if that gives any of their belongings more meaning. They want ready-made caretakers when they're old. They want mini replicas of themselves, little minions who they can manipulate into doing the things they never had the guts to do themselves. They want trophies, Kathryn. What's more selfish than that?'

My mouth opens and closes, like a fish that's found itself on dry land, gasping for the cool escape of familiarity.

'My— my children aren't trophies,' I stammer. 'I love them, I'd do anything for them. That's not selfish!'

Somewhere at the back of my brain, my subconscious recognises that she's baiting me. That I'm just another plaything for her, someone new to torture. But I can't help myself. I know I'm rising to her twisted taunting, but I won't be called selfish. Not by this madwoman.

'Sure,' she says, a sharp little puff of breath escaping her nostrils, a muffled laugh at my insistence. 'It looks like you gave Amy a lovely middle-class life, probably better on the surface than what we could have given her, to be honest, but, on some level, you wanted her for you. For your purposes. I'll admit that the things you wanted kids for was probably less ... unsavoury ... than my reasons, but in the end, kids are just adults' playthings, aren't they? Sugarcoat it however you like, but babies aren't much more than dolls for you to dress up and pass around to impress your neighbours. Accessories that make you feel good about yourself because you're, I don't know, passing on your superior genetics or something.'

I try to tune her out as she delivers her soliloquy. As soon as she started comparing the two of us as mothers, I understood. She's deranged. This is nothing more than the ravings of a lunatic. Instead of focusing on her words, I tell myself that I'm safe, that she's chained to the table, that she's locked up for life without hope of ever being released.

And I remind myself that the reason I'm here is for Imogen, not to justify my parenting. I ignore the fear that's pounding urgently at the back of my eyes, warning me to run, to forget this insanity, to be done with this woman. I can't leave. Not without getting what I came for.

I wait until Sally pauses for breath. She peers at me, suddenly curious as to why I'm not reacting. I cross my arms over my chest.

'So, have you heard from her?'

'Who? Amy? Oh yeah, of course. We're thick as thieves, my daughter and I. Go shopping every week, share clothes, do each other's nails, pillow fights, the works,' she sneers.

'She could be in danger,' I say, ignoring her sarcasm. 'She's been missing for almost a week now.'

'Is that so?' Sally shrugs, her tone laced with boredom, as she inspects her ragged fingernails. I try not to think about what those hands have done, the pain they caused the children who weren't as lucky as my daughter. She got out alive. Almost completely unscathed. She hadn't reached the 'prime' age yet, it was revealed in the trial, as Tim had tried to justify their sick rituals.

And then it dawns on me that I had this all wrong. That I was stupid for following my irrational, emotion-driven whim. Of course Sally doesn't care that her daughter is in danger. Sally created danger for her children, she didn't protect them from it. For her, love is something sick and depraved, a need to harm rather than to shelter, a compulsion to destroy rather than to build. I'm suddenly exhausted, all of my momentum halted instantly by this solid realisation.

I move to stand and Sally straightens up.

'Wait,' she says, her tone transforming from arrogant and taunting to something softer. There's a hint of desperation in her voice. She wants me to stay. It must be lonely, being Australia's most hated woman. Being in a maximum-security prison for life, with no visitors, no friends outside, and plenty of enemies inside, if those scars are anything to go by. And then I understand. I have the upper hand here. She may repulse me, but I have the power.

I stand, silent and resolute, my arms crossed over my chest.

'I don't know where Amy is,' she says slowly. 'But there is something you should probably know.'

I raise an eyebrow. I can't tell if she's lying, manipulating me to get me to stay.

'Honest,' she says, splaying her fingers out, pleading.

I sit down again without a word and wait for her to tell me whatever it is that she knows.

'About a year ago,' she begins, 'I received a letter. Now, I should point out that I get quite a few letters in here. Fan mail, you know? Proposals. Not that I'd ever do that to my Tim, but it's a nice little ego boost, I'm not going to pretend otherwise.'

My stomach curdles. What kind of man would propose to this woman? Surely the police should look into the sort of person who wants to be romantically involved with a serial killer and child torturer? I blink away the visions of Sally in a wedding dress, smiling and holding hands with someone equally deranged.

'Do you have a point?' I ask curtly.

'Oooh,' she crows. 'You think you're better than me, don't you? You think you're some kind of superior human and I'm just a low-life bogan you can look down on.'

Right on all counts, I think. But I ignore her and wait. If she has something to say, she'll say it. She looks so smug, I know she won't be able to help herself. I focus on

Imogen, on getting her home, on this being nothing but an unpleasant and distant memory the moment I walk back out the door and into the blaring sunlight.

'OK,' she mutters when I fail to react. 'So, I received a letter from some guy I've never heard of. He said he thinks maybe I'm his mum.'

'Tristan,' I say, deadpan. She straightens a little. Frowns. I resist the temptation to smile. 'I'm not an idiot, you know. I didn't come here without doing some research.'

She stares back at me, her expression unsettling. Then she gives the smallest of shrugs. 'Right. Guess that part's not news. So I wrote back, told him I certainly didn't call any of my children Tristan. What kind of pretentious name is that, anyway? Not as bad as Imogen, but still. So he wrote to me again, telling me that his name was changed when he was little, and that no one will tell him anything about his real family or his past, but he has enough memory to piece bits of it together.'

I know what's coming before she says it. I don't know why I expected more from this visit, but something in me expected to find out something that we didn't already know.

'He said that he thinks his name was Brad,' Sally says, her voice low, conspiratorial. 'And that he wants his family back together again. Looks like he's got what he wanted, don't you think?'

Chapter 42

KAT

'Right, yeah, I pretty much expected that,' I say mildly. 'But I want to know what he's planning, exactly.'

Sally's eyes bore into mine. This time I don't flinch. I don't look away. My strength builds as I think about her crimes. Spineless, cowardly crimes. Crimes where the victims were entirely dependent on her. Where they couldn't fight back. She's dangerous, yes. But not to me. Even if she was given the chance, I doubt she'd come for me. She thrives on power; dominance. I wouldn't go down without a damn good fight.

She seems to sense the change in me as she shifts in her chair, sits a little straighter, tries to look more threatening. I stay completely still. This is a game, and I intend to win it.

'Well, when he came to visit me—'

'He came here?'

'He's my son. Of course he visited me.'

'How? Surely they would have flagged that.'

She laughs, a throaty, raspy laugh that I've heard a hundred thousand times before. It's Imogen's laugh. The noise pinches at my confidence, stops the air from reaching my lungs. For a few seconds, I'm convinced I can't breathe. The grim, grey walls are closing in on me, and I'm going to die here in this prison, with no one but Sally Sanders to keep me company.

My fingers tingle, and my vision begins to blur. My heart is beating so wildly that I'm certain this is it for me. And then Sally laughs again and my panic shifts, morphs, is replaced by anger. The attack subsides, and my lungs flood with oxygen once more. Panting, I force myself to regain my composure. The stakes are too high to give in to this. I need to find out what Brad is doing.

'Oh, you rich city folk are all the same,' she says mockingly. 'You see the rules, and you think of them as restrictions. Some of us, the creative ones, we see them as ways to come up with alternative solutions. He got a fake ID. Obviously. It's not that hard, if you know who to speak to, and you have the money for it, which he does. The mines pay well, and you can keep to yourself out there, so he tells me. He works hard. We taught him that, having a good work ethic.'

At this she puffs her chest out with pride. I don't give myself a chance to feel sick, to let her reactions sink in. My armour is up. I'm going to get my answers.

'Impressive,' I lie. I'll tell her what she wants to hear, so long as she pays me back with the truth. 'So he came to see you. What did he say?'

'Well, he told me all about the miserable life the authorities forced upon him after they took his family away. I'd say I'm better off in here than he was out there as a little boy, fending for himself, getting passed from family to family. Should have stayed with me, with his mum. Where he belongs. Doesn't say much about justice when a kid has a worse life than a convict, does it?'

That familiar guilt comes hissing to the surface again, as it always does when I think about Brad, about the life he had, a stark contrast to that of his sister. But instead of indulging my conscience, I shift it, like a puzzle piece, slotting it neatly into its rightful place. As awful as childhood must have been for Brad, it's not my fault. It's not the fault of the families who tried to take him in, who tried to make him one of their own. It's the fault of just two people, one of whom is sitting right in front of me. The sense of absolution is swift, overwhelming. My shoulders loosen, just a tiny bit, as I realise the truth of the issue.

'He told me about you, too,' Sally says, and I freeze. My skin erupts in goosebumps.

'Me?' I squeak.

'Yeah, you. He told me about a family. About a woman who rejected him, left him to be passed around from home to home, who took his baby sister away from him.'

'I saved her,' I say fiercely. 'I took her away from you.'

'That may be how you see it,' Sally spits, 'but we don't look at it the same way. Family sticks together, above all else. That's the way we work, us Sanders. We're loyal. We don't tear families apart.'

'Oh yeah?' I ask, my voice rising, rage bubbling hot in my chest. 'Maybe you should have thought about that before you tortured your helpless children, you worthless excuse for a mother. Maybe you should have taken care of your kids instead of neglecting them and abusing them, and God knows what else—'

'Guard!'

She's not looking at me now. She's gesturing to the guard in the corner, a flick of the head that brings the woman in the uniform strolling over, hands on her hips.

'Visit's over,' she says as the woman approaches.

'No,' I pant, breathless. 'I'm not done yet, I don't have what I need.'

'Oh, honey,' she croons, patronising. 'Even if I knew what my boy was planning on doing, you can get stuffed if you think I'd tell the likes of you. I don't want my daughter in the hands of a stranger.'

The guard steps between us and motions for me to leave.

'Please,' I gasp, but she shakes her head as Sally bursts out laughing, that low, rasping noise igniting a flare of longing for Imogen, and a blaze of hate for this poisonous, dangerous woman.

'I'll be seeing you around, Kathryn Braidwood,' Sally says.

I frown. She's delusional if she thinks I'll be back.

'I've got a court hearing coming up. Bet you didn't know about that. There was an issue with some of the evidence presented at my trial, all those years ago. Which means I might actually get out of here one day. And it might be sooner than you think.'

I stare at her, appalled, then look to the guard for confirmation. She offers no reaction. Surely this can't be true? She was given life with no eligibility of parole. She's lying. She has to be.

There's a clink of chains as Sally's untied from the table by a second guard. As she's led away, shuffling in her shackles, she gives another throaty laugh, stops, and looks back.

In that moment, our eyes locked in silent battle, I know I've made an enormous error. I should never have come. I should have trusted the police to do their job.

'And when I do get out,' Sally cackles as she turns to leave again, 'I know exactly how to find the person who stole my daughter ... and rejected my son.'

Chapter 43

KAT

Fifteen Years Ago

'And what about Brad?' Monica asks.

It's been two weeks since we agreed to adopt Amy. Fourteen days, two meetings with the adoption agency, dozens of forms and hundreds of the most difficult conversations Dylan and I have ever had.

The problem is, neither of us is passionately convinced either way. Every time we've tried to talk about it, one of us will suggest a point to consider; either for or against adopting Amy's older, traumatised brother. It'll be a good point, well made, evenly delivered. The other person will counter, and then we'll stay in whichever camp we started in, vehemently arguing for and against. The next time, without meaning to, we'll switch sides and argue the same points as before, but in reverse.

It's an impossible choice.

On the one hand, an abused, neglected, traumatised child needs a home. That much is irrefutable. He deserves the kind of life he's been denied in his five short years. He deserves the kind of life that we could give him. Besides, he's Amy's brother, and we learned in training how important it is for siblings to stay together. It gives them a sense of security, of familiarity, of belonging.

On the other hand, this particular child has been so badly

affected by his parents that he's riddled with behavioural issues and anger management problems. It's to be expected – of course it is. But so far, in the emergency foster homes he's been placed in, he's lit a fire in his bedroom, punched another child, bitten a carer and urinated all over a family's dinner while standing in the middle of the dining table. The agency has advised his current foster carers to keep him locked in his room at night, for their own safety.

Sure, Amy might present her own set of behavioural problems. She's experienced her own trauma; it's inevitable that there will be some effects, somewhere along the way. But bringing up a baby is a very different undertaking to bringing home a five-year-old child who can remember his trauma, who has already been shaped by it.

There's concern for Amy's safety, too. Not that Brad has shown any indication that he'd harm her. If anything, he seems to be her protector, her keeper. But if they grow up together, there's no way we'll be able to keep her past from her, because he remembers where they came from. And if she finds out, it means at eighteen she'll have legal access to her records, which means she'll work out who her parents are, if she hasn't already figured it out by then. Most adopted children want to meet – or at least contact – their biological parents, and there's no reason to believe Amy won't feel the same way. But her parents are so dangerous, so cruel, that the authorities want to limit any chance of her having any kind of contact with them.

So keeping Brad with her could, in the long term, put Amy in serious danger.

And yet tearing them apart could ruin a little boy's life.

It's been a hellish two weeks. Even now, sitting in Monica's office, signing more papers and entering into more discussions about changed identities and suppressed records and psychological monitoring, I still don't know what our answer is going to be. I'm torn.

Well, no. That's not entirely true. I think I've finally decided what our answer should be. Maybe I've known all along. But that in itself is tearing me up, because I know I'll probably regret it. And I'll definitely feel guilty for a long, long time. But at least I'll know. It's the not knowing of the other option that I'm not sure I can handle. It's the fact that anything could happen. Of course it could be rewarding and joyful and the best thing we ever do. Or it could be a disaster, and it could bring danger and chaos and distress into our lives.

I glance at Dylan. His head is bowed, and he folds one hand into the other, cracking each knuckle, one by one, a series of soft pops.

My heart sinks as I realise I'm about to say the words I haven't been able to bear uttering before. I've barely let myself think them.

'I don't think we can,' I say, wincing as I prepare for judgement, or worse, disappointment.

'I understand,' Monica says gently, and I think she genuinely might. 'It's an incredibly difficult decision, but I can see you've put a lot of thought into this, and in the end, it has to be right for your family.'

I nod, tears building on the rims of my eyes.

'And besides,' she continues, 'we don't even know what's best here. It's a completely unique situation, and regular procedures don't really apply. So this might be the best thing for Amy, after all. What we're most focused on is getting her into a stable, loving home so that she at least has a chance at a fresh start.'

'Can we . . .' Dylan lifts his head as though he's suddenly

221

thought of something important, but the words fade as he trails off.

'What is it?'

He shakes his head. 'I just . . . I feel like we're making this decision based on what we're seeing on paper. We haven't even met the poor little guy. What if . . . I just think it'd be a good idea to meet him before we give our final yes or no. Can we do that?'

Monica pauses, tapping her pen against her bottom lip. I hold my breath.

'Look,' she says, 'it's not standard procedure, but then again, none of this is. I think we can probably make that happen. What do you think, Kat?'

I smile weakly and nod, because I know that's what I'm supposed to do. But I don't want to meet him. I know that seeing him in the flesh and looking into his eyes isn't going to change my mind. All it's going to do is make me feel more guilty.

I can't do it. I can't take him.

And I hate myself for knowing that.

Chapter 44

IMOGEN

It was still early, and yet Imogen's whole body seemed to be oozing sweat. She'd woken up gasping and drenched, the heat like a blanket, smothering her. The little cabin, all dark and shaded by gums, had been outdone by the rising temperatures and was now retaining more heat every day, making it feel like an oven.

She pulled herself out of bed, splashed some tepid water on her face and went in search of Brad. She wanted to be around him, stay near him, to be within sight of the only person who wanted her around. Whenever he wasn't in her direct line of sight, Imogen began feeling anxious, worried that he had run off and left her with no one and nothing. The fear would bubble and build, tears forming behind her eyes, until inevitably he'd return, having only been gone a few seconds, and she'd want to weep with relief.

The same panic was creeping up in her as she peered into the living room and the bathroom. Both were empty. As Imogen looked around for another door, the one that would lead to his bedroom, she realised that there wasn't one. Guilt pinched her stomach. Where had he been sleeping? And where had he gone? Hands shaking, she tried the back door and, knees weak with relief, she found Brad outside, lying face up on a pile of sofa cushions under the tiny corrugated iron porch.

'Hi,' she said, her voice still thick with sleep. She cleared her throat, and her skin tingled as the slightest breeze breathed across it.

'Morning,' he replied, throwing her a cushion.

She sat heavily, her spine still tingling from the horrifying split second when she thought he'd left. She hated being like this, so needy and paranoid, but she couldn't stop it. Brad was all she had. She couldn't bear to lose him, too.

'Brad?'

'Amy.'

'Where have you been sleeping?'

'Oh, just on the sofa,' he said.

Her hands flew to her face in shame.

'I'm so sorry,' she said. 'I didn't mean to take your room, you can have it back and I'll sleep on the sofa—'

'Over my dead body, little one,' he said firmly. 'My baby sister isn't sleeping on a sofa, OK?'

'I'm not a baby,' she mumbled.

'You are to me.'

He smiled widely, that dimple in his cheek getting even deeper, his caramel eyes filled with affection, and her heart flipped over. She didn't need to worry about him leaving, she decided. He wanted to be there, wanted to be with her.

Unlike her own family.

Her heart dropped again, as it did every time she thought about that message from Kat. She couldn't understand the things she'd said, the way she'd just dismissed her daughter – adopted or not – without even trying to speak to her. If she hadn't seen the message with her own eyes, she'd never have believed Kat was capable of such cruel words. Imogen's

224

whole body ached when she thought about it. She tried to focus on something else instead, like her rumbling stomach.

'You hungry?'

She nodded, and Brad pulled a bag from behind him, the brown paper dark where grease had soaked through.

'When did you...?'

'Oh, I was up early; too hot. And I was starving. So I thought I'd do a Maccas run for us. I mean, it's not exactly fresh any more, but it's still warm. I got us a bacon and egg McMuffin each and some hash browns. And coffee.'

'Thank you,' she managed a weak smile and took the proffered bag from him, rummaging through it for one of the wrapped muffins and two hash browns. Her appetite had reappeared with a vengeance, and the salty, fatty smell of breakfast made her mouth water.

For a few minutes they sat in comfortable silence, eating and sipping, Imogen trying to contain the barrage of questions she still had for him. Eventually, though, she couldn't hold them in.

'Please can you tell me about our family? Our parents?'

'Yeah, of course,' he said, mouth full of food. 'OK, where do I start? Right, so I've told you your name is Amy. Amy Sanders. And you were born in Victoria.'

'Victoria!'

'Yep, you're not an Adelaide girl. You're from the outback.'

Imogen glowed with a strange kind of pride for her newly discovered beginnings.

'Wait. Am I really sixteen? Is my birthday a lie too?'

'12 January?'

'Yep, OK, so some things are real then,' she said, relieved.

'We have an older sister,' Brad said, and Imogen's jaw fell open. She'd never had an older sibling before, and now she had two. She felt like she was getting emotional

225

whiplash; the excitement of a new family, and all the possibilities ahead of her, followed by crushing disappointment and rejection. Then more joy and hope and expectation. It was hard to keep up, but she let herself be carried by her emotions, helpless to stop them.

'Where is she?'

'Well, that part I don't know yet,' he said.

Imogen frowned.

'I should back up. We were all separated – our parents, us. The one thing I want you to know, and never ever doubt, is that our mum and dad loved us.'

Imogen swallowed. Tears prickled behind her eyes, but she blinked until they disappeared. She desperately wanted to believe him.

'Why did they give us up then?' Her voice cracked on the last word, and her eyes filled with hot tears.

'They didn't,' Brad said, leaning over to grip her hand. 'Amy, listen to me. They didn't give us up. We were taken from them.'

'By who?'

'The government. Social workers. People who decided that our parents weren't doing a good enough job. And yeah, OK, they weren't perfect – I know that, and they'd admit it – but they loved us. We were a family.'

'So where are they now?'

'I'll come to that,' he said.

Imogen wanted to press him, to know right then, but he seemed to be on a roll, his hands waving as he spoke, his face getting more animated. She didn't want to interrupt.

'So Kimberley – that's our sister – was taken away and given a new identity – we all were. I've been trying to find her for ages but haven't managed to find her new name so far.'

'Well, how did you find me?'

'Now that, little sis, is a good question,' he said with a smile.

Imogen glowed with pride.

'You see, I was there when you were taken away from me. I was supposed to go with you, but the people who adopted you didn't want me, too.'

'Wait – Kat and Dylan were going to adopt you, too?'

With every new snippet of information she was given about the couple who raised her, Imogen's hatred snowballed into something huge and unstoppable.

'Well, they were at least considering it. They came to meet us. I remember it so clearly, even now. I was five, and you were just a baby, totally helpless. They turned up at the foster home we were in, and I could hear them talking. They didn't want me. I'd pushed the memory away, hadn't thought anything of it for ages. And then one day I met someone at work whose name was Braidwood and that day just flooded back to me. I remembered overhearing the social worker calling the couple who took you Mr and Mrs Braidwood. Once I'd remembered that, I realised that maybe I could find you after all. It didn't take too long to find a couple called Braidwood with a daughter Amy's age, thanks to Facebook.'

Imogen was still reeling from the revelation that she could have grown up with Brad, that their entire childhood together had been taken from her. She wondered how different her life would have been if she'd had an older brother around, someone who was looking out for her. She wished she'd known that life.

'Why didn't they want you?'

'I was damaged, apparently.'

Imogen didn't know what to say, how to apologise for the

227

behaviour of the people she'd been chosen by. There were no words that could bring back what they'd lost. She felt guilty, although deep down she knew that it wasn't her fault.

'But the good news is that I found you,' Brad said suddenly, breaking the silence. 'And together, I'm sure we can find Kimmy. And then we can be a family again.'

'Are we going to find our parents?' she asked. 'Where are they?'

'I'm going to tell you, little one. But when I do, I want you to keep an open mind, OK? And remember what I said before . . . our parents loved us. They still do.'

She nodded, her skin tingling with nerves. She didn't know what he was going to tell her, but she knew that she trusted him. He was her family, her real family. He was all she needed. He was all she had. It didn't matter what he said, in the end. Nothing mattered but them being together.

'Our parents,' he said softly, 'are in jail.'

Chapter 45

KAT

I dial Owen Griffin's number as soon as I'm back in the safety of my car. I can barely breathe, but I need to know.

He picks up as I'm turning out of the prison car park.

'Is it true?' I say, in lieu of a greeting.

'Sorry, is what true? Is that you, Mrs Braidwood? Did you get what you needed from Sally?'

'Is it true that she's making an appeal? She said there was some bad evidence in her trial or something, that she might get out of there one day.'

There's a hissing noise as Owen inhales sharply. 'She said that?'

'Right as I was leaving,' I tell him. 'She has to be lying, right?'

'I honestly don't know,' he admits. 'I mean, she *is* going to make an appeal. I have no idea whether it could possibly be successful.'

'But you told me you haven't spoken to her for years!'

'I haven't,' Owen replies quickly. 'She found another lawyer, one who thinks she has a case. She contacted me to get all of the original files.'

'And you didn't think to tell me that?'

'No,' he says, sounding surprised. 'I didn't. You're after information about your daughter. Not her current legal status.'

I hang up, frustrated. He calls me right back. I reject the call. And the next one. He leaves a voicemail, which I ignore.

As I enter the freeway and overtake a semi, my heart begins to slow to its regular rhythm. My fear is absorbed once again into my bloodstream, a low thrum rather than a screaming, front-of-mind presence. I'm nowhere near her. I'm safe. For now, anyway. I can't think about Sally's appeal, or the fact that there's even the slightest possibility of her being back on the streets again in the future. I have to get home, and keep my sights on what matters: Imogen.

Although my visit with Sally didn't offer me any solid leads to follow in terms of what might have happened to Imogen, she did confirm that Brad wanted to get his family back together again. He'd been to see her, albeit under a different name—

My stomach does a flip. A different name. I reach over to my phone and scroll through my recently dialled numbers. When I find the one I need, I hit the call button. As it rings, my heart rate picks up again, and I press my foot down to speed past a caravan.

'Hello, Constable Troy Monroe speaking.'

'Troy, it's Kat Braidwood.'

'Kat! Are you OK? Dylan told us you'd taken off, he's been worried sick about you.'

'I'm fine,' I say. 'I've been to Melbourne to visit Sally Sanders, and—'

'You bloody what!' It's an explosion rather than a question.

My cheeks heat up as the shame of my rebellion surfaces. 'I know, I'm sorry. I really am, and you can yell at me all you want later, OK, but I have some information that might help.'

Troy tuts and sighs, as though I'm a naughty toddler

who's misbehaved and he's trying to decide how to punish me. After a beat, he sighs again.

'Fine,' he says, 'but I'll be having some serious words with you later about meddling with a police investigation and putting yourself in danger. What have you got for us?'

'Sally said that Brad's visited her in prison before,' I say.

'She's lying,' he replies gently. 'We checked those records, in our initial search for Brad. There's no Brad on her visitor log, and no Tristan, either.'

'She said he used a fake ID,' I argue. 'Which means he might have another name you guys don't know about. And I guess some kind of disguise?'

'We'll look into it,' Troy says.

I try not to scream down the phone, to demand that he stops messing around and starts seriously looking for my daughter. Surely they can do better than this? If I could get this information, how could they have missed it? And what else have they overlooked? I hold my tongue, though, and manage to rein in my anger enough to say calmly: 'I'm worried you're not being thorough enough about this, and not taking Imogen's safety seriously.'

'I assure you, we're doing all we can. I know it might feel like we're not, because you're not seeing us at work, but we do know what we're doing here. Keep in mind, Kat, Sally might have just been saying this to get a reaction from you. We might not have missed anything.'

I consider his words. Perhaps he's right. Maybe she was playing me.

'Maybe,' I concede.

'I know this is incredibly difficult for you. But please leave this to us from now on, OK? We really do know what we're doing.'

'OK,' I say meekly. I'm embarrassed now that the initial

231

adrenaline has worn off, now that I'm left empty-handed, no closer to finding Imogen than I was before.

'And, Kat?'

'Yeah?'

'Do me a favour and give Dylan a call, will you? Just let him know you're safe. Poor bloke's going out of his mind.'

I promise I will, then hang up and stare at the road as it whirs past me. My hands are cramped from gripping the steering wheel so intensely. I let out a long, slow lungful of air and relax my fingers. My knuckles immediately flood with blood and the colour returns to them. I reach towards my phone, and then hesitate, my hand shaking as it hovers to my left.

No point putting this off, I tell myself. Besides, I promised Troy. And Dylan does deserve to know that I'm all right.

He picks up after half a ring, his breath heavy as though he's been running.

'Kat, thank God, are you OK?'

'I'm fine,' I say wearily. 'I'm on my way home.'

'Where the hell are you?'

I sigh. I'll have to tell him what I did eventually, anyway. Might as well get it over with.

'I'm in Victoria—'

'Victoria? What the hell—'

'I went to see Sally. Sanders.'

There's a brief pause. I wait for the explosion I know is coming, and after a few seconds, when my confession sinks in, it arrives.

'Are you out of your mind? What the hell is wrong with you? Why would you do something so stupid, so... so bloody reckless?'

I let him rant at me for a few minutes, keeping my eyes on the horizon while he exhausts himself. There's nothing out here on the freeway. It's flat and dry as far as the eye can see, an occasional dusty grey bush the only landmark. It's hypnotic after a while. The kilometres tick past, but the landscape remains exactly the same. Bleak. Dead. Hopeless.

'Kat?'

I blink quickly, my attention back on Dylan, on his raised voice. 'Yes, sorry, what?'

'I asked if she said anything. If it helped; meeting her.'

'I don't know,' I admit. 'She did say that Brad visited her in prison using a fake identity. And, before you interrupt, I've already told the cops.'

'That feels like a pretty massive bit of information for them to have missed,' Dylan says, his volume lower now, the fight gone from his voice.

I murmur my agreement.

'Are you all right?' he asks.

'I don't know,' I say, a sob creeping up my chest. 'It was so awful meeting her, hearing her try to act like she's a great mother and I'm this terrible human.'

My eyes well up and I blink the tears away.

'She said that Brad mentioned us when he visited her. Not us specifically,' I add as Dylan starts speaking over me. 'Just that he remembers a couple choosing Imogen – Amy – and rejecting him.'

As I'm speaking, new thoughts are forming, new connections are being made. And as they are, my stomach plummets.

'Dylan,' I whisper. 'What if this isn't just about getting his family back together?'

'What do you mean?'

'Well, what if it's about revenge?'

There's silence over the phone as the idea takes root. The road hurtles past, a blur of black and white. I almost don't say the words I'm thinking, can't bear the idea. They catch in my throat as I force them out, the horror of it coming out as a wheeze.

'What if he wants to get back at us,' I say, 'for taking his sister away?'

PART THREE

Chapter 46

IMOGEN

She didn't think she could handle any more bombshells about her past. She'd had enough for a lifetime. These new truths were slamming into her brain, the force of their impact almost blinding her with a sharp, insistent pain. She winced as another blow caught her behind her eyes.

Finding out she was adopted would have been shock enough. But then there was the discovery of her older brother, the news that she had an older sister somewhere, that her adoptive parents kept her and Brad apart and, finally, learning that her real parents were in prison. It was too much.

As soon as the words had left Brad's lips, she'd burst into tears, unable to control the tide of emotion that had been building inside her. Her sobs were loud and messy, like parts of her had come loose and were being expelled from her lungs. She didn't know how to stop it, or slow it down. Her grief was like a black hole, sucking up any light that dared to come too close.

Brad had leapt over the cushions to hold her, wrapping her in his arms and rocking her gently, whispering that it was going to be OK, that he was there, that he wouldn't let her go. Eventually, the sobs had subsided, leaving her numb and frozen to the spot. She couldn't have moved if she'd wanted to, but she didn't want to.

She didn't know how long they sat there for, her brother's hands clasped together at her side, her ribs pressing into his, small puffs of his breath warming the top of her head.

'Let's get you inside, shall we?' he'd asked eventually.

She hadn't replied, so he'd picked her up and carried her back into the dark, where he lay her gently on the sofa, pulling the armchair close so he could hold her hand.

She stared at a small stain on the knee of his jeans, a single point that she concentrated all of her attention on. It was the only way to stop the anguish. And she needed to stop it. If she didn't, it would consume her completely until there was none of her left. Just the dry husk of a girl whose whole world was pulled out from under her all at once.

'I'm sorry, Amy,' Brad said, stroking her arm. 'I shouldn't have told you, I knew it was too soon.'

She tried to shake her head, but all she managed to do was blink. It was her fault, not his. She'd been the one who wouldn't stop asking where their parents were. She had so many more questions, but every time she began to think about all the things she didn't know, she'd be battered by another crashing wave of emotion and she'd start falling apart again. Maybe there were some things it was better not to know.

'I'm going to call Kat,' he said.

'No,' she managed to croak. 'Please don't.'

'Amy, this is serious. I'm worried about you.'

'I don't want to see her. And, anyway, she doesn't want to see me.'

'Oh, little one,' he said. 'I know this is so hard. I wish I could take all of your pain away, but I just want to help. What if I get Kat to bring some of your things. Would that make you feel better? Do you think maybe some of your clothes and, I don't know, just some familiar stuff, would help?'

Imogen thought about it for a second. She did miss having her own clothes, clothes that fitted properly and smelled like her. She missed her phone, too, but Brad told her she'd thrown it out the window of his car on Saturday night. She couldn't remember, but she'd been feeling reckless when she left home, so she must have done. More than anything specific, though, she just missed having anything of her own, anything that tethered her to the world. Right now she was just floating, in someone else's space, in someone else's identity. Maybe having some things that she recognised would remind her that she really did exist.

'OK, but please don't make me see her.'

'I won't. I promise. I think you need to rest for now, anyway. I can get her to come and bring your things and you can have a bit of a sleep. I actually got you some vitamins this morning, when I was out getting breakfast. Will you take one with some water? I need to make sure you're staying healthy; you're still recovering from whatever that was you had, and I don't want to risk it happening again.'

She nodded, grateful to her brother for knowing exactly what she needed. A tear escaped from the corner of her eye.

'Thank you, Brad,' she said. 'I don't know what I'd do without you.'

'You don't have to be without me,' he said. 'You never have to be without me again.'

She squeezed his hand, unable to put into words how she felt, how much she owed him, how much she loved him already, after only knowing him for a few days. He squeezed it back, then got up to pour her a glass of water. She took it gratefully, the cool side of the glass providing a tiny bit of relief from the heat of the day.

It was only after taking her first sip that she realised how thirsty she was, and with just a few gulps the water was gone. Brad refilled it, then handed her a pill. She looked at it, then back to him.

'Vitamins. You need it, Amy.'

She slipped the tablet onto her tongue and chugged the rest of the water. Then Brad carried her back to the bedroom, placing her on the bed. She felt empty, wrung dry. She wanted this day to be over. She wanted to fast-forward to the part where life felt normal again, where she and Brad and Kimberley lived together, making up for all of the time they'd lost, and where she didn't feel constantly confused and sad and angry.

'Don't go,' she whispered to Brad, grabbing his arm as she curled up on her side.

'I'm right here, little one,' he said, stroking her hair.

She let her eyes drift closed, and as sleep claimed her wearied mind, she decided that Brad was the kindest and most gentle person she'd ever met. If he turned out so great, then their parents *couldn't* be bad people. It was impossible.

Her lips stretched into a drowsy smile. Maybe being Amy would turn out OK.

240

Chapter 47

KAT

My head spins as petrol fumes hit my lungs. I breathe in deeply, enjoying the sudden lightness, the sweet chemical scent that overpowers everything else. The pump jolts in my hand and I'm brought back to my senses. The tank's full, and I need to get back home, need to find a way to get to Brad so I can find Imogen.

Because if it's me he's really after, and if taking Imogen is just a way to get revenge on me – on us – then she could be in more danger than we thought. Revenge is a completely different beast from reunion; it's driven by rage and injustice, not love. If he's hell-bent on retribution for what he saw as our unforgivable act – taking his sister and leaving him behind – then there's no telling what he'll do to get even. What if he wants me to feel what he did, the loss of the girl he knows as Amy, who I know as Imogen? The thought rages inside me, a blaze that scorches my heart, my lungs, the marrow inside my bones.

I slam the car door closed and start the engine. Only three hundred kilometres to Adelaide, and a full tank to get me there. I should be home before dark. I'll be there to kiss Jemima goodnight, to sit with Dylan and work out what the hell we do next, how we keep fighting, keep searching, keep believing that we'll get our daughter back. I pull out of the petrol station and back onto the highway.

The only comfort I have is that Brad wants her with him. I have to believe that no matter how much pain he'd like to cause me, he doesn't want to hurt his sister. Although ... perhaps, with genes like his, his idea of love isn't the same as the rest of us. If he loves the way his parents did ... I shake my head. It's not worth thinking about. Giving in to thoughts of his DNA only leads to thoughts of what's running through my own daughter's blood, and I refuse to believe the worst of her.

Besides, if there's one thing I am certain of when it comes to Imogen, it's that she's strong. I think about the girl I saw in the school nurse's office just last week, her face bloodied and bruised, and I know that Imogen wouldn't go down without a fight. She wouldn't let herself be hurt. But the relief is fleeting. If she does fight, maybe that will anger him. Maybe that will make things worse.

I let out a scream of frustration and punch the steering wheel. It feels good, so I let another scream tear up my throat, contracting my lungs until I can scream no more and I have to gasp for breath, and then I let another one rip, all of the fear and confusion and anger and what-ifs escaping in a burst of noise and emotion. I slam my fist against the wheel again and again, the car horn blasting in time with my grief, and I relish the pain as the side of my hand becomes bruised and tender.

Spent, I slump back in my seat and hit cruise control. I take my feet off the pedals and watch the nothingness whir past me. There's not another soul on this stretch of road. It's apocalyptic. Nothing but dust and bugs and, occasionally, a snake writhing its way across the shimmering road, graceful as water and utterly deadly.

I reach for the radio, needing something to distract me from my own thoughts, and to keep me awake on the monotonous drive home. All the way here I was pumped up on adrenaline, imagining what I'd say to Sally, picturing a triumphant moment where she, cowed by my love for Imogen, confessed to knowing exactly where my daughter is being held. Now I'm deflated, confused, scared, ashamed and exhausted. But I can't let myself fall asleep on the road. Imogen needs me.

As I press the audio button and scroll through my play-lists, I spot a notification above my messages icon. I didn't hear my phone beeping. Frowning, I tap the message to open it. It's from a withheld number. When the message appears on my screen, I'm jolted awake, the movement so sudden that I swerve unintentionally, my car veering until it's almost off the road.

I hit the rumble strip and the tyres protest loudly. My bones rattle as I pull the wheel sharply, navigating back to safety. It's not safe to pull over; there's nowhere to stop. Instead, I slow down, take a couple of deep breaths, and read the message again slowly:

Remember me? the text begins. *It's the child you left behind, the one you rejected. I'm back – I've come to take back what was never yours. But I can see you won't give up. So why don't we let Amy choose? Her real family, or the people who lied to her for her entire life? I'll send you an address tonight. Come alone. Don't even think about telling your husband, and definitely not the cops, or you'll never hear from us again. And Amy will be gone forever.*

Chapter 48

SALLY

To some extent, I can understand when outsiders – people unfamiliar with prison life, the portion of society that believes those of us behind bars are other, somehow – underestimate me. After all, they want so desperately to be removed from who I am – from what I am – that they're willing to deceive themselves. They're convinced that I must be lesser than them, intelligence included, if I've ended up behind bars.

It's a flawed argument, honestly. If you thought for more than a second about the kind of morons you encounter day to day – in your job, at the supermarket, on the roads – you'd know that incarceration and a deficit of intelligence couldn't possibly be linked. But I know you don't stop to think about that. You don't want to. I get it.

What I don't understand is when people on the inside assume I'm a woman of lesser intellect, simply because I'm here. Of course, just like on the outside, there are people in prison who are utter imbeciles. It's a statistical certainty, whether you're in prison or in a boardroom. But sometimes I think people just decide that because of what I did, I must be mentally defective.

I'd like to state here, for the record, that I'm not. I am, in fact, quite intelligent.

244

And, frustrating as it is to have my fellow criminals mis-judge my intellect, I can't deny that it works in my favour.

If any of the degenerates in this place knew what I was really doing in the library every day, they'd want a piece of my brainpower. They see me, tucked away in the reference section, legal tomes spread before me, and they think it's just a cover. I mean, sure, it's a great spot from which to run my business, but that's just a bonus. I'm not there for the transactions. I'm there for my babies. To protect them. Because they're not safe out there all alone. They're exposed to too much, at the mercy of people whose intentions I can't be certain of.

So, yes, I am trying to appeal my case, just as I told Kathryn. If I can get out of here, then I can look after my babies once again; I can make sure they stay safe. We can be a family, and that's all I've ever wanted.

Do I think I'll get out? Well, that depends. It all hinges on whether I'm willing to betray my Tim, throw him under the bus for the greater good – the well-being of my children. My new lawyer – the one Brad hired for me, using his savings from working at the mines all those years – tells me that nothing I can do will change Tim's future. Me stabbing him in the back, claiming it's all his fault, that none of it was my doing, won't make his sentence any longer.

But it's not like there's any guarantee I'll be released, even if I do the unthinkable. Because even if it won't change his future, Tim will know what I've done. There's no worse thing anyone can do to another human than betray them.

Oh, you think what I've done is worse? That's cute. Clearly you've never been betrayed; not really. I have. By my own daughter. That pain was greater than losing all the rest of them put together. If Tim turned on me, I don't think

I'd survive it. And I don't think I have it in me to put him through that.

So I'm doing all I can to read up on my rights and find a way out of here – and of course, I'm so grateful that my boy is helping – but in the end, I might not succeed. And if I don't, I need to make sure that my babies are safe without me. I may be incarcerated, but I'm not helpless. As I said, I'm smart. And I've got time on my hands.

I'm glad Kathryn came to see me. It confirmed to me what I've long suspected, that she feels a sense of ownership over what's rightfully mine, and she intends to find and reclaim what she believes is her property. It's almost charming how sincere she is, how much she truly believes that Amy is better with her, playing the role of Imogen Braidwood, blithely ignoring the things that lurk in her blood.

But sorry, Kathryn, you don't get to make that choice any more, no matter how eager you are.

It's lucky, really, that I have Brad on my side, a willing helper, someone to carry out my wishes while I'm stuck in here. He's my hands and feet, my action man. It was something of a surprise when he came back into my life, if I'm completely honest. I suppose maybe I'd started to believe some of the things they say about me, about my abilities to parent. Fifteen years of being told you're the scum of the earth, with no one telling you otherwise, isn't exactly great for the old self-esteem.

But then that letter arrived, the one where a stranger named Tristan said he thought I was his mum. When we'd established that Tristan was actually my Brad, I told him that he was welcome to come and see me, although he'd need to use another name. Obviously our communication was more subtle than that – there are people monitoring all of my letters – but I'm simplifying it for you. I don't want to lose anyone here.

He turned up, in the guise of a journalist, and I'd known the second I laid eyes on him that he was mine. He knew it, too. There was an instant connection, the kind of recognition that you only find with someone who shares your flesh and blood.

He told me about his life, about the family who rejected him and took Amy, about the people who took him in and then kicked him out, and my blood ran cold. All these years, all that danger. I would never have let that happen to him. I would never have exposed him to risks like that.

And it was in that moment that I knew, with total certainty, that I'm a good mum. That no one else ever could – or ever will – do a better job.

And I realised that maybe I could still protect my babies. One of them, at least. It would just take some time, and a lot of careful planning. But I was up to the challenge.

Chapter 49

KAT

My vision blurs. I can't tell whether I'm going to throw up or faint. Maybe both.

The engine ticks and pops as I sit in the driveway, too exhausted to move.

The front door opens, and Dylan rushes out, opening the driver's door and embracing me awkwardly as I sit, still buckled in, unsure how to react, how to deal with the information I've been analysing for the past few hours on the road.

'Oh my God, I was so worried about you, I'm so glad you're safe. Come inside, let's get you some coffee.'

I nod as he reaches in to unbuckle my seat belt, and I allow myself to be led into the house, Jemima waiting for me as soon as I walk through the front door.

'Mum, you're home!' she says, as I wrap my arms tightly around her.

I'm not sure what Dylan has told her about my absence, but she doesn't seem distressed, or angry. I'm grateful to him for protecting her from the truth: that her mother took off without a word and drove interstate to chat with a serial killer. I close my eyes, and breathe in the sweet smell of her freshly washed hair, wishing I could absorb her innocence. I tighten my arms around her.

248

'Ooof, Mum, I can't breathe,' she moans into my chest.

'Sorry,' I say, letting her go and wiping tears from my cheeks. 'Now, young lady, it's almost bedtime, isn't it?'

'Not yet,' she argues. 'It's only eight. And I've done all my homework. Can I have an iced chocolate before bed? Please?'

She looks between Dylan and me, and I relent instantly. She drags us to the kitchen, where Dylan makes three iced chocolates, complete with whipped cream and sprinkles. We sip in silence for a few minutes, the sugar slowly bringing my strength back, the familiar surroundings comforting the turmoil in my head.

'I wish Immy was back,' Jemima says suddenly, and I think I might crumble right there at the kitchen table.

'Me too, love,' I say, reaching across to grab her hand, needing to cling to something so I don't fall apart.

'Do you think she'll come home soon?' Jemima asks, her eyes wide and pleading, voicing the question I'm too scared to put into words, in case I get the answer I don't want to hear.

'Of course she will,' Dylan says, a little too loudly, a little too vehemently.

I try to swallow the lump in my throat, and squeeze Jemima's hand even tighter. She doesn't squeeze mine in return.

'I'm tired,' she says quietly. 'I want to go to bed.'

I stand next to her, folding her in my arms.

'OK, love,' I say into her hair. 'Let's go get you ready.'

I lay on top of the covers beside Jemima, stroking her hair until her breath becomes rhythmic and slow. She's fast asleep, the stress of the past few days sapping her usual resistance to bedtime. She stirs gently, and I whisper *shhhh* until she stills again. I curl up next to her, my chest tightening as I try to imagine what this must be like for her.

Imogen and Jemima are close; closer than I expected them to be at this age. As they got older, I figured that Immy would become moody with teenage hormones, pushing away an annoying little sister, distancing herself so as not to damage her social life, delicate as that can be for high-school kids. The hormones did make her moody. Just not towards her baby sister.

They were always whispering and conspiring in one of their rooms, conversations I'd never be a part of. Sometimes I'd hear a blood-curdling shriek or an almighty crash and I'd think that we'd reached the moment when they couldn't stand each other, when their love transformed into sibling rivalry, or worse. But every time, after a few panicked seconds, I'd hear a peal of laughter and my heart would swell. As an only child, I'd never experienced that. I'd only ever had my parents for company, a relationship that had never involved laughter or secrets or play-fighting. I didn't have a confidante, aside from the brief existence of an imaginary friend named Casper, and I always longed for a sibling, a constant companion who would turn my lonely, listless weekends into boundless adventures. But watching Imogen and Jemima mended that part of me. I never had it for myself, but I got to provide it for my girls. I got to see it happening before my eyes.

To have it, and then to lose it . . . that's a tragedy I can't imagine. But it's what Jemima's going through now. She might only be twelve, but she's perceptive, and I know she'll understand the realities of what's happening. She'll have thought through all of the possible scenarios, she'll have considered the idea of never seeing her sister again. Her potential heartbreak is unbearable.

A small voice in the back of my mind reminds me that what Jemima is going through – that pain, that loss, that grief – that's what Brad had to go through when he was just five, when he didn't have any family left, when he was confused and scared and without another soul on his side. Only in his situation, no one was working to get his sister back to him. Something inside me tears, a seam coming undone, stitch by stitch, and I almost howl with the pain of it.

So this is my fault. I did this to Brad. I took his only ally, I broke that bond.

Heavy-hearted, I creep out of Jemima's room. I need to get to Brad. I need to look into his eyes, tell him that I'm sorry for not taking him, too; for stealing Imogen away from him. I need him to understand that my daughter's life is good and that, whatever he's been through, she deserves to live the life she's been given, and to live it well. Maybe we can arrange visits, some kind of supervised time together, so she can get to know her brother, without any possibility of him hurting her. I don't know. All I do know is that if I can just look at him, talk to him, reason with him, I'll get through to him.

I have to.

There's a problem, though: Dylan. I don't know how to get away from him without raising his suspicions. I only just got home after taking off without an explanation, so I'm pretty sure if I did it again, Dylan would follow me, demand an answer.

I should just tell him, tell the police, let other people decide how to handle this. But Brad told me not to breathe a word to anyone, told me there would be consequences if I did. I don't know how he'd know, but I don't think I can risk it.

I almost think I've decided, until I realise that I can't trust my own judgement. I drove over seven hundred kilometres

251

to meet with the country's most dangerous woman, for goodness' sake. Clearly my decision-making skills aren't in any condition to be making a call this important alone.

I want to go to the police. I want to let Dylan in, present the evidence as a team, and then trust the authorities to take care of it all. But Imogen's life could be at stake. And if the police managed to miss information as important as Brad visiting Sally in prison, I'm not convinced they'll be able to do much to help. It's too big a risk. I can't do it.

For now, I need to follow Brad's rules, play his game the way he wants it to be played. For Imogen's sake.

I walk into the living room, so absorbed with trying to work out how I can get away undetected, that I don't notice Dylan standing in the middle of the room, phone in his hand and a deep frown on his face.

'Kat,' he says, and I look up sharply. Was I thinking out loud? Did I just let slip what I'm planning? 'I just got off the phone with the cops,' he says, and everything stops. Every time the police call, there's the chance that it's the worst news imaginable. Every single time, my brain immediately goes to the darkest of places. 'They haven't found her,' he says in a rush as he sees my reaction. 'It's nothing like that. They just found the ID of the man who visited Sally. He called himself Dylan.'

I can feel the blood rushing from my head. I lean on the back of the sofa for support.

'What?'

'I know. Dylan Anderson. But still. Apparently he dyed his hair, grew a beard. His ID was fake, but it was so good it wasn't picked up. He said he was a journalist, that he was writing about Satan's Ranch, he had a press pass and everything. No one batted an eyelid. They think there were letters, too. They should have more information soon.'

'OK,' I say slowly, trying to focus, 'so why did they want to speak to you?'

'They want to do another press conference tomorrow,' he says. 'With more information on Brad. They want to reveal his real identity, share all the aliases he was using, in case someone's seen him.'

I have to sit down.

'But,' I whisper, 'once they reveal his real identity, everyone will work out the truth about Imogen, about who she is.'

'Honey,' he says gently, sitting beside me and taking my hand. 'What is there to hide any more? Who are we hiding from?'

I slump back on the sofa. For so long, for so many years, we've been concealing this huge, life-changing truth, careful not to let slip, careful to keep the paperwork behind locked, steel doors, careful to never let on that Imogen isn't a Braidwood. To simply let that go now feels so wrong, feels impossible somehow. And yet holding on is impossible, too.

'I'm scared for her,' I admit. 'I'm scared of what people will say about her, about what she'll go through if people know. It could ruin her life.'

'I'm scared too,' he says. 'But not telling the truth could put her in even more danger. Immy's a fighter. You know she is. She'll be OK.'

Brad's message swirls in my mind. *Why don't we let Amy choose?* I just need to convince her to choose us. If I can get her back tonight, there will be no need for anyone to know who she is. I can save her. I can save her life, and I can protect her reputation. Her future. I have to, or all of our hard work will have been for nothing. She'll be hunted down by the press, she'll be known not for who she is but for what her parents did. I'm not going to let that happen, not after everything we did to keep her real identity hidden. I just have to find a way to get away from Dylan, to go and meet Brad, to put an end to all of this tonight.

'OK,' I say, nodding. 'If it's going to get Imogen back, then they should do it.'

'They want us to come down to the headquarters again to go through the messaging.'

'Now?'

'Yeah, the press conference is first thing. They said the media specialist is still there and is willing to walk us through what we'll be asked to say tonight.'

The opportunity to slip away and meet Brad is narrowing.

'Jemima's fast asleep,' I say quickly, trying to work out how to do this and also see Brad. 'I'll call Linda and see if she can come over.'

'She's out tonight,' Dylan tells me. I look at him questioningly. 'She told me earlier. She and the kids went to her parents'.'

'Well, I don't want to wake Jemima,' I argue. 'She's exhausted. She doesn't need any more disruption. Or any more trips to the police station.'

Dylan sits back, frowning.

'You're right. How about I go to the station now, and you stay and look after Jems? It's not ideal, but I can pass on anything they tell me, and Jemima can stay sleeping.'

And just like that, I have my window.

Chapter 50

KAT

The house is eerily quiet. I can't keep still. Since Dylan left, I've been pacing the living room, my phone in my hand, willing it to buzz with the address Brad said he'd send. My up-and-down route has taken me to the kitchen more than once, where I've opened the fridge and stared longingly at the bottle of wine that's taunting me from the shelf in the door. I could do with something to calm me down. But I need to be alert. I need to be ready.

I close the fridge firmly and resume my pacing in the living room.

'Come on, come on, come on,' I mutter under my breath.

What if he doesn't text me? Or what if it's too late, and Dylan's already home by the time I get the address and I have to come up with another plan to get out and meet with Brad? My stomach has worked itself into a knot so tight that every so often I have to stop pacing and fold my body over, clutching my abdomen until the cramps subside.

It's during one of these fits of pain that my phone buzzes in my hand, forcing a yelp from my lungs. I stare at it, the message wobbling before my eyes as my hands shake with anticipation and fear. There's just an address, which I recognise to be somewhere up in the hills; nothing else.

'Jemima,' I whisper as I shake her awake. 'Jemima, come on, we have to go.'

She groans and rolls over. I wince with the shame of what I'm dragging her into. I shouldn't be taking her with me, but I don't have a choice. If I'd told Dylan to take her, there would have been no reason for me to stay behind. Linda's not around to look after her. And there's no way I'm leaving her at home alone. For all I know, this is a decoy and Brad plans to take my other daughter from her bed while I'm off trying to find him. No way. I know it's dangerous to take her, but right now it's the safest option.

I shake her gently again.

'Jems, my love, we need to go, OK? Grab your blanket and you can sleep in the car.'

'Where are we going?' she murmurs.

'Don't worry,' I say, ignoring her question and lifting her from her bed.

She protests and wriggles, but I hold her tightly and carry her down the hallway, out the front door and onto the back seat of the car. I buckle her in and put a blanket over her. It's far too hot, but once the air conditioning is on, she'll be OK. Besides, she's asleep again already, dead to the world, completely trusting.

I start the car and tap the address from Brad's text into my maps app, then I rest my phone in its cradle on the dashboard. The app tells me the journey will take half an hour. I grit my teeth. At this time of night, with no traffic, I think I can make it in twenty minutes.

I peel out of our street and along familiar roads, lit by the yellow glow of the street lights. I don't notice that I'm holding my breath until my lungs are burning and my head feels light. I breathe out and gasp for more air as I turn off the main road, where the street lights become sparser, the road narrower and the houses fewer and further apart. Before long, there are no lights at all, and I can see only by the white glare of my headlights, the old, twisted gum trees on either side of the road flashing like gnarled ghosts, taunting me, daring me further in. I press my foot on the accelerator and speed up, past a caravan park and further into the bush.

Here, the road is a single lane. If anyone was coming towards me, I'd have to stop and reverse, but there's no one around. Few people live this far out, and fewer still would be driving around at this time of night. There's nothing in this isolated part of the hills. Only a smattering of homes, and hardly any mobile phone signal. No signs of life. No one to see a young woman who doesn't belong, who shouldn't be here, who the whole city is searching for. No one to hear a scream.

Dread swells inside me as the road narrows even further and all signs of civilisation are swallowed by the darkness I'm leaving in my wake. Rocks jut out towards the car menacingly, while on the other side of the road, dry branches scrape and squeal against the paintwork. I flinch at the noise, but press the pedal down even further, hurtling towards the unknown. Towards Imogen. Or towards a trap. I don't know which it is, but I'm willing to take the risk.

Without warning, I'm at the end of the road. Following my phone's directions, I take a tiny dirt track to the right, past a quaint homestead and into the trees and the bushes and the pressing darkness. I slow down, in part because the road is so treacherous, but also because I don't want to draw any more attention to myself than I need to. It'll be dead silent out here; the car's engine will sound like thunder. I creep along the track and consider turning my lights out, but I don't want to risk crashing into a tree. I settle for keeping them on, but on the lowest setting. I reach over to turn my phone screen off, noticing as I do that the coverage out here is weak, flitting between no signal at all and a single bar. I press the button and the device goes black, the ghost of its blue glare leaving a rectangle of blinding white in my vision. Bright yellow eyes shine from up ahead, and I jump, until they disappear and I realise it was just a possum.

Looming ahead I can vaguely make out a ramshackle structure that looks more like a shed than someone's home. I switch the headlights off and roll the car to a gentle stop. Then, slowly, I reverse for a hundred metres or so. I open the passenger side window and turn the engine off, its soft pops sounding like fireworks in the inky silence. I slowly step out into the stiflingly hot night, trying to make as little noise as possible. Closing my door gently, I open the back door and shake Jemima awake again.

'Mum,' she mumbles, her eyes still closed. 'Where are we?'

'I'm just going to speak to someone, but you have to stay here, OK, love?'

She mutters something in her drowsy half-sleep.

'Jems? Listen to me, OK? Even if you wake up, I need you to stay here.'

I emphasise the last two words, but she's out already. Her sleep is a deep and marvellous thing. I will her to stay unconscious like this until I return with Imogen, and I pray that nothing goes wrong. My instinct tells me I should lock the doors, close the windows tightly, keep her safe. But I don't know how long I'll be, and in this heat, she'd suffocate in minutes without a window open. And if she needs to run, for whatever reason, I want her to have the best chance of a quick escape. I can't put her in any more danger than I already have by bringing her here. I close her door very slowly, very gently, and step towards the house that I can no longer see, but which I know is there.

Each step makes a crack like gunfire as dry twigs and leaves snap beneath my feet. Even as my eyes adjust to the dark, I'm walking blindly, the stars and moon blotted out by a blanket of clouds, a sign that the heat has built and swelled to the point where it has to burst, where a storm will provide a short-lived release. I desperately need the sky to clear, though. I need to see what I'm walking into.

A door creaks. It's close. Almost close enough to touch.

'Imogen?' I call out into the darkness.

And then a light is switched on and I'm blinded. A voice calls out, cutting through the brightness like a laser.

'Hello, Kathryn. Long time no see.'

'Brad,' I say, being careful to keep my voice calm and steady. I hold my hands out, a gesture of surrender. I still can't see anything; the spotlight is pointed directly at my face. I'm like the possum that was just in my headlights: utterly stunned and frozen to the spot. 'I'm here to talk. I know I've hurt you, and I'm sorry. Can we talk about it? Please?'

I step forward, tentatively, hoping to bridge the gap, hoping he'll let me try.

There's a rustling sound, and a whoosh. A flash of a shadow across the light, the blinding glare again and then a hollow crack.

The world jolts for a moment before descending into nothing.

Chapter 51

IMOGEN

'Amy,' Brad called from somewhere else in the house. His voice sounded urgent, but she couldn't muster the energy, or the interest, to get up. She kept her eyes closed.

She had barely moved for hours. The sickness was back, just like Brad had feared. Had she pushed herself too much, too quickly? Was it her own fault that she felt so bad again? Her head was spinning, her eyes were heavy, and she knew that if she dared to roll over, or sit up, the nausea would hit.

She lifted an eyelid carefully, cautiously. It was dark. She couldn't have said what time it was, she had no concept of how long she'd been lying there.

'Amy!' Brad called, this time more urgently.

With a cry of pain she heaved herself up, her head pounding and her mouth dry. She staggered to the bathroom, threw up and then gulped rusty brown water straight from the tap.

Brad was still calling her, so she stumbled out to the living room. He wasn't there. The front door was wide open, and he was shouting from outside.

She stepped around the sofa, and that was when she saw it.

A shape on the ground, just beyond the door, lit by a bright light attached to the front of the house. It looked like a sensor light, the kind Dylan had installed to scare away intruders. She had no idea who would bother intruding all the way out where they were – wherever that was. What would anyone be after? There was nothing worth stealing, she was certain of it. But someone *had* turned up. Someone *had* intruded.

Only they weren't intruding any more. They were lying on the ground, not moving.

She stepped outside into the bright light and walked towards the shape on the ground, her heart stammering in her chest.

'Are they . . . ?' She didn't dare say the word.

'She's not dead,' Brad said, and Imogen's shoulders dropped in relief. Then as his words settled, she turned to face him sharply.

'She?'

Her heart pounded more furiously, her headache intensifying.

'It's Kat, Amy. She turned up while you were asleep and started threatening me, saying that she'd changed her mind and was going to take you back. I was trying to reason with her, I just wanted to talk, and then she came at me. It was all so fast, I couldn't see if she had a weapon or something. I just reacted. I don't know what to do, she's been out cold for a couple of minutes.'

Imogen's eyes focused for a second, taking in the shape of Kat crumpled on the ground in a floral dress. She wasn't moving. Without thinking, she rushed to Kat's side, tugging her shoulder so she rolled onto her back. She heard a slight groan and felt a rush of relief, followed quickly by confusion and that same anger that had been simmering away for days. Why would Kat change her mind? Why would she want her back now, after saying that she didn't? What was happening?

Imogen didn't want to go back to Kat and Dylan's, didn't want to leave Brad to return to a family that wasn't really hers, where she wasn't wanted. Where she didn't belong.

'We need to do something,' Brad said, his voice right in her ear. His breath was hot against her skin, and she recoiled from the noise. The sharp pain behind her eyeballs was getting worse. She needed to lie down, or be sick again, but she couldn't, not when Kat was lying helpless in the dust.

'I don't know how to help,' she whispered. 'I don't know what to do.'

Silence descended on them and time seemed suspended as she waited for Brad to take control, to fix everything.

'It's going to be OK, little one,' Brad said eventually, and she let her breath out with a hiss. 'You go get some water for her, I'll take her to the shed out the back.'

She stared at him. 'But—'

'You're sick,' he interrupted. 'You need the bed more than she does. And I need to stay close to you, to monitor you. There's no room in the house. Besides, she'll be out of here in no time.'

Imogen hesitated, trying to make sense of what was happening, unsure whether what Brad was saying made sense. It didn't feel right, but then again, nothing felt right. Her head was spinning, and she swayed.

'OK,' she said, knowing she was incapable of arguing, even if she wanted to.

She fumbled her way inside, feeling like her throat was being squeezed by an invisible, unrelenting fist, its grip tightening millimetre by millimetre. She stopped to force air into her lungs, to tell herself that it was going to be OK, although she wasn't sure if she believed it. Her mother, who wasn't really her mother, had come here and attacked her brother.

Her hatred towards Kat, fierce and unyielding and gathering intensity, lodged in Imogen's stomach. She was so angry with her, so hurt, that she thought she'd be fine never to see her again. Which would suit Kat just fine, since she'd rejected her, said she shouldn't bother coming home. But then Brad said she'd turned up wanting Imogen back. She let out a moan, her already muddled head swirling with too many emotions, too many questions.

She hated Kat. She knew that with certainty. And yet, seeing her like that, crumpled on the ground, weak and in pain – that wasn't what she wanted, either. What she wanted was for Kat to understand, for her to acknowledge the destruction she had caused, the damage she'd done to Brad, to admit that she'd been wrong. And she wanted Kat to let her stay there, with Brad, where she belonged. She wanted to be wanted, but she also wanted to be left alone, to not have to face her adoptive family, to start afresh without having to confront the pain and betrayal.

But Kat was there now, out the back, in the woodshed, and Imogen was left with no choice but to confront her past.

A giggle rose up in her chest, a bubble of mirth that came from nowhere, that made no sense. She stared at the pram against the wall, wondering what Brad wanted with it, after all. She shook her head. She needed to concentrate, she just didn't know how to.

Kat. She needed to work out what was happening with Kat. She drummed her fingers against her thigh. She wondered if maybe Kat did want her to go back to that house where the truth was hidden in the shadows and darkness ran rampant. She couldn't go back. She knew – the knowledge echoing deep in her marrow – that she wouldn't go willingly.

The room spun perilously as she tried to sort her jumbled thoughts into some kind of order.

Water. That was what she'd come inside for. She held a glass under the tap and filled it with the tepid, brown liquid that sputtered out. The house wasn't plumbed, so the water came from the tank outside, and that was slowly empty-ing thanks to the relentlessly dry summer. A few wrigglers struggled against the side of the glass. Imogen tried to fish them out with her finger, but her co-ordination was off, and her arm was too heavy, so she gave up and walked outside towards the shed, light filtering through the gap under the door.

When she got close, she stopped for a second and lis-tened. Low, urgent voices reached her from behind the door, but they were too muffled for her to make out the words clearly. She wanted to hear what they were saying. She needed to know, because she knew that it must be about her. Leaves cracked under her bare feet, and she winced as something sharp dug into the skin between her toes, but she pressed forward. Opening the door, the reality of what was happening flooded over her, cutting through her hazy mind, causing her stomach to lurch.

'Oh, hey, Amy, there you are,' Brad said casually, as though he was sitting in the living room, arm flung over the sofa like it was just a regular moment. 'Come in.'

As her eyes flickered over the details, her brain tried to calculate what she was seeing. But there was a fog stopping her from forming a clear thought, and it wouldn't lift, and all she could do was obey.

She stepped inside. The door swung behind her with a dull *whap*. She took a shaking breath and closed her eyes, hoping that when she opened them she would wake up, the scene before her just the memory of a sickening hallucination, a symptom of her illness. She squeezed them tight, then opened them once more. Everything remained the same.

Her brother was standing to her left, hovering over a wooden bench. Kat was tied to the table, her limbs immobile, her face twisted in fear. And glistening above her, clasped in Brad's hand, was a very long, very sharp blade.

Chapter 52

KAT

Pain floods my senses, dragging me back to consciousness with a sharpness that forces the breath from my lungs.

'Wakey, wakey,' a voice whispers, so close to my ear that wisps of my hair dance across my cheek. It makes my skin crawl, although I don't know who the voice belongs to, or where I am, or if I am OK.

Gingerly, I open one eye just a crack, closing it again quickly as my head screams in protest against the light. I'm lying flat on my back, directly underneath a bare yellow bulb.

Think, Kat, I tell myself. I strain to remember where I am, or who I'm with, and then, like a dam being opened in my memory, it all comes back to me with brutal force. I attempt to sit up, gasping with panic, but I can't move. I try again, harder this time, but there's something stopping me.

I open both of my eyes, bracing myself for the pain of the light, gritting my teeth and screaming into my closed mouth as my eyelids fly apart. Instinctively, they try to close, but I battle against my nature and force them wider.

Brad's face hovers over mine, but I keep my eyes averted. I'm not ready to face him yet. I have to understand what I'm up against first. I twist my head one way, and then the other, looking down along my body to get a read on the situation. It's bad. I'm lying on a wooden table in what looks like some kind of shed. I'm held down by rope, the thick cord wrapped around and around my torso, my legs, my arms. My wrists are tied separately, and I think my hands are roped together behind my back, but I can't feel them to know for sure. The pain in my skull is almost blinding, like someone's slamming a hammer against the back of my head over and over again.

I have to block out the pain. I have to focus.

'Where's Imogen?' I whisper to Brad, the possibility that she's not here, that she's being kept somewhere else, blossoming in my chest.

'Oh, you mean Amy? She's just getting you some water,' he says, oozing nonchalance.

My stomach sinks. She's here, which is good, but it also means that she's in danger.

'In the meantime, I reckon it's high time we had a little chit-chat, don't you?'

His accent is thick, his voice low and simmering with a rage he's not bothering to conceal.

I try a direct approach, hoping it'll get through to him quickly.

'I know you're angry at me for taking Imogen away from you—' I start, but he slams his fist on the bench with such force I'm certain he's broken a bone in his own hand. I'm too stunned to continue.

'It's Amy,' he hisses. 'Not Imogen. Her name is Amy Sanders, and she is my sister. She's not yours. She's mine.' His volume increases with every word, until he's almost shouting.

I close my eyes to try to think. I can't afford to make him angrier than he already is. I need him calm. Rational, if that's even possible.

'OK,' I say quietly, my voice steady. 'Amy. I'm sorry that we took her. We should have taken you, too. I regret that, now. I was wrong to break you apart.'

He looks surprised; those caramel eyes, so similar to Imogen's, so similar to their mother's, widen for a moment. But then he frowns again, and it's not his eyes I'm looking at any longer. It's the muscle pulsing at the side of his jaw, the vein in his neck that's bulging dangerously. It's his fists, clenched and ready for destruction.

I open my mouth to speak again, to ask him to give Imogen the choice, but he shushes me impatiently. He turns his back to me, this young man who could have been my child, if I'd been braver, more compassionate, if I'd been willing. Instead, he's a stranger. A man shaped and moulded by his loss, his pain, his rejection.

I need to reach him, to bridge this gap between us, to tell him that I understand who he is, that I know why he's so angry, that it's OK to feel like this, that maybe there's a way to keep him and Imogen in contact, for them to rebuild their relationship. I'm picturing weekends spent visiting Brad at his home, somewhere clean and in civilisation. He'd be under house arrest, of course, but we'd drop by with Imogen, and they could spend the day together, Dylan and me within easy reach, giving them the privacy they need, but still at a safe distance. I imagine laughter coming from the next room, the two siblings reunited.

But then he turns around again and I know without a doubt that my fantasy is just that: a dream, a figment of my imagination. Because Brad doesn't want me to come out of this alive; the knife glinting in his hand is proof of that.

The door swings open, and my pulse ramps up its pace. I can't see, but I know it must be Imogen.

'Oh, hey, Amy, there you are,' Brad says, and my heart leaps into my throat.

I can't see if she's hurt, if she's OK, if she hates me. I have no idea what to expect.

'Come in,' my daughter's brother says, and the door closes with a slam.

I hold my breath, hoping I can catch the sound of Imogen breathing, hoping to feel her with me. I turn my head again, and she steps into my vision. A sob leaps from my chest.

'Oh, Immy, my love, I'm so sorry—'

My head jolts backwards as Brad's fist connects with my jaw, and a fine spray of blood shoots into the air, raining back down on me in a red mist. The pain lands on me soon after, a searing heat that spreads from my chin all the way up my face to my forehead and around my temples. It's excruciating, so consuming that I can't focus on anything else. It takes all of my concentration to remain conscious, to not give in to the delicious darkness that's hovering at the edges of my vision. My daughter needs me. I need to be alert.

I blink my way out of the tunnel and force my eyes to focus on Imogen. She looks different. Older. She's wearing clothes that are too small for her. They're plain and functional, and nothing like the bright, stylish clothes she usually wears. Her hair is greasy and pulled back in a ponytail, and she's swaying ever so slightly as she stands, staring at Brad, the knife now dangling loosely by his side. I try to catch her attention, to get her to look at me, but her eyes are glazed over. She seems far away, like she's in a dream. She's not herself. With horror, I realise that he must have drugged her, and my stomach clenches with red-hot rage.

'Brad, listen,' I say as calmly as I can manage. 'This is

between us, OK? Let your sister go, and we can work this out, just you and me.'

He shakes his head.

'No way,' he growls. 'I've only just got my family back. There's no way I'm going to give that up now.'

'I'm not asking you to give anything up,' I plead, but he doesn't hear me.

'Liar,' he spits, reaching forward to turn Imogen towards him. 'Amy,' he says, his free hand on her shoulder.

She looks up at him and her expression makes me ache. She is completely captivated by her brother, that much is clear. What has he said to her? What lies has he told about where she comes from, about who her biological family is, about who I am? I can't see his face, but whatever she sees makes her smile. She sways again slightly. I'm desperate just to look into her eyes, for her to look into mine so she can see that all I want is for her to be safe and out of harm's way.

She's holding a glass, her hand trembling. I take a shaking breath. I need to get her attention.

'Water,' I whisper. 'Please. Can I have some water?'

Brad spins around. I ignore him and keep my eyes focused on Imogen. Slowly, slowly, her gaze slides from her brother, along the bench, landing on my arm, then my shoulder, then my chin, and finally, after what feels like forever, my baby girl is looking into my eyes.

'Imogen,' I breathe, my muscles relaxing with the relief of having made this connection with her at last. I know what's behind those eyes. And she knows what's behind mine. It's enough. It has to be.

I don't see Brad's fist coming for me again. I just hear his furious voice.

'Her name,' he roars, 'is Amy.'

Everything goes black again.

270

Chapter 53

KAT

When I wake, seconds or minutes or hours later, the pain in my head reaching a crescendo, Imogen and Brad are huddled in the corner of the shed, whispering furiously. I can't hear what they're saying.

I cough, and they both turn to face me. Imogen has a strange look on her face. I think it's fear. But she can't possibly be scared of me ... can she? I need to know what he's been telling her.

'Your real mother,' I say quietly, steadily, keeping my eyes focused on her, 'is in prison.'

'I know that,' she says defiantly, her lower jaw jutting out. I've seen this look a thousand times before. I know my daughter, even if she thinks I don't. I know how to get through to her. Her life might depend on it. Mine definitely does.

'She did horrible things to her children,' I say. 'To you, and to your brothers and sisters.'

Brad rushes forward with a growl, but Imogen puts her hand out to stop him, and my heart leaps with hope. Unexpectedly, he freezes. So maybe he doesn't hold all of the power, after all. That's promising.

'The house you were born in,' I continue, 'it was nicknamed Satan's Ranch. There were more, more children, who didn't survive. The things she did to you, to all of you, the things they both did...' I trail off, swallowing hard, desperate to keep my emotions in check, to serve my daughter the facts, bare and unadorned, so she knows what it is she came from. What it is we rescued her from. But saying the words, voicing the horror that we've so deliberately tried to keep her from, it makes my stomach turn.

'Brad?' Imogen turns to face him, a look of pure, innocent inquisitiveness in her eyes. My heart cracks like the scorched ground outside, a fissure so deep I'm certain it'll never be repaired. Once she knows the truth, she'll never be the same. How could she be?

'She's lying,' Brad says with a laugh. His body language is casual, as though I'm nothing more than a nuisance. He's smart. He knows exactly how to manipulate her. 'She doesn't want to lose, Amy. She thinks this is some kind of battle, me versus her, and she'll say whatever she needs to in order to win. You know she's a liar, Amy. Have I ever lied to you?'

'No,' she whispers.

My stomach plummets.

'Exactly. You can trust me. I didn't lie to you, I told you that Mum and Dad are in prison, but that's not because of some kind of satanic ranch. It's because they were misunderstood.'

'Misunderstood?' I explode. 'Is that really what you think, Brad? They chained you to your beds and starved and tortured you, for God's sake. Immy, they didn't love you. Not really. They don't know what love means.'

Tears wobble on the rims of Imogen's bloodshot eyes. She's so pale. So thin. She's only been gone for a week, and this is what he's done to her. She turns once again to face her brother.

'Amy,' Brad says slowly, gently, like he's talking to a toddler. 'Our parents love us. They love you. I know they do. Because they told me so. And I was saving this for a time like now, when I knew you needed to hear it. Last time I went to visit Mum, she gave me this. I think you need to read what she had to say. To you.'

He pulls a piece of paper from the back pocket of his jeans. It's folded into a small square, and it's soft and crinkled, as though it's been opened and read and reread a hundred times. He holds it out to Imogen, her questioning eyes still locked on him. I watch, helpless, as she reaches out a trembling hand to take it. She's eating up everything he's saying. She *wants* to believe him, wants me to be wrong, to be the bad guy. I don't know how to stop this, how to make her change her mind.

She unfolds the paper, and holds it up with two hands, squinting through the fug of whatever substance it is he's given her to read it.

'Out loud,' Brad says to Imogen. 'Read it out loud so your liar of a fake mother knows that she's wrong about our mum.'

Imogen glances briefly at me. In the split second when our eyes meet, I try to convey everything I'm feeling for her without saying a word. But she looks away again just as quickly and focuses on the letter.

'Dear Brad,' she reads quietly, 'I want you to know how much I love you. You are my son, and I'm so proud of you for carrying on the Sanders name. We might not be perfect, but we are family. And family always sticks together. For years, we've been shown as the bad guys, as inhuman, your dad and I. And I know we weren't the perfect parents, but we love you, we always have. That much I can promise. I hope

273

you do succeed in finding your sister. If you do, tell her I love her so much. She'll always be my baby girl.'

Here, Imogen's voice, slurred and thick from whatever's pulsing through her bloodstream, begins to shake. My heart sinks lower and lower. I want to scream, to make her understand that she's *my* baby girl. That what her crazed shadow of a mother offered her was nothing like love, was a warped and distorted version of it from someone so broken she can't understand what love really means. But if I speak, I know I'll be silenced. And I'm not sure how many more times I can endure being beaten before I pass out for too long to save my daughter. As it is, I'm queasy and feeble. I need to find another way to get through to her, and quickly.

'Ask her if she still has the birthmark right above her belly button,' Imogen reads, then stops, covering her mouth with her free hand.

I know that birthmark is there. I've seen it a thousand times, a hundred thousand times, when I've changed her, cleaned her, bathed her. But she doesn't want to hear about all the nappy changes and sleepless nights and child therapy sessions and late-night sheet changes and nightmares and the patience I needed to get through the tantrums she didn't understand, couldn't understand, because she didn't remember, not really. She just wants to hear from the woman whose genes she inherited.

'Tell her,' Imogen whispers, her eyes wide, 'that I have a matching one. Tell her we have that in common. Tell her we're still connected, even if we can't be together.'

Imogen's crying now. So am I. I've lost this battle. I've lost my daughter. As I fall apart on a wooden bench in a hot shed in the middle of nowhere, Brad folds Imogen into his arms and whispers something into her ear. She nods, sobbing, her shoulders heaving, and he strokes her back and keeps whispering, his voice too quiet for me to hear, until Imogen's breathing slows and her sobs subside.

Brad holds her out at arm's length, looking right into her glassy eyes.

'You see?' he urges her. 'You're connected, you and Mum. And so are you and I. We have a bond that can't be broken. Not by anyone, no matter how well you think you know them, or how well they think they know you.'

She nods, sniffing, and runs her forearm under her nose.

'Good,' Brad says. 'So now that you know the truth, we need to do something about her.'

He turns to look at me, his eyes shining with glee.

My blood turns to ice in my veins.

Chapter 54

IMOGEN

Brad held the knife out towards her. The blade winked in the light that was coming from a single bulb, suspended from a cord above Kat.

She looked at him, confused.

She couldn't think clearly. She wanted to soak up every word of the letter she'd just read, but she couldn't do that when her mind was swirling and Kat was tied to a bench and there was a knife in Brad's hand.

Why was Brad holding a knife? Why had Kat been tied up like a prisoner?

She knew that she should be focusing, that she should be getting answers to those questions, but her thoughts kept circling back to the fact that she had a letter, that her mum had reached out to her, that they shared a connection. Her insides glowed with that knowledge, with the thrill of reading words meant solely for her, coming from the woman she had been desperate to know since she first learned the truth about Kat and Dylan.

She could have sworn the birthmark on her stomach was pulsing, reminding her of its presence, of her link to her mother. This snippet of information, this glimpse into who her mum was, it was too precious to have out in the open, too valuable a treasure to waste on an audience. She wanted to go back to bed and turn it over, inspect it from every direction, watch it sparkle in the light, get to know every millimetre of its surfaces.

But Brad wanted her here. With him. He wanted her to do something. Only she didn't understand what that was.

She stared at him, not moving, until he thrust the knife towards her. She jumped backwards.

'Amy,' he said gently, 'I need you to take the knife. Will you take it, please?'

She reached forward and curled her fingers around the handle carefully. It was made of wood; smooth, with the natural grain curving and whirling around it. It was beautiful. Mesmerising. She stared at it for a few seconds before turning her attention back to her brother.

'What's this for?'

He jerked his head towards Kat, who was tied to the wooden bench in the middle of the shed, her face covered in blood. She was badly injured, and as the teenager absorbed the state of the woman who had betrayed her, she felt a pull somewhere deep inside her, a tug of something familiar, something she thought she'd shed along with the rest of her unwanted identity.

'You want me to cut the ropes?' she asked, more alert now.

'We have to get rid of her,' Brad said, matter-of-factly.

'Well, I doubt she can drive herself home. We'll have to call someone to pick her up, probably—'

'I don't mean that we're going to let her go,' Brad said pointedly, and she felt a sudden jolt of clarity.

She dropped the knife with a clatter.

'What? No. No way, Brad. What? That's crazy!'

Kat made a hissing sound that could have been a sigh of relief. Brad whirled around, picking the knife up from the concrete floor and holding it against Kat's throat. Her eyes widened in fear. Imogen's chest tightened. She couldn't move. She didn't know if she wanted to.

'One word – a single syllable – and I promise you, you'll regret it,' Brad growled. Kat whimpered in response, a pathetic, childlike sound that grated on Imogen, made her feel even more agitated. She needed to lie down. She needed sleep. Her head was thumping with a ferocity she didn't know was possible. It was like something was trying to break out from the inside using an ice pick. Her stomach was in knots, whatever was left in there threatening to come up every few minutes, and the walls were spinning alarmingly fast.

'Amy, listen,' Brad said, circling both of her wrists gently with his free hand. 'Look at me.'

She did as she was told, meeting his caramel eyes with her own. She studied his irises, hoping to understand him, to get a better read on what he meant, on what he was trying to say, on what he was going to do next. But she couldn't focus. Her eyelids felt heavy.

'Kat wants to break us up,' he said, and she knew that he was right. Why else would she be there? Why else would she have attacked him, or made up all of those awful things about their mum? Kat was desperate – she wasn't making sense, with her claims about Satan and chains and starvation. If their parents really were so terrible, Brad wouldn't be standing up for them. He wouldn't be trying to reconnect with them. 'If we let her go, she'll find a way to get me out of the picture for good. She'll tell the police that I'm dangerous, that I'm exactly what they think our parents are. I'll never get to see you again. Do you want that, Amy? Is that what you want?'

'No,' she shouted. 'Of course I don't want that, but, Brad . . . we don't have to hurt her. No one has to get hurt.'

She hated Kat. She'd be satisfied with never having to see her again, never having to speak to her. But she didn't want her injured, or worse. She just wanted to start her new life with Brad, find their sister, meet their parents.

'Please,' she whispered.

'She's already hurt,' he said, looking over at the limp, blood-soaked body on the bench. 'Who's to say she'd be OK even if we let her go?'

She shook her head. 'No,' she said firmly, her jaw set. 'No, I can't. I won't hurt her. We don't need to, we can just run away. We don't need to stay here. Let's just go, then we can be together and no one gets hurt. Why can't we go now?'

It took a couple of seconds to register the look in his eyes, but then she realised. It was pity. He felt sorry for her.

'Oh, little one,' he said, condescension dripping from his voice. 'Always thinking the best of people. If we leave her, we might get away. You're right about that. But don't you want to meet Mum?'

She nodded uncertainly. She was being backed into a corner, she could feel it. But she didn't understand enough about what was happening, or what happened next, to know how to fight it. And she did, she really did, want to meet her mother; the woman with a birthmark that matched her own.

'You think Kat will let us go visit her, huh? The authorities will have all kinds of alerts on us. The moment we even attempt to see Mum, the cops will be all over us and we'll be split up again, and I'll spend the rest of my life behind bars for what? For letting her go? No way.'

Imogen tried to think through what Brad was saying, to separate facts from fear. She desperately wanted to meet her mum, but she was also certain that there had to be a way for that to happen without Kat being harmed any more.

'But if we ... if she's hurt ... they'll be looking for us, anyway.'

He shook his head violently.

'They didn't find you,' he said triumphantly. 'Why would they find her?'

Something sparked at the back of her mind, but she couldn't grasp what it meant. She squeezed her eyes closed and tried to find clarity. She didn't want to listen to what he was saying, but she couldn't deny the truth of it, either. If they ran, Kat wouldn't stop looking. And now she'd heard them talking about visiting their mum in prison, of course she would try to find them that way. Of course she'd put a stop to it.

She felt like she was being torn in two. The pain was unbearable. She didn't want to have to choose between her family and murder. She couldn't make that kind of decision.

'I can't,' she said.

'You have to,' Brad said.

'Why?' she asked. 'Why do I have to decide? That's not fair.'

'I'm disappointed in you, Amy,' he said, and the crack in her heart split even wider. 'I moved across the country for you. I found you, I told you the truth when no one else would. I nursed you back to life. I've done everything for you, and now you're saying that *this* isn't fair? What would you know about unfair? You got chosen, you got a family. I was left with nothing.'

'I'm sorry,' she whispered, shame building inside her. He was right. She'd had safety, and stability. And even though it had been a lie, at least she hadn't had to live with knowing, for all of these years, what had been taken from her. She owed him her life. She owed him her loyalty. But was this the price? Was this the only way? Her mouth was dry. She was sweaty and sick, bile bubbling bitterly at the back of her throat.

The siblings stared at each other.

'So what's it to be, Amy?' Brad asked, holding the knife out towards her. 'Or should I just call you Imogen?'

Overwhelmed with guilt and confusion and fear, she took the knife from him and held it in her shaking hand, grief radiating from her in waves.

She wasn't Imogen. She wanted to be Amy, to belong in the Sanders family, to prove that she belonged, that she was worthy of all that her brother had sacrificed for her. She wanted him to see, wanted him to understand, that she *was* loyal to her family. That she *did* care what happened to him, even if no one else ever had.

Brad smiled, that dazzling smile that made her feel special, that made her feel like she belonged. And then he nodded. Just once. A glint in his eye. A promise that they were in it together.

She gripped the knife tightly in her fist and took a shaky step towards the bench.

Chapter 55

KAT

'I trust you,' I blurt out as my daughter steps towards me, the knife held in her right hand.

Brad steps between us, his fist raised, his face a picture of unbridled rage. I wince, preparing for another blow, but Imogen touches him on the shoulder and he turns, surprised by the contact, to look at her. She shakes her head, just slightly, and his whole demeanour changes. His arm drops, and his body relaxes. He steps aside again, allowing his sister to take charge, handing the control over to her completely.

She stops, pauses, then takes another uncertain step in my direction.

'I trust you,' I say again, this time with more conviction. 'I always have trusted you. I was just scared. I was so scared that you'd hate me, that you'd never forgive me. And I was so wrong not to tell you, my love. I shouldn't have kept something this big a secret from you. I just wanted to protect you, from the truth, from being hurt. I wanted to keep you out of harm's way. And I wanted you to be happy.'

'You didn't want me to be happy,' she sobs. 'You just wanted to *own* me. You just wanted me all to yourself. You knew if you told me the truth I'd want to know my family. My *real* family. You were scared, weren't you? You were

282

scared that I'd choose them over you. Well, I guess you know for sure, don't you?'

'Imogen—'

'My name,' she whispers, tears streaming down her cheeks, 'is Amy.'

The conviction in her voice – the certainty that she belongs to the man beside her – turns my stomach. She's right, though. The girl in front of me isn't my Imogen. This girl is confused, she's hurting, and she's lashing out.

'It was,' I say. 'But you're Imogen now. Don't you remember what it's like to be Imogen? You're an amazing volleyball player. You're going to be on the national team. Nationals! Coach Cresswell has been talking about the Olympics! That's who you are. You're a friend, Imogen. Paige and Maddie and Esther, they miss you so much, and they're so worried about you. They love you. They love Imogen. And Jemima? Oh my goodness, my love, she misses her big sister so much.'

Something flickers behind my daughter's eyes at the mention of her little sister. I cling to it.

'She's been absolutely lost without you,' I tell her. 'She cries herself to sleep at night. She just wants to see you again, to tell you about school, to share an iced chocolate with you before bed.'

Imogen blinks, shakes her head, looks up to Brad and back down to me.

'You're a liar,' she spits, her tongue darting out to the corner of her mouth and back in again. She's scared, but she's trying to act tough. For Brad. 'Everything that comes out of your mouth is a lie.'

'I'm not lying,' I insist, but she raises the knife up, her arm no longer shaking, and my insides liquefy. I didn't think she'd do it, even while Brad was manipulating her, telling her what she wanted to hear, convincing her. But now . . . now, I'm not so certain.

'You've lied to me my entire life,' she cries, her eyes flashing with anger. 'My whole life has been fake. And now you want me to believe you? Now? When you're just trying to save your own skin? Why should I? Why should I believe a word that's coming out of your hypocritical, lying mouth?'

I close my eyes for just a moment in an attempt to find clarity, to come up with a way to get through to her, but I don't know how. She's furious, and I can't blame her. She's confused. She's being pulled in two different directions and being made to choose between her two worlds. One that she knows, that's familiar, but that she resents. The other that she doesn't know, doesn't understand the dangers of, but is desperate to be a part of.

'I went to see your mum,' I say, realising that she'll want to hear this.

The change in her eyes is instant. She's hungry for information, greedy to know what her biological mother is like, a woman who shares a birthmark and eye colour with her daughter, and little else.

'She's lying,' Brad growls from over her shoulder.

She flaps her hand, dismissing him.

'Are you lying?' she asks me.

'No,' I breathe. 'I drove to Victoria. She's in a maximum-security women's prison there. I wanted to know if she knew where you were.'

Imogen doesn't react. She's swaying slightly, one arm hovering above me, the knife clutched in her fist, the other by her side.

'She has the same eyes as you,' I continue, spotting a chance to talk, at least. To stall. Although what I'm stalling for, I don't know. Dylan might still be with the police, talking about tomorrow's press conference. And even if he's not, even if he's home, he doesn't know where I am. He might try to look for me, but if we couldn't find our daughter, how would he find me?

Imogen's eyebrows flicker into the smallest of frowns. She doesn't trust me. She doesn't know if I'm telling the truth or not, not when she believes her whole life has been a fabrication.

'And the same laugh,' I add. 'You look alike, but you also share some features with your father, like your chin.'

I don't know much about Tim – he never made as many headlines as Sally, and there are fewer photos of him online – but as far as I know, their chins are where the similarities end. Thank goodness.

'What did she say?' Imogen asks, the need in her voice palpable. 'About me?'

'Oh honey,' I whisper, my fragile heart shattering on my daughter's behalf, 'I'm sorry, but she didn't really talk about you.'

'She's making this all up,' Brad says, a warning in his voice. 'Mum loves you, Amy. Don't believe her lies, she's just trying to turn you against us.'

'I'm not,' I gasp. 'I promise I'm not lying. Look, honey, I was wrong to keep the truth from you. You're right – I was scared about what that would do to you, what it would do to us – our family. I should have trusted you with the truth, let you make your own mind up. But we love you, and we saved you from what would have been a horrific life . . . and not a very long one, given what happened in that house.'

I stop, trying to decide whether to reveal the appalling details of what took place inside Satan's Ranch, or whether, even now, she should be spared the horror of knowing. I take a deep breath, looking into those beautiful amber eyes that are as familiar as they are mysterious, that hide a universe of feelings and thoughts, that view me as the enemy. And I'm certain that, in spite of what she now knows, even as she's contemplating killing me, she believes in the goodness of others. That she believes the world is fundamentally right, a place where parents love their children and where justice always prevails. And I know that finding out what her first few months on this earth looked like would crush her.

'Your parents didn't love you,' I say eventually. 'They don't understand love, they're not capable of it. I can show you the articles, but I don't think you want to know. The things they did . . . I swear that all we ever wanted was the best for you, and for your safety. The decisions we made, right or wrong, they were to protect you. You're our daughter, you always will be. You're Sally and Tim's daughter, too, but that doesn't change the fact that you're our baby and we love you no matter what. Nothing can change that. Do you hear me? Nothing.'

Tears are running down the sides of my face, mingling with blood, pooling under my neck. Imogen's eyes are welling up, too, but she tries to brush her tears away, tries to hide the fact that I'm getting through to her.

'If you love me so much, why didn't you look for me? Why did you tell me not to come home?'

My body is battered and raw, and yet this blow hurts more than any of the others. Not look for her? How can she think that? My eyes flit from Imogen to Brad, whose curled lip and disdainful sneer answer my questions. So that's how he turned her against me so quickly, I realise, and my heart breaks for what that must have felt like to Imogen.

'Oh, my baby,' I whisper. 'We *have* been looking, I promise. We haven't stopped looking. We'd travel to the ends of the earth to find you.'

'Amy,' Brad growls from the corner. 'Amy, I've told you this. You can't trust her. Trust *me*.'

'Darling,' I say now, as calmly as I can. 'You don't have to do this. You don't have to make any decisions right now, OK? Just put the knife down, and we can talk, and work out what to do next. You don't have to choose between me and him. I'm not going to make you. I can take you to visit your mum. I can help you find out the truth about your family. I know that's what you want. But if you hurt me, my love, then we can't help you. Then you'll be in trouble, and there will be no taking it back. Do you understand?'

'Are you going to shut this bitch up?' Brad yells, his patience gone, his anger in full force. 'Or are you going to choose her? Because, Amy, I'm telling you, you pick her over me and that's it – we're over. If I can't trust you, then we're not really family.'

Imogen's face turns pale, and her hand moves, ever so slightly, back towards her body. Then she freezes again, immobilised by indecision, by the total unravelling of her world as she knows it. She closes her eyes, just for a second, but I know her well enough to understand what's happening. She's thinking, she's weighing up everything I've said, everything Brad's said, everything she knows and everything she doesn't.

I am desperate – it's a longing that seeps into my bones – to take this burden from her, to have it crush me instead. But I can't. It's hers. I have to let her make her own decision. I have no choice. I have to trust her.

'I love you, Imogen,' I whisper.

And then I close my eyes.

Chapter 56

IMOGEN

'I love you, Imogen.'

The woman on the bench closed her eyes in surrender, and the teenager's heart felt like it was being squeezed, drained of everything good and true. The pain was physical, and it took everything in her not to cry out, to fold over, clutching her chest and screaming with the agony of it.

She wanted someone to tell her what to do, to tell her the right choice and to help her untangle the strands of truth from the mess of lies she found herself staring at. Had Kat been looking for her? She sounded so sincere, but then again, she was an expert at deception. And even if she had been looking, did that really change anything? Did it make up for the awful things she'd done?

Imogen wanted to know why, when she knew that she belonged with Brad, and that he deserved her unquestioning loyalty, she couldn't bear the idea of hurting Kat. She wanted to be Amy, to embody who she was born as. She just didn't want anyone to get hurt. She didn't want Kat to die. She didn't want to be a murderer.

She wanted to run out of the shed screaming, Brad beside her, and keep running until they couldn't breathe and the scene before her was just a distant memory. But she knew that if she did that, she'd have let her brother down. Would he still want to see her, if she betrayed him like that? She couldn't bear to think about how it would feel to be rejected by him, too.

What he was asking her to do was wrong. She knew that. And she knew that she didn't want to do it. Of course she didn't. She wasn't a monster.

Was she?

If what Kat had told her was true – and she didn't know if it was, but she couldn't really tell what was fabrication, what was manipulation, and what was real – then the grotesque and the monstrous … it ran in her blood. It was imprinted in her DNA, a part of every cell in her body.

Imogen wouldn't do what Brad was asking. Not in a million years. But Amy? Well, she didn't really know Amy; not yet. She wanted to get to know her, wanted the chance to be her, to try her on and wear her in. She wondered what she would do if she'd been Amy for her whole life instead of pretending to be Imogen for so long. Would she do what Brad had asked of her without hesitation? Or would Amy still know that what he was asking was too terrible to bear?

She tried to picture every possible outcome. If she dropped the knife, refused to do what Brad wanted, would he let Kat go? Even if she was brave enough to refuse the one thing he'd ever asked of her, even if she made that choice, would the end result be any different? Would Kat be allowed to go free?

And then another thought forced its way to the forefront of her mind. Would *she* be allowed to go free if Brad didn't believe she was loyal, if she betrayed him, just like Kat had? He had changed in Kat's presence, become angry and vengeful, nothing like the gentle, nurturing brother who had pulled her back from oblivion. She didn't recognise this

289

version of him, didn't know how he'd react, what he was thinking. A shudder reverberated up her spine.

There was no right answer, no way that things could end without her being heartbroken, without Kat being in danger. And that was the best-case scenario.

Perhaps it was better if she just did it, did what Brad wanted, drove the knife into Kat's chest. The thought horrified her, but maybe she could do it in a way that would hurt – of course it would hurt – but not kill. If Brad saw that she was willing, that she was worthy of all the sacrifices he'd made, maybe Kat would be OK and she and Brad could still be together.

Yes, she decided, her birthmark pulsing again, a reminder of who she was. That could work. It would prove to him that she really was on his side, that she loved him just as much as he loved her. But Kat wouldn't die. No one would die. She wouldn't become a killer.

She racked her brain, wishing she'd paid more attention in biology to know exactly where the knife could go without causing life-threatening damage.

She needed to act before Brad got impatient and decided her future for her. Her hand trembled. She knew this was the only way to make sure that everyone got out alive, that she could be with her family, but she still wasn't confident that she could do it. Even if she knew exactly where the knife needed to go; even if it might save Kat. And her.

She held the blade over Kat's heaving chest and tried to picture everything that made her angry about the bleeding, terrified woman beneath her. If she was going to hurt her like this, risk her life, even, she needed strength she didn't have. And short of courage, she figured that anger would probably do the same thing.

She made herself remember the moment when she

opened that email and discovered that her life had been a lie. She thought back to the fight they'd had about Emerald, when Kat completely refused to trust her. A flicker of understanding ignited somewhere deep inside her. She tried to tamp it down, but it came rushing at her all at once. Kat was scared that she would turn out like her parents, she realised. All this time, Kat had been worried that nurturing wasn't enough; that her adopted daughter's nature was rotten.

She tried to conjure rage at the idea of Kat believing that she wasn't fundamentally good. But, instead, she felt resignation. Here she was, a knife held over Kat's beaten body. Perhaps she was right not to trust her.

She shook her head. She needed the burn of anger. She needed something to fuel her into action, not acceptance of her adoptive mother's behaviour.

'Think of the lies she told you, Amy,' Brad whispered beside her, as though he could read her thoughts. She could feel his excitement from where she stood; it was like electricity crackling off of him. They were connected, feeding off one another's energy, her brother seeming to know what she was going to do before she even moved. A thrill rippled along her nerves, all the way to her toes, the tips of her fingers. She took a breath. He was right. Kat's lies. That was what she needed to remember, that's how she would get through this.

Memories whirred through her mind, and she tried to grab hold of one, of anything that would ignite her anger, but it was like trying to snatch a dandelion seed in the wind. Her thoughts were jumbled, the information she had been given all swirling around her, a tempest of secrets and lies and truth.

'Amy is damaged,' Brad hissed beside her. 'Remember?

That's what she said in that message she sent me, before she came here to ruin your life again.'

Fury burst behind her eyes, red-hot and blinding. Damaged. That *was* what she had said. Her heart pounded. She focused on Kat's chest, moving up and down, up and down, faster and faster. Her eyes were squeezed closed, her hands balled into tight fists.

She mouthed the word *sorry*, knowing Kat would never see it, never know the truth, but needing to say it anyway, and then she closed her eyes and lifted the knife higher and higher.

And as it hovered there, another thought popped into her mind, unwelcome now, when she had come to a decision already, when she needed to take action.

'Amy is damaged,' Brad had said. That was the message Kat sent to him.

Except she knew. She knew without any flicker of hesitation. To Kat, she was Imogen. Kat would never call her Amy.

Chapter 57

KAT

My body is clenched, ready – as ready as I possibly can be – for the pain of a blade slicing through my skin, into my muscle, piercing my vital organs, ending me. My eyes are squeezed tightly closed, but I can see it, visualise the flash of the knife and the searing agony that will follow. And it's OK; I understand. Imogen doesn't have a choice.

If she disobeys her brother, there's no way of knowing what he'll do. This is the best chance she has of getting out of here alive, whether she grasps the truth of that or not. But I understand. I want to tell her that I get it, that it's OK, but I don't think I can move, or speak, and I don't want her to hesitate. She needs to do this; she needs to do what it takes to survive.

I lift one eyelid a sliver, just enough to see my beautiful daughter one last time. Her eyes are tightly closed, the knife held above me with both of her hands. She mouths something. I think it might be *sorry*. My stomach wrenches, but I barely notice the dull ache that remains after the spasm is over. Nor do I notice the pounding in my head, or the red-hot burning sensation that's shooting up my arm.

The pain doesn't matter any more. Nothing does, because this is how it ends. My life, punched out of me in a dark shed in the hills, by the hand of my eldest daughter, while my youngest sleeps, unaware, in the car outside.

I wish I could go back, could explain to Imogen that she has been loved – so completely – since we first laid eyes on her. That we chose her, that we loved her fully and fiercely, and that we'd always protect her from anyone who tried to hurt her.

Except that promise would be a lie. Look at how badly I failed, look at how I neglected to protect her when it mattered the most.

I want to groan, to scream with the shame and self-loathing of it all, of the utter failure I am, at the nightmare I've created for the people I love most in the world. All along, all I needed to do was believe that she isn't her parents. And rest in the knowledge that we've done a good enough job of raising her, of nurturing her, of loving her, that she'd make the right choice if faced with something unthinkable. Something like this.

But I was paranoid, I was scared, and this is all my fault. All I can do is hope that she'll be OK, that she'll survive, and that one day she'll look back and understand how much I love her, how I adore her regardless of her choices, or her background.

I think of Dylan. Of Jemima. I know they'll be OK together. He's an incredible father, and she's strong and brave. They'll find a way through this.

I breathe out slowly, deeply. I'm ready.

Seconds pass, and I will Imogen to just do it, to get it over with. More seconds tick by, and then out of nowhere there's a shriek, high-pitched and piercing. My eyes fly open and land on Brad, who's looking directly at me, his face a picture of disbelief. His eyes are bulging, that golden colour almost hidden by his dilated pupils. My mind is frantic. What is happening? Why am I still conscious? Where is Imogen?

My eyes flit back and forth until they find her. She's standing back from the table, both hands clamped over her mouth, staring at her brother. The three of us are frozen in this strange tableau for what feels like eternity, me alive, but not comprehending anything. It dawns on me, the facts clicking into place, that Imogen is no longer holding the knife. Brad still hasn't moved; he's been halted by something that, judging by his expression, he can barely believe.

And then, as though a fast-forward button has been pressed, Brad sways once, to the left, then to the right, except it's not a sway, it's a fall, and he's out of my view, replaced by a face so familiar and yet so out of place that it takes a moment for me to realise, for me to understand that it's definitely her, that it's not a hallucination.

My daughter is in front of me, where Brad was standing just a second ago.

But it's not Imogen.

It's Jemima.

Chapter 58

KAT

'Jemima!' I choke, still not able to grasp what's going on.

My twelve-year-old daughter's face is completely blank. She's standing still, one arm lifted out in front of her, the other pressed rigidly against her side.

Before I can arrange all of these new pieces of information into place, Imogen screams, long and loud and swelling with such emotion that it slices through my heart. She throws herself down to the ground, to where her brother just disappeared.

I'm immobilised. Even if I wasn't tied down, I don't think I'd be able to move. I'm frozen, staring into the eyes of my youngest daughter, trying desperately to understand what's happened and what to do next.

'Jemima, what are you doing? You shouldn't be here!'

She doesn't move. My thoughts are spinning, a whirlwind that's gathering pace, gaining momentum, drowning out logic. I need to get out of here.

'Help me,' I gasp, and Jemima blinks.

Something flickers in her eyes and then she moves, stepping around an object I can't see but which must be her sister hunched over Brad. Calmly, methodically, she begins untying the ropes that are strapping me down.

'Jemima,' I pant. 'How did ... what ...?'

My sentences stutter and start, but there are too many questions, too many layers, to articulate them all.

'It's OK, Mum, you're going to be OK.'

I want to wail at my little girl's assurances, to grip her and never let go, to let myself melt into her arms, but I can't. I need to get my children away from here, to safety, away from Brad. He's dangerous. He wants to tear us apart.

But why is he on the ground?

I try to sit up, but my head is screaming and my arms won't work. Jemima lifts the glass that Imogen brought in to my lips and I tilt my head and gulp down the warm, metallic water, not caring that it's brown or full of wriggling mosquito larvae. The liquid hits my stomach with such force that I almost bring it up immediately, but I wait a second, swallow again, and steel myself to get up.

Slowly, gingerly, I wriggle my fingers, waiting for the blood to pump back into them. When it does, the pain is almost unbearable. Ignoring it, I haul myself into a sitting position, the room spinning as the blood rushes from my head. I close my eyes for a second, and when I open them, the sight that greets me makes my stomach curdle.

Blood is everywhere. The floor is slick with it, a red pool that's spreading, leaking, crawling like a macabre glacier across the concrete. Brad's body is limp and still, the knife lying next to him, the blade dark red and dripping. Imogen is huddled by his side, heaving with sobs so deep and so consuming that they wrack her entire body. I watch her convulse again and push myself off the bench, crying out in pain as my feet hit the ground and the jolt reverberates in my tender head. My legs give way and I collapse onto my knees.

Kneeling in the blood, still warm, now seeping up the hem of my dress, I wrap my arms around Imogen and hold her with as much strength as I can muster. Her cries grow louder and I press my face between her shoulder blades, wishing I could absorb her pain, wondering if she will ever recover.

'Mum,' Jemima is shaking me by the shoulder. 'Mum, can we go? Please?'

I look up at her, her brown eyes wide and pleading. Countless questions clamour for priority in my mind. What happened? How did Jemima get in here? What has she done?

Jemima pulls at my dress. It doesn't matter what happened. We're safe now.

'Immy,' I say, gently tugging her towards me. 'Immy, we have to go.'

'NO!'

Her scream is primal. This is not my Imogen here, covering her brother's body with her own, gasping for breath between sobs. It's Amy.

The girl who, just moments before, was holding a knife above my body, eyes closed, poised to kill.

Chapter 59

IMOGEN

She didn't see Jemima coming in. She didn't hear her. None of them did.

If she'd known her younger sister was outside, if she'd known there was a possibility that Jemima could become involved, could find herself in the room with them all, things might have been different. Maybe she would have convinced Brad to run, to get away and leave Kat in peace and worry about the consequences later. Maybe.

She hadn't flinched. Jemima, that is. Imogen had been standing, the knife held over her head with both hands, trembling, trying to find the strength she needed to do the only thing she could think of to get everyone out of that shed alive, trying to separate facts from lies.

There hadn't been a sound; there had been nothing to warn her. Out of nowhere, a sharp burst of pain had exploded in her stomach. The air had left her lungs with a gentle *ooof*, and she must have leaned over to grab the part of her abdomen that sang with pain. She didn't even notice the knife being wrenched from her hand, was still trying to work out what had happened, was trying to protect the part of her that was wounded. She was disoriented.

So she didn't see the knife – the same knife she'd been holding just seconds before – going into her brother's body.

She wasn't looking, the moment when Brad felt the blade slicing through his flesh. She felt his hand brushing her arm, looked up at him, her movements slow and dreamlike, and saw his wide eyes, spotted the fear and surprise written across his face. In that moment, he was just a little boy, lost and alone and confused.

She knew, with terrifying certainty, what had happened. She sensed Jemima's presence before she saw her. She might have screamed, then, although she couldn't be sure if it was her or Kat or even Brad. It wasn't Jemima. As Brad swayed and collapsed, Jemima just stood, stock-still, watching as the scene unfolded before her.

When he dropped to the ground, Imogen threw herself on top of him. He was lying on his side on the hot concrete, blood seeping from the wound in his back, where the knife that Jemima had snatched from her hand – the knife intended for Kat – had punctured his skin.

She didn't know how long they had been lying there. She could feel his breath, each one shallower and shorter than the last, against her cheek, and she knew that he was dying. Sobs burst from her, a flood of fury and loss and abandonment. Because that was what he was doing: he was leaving.

'Don't go,' she whispered into his ear between cries. 'Please don't leave me. Not when I've just found you.'

'Amy,' he croaked, his face so pale she was sure he was fading into nothing, as though he could eventually disappear altogether. 'I love you.'

'I love you too,' she wept, and she knew it was true. She was connected with him, tied by strands she couldn't see or explain or understand. All she knew was that they shared the same blood, the same DNA, and that made them part of one another.

But he was leaving her, and she would never have the

chance to find out what it was like to have a family. Not really.

His eyes fluttered, the movement so fragile and innocent that it crushed her heart.

'I'm scared,' he said, his voice barely audible. But she heard him. She gripped his hand tightly. He tried to squeeze back, but his fingers just curled weakly around hers.

'I know you are,' she said, instinctively knowing the words that would comfort him. 'But I'm here. We're together. That's what matters, Brad. I'm here.'

She repeated those final two words over and over again, until long after she knew that he was gone. His chest was so still, his breath no longer whispering against her skin, his eyes closed. There was no more flickering. No movement in his hand, still wrapped around hers. For a few seconds, there was silence. The world, it seemed, was holding its breath.

But her grief was too expansive to stay trapped inside her body. If she didn't release it, it would tear through the flesh of her lungs to find a way out. She wailed, her ribs aching and her eyes burning, her loss a physical presence that was coursing through her, swirling around her, pouring out of her.

Arms found their way around her shoulders and squeezed tightly, like they were stemming the flow of blood from an open wound. But it was useless. She knew that nothing could stop her from falling apart. She let the arms hold her, though, as she screamed and cried and raged.

'Immy,' Kat said after a while, tugging her away from her brother's body. 'Immy, we have to go.'

'NO!'

She shrugged Kat off, and clung even more tightly to Brad's body, twisting her arms around him as though he would know, from wherever it was that he had gone, that she was not going to let him go that easily, that she wouldn't leave him. Not again.

'Baby,' Kat whispered in her ear, 'we need to go. Your sister, I think she's in shock. I know you don't want to leave, but think about Jemima, OK? Do it for her?'

Jemima. Of course.

Her mind struggled through the cloud of her pain to find clarity. She tried to cling to the facts: Brad was gone. She didn't know where their older sister was. She couldn't live with her real parents. The only place she had left was Kat and Dylan's house, the place she'd called home until less than a week ago. She'd failed Brad. She'd let him down, let her fear get the best of her. If she'd acted faster, stopped deliberating and just done what he'd asked her to, they'd be gone. Jemima never would have done what she'd done.

But she *had* done it. Jemima had taken the knife from her hands and plunged it into Brad's back. Imogen knew that, ultimately, his death was her own fault. And now the only place she had left to go was the very place she'd tried to escape.

Rage bubbled up as she thought about what Jemima had done. Staring at the handle of the knife, now lying on the concrete, she imagined herself grabbing it, spinning around and hurling herself at Jemima, taking revenge for what she'd done. But just as quickly as the thought arrived, she dismissed it. She wasn't going to hurt Jemima. She couldn't. It wasn't who she was.

With tears coursing down her cheeks, she nodded.

'Let's go,' she whispered.

She felt herself being lifted from the ground, carried like a child away from her brother, away from all of that blood, away from the shed where she had lost herself forever.

Jemima reached up and took her sister's hand, which was

limp and sticky. Imogen didn't have the strength to tear her hand away. She couldn't do anything, couldn't feel anything.

The three of them left the shed and walked around the side of the little shack that had, in such a short time, become her home. As they passed the living room window, Imogen caught a glimpse of the awful floral sofa and that stupid pram that Brad never explained to her, and she realised, with a fresh wave of grief, that she would never know. She would never have all of the answers.

Kat was whispering in her ear, and then there was noise, and light; so much light. Voices. Shouts. It was too much, she thought. And then she slipped into unconsciousness, held in the arms of the woman who raised her; Kat's once again.

Chapter 60

KAT

'Thank God,' Dylan says, dropping to his knees as I approach him in the floodlit space beyond Brad's house. His face is streaked with tears, his arms flung out as though he's surrendering.

Someone, I don't see who, takes Imogen from my arms, tries to get me to follow them, but I fall on my knees onto the dirt beside my husband, and I let him hold me while I say, over and over again, for my own reassurance as much as for his, 'Imogen is OK. She's OK. Imogen is OK.'

'I know, my love,' he says, taking my face gently in his hands and tipping it up so I'm looking directly into his eyes. 'I know. She's safe. You're all safe. It's over.'

I stare at him until my breathing becomes steady again, but then my eyes flicker left and right.

'Imogen ... where ... ?'

He senses the panic in my voice, the same fear pressing against my ribs as that very first day when Imogen went missing. Brad's gone, I know that. But logic doesn't stop the fear from rising once more. I can't see my daughter. Can't be certain she's OK.

'There,' Dylan points to my left, where two police officers are wrapping Imogen in a blanket and offering her water to drink. Jemima is standing next to her sister, still gripping her hand. My shoulders drop.

We stay like that, collapsed in the ochre dust, our girls safely with the police, until more sirens and lights fill the air around us. An ambulance has arrived. It must have been called as soon as we stepped out of the house. Dylan carries me to the van as it pulls off to the side, beside the fleet of police cars, their bright white headlights all pointed towards the house. Our daughters are just ahead of us, their hair gleaming red and blue in the lights, their hands still linked.

Officers stormed into the property as we walked out. They must have found Brad by now. I shudder at the memory of the scene we just left behind, at what they've had to walk into.

As I take a seat in the back of the ambulance, opposite Imogen and Jemima, I let myself be examined by the medics, who talk to me in calm, gentle voices that do nothing to quiet the panic that's started building inside me. I'm not worried about Imogen's safety. She's being taken care of now. But they're going to want to know what happened. They're going to want to know how Brad died, who drove the knife so deeply into his back, through his ribs, into his vital organs. They can't know the truth. They can't. Jemima saved us. She brought our family back together again. She can't be punished for it. I try to speak, try to make sure that the girls understand, but all that comes out is an incomprehensible mumble.

'Concussion,' a medic says to Dylan.

I try to protest, to stand, but Dylan puts a hand firmly on my knee.

'Just try to relax,' he says. 'It's over. Just rest now, and don't worry about anything, OK? The girls are fine. Everything is going to be all right.'

He keeps talking, a stream of reassurances I can't hear for the deafening anxiety that's clamouring inside me. I want to argue, to make him understand that nothing's OK, that this nightmare isn't over yet, but I'm so weak, so tired, and my muscles won't work anyway, and then I drift, and the voices and faces blur, and I try to fight it but in the end, my body's fight is stronger, and I sense myself slipping, submerging into the darkness all over again.

Chapter 61

KAT

My eyelids flutter open and I close them tightly again, a defence mechanism against the harsh white light that burns at the back of my eyeballs. It's blinding. I'm lying down, although I have no idea where I am. I try wiggling my fingers. They brush against fabric; not soft, but comforting anyway. The air smells clean. I try again, squinting against the light, opening my eyes slowly, slowly, until they adjust.

As the scene comes into focus, the sounds of a beeping monitor and the gentle squeak of shoes in the hallway come into focus. And the wheeze of my own laboured breathing. I'm in a hospital.

I lift a hand to my head, and my fingers touch some kind of dressing. I wince.

'You're awake,' Dylan's voice announces.

I turn my head slowly and his face fills my vision. He's beaming.

'Hi,' I say.

'Hi,' he says back, and in that tiny word there is an entire ecosystem of loss and relief and fear and hope.

'The girls—'

'They're both OK,' he replies, taking my hand. 'They're just down the hall, two rooms next to one another. Jemima is being treated for shock, and Imogen needed a bit of extra

307

help to flush out whatever was in her system and get some nutrients back in her, but they're going to be completely fine.'

I sigh, relieved, until the scene in the shed comes flooding back to me, not blurred and distorted, but with a crushing clarity that leaves me breathless.

'Are you OK?' Dylan asks, looking around for someone who can help me. 'I'll get a nurse.'

'No,' I say, my voice raspy. 'I'm OK, I'm just remembering it all. How did you . . . ?'

'How did I know where you were?' he asks. I nod. 'Jemima called. She woke up in the car, alone, and didn't know where you were. She was scared, but she spotted your phone in the front and she called me. The signal was terrible, she kept dropping out, but she eventually managed to send me a pin to her location. I was at the police headquarters, so we raced over there straight away.'

'But how did you know . . . ?'

'What, that you were in trouble?' Dylan laughs. 'I do know you, you know. And I know you wouldn't have pulled Jems out of bed in the middle of the night unless it was really important. And unless you really didn't want me to know.'

I try to smile, but it doesn't work.

'I'm sorry,' I say. And I mean it. 'I should have just told you. I was so scared, he told me not to tell anyone, and I didn't know what he might do . . .'

'It's OK. We're all OK.'

I close my eyes and breathe in. Then out. Trying to steady my nerves, trying to still the turmoil inside.

'Is Brad . . . ?'

'Yes, he's dead,' Dylan says, his voice dull. 'The police need

308

to ask you about that, actually. They said they'll come back when you're awake. They've spoken with Imogen already.'

I try to sit up, but the movement causes fireworks behind my eyes. I moan and collapse into the pillow again.

'What did she say?' I ask weakly, my eyes squeezed closed as though that will stop the hammering inside my skull.

'The truth... presumably.'

His words hang over us, a challenge. I don't dare to open my eyes, don't allow myself to show him my fear. Because, just like the moment in that shed when the knife blade was pointed at my chest and my life was in my daughter's hands, I need to trust her.

I almost laugh at the version of myself who, only a week ago, didn't trust Imogen when the worst thing she'd been involved in was some stupid fight at school. We've come a long way since then. I've had to trust her with my life. And now I have to trust her with her sister's. Our family depends on it. It depends on her.

Only I'm not sure which *her* I'm talking about. Is it Imogen we'll be taking home with us... or Amy?

Chapter 62

IMOGEN

'I know this is hard,' the policeman said gently.

Imogen tried not to look him in the eye; she couldn't cope with his pity, or that sympathetic head-tilt everyone seemed to be doing. If she acknowledged his sympathy, it might cause a tiny crack in her facade, burst her wide open, expose all of her to the world. To herself.

It had only been a few hours, so she'd had to think quickly. She knew that they were going to ask her what happened in that shed, and she knew that her answers would change the future. For her, for Jemima. For everyone. The balance of power was weighted heavily on her – was all on her, really. She didn't want that kind of pressure, didn't trust herself with big decisions, especially not now, not after she'd cost Brad his life.

Since Kat had carried her out of the shed, covered in blood, and empty inside, she hadn't spoken a word. What could she possibly say, now that Brad was dead and Jemima had killed him?

She'd gone around and around in circles in her mind, trying to decide how to carry on, desperately hoping to make sense of it all, but she still didn't know what she'd say when they asked. And now they were asking.

She was lying in an uncomfortable single bed, covered

in stiff white sheets, in her own hospital room. The nurses had explained that she couldn't go home yet. Apparently she was in shock, and there were substances in her bloodstream that needed to be flushed out before they could let her go. At the back of her mind, Imogen knew what that meant, what they weren't really telling her about the last week of her life, but she wasn't ready to face it. She couldn't cope with that, too. Not just yet.

In the meantime, the cops were here, and they wanted to hear, in her words, what had happened.

'I know this is hard,' the policeman repeated, looking down at his notepad. 'But we need you to tell us what happened. We need to hear it from your point of view. From the start.'

She'd rather just forget, block it out, never have to think about it again, but as soon as a sliver of memory appeared in the gaps of the walls she was trying to put up, the truth enveloped her, and emotions formed like a hurricane, building force, gathering intensity, in the back of her throat. She swallowed them down.

She let out a long, slow breath. She closed her eyes tightly and opened them again. And then, without planning her words, she took another deep breath, and let her instincts take over.

'The start?' she began. 'Well, Brad got in touch with me on Facebook one day, out of the blue. I didn't know who he was, and I'd never heard of him before, but he told me that I might want to consider getting a DNA test.' She swallowed. 'I ignored him at first, just thought it was spam, or some creep trying to get hold of me. But I don't know, I guess I'd always felt like a bit of an outsider, like I didn't belong. I was so different. I just... Well, anyway, I guess his words just ate away at me for a few weeks, so one day I ordered the DNA test.'

'We found Brad's messages,' the officer said, surprising her. Those messages had been private. What else did they know about her that she'd rather keep hidden? 'We noticed that after a while, your communication with Brad on Facebook stopped. Can you tell us how you kept in touch with each other after that?'

'I . . . He sent me a phone,' she admitted. 'Just an old lame one, like, it didn't actually do anything except send texts and make calls. It arrived one day after he'd stopped replying to my messages and I told Kat the parcel was something for school. She didn't suspect anything.'

'What happened to that phone?'

'I don't know,' she said quietly, trying to remember the night they had met. He told her she'd thrown her phone out the window of his car. 'I can't remember.'

'OK,' the cops exchanged a look. 'That's OK. Can you tell us about the night you ran away? Why did you decide to meet with Brad then?'

'I got the DNA test results,' she began, closing her eyes to bring the events of that evening into clarity. Her fingers curled into fists as she remembered how betrayed she'd felt, how her anger had been so intense that she'd thought she might explode. 'Brad was the only person I could talk to about it,' she continued. 'So I messaged him, and I told him what the test results said, that I was adopted. And then he messaged me back and told me he'd come and get me, that he'd look after me.'

She paused. The policeman who had been asking her questions was scribbling notes in a little notepad that was balanced on his knee. The other cop, an older guy, friendly looking, was nodding at her, smiling warmly.

'So you arranged to meet?' the scribbling cop asked.

She nodded. 'Yeah. Brad said that I should sneak out the house and meet him down on Jetty Road. It's not far from home, and it's usually busy enough that no one would pay too much attention to me.'

'Were you planning to run away, to stay with him, or did you intend to come home again?'

'I didn't . . . I hadn't thought about it,' she admitted sheepishly. 'I was just so angry with Kat and Dylan, so I wanted to get away, I didn't want to see them or speak to them. I just wanted to speak to Brad, to find out how he knew about me being adopted. I wanted answers.'

'So you met him on Jetty Road?'

Imogen nodded. 'Yeah. I climbed out my window and jumped the fence to go over the neighbours' backyards for a block or so. And then I ran to Jetty Road and waited where Brad said, outside the hairdresser's, in the little alleyway bit. He pulled up just after I arrived—'

'How did you know what he looked like?' the older policeman interrupted.

'I didn't,' she replied. 'He told me to look out for an old Nissan Pulsar, white, with a blue stripe down the side.'

'OK,' the young policeman said, his words slicing through her memories. 'So what happened then?'

'I got in the car, and he drove me somewhere. To the house.'

'Did you know where you were?'

'No,' she said. 'I got really sick when we got to his house, so I can't really remember a lot from when I met him. Just from when I started getting better . . .'

A mass of emotion bloomed in her chest. Those few days had been filled with so much hope, and love, and security. Things she thought she might never feel again.

'Did you try to leave?'

She frowned. 'Why would I have wanted to leave? He was taking care of me.'

'OK,' the policeman said gently. 'That's OK. So what happened at the house?'

'Not much.' She shrugged. 'I was in bed for most of it, but when I was up and about, we sat and talked.'

'Did Brad mention what his plans were? You weren't going to stay there forever, were you?'

'He didn't say,' she replied, exhausted suddenly. She wasn't sure what they expected her to say, what they thought had happened over the past week. There was nothing to tell them, no big secret. She was with her brother. They had been spending time together, getting to know one another. It was as simple and as wonderful as that. 'I'm tired,' she said. 'And I don't know anything that's going to help you. Please can I go to sleep now?'

'We won't keep you for much longer, Imogen,' the older policeman assured her. 'But it's important that we find out what happened last night when your mum – when Kat – came to the house. Do you know how she found out where Brad was keeping you?'

'He wasn't keeping me,' she snapped, angry. 'I wasn't kidnapped.'

'Right,' the young policeman said, his hands up. 'But do you know how Kat found out where you were staying?'

'Brad told her,' she answered, her anger dissipating and turning into confusion. Why did they need her to answer this? Shouldn't they just ask Kat? 'She'd said she didn't want me to come home, so Brad asked if she could at least drop some of my stuff off at his place. Then when she came, she said she'd changed her mind and wanted me to come back after all. She attacked Brad.'

314

The cops exchanged a glance. Something in the back of Imogen's mind twisted. The words sounded wrong in the air. Something was missing, only she couldn't understand what it was. She pushed the thoughts away. It didn't matter any more. Brad was gone. She blinked away the tears that welled up in her eyes.

'Imogen,' the older cop said kindly. 'Kat and Dylan have been looking for you relentlessly since you left. Kat wasn't in touch with Brad before last night.'

'But he showed me her message,' she said, her confusion amplifying.

'I don't know what message you saw – we'll look into it – but I can assure you, Imogen, Kat wanted you home. Don't ever doubt that.'

The clock above the door ticked into the silence that expanded around them. Imogen tried to adjust her recollection, to recalibrate the facts. But it was messy, and she was so tired, and all she wanted was to be alone with her memories of her brother, to relive every moment without anyone muddying the truth.

'If we can just go back to when Kat arrived at Brad's house,' the young cop said, clearing his throat. 'What happened when you saw her lying there?'

'I ran over to check that she was OK,' she explained. 'I asked Brad to take her inside. I wanted to get her some water. He said that there wasn't enough room in the house, so he'd take her out the back. He carried her off, and I went inside to find her something to drink. I took a glass of water out to Brad's shed.'

'This is really helpful,' the older cop said. 'You're doing a great job, Imogen; you're really helping us. Can you tell us what happened when you got to the shed?'

She squeezed her eyes closed. She had replayed those few

minutes over and over again in her mind. The scene was printed in her memory forever. But so were the words that Kat had whispered in her ear as they left the horror of the shed behind them, before they were swept into ambulances and wrapped in blankets and told that everything was going to be fine.

Once upon a time, she'd believed that telling the truth was always the right thing to do. She'd seen the world in black and white. But now she understood that every decision in life was a compromise, shades of grey painted by so many factors. Right wasn't always right, and wrong wasn't always wrong. Just like her identity, the truth was ever-changing, determined by so much more than cold, hard facts.

She couldn't say for certain who she was, or what she believed, any more. She was no longer the naive, lost girl who ran away from home, driven by the sting of betrayal and the promise of something more, something she believed would make her whole. Nor was she the confused, angry girl who stood over Kat in the shed, desperate to earn her brother's love, desperate to belong. She guessed that she was something in between. A little bit of a Braidwood, a little bit of a Sanders. Light and dark, coexisting.

And so she forced aside the image of Brad, a halo of blood spreading from beneath his limp body, and began speaking, her voice clear and strong, her eyes locked with those of the policeman.

Chapter 63

KAT

'And can you describe what happened next?'

I hold Troy's gaze. His expression is neutral, probably well rehearsed so as not to give away his thoughts. I hope my face is equally impassive, that he can't detect my pounding heart or the bead of sweat slowly slipping between my shoulder blades. He can't see the wrestling match that's going on in my mind, the desperate scramble to reach a decision, to know with certainty the right thing to do.

I breathe in deeply. It's shaky, my chest not working as it should. The police mistake this for me having a hard time reliving my trauma, and they respond with sympathetic looks.

'We know it's difficult,' Ruben says gently. 'Take your time.'

I nod and drop my head. My hands are resting on the starched white sheet, both wrists encircled with black bruises, and on top of the black ring around my left wrist, a plastic hospital band, identical, no doubt, to the one Imogen is wearing just a few doors down.

When I look up again, I spot scribbled writing in Ruben's little black Moleskine notebook. I can't see what his words say. What Imogen said.

Without knowing, I have to make a decision. I have to

say the words I've rehearsed in my head and believe – trust – that Imogen and I are in this together. That we'll do what it takes to protect this family.

Only ... I have no idea what Imogen is thinking. Not only did her little sister kill her brother, but just hours ago, she stood with a knife suspended above me, looking for all the world as though she was considering plunging it into my chest. If it hadn't been for Jemima coming in ... I shudder. I don't know. I don't have all of the information, and I don't know how to make a decision.

If I tell the truth, the whole truth, then Jemima will be dragged into all of this, she'll be made to justify her decision to defend her mother and save her sister from doing something awful. She'll be forced to relive it over and over again, and maybe even be a witness at a trial – I don't know how these things work. There's no way to ask without giving the truth away.

If I say what really happened, but Imogen has told the version of the truth we agreed upon, or rather, that I whispered to her in a panic – *Say you did it in self-defence, keep Jemima out of it* – as we walked out of Brad's home and towards the flashing blue and red lights, then we'll both have some explaining to do.

And yet, if I tell our version, and Imogen has told them what actually happened in that shed, if she isn't loyal to this family, if she's angry about what happened to Brad, about the lies, about everything – and, honestly, I can't blame her if she is – well, then there will be no protecting Jemima. And then there will be more questions, and it could be so much worse than just telling the truth in the first place. It's a gamble, however I play it.

But in the end, I know there's only one decision I can

make, only one way to keep my family intact. I have to trust Imogen.

Because isn't that what she wanted all along – for me to trust her? And here I am, having to find the faith that she will lie to the police to protect the sister she's not even related to. To protect the girl who killed her biological brother. It's ludicrous to think that she'd choose to do that.

I try to imagine what I'd do in the same circumstances, but I can't picture it. I don't know. I can't fathom what my daughter is going through.

And so I take another deep breath, less shaky this time, and I take the leap.

'I woke up in the shed,' I say. 'I didn't know where I was, but I could tell I was tied to something. I couldn't feel my hands, and my head had been hit, I think. I tried talking to Brad, but he was angry; he wouldn't listen. Every time I spoke, he'd hit me again. I was slipping in and out of consciousness, so I don't know how much I was awake for, but I do know that he had a knife. I thought he was going to stab me. And then I heard Imogen coming in, and I tried to call out, but he hit me in the head and I passed out again. When I came to, he was on the floor and Jemima was helping to untie the ropes that I was held down with. I didn't see what happened.'

Ruben scribbles in his notebook. Troy looks at me, sizing me up, weighing my words. I breathe a silent prayer that my story matches Imogen's, that this isn't the beginning of another nightmare. I take a slow, controlled breath, and hold it in. I can't meet Troy's eyes. I look down at my hands and softly stroke the shackle-like bruises.

'How did Jemima come to be in the shed?' Troy asks after what feels like hours.

I look up at him in surprise, letting out the breath in a

rush of relief. He isn't questioning my story. Does that mean it's the same as Imogen's?

'Uh . . . I don't know,' I say, trying to shift my focus to the question I'm being expected to answer. 'I left her in the car. She was asleep – fast asleep – and I didn't want to disturb her. But I suppose she must have heard a noise, or woken up and come to investigate. I don't know.'

'OK,' Ruben says, snapping his notebook shut. 'Thanks for your help, Kat. I think we have everything we need from you for now, although you will need to come down to the station once you're released from here to sign your witness statement. But it's a fairly straightforward case of self-defence from what you and Imogen have told us.'

I don't hear the rest of his words. I'm light-headed, dizzy with the knowledge that maybe, just maybe, this is all over. I try to act normally, to nod and smile in the right places, to say goodbye, but I'm barely aware of what I'm doing. The same single sentence is repeating in my mind, over and over again, until it's branded onto my brain.

Imogen is back.

My daughter is back.

It's all I need. This knowledge, the fact that she did what she needed to in order to protect her sister, it quiets the symphony of doubt that's been playing in my mind on a loop.

Imogen feels a connection to this family, and however tenuous that might be, it's enough that she lied to protect us. She didn't have to say what she did. She didn't have to be loyal.

As the police officers leave, a smile spreads across my face until I'm grinning unreservedly. I close my eyes and let the relief wash over me, content in the knowledge that Brad is gone and no one is trying to split up my family, that Imogen doesn't want to sabotage us. I know we're a long way from forgiveness, and I'm certain there will be hard days ahead, but all that matters is that Imogen is where she belongs. With us. Safe.

'Kat?'

My eyes fly open in surprise. I didn't hear any footsteps, but standing in the doorframe is a beautiful blonde young woman, a little gaunt, with dark circles under eyes that were never there before, but still unmistakably my daughter. She's holding onto a metal pole, at the top of which is a bag of liquid, leading into her arm.

'Oh, Immy,' I sob, and she steps tentatively towards me, once, twice. I hold my hands out. She stops and looks at them for a second, deciding, judging, grappling. Tears flood down my cheeks as I wait. And I trust. And then slowly, almost robotically, she extends a hand towards me. I reach further and clasp her fingers between mine. 'Imogen,' I say, my voice high-pitched with emotion. 'I'm so sorry, my love. I'm sorry. For everything.'

She nods. Her lips are pressed tightly together to form a straight, harsh line. Her eyebrows are moving closer together, a frown taking over her pretty features.

Normally, I'd fill this awkward silence. I'd erase it with words, with supplication, with anything that could convince her to forgive me, to want to be my daughter again. Because, after all, now it's her choice. I chose her as my daughter all those years ago, and now it's her chance. Her time to decide. She could walk away, and no one would blame her. Or she could see past my lies, understand that I only told them to protect her, and accept me as her mother. But I can't make that decision for her.

My chest squeezes as I consider the risk. What if she walks away? What if saving Jemima had nothing to do with her wanting to be part of this family, and everything to do with wanting to get away faster, to have this whole ordeal over and done with as quickly as possible so that she could escape us, unfettered by legal proceedings?

A lump builds in my throat and threatens to choke me. Imogen's gaze flickers between my left eye and my right, as though she might see something different in each. It takes every ounce of strength I have, but I stay quiet. I let my pleas die in my throat.

And I wait.

After seconds, or hours, I can't tell them apart, she shuffles one foot. Just by a centimetre, almost imperceptibly. But I see it. She moved closer. I try to keep my elation hidden, but it's too much. Another sob bursts from my chest, and I pull on her fingertips with my own, the movement propelling her forward.

And finally, finally, she's back in my arms. Where she's always belonged. Where I can love her and protect her and never, ever lie to her again.

Chapter 64

IMOGEN

She hovered in the doorway and watched for a minute, waiting for her heartbeat to resume its normal rhythm. The nurse had tried to stop her, but she'd begged to be let out of her room, to go for a walk. In the end, she'd had to compromise. She could go, but she had to take the IV drip around with her. The wheel squeaked as she shifted to the right.

From where she was standing, Jemima looked tiny. Fragile, even. She was asleep, covered by starched white sheets and surrounded by machines that looked like they would harm rather than heal. But Jemima wasn't attached to any of them. She was fine, the nurses had assured her. Just in shock.

She didn't want to say so to the nurses, but she doubted the girl was in shock. She knew Jemima well enough to be certain of that.

The younger girl opened an eyelid, just a sliver, then clamped it closed again.

'I know you're awake.'

Jemima sighed and opened her eyes fully. 'Don't be mad, Imogen.'

'It's not Imogen. It's Amy,' she replied wearily. She wasn't sure if that was true either, but she wasn't ready to let go of it yet. Her name was one of the only things linking her to her real family. And besides, she wasn't Imogen any more; not really. She might look the same, sound the same, walk the same... but inside, she'd changed. That girl from before, she was lost.

'OK, Amy, then,' Jemima said. 'Are you mad?'

'Of course I am,' she muttered, but she wasn't sure if that was the right way to describe how she really felt, or if she'd ever be able to put her anguish into words.

Jemima narrowed her eyes. 'I'm not going to apologise. I did it because I had to.'

The older girl set her jaw and stared. She wasn't going to back down, just because Jemima wanted her to.

'You know it's true! If I hadn't, you would have killed Mum—'

'I wouldn't—'

'How do you know? I know I'm only twelve, but I could tell you were spaced out on something. And besides, you were so mad at her, and you wanted to be with your brother, and I know you were thinking about it, OK? There's no point pretending with me.'

'How do you know he was my brother?'

Jemima rolled her eyes. 'Mum and Dad think I'm an idiot, but you know better than that. Besides, it's called listening.'

She didn't say anything, but she didn't have to, because Jemima kept talking.

'And so you might have killed her, or seriously hurt her, and then what? Run off with Brad; been a fugitive? Even if you didn't stab her, Brad probably would have, and then you, for good measure.'

She winced. She hadn't allowed herself to imagine that scenario again, the one where she refused to do what Brad had asked her to do. She had no idea what he would have done. The brother she thought she knew – the kind, sweet guy who had cradled her when she was sick – seemed so hard to find among the whispers she was hearing now. She wanted to understand, to sit down and listen to his side of the story. But now she'd never find out, would never hear it from him.

'Imog— Amy, don't be moody. It's over. I can't take it back. And besides, things are going to go back to normal now.'

'No. They're not.'

There was a pause as the two girls sized each other up.

'If I hadn't done what I did,' Jemima said, sitting up in bed, growing animated, 'I'd have lost you. And maybe Mum, but almost definitely you. I couldn't let that happen. I needed you back at home.'

'Ah, so there it is,' she said bitterly. 'That's the truth, isn't it?'

'Amy,' Jemima whined.

'What?'

'I know you don't believe me, but I am sorry that you don't have your brother any more. I'm just not going to apologise for what I did, because I didn't want you to die. And really, if you actually put yourself in my shoes, I didn't have another option.'

Imogen had considered that; she'd tried to understand what she would have done if their roles had been reversed. When Jemima had walked from Kat's car into that shed, there were only two outcomes: either she stopped Brad, or he would have taken her family from her. And for Jemima, the Braidwood family was the only one she had. She didn't have a secret set of siblings to run away to when things turned sour. She didn't have anyone else to bail her out.

'Amy?' Jemima asked tentatively.

325

'Yeah?'

She felt her anger deflating, and resignation setting in. Not because she could forgive the young girl on the bed for what she'd done, but because maybe she could understand it. Maybe she understood it more than she would let herself admit. And because this wasn't Jemima's fault; not really. She hadn't lied to her older sister for her whole life. On the contrary, she'd been utterly honest, and completely herself. Jemima hadn't kept the truth from her. And yes, she had stabbed Brad. That would never be erased, could never be taken back. But she'd been faced with an impossible choice.

They both had. The only difference was that Jemima was the one who had had the guts to act on it.

Exhausted, she let her arms drop to her sides.

There was no point fighting it any more. She knew Jemima. She knew that being angry – fighting – wouldn't do any good.

'This doesn't change anything between us,' Jemima whispered.

Imogen wasn't sure if it was a question or a statement. She shrugged. 'You know we're not sisters,' she said.

'So?'

Imogen shrugged again. She wondered if it mattered. She wondered if it should.

'None of that matters now that you're back,' the younger girl said, as though reading Imogen's mind. 'When we go home, things are going to go right back to the way they were.' She smiled brightly.

Imogen's stomach plummeted. It was exactly what she feared.

Chapter 65

KAT

'Muuuummmm,' Jemima's voice whines from the kitchen table.

I laugh. I've been doing a lot of that lately – laughing. Everything feels light now, in a way it didn't before. Because now I know what I could have lost. I know what could have happened. And yet somehow, impossibly, I am fine. My family is safe. And that thought, which I've woken up with every morning since that night in the shed, makes the smiles, the laughs, come easily.

'What is it, Jems?'

'Immy took four pancakes instead of three!'

I close the fridge and bring the punnet of strawberries to the table. I eye Imogen's plate and raise an eyebrow at her.

'I didn't do it. Dylan, you saw! Tell Kat I didn't do it!'

Dylan and I share a bemused smile. Since we came home, Imogen has taken to calling Dylan and me by our first names. At first I was too worried about upsetting the delicate balance we'd achieved to bother demanding the traditional 'Mum' and 'Dad', but now it just feels like we've let it go on for too long to start arguing it. It grates on me every time, but I suppose, after all, we're not her mum and dad. Not in the biological sense, anyway. Demanding that she labels us as such would probably be hypocritical. I hope one day she'll see us as her parents again, but I know that trusting us again isn't something that will happen overnight. I'm trying to be patient, to remind myself that having her home is enough.

I laugh again as Dylan steals a pancake from my plate and slaps it on top of the pile in front of Jemima. She looks delighted. I stick my tongue out at Dylan and swipe the pancake at the top of his pile, adding it to my own. Laughter bounces off the walls as the girls tuck into their breakfasts with zeal before they can be stolen from under their noses.

I sit back and absorb the scene for a moment. I can hardly believe the difference these past few months have made to the way we look, the way we interact. This family has been transformed by the truth; the brutal, heartbreaking, raw truth. I'd been so scared of it coming out, of the lies I'd been telling coming to light, that I was trying to control everything. I acted like my own daughter was the one who couldn't be trusted, like she was the real danger.

And then my worst fears came true, and they were so much worse than I'd ever imagined, and yet... I survived. *We* survived. And now there's no more hiding. Imogen knows where she's come from. She knows who she is.

For the first few weeks after we got home, Imogen was still trying to process everything that had happened. She made us call her Amy for a few days but dropped it soon after she began the search for her uncensored history in earnest. She was hungry for information. Ravenous.

Once the floodgates were opened, the questions kept coming, faster and increasingly more confronting. I sat her down with my pile of paperwork, with the newspaper cuttings and the adoption certificates. We submitted a request for the transcripts of her parents' trial, and we pored over them together, united in grief and horror and the total inability to understand why.

Imogen wrote to her mother, a beautiful letter that she let me read, a heartfelt attempt to get the answers she so desperately craves. Her hand shook as she slid the envelope into the mailbox, and I mentally willed Sally to do the right thing, to give her daughter the closure she needs. No reply has arrived yet.

She's been seeing a counsellor, too. I've been to a couple of sessions – family reconciliation, they call it. Imogen told me how angry she was that I kept her identity a secret for all of her life, how much she resented the years she never got with her brother. I apologised, told her how afraid we had been for her. I explained that the authorities had believed it was the best way forward all those years ago, too. And I admitted my fear that she'd choose them over us. We cried some more. Hugged. Went out for ice cream afterwards.

I considered sending Jemima to speak to someone as well. But then she'd have to say why she was there – she'd have to admit that she's the one who stabbed Brad. And no one knows that, not even Dylan. It's our secret. Us Braidwood girls. We're bound by it, this shared knowledge of what Jemima did to save her sister; to save me. Whether I was being saved from Imogen, and whether Imogen was being saved from herself, or whether Brad was the one we were being protected from, that's the one thing we haven't spoken about. That's the part I don't let myself think about.

That, and the question of what my youngest daughter, the daughter I carried inside me for nine months, the daughter who shares my DNA, is capable of. I've told myself it was self-defence. Repeated over and over again that it's nothing to worry about. I'm good at repressing deep fears. It's what

I did for fifteen years before Brad came along and changed everything.

I don't want to let myself acknowledge the thoughts that lurk in the wings. Because if I do, I'll be forced to ask questions I don't know how to put into words. I'll have to face myself, delve into my own soul and uncover the truth of who I am, of what's in my blood, of my shortcomings. I'll be compelled to ask the questions I don't think I want to know the answers to. Questions like: is darkness lurking inside all of us? Is it something we inherit, like the ability to curl your tongue? Or does it appear later in life, formed by circumstances and experiences . . . and parenting? I can't face those questions. And I don't need to.

We're fine. We're safe. Jemima was acting in self-defence. Imogen isn't Amy. Everyone is OK.

When I wake up in cold sweats, a scream echoing on my lips, Dylan's breath at my ear telling me I'm safe, his arm around my sweaty body, holding me tight, I don't tell him about my nightmares. He assumes he knows, he's working from the official story. But what I see is Imogen – Amy – towering over me, knife in her hand, resignation on her face. I want to believe that she'd have turned the knife on Brad instead of going through with it. But in those moments in the dead of night, when the nightmare is still prickling on my skin, I'm not so sure.

I shake the thought away. I trust Imogen. She's proven where her loyalties lie. Whatever may have happened, she didn't have to make that choice, in the end. Jemima made it for her. And now Imogen and I are forgetting what could have been and are focusing on letting Jemima get on with it, on making sure the way things happened is kept between us.

As far as Dylan is concerned – and as far as the police and

media are concerned – Jemima woke up in the car, scared and confused, and wasn't sure what to do. She found my phone, still in the cradle at the front, and somehow got through to Dylan. She sent him her location, then their connection was lost and she heard a scream. This, of course, is all true. When she came into the shed, however, that's when our version of events deviates from the truth.

They found two sets of fingerprints on the knife: Jemima's and Imogen's. But my clever daughter told the police that after *she'd* stabbed Brad – in self-defence – Jemima had come in and had pulled the knife out. They didn't question it. The girls were both covered in blood, and there was no way to decipher spatter patterns in all of that mess. The height of the stab wound was questioned, but as Imogen had been in a struggle with Brad, they deemed it conceivable that she could have stabbed him from an unnatural angle.

As far as the police are concerned, Brad's death was far from a tragedy. It was a case of a kidnapper who died when an innocent girl defended herself. And we've been left to get on with our lives, to be a family again, to carry on.

Sometimes I catch myself staring at Jemima, remembering the moment in the shed when Brad's body swayed and fell, when my daughter came into view and the truth dawned on me. And I watch her. I wonder what really went through her mind on that terrifying night. I wonder how much she knows, how much she understands. And I look for signs. Until I remember how all of this started, how I made my family implode by not trusting them. And I remind myself of the promise I made when I was lying on that table, staring at the naked bulb and knowing I was about to die. I told myself that if I survived, I'd always trust my family.

I'm doing my best to keep my promise. I don't want to tempt fate. I don't want to be the cause of my family's downfall again. Besides, I have to trust my daughters, now. They hold a secret that could destroy me.

No one suspects that what we've said, the three of us Braidwood girls, is anything other than the truth. We're united by our lie, bonded by the threads of what actually happened in that dark, hot shed, the truth woven tightly with our statements to the police, so that from the front it's a neat and tidy picture of a family doing what needed to be done to stay safe. It's only from the back you can see the loose threads, the knots, the mess.

It's our mess, though. Ours. Together. And that's what matters. Besides, we're all entitled to secrets, aren't we? We're family, and family protects one another.

Because, in the end, as Sally Sanders so rightly told me, *family sticks together, above all else.*

Chapter 66

IMOGEN

'Immy?'

Imogen snapped the top of her laptop closed and spun her chair around, her heart pounding. Her bedroom door opened fully to reveal a pyjama-clad Jemima.

The younger girl padded into Imogen's room and sat cross-legged on the floor, which was plastered in newspaper clippings, articles printed from the internet and case notes that had arrived after Kat's freedom of information request was granted.

Jemima picked up the sheet of paper closest to her left hand, a copy of an article that was written during Tim and Sally's trial, and stared at it for a while.

Satan's Ranch Shocking Torture Revelations, the headline screamed.

Imogen didn't need to reread it to know what it said. She'd studied every word of every document in her bedroom, and she knew them all by heart.

Today concluded the sixth day of the trial of Sally Sanders, the woman charged with the torture and murder of her own children on the Victorian property dubbed Satan's Ranch. The prosecution's key witness, the fourteen-year-old daughter of Sally, told today of the torture endured by the children under the woman's care. Speaking via a video link to protect her from those who had abused her, the daughter, whose identity is being withheld for her privacy, revealed that the children were routinely starved, physically abused and kept as prisoners on the property. None of the children who lived there had ever set foot outside the torture chamber they called home.

When she'd first come back home, Imogen had been voracious, needing to learn every single detail of her past, desperate to connect to anything that would make her feel close to Brad again. Nothing worked. Learning about her biological parents' deeds only made her feel worse, which she hadn't thought was possible.

Brad had been adamant that their parents weren't the monsters the world saw them as. But she'd seen the evidence, read the trial transcripts. She'd seen photographs of Kimberley's scars, X-rays of Brad's tiny, shattered bones. She knew the truth. It was undeniable.

'Have you heard back from her?' Jemima whispered, her eyes wide.

Imogen's heart stopped for a second, until she realised that Jemima was talking about her mum.

'No,' Imogen said, relief flooding her.

Jemima's shoulders dropped, disappointed. Her fascination with Sally bordered on obsession, which didn't surprise Imogen, but it had meant that her own interest in hearing from her birth mother was waning. The letter had been part of her therapy. She'd done what she'd been told; she'd reached out. She'd asked the difficult questions, the questions she didn't really need the answers to. Because those answers wouldn't change anything. They wouldn't bring Brad back.

'Did you need something?' Imogen asked, unsettled by Jemima's presence.

'Oh. Yeah, a Picnic.'

'Please?'

'Just give me the chocolate, Immy. Mum wouldn't let me have anything before bed.'

Imogen sighed and rolled her chair over to the wardrobe, where she plucked a chocolate bar from her hidden stockpile, handing it over. She knew better than to argue, or worse, to refuse her little sister's demands. If she didn't give Jemima what she wanted, when she wanted it, she could expect something she cared about to be destroyed: a painstakingly written essay, a friendship. Her brother.

Jemima tore the Picnic open and ate the whole thing within seconds. She threw the wrapper on the carpet and stood up, smiling to reveal chocolate-covered teeth.

'You'd better brush your teeth,' Imogen warned. 'Or Kat will know.'

'Don't worry.' Jemima grinned even more widely. 'It's our little secret.'

Secrets. They were like currency in the Braidwood house. Imogen was hoarding a stash of her own.

Kat believed that the secret she shared with her daughters was the only one lurking in their home, but that was just a tiny snippet of the full, twisted picture. She was clueless, her vision blinkered by love, or perhaps by the fear of looking directly at the truth in case it was too much for her to bear. Kat was a coward, Imogen had realised lately.

In her darker moments, she let her thoughts wander, let herself go back to that night, to that moment, the knife solid in her hand, Kat's helpless body stretched out beneath her, her mind racing, her stomach churning, her brother urging her on. She let herself imagine what would have happened if Jemima hadn't come in, if she had driven that knife down, through skin, muscle, sinew, organs. If Brad had lived. If she'd done what he wanted her to do. If she'd known exactly where that knife could enter Kat's body without killing her. If Brad had let Kat live. If they'd run away and Kat believed that Imogen had tried to kill her.

She knew that there was no point wondering *what if*, because there was no such thing. But still. Since looking into the truth of her parents, since reading articles that made her skin crawl, and poring over trial transcripts that left her feeling like her chest was shrinking, she'd had to ask herself the same questions that she knew Kat had spent Imogen's whole life trying to answer. Did that same darkness flow through her blood? Was violence imprinted on every cell in her body? Was cruelty twisted into her DNA?

But, unlike Kat, Imogen had found the answers. She knew that evil wasn't inherited. It wasn't passed down from generation to generation, like a medical disorder, or an attached earlobe. Nor was it learned.

Brad, she knew, wasn't bad. He'd been hurt and rejected and abused and traumatised, and he was looking for his mother's approval without questioning her motives. He was misguided. And maybe a little too desperate, a little too trusting. But he'd loved Imogen. He'd cared for her when she was sick – and yes, he had been the one to make her sick, but that didn't mean he cared any less. She *knew* that, no matter what anyone else said. They didn't know. They hadn't been there in his tiny ramshackle house up in the hills. They hadn't looked into his eyes, seen his kindness, his capacity for good. He wasn't bad; not by birth, and not by circumstance.

Neither was she. For a while there, she'd wondered. She'd thought maybe the evidence was obvious, that there was no way to escape the science of who she was. But she knew better now. She understood that the only thing that created evil was plain old bad luck. Nothing more, nothing less. Some people were just born bad, regardless of what their family tree said. Her biological parents certainly were. And yes, perhaps their upbringings brought the very worst out in them, maybe their environments enhanced their propensity for destruction. But it was in them, it was part of them, based not on their parents' genes but on random chance and their own bad decisions.

Imogen knew all about bad luck. Hers had been terrible. It wasn't enough that she'd been born to abusive, murderous parents. Fate had decided that she should be placed with a family who bore evil of their own.

Jemima didn't inherit her hatefulness. Kat and Dylan, for all their flaws, were decent enough parents. They were well meaning, even if they were seriously delusional about their precious baby girl. They loved Jemima, provided for all of her needs. They cared for her, and thought the best of her. Her environment hadn't shaped her into the monster she was. She was just born like that. Pure chance. An awful, cosmic screw-up that meant Imogen was in just as much danger in the home she'd been brought to for safety as she had been in Satan's Ranch.

Which was why, when Brad messaged her, when she learned the truth and was offered an escape, she'd jumped at the chance to get away. It had never been her blonde hair and pale skin that had made her feel out of place in her own home. It had been the fact that she couldn't bear to be related to the monster in the room next door. The promise of a new life, a new family . . . it was far too tempting to pass up. After all, what could possibly be worse than the one she'd been brought up in?

Her throat squeezed at the memory of how horribly things had gone wrong. She should have known that Jemima would find a way to ruin everything, to take her new family away from her. It certainly wasn't the first thing she'd destroyed. It probably wouldn't be the last.

Imogen was doing her part to make sure the destruction was kept at bay. She had learned over the years how to handle Jemima, how to slow the frequency of attacks. She knew that any money she earned – pocket money, babysitting, random errands for Dylan – had to be safely stored at a friend's house. She changed her laptop password once a week, using a complicated combination of letters and numbers. She slept with a tripwire across her bedroom door so that Jemima couldn't make good on her worst threats.

But her biggest lesson was to simply go along with the younger girl's plans, to let everyone believe that Jemima was innocent, no matter what she'd done. If she did that, Jemima would let her older sister get on with her life, relatively unscathed. After all, she needed her around. She needed a scapegoat, like in the case of Emerald.

That poor girl. The only mistake she'd made was being in Jemima's path at the wrong time. Imogen had made the same timing error, rounding the corner from the art building towards the maths block just as Jemima had launched herself at Emerald. She'd spotted the look of utter fear on the girl's face – a look she recognised, that she *felt* deep inside – as Jemima had attacked, knocking her to the ground before kneeing her in the stomach, the chest, the face, continuing her assault, even when it had become clear that her victim wasn't fighting back. Imogen had run over, pulled her sister off the older, much larger girl, and had been faced with a dishevelled but eerily calm Jemima.

'Why did you stop me? I wasn't done.'

'She's badly hurt, Jems! You have to stop. You can't explain this one away.'

'You're right,' Jemima had said, and Imogen's stomach had lurched with hope. Maybe, just maybe, now would be the moment when Kat and Dylan would see Jemima for who she truly was – for what she was capable of. All those other times she'd covered for her, they weren't this bad. Maybe now they'd stop her, find a way to put an end to the violence and scheming and relentless psychological torture.

But Jemima had smiled, that innocent, terrifying smile, and Imogen had known that there wouldn't be an end.

'But *you* can,' she had said.

'I'm not taking the blame for this,' Imogen had cried, knowing even as she protested that she didn't have a choice.

'Sure you are. Say she was bullying someone, or that she looked at you funny, or don't say anything at all. I don't care. It's either that or I'll get you kicked off the volleyball team.'

'You wouldn't.'

But she knew that Jemima would. She didn't know how, or when. But she'd find a way. She always found a way to make good on her threats.

'I'm going to be late for English,' Jemima had said brightly. 'And I need to clean up first. Good luck.'

When Jemima was out of sight, Imogen had only hesitated for a second, her heart plummeting, before speaking to Emerald calmly and clearly. With resignation.

'If you say that I did this, and if you swear that you won't breathe a word about what really happened here – and I mean to no one – I'll make sure she never bothers you again. OK?' It was a promise she couldn't keep, but she couldn't think of another way.

Emerald had stared at Imogen, her brow creased into a frown of confusion, blood smeared across her face.

'Look, we don't have much time. Do we have an understanding or not?'

Emerald had nodded, then burst into tears. Imogen had felt awful for her, but she'd had to get some blood onto her hands, so she swiped her palm across the girl's tender face, wincing as she groaned in pain, then rubbed it over her knuckles. She'd messed up her hair, pulled the top button of her shirt loose, and then a teacher had rounded the corner, taken one look and had drawn the conclusion that Imogen knew she would.

And, of course, with Kat believing, somewhere in the recesses of her mind, that Imogen's blood was tainted with the Sanders legacy of violence, she'd drawn her own conclusions, too.

If only Kat knew about her biological daughter's tendencies. What was hidden behind that sweet smile and those big brown eyes, so similar to her own. Kat was terrified that her youngest daughter was damaged, traumatised by what she'd had to do to save Imogen, to save them all. But Imogen knew the truth. Jemima hadn't liked it when Imogen was missing, when all of the attention was focused on getting her home. And she'd realised that, without Imogen around, no one would be there to take the fall when she needed an out.

Self-defence sounded plausible enough, but Imogen knew that Brad's murder was nothing to do with Jemima protecting her family, and everything to do with her wanting to get her own way. Imogen had seen the look of pure satisfaction on Jemima's face after she'd buried the knife in her brother's back.

She couldn't tell the police the truth about what happened in Brad's shed – Jemima had made that perfectly clear, whispering her blood-curdling threats in the flashing red and blue lights of the ambulance. She was at the twelve-year-old's mercy. For now.

Jemima thought she had her older sister right where she wanted her, and Imogen let her believe it. She had to; it was the only way she'd survive until she could escape again. The lawyer had emailed that afternoon, a coded message to an email address no one else knew about. The emancipation application was under way. And if, by some miracle, that was granted, she could safely access the money that Brad had left her, hidden in secret accounts, his savings from years at the mine and from selling his apartment. If all went to plan, Jemima wouldn't be able to get her hands on it. She wouldn't be able to touch Imogen. It wouldn't be easy. But she had to try. She had to get away from her brother's killer.

She just needed to make sure that Jemima didn't find out first. The fear kept her awake most nights, a constant panic that this, her only chance to break free and create her own life, would be taken from her, too. Because if Jemima discovered her secret, knew that she was going to be left exposed, without anyone to take the fall, Imogen didn't know what she would do. Didn't know what she was capable of. She feared for Kat and Dylan, too, but not enough to tell them the truth. They wouldn't believe her, anyway.

In the end, Kat hadn't been wrong to question her

daughter's nature, to wonder whether life had handed her a bad apple.

All this time, she'd just been looking in the wrong direction.

Chapter 67

SALLY

All's well that ends well, I suppose. OK, so it didn't exactly end *well*, as such, but there are some silver linings to this particular storm cloud, dark and heavy as it is.

At least he tried; my boy. He followed my instructions. He played his part in trying to protect my baby, to get her away from the world and all that could harm her. To balance the scales of justice. He did his best, as far as I can tell.

His only mistake was not preparing for the fact that Amy had been brainwashed by her adoptive family. It was always going to be a risk, although we couldn't plan for that, not really. We just had to hope. If all had gone as we'd have liked it to, Kat would be out of the way, we'd know for certain whose side Amy was on, and Brad would have his sister back.

We do know whose side Amy is on, so I suppose one out of three ain't bad. And my boy didn't get arrested. Death is an upgrade on prison, believe me.

I wish I had a garden here. I accept that I won't be able to lay my boy in the ground myself, like I did the others. But I'd at least plant him a rose if I could. The Prince, rich and crimson, a fitting tribute for the one who spilled his blood to try what I couldn't. My son is a hero, and I couldn't be more proud.

I'm sad that he died. Of *course* I'm sad. But we all die, one way or another. Besides, he suffered while he lived. He was ripped from his family, placed in home after home, abandoned and rejected, made to feel like he was damaged. He didn't live a good life. But he died a good death, and for that I am grateful. And despite my plan not going smoothly, at least he got the one thing he really wanted: he got to be with his sister.

It's a shame that the world won't know what he did, who he was. He'll die anonymous – his identity hidden to protect Amy, not him – a stranger despised by the world, misunderstood and judged for something no one will ever try to comprehend.

I understand, though. I know he wasn't just a 'mentally ill drifter' who 'took Imogen'. I know he was a caring brother who tried to save his sister from a life she was never supposed to live.

It's too bad she doesn't realise that.

The drugs should have made her more pliable. I put Brad in touch with an ex-cellmate of mine, a woman who made a good few years in here just fly by. She's an expert at what she does, so I have no doubt that she'd have cooked up the perfect recipe and supplied him with the right dosage. Amy should have been more compliant. Kathryn should be dead. I guess I didn't account for that bullheadedness that so many Sanders children exhibited over the years. I should have. I only had to look at Kimmy to know that it could come out at any moment. After she betrayed me, Kimberley disappeared. Vanished. We never managed to track her down, Brad and I. I wonder if Amy will achieve what we couldn't.

She's back with the Braidwoods, now. I suppose fifteen years of brainwashing can make a teenage girl conflicted. She was taken from me so young that she doesn't know any better. I'm trying not to hold that against her. She is my daughter, after all, whether she followed the plan or not.

I got a letter from her, right after it all happened. She was so apologetic. So sorry that Brad had been killed the way he had been. She was heartbroken by the death of her brother. I was glad she was upset; after all, she was partly to blame. Brad and I didn't spend the better part of a year researching, planning, writing carefully coded messages and putting everything in place for her just to get him killed.

But, I have to remind myself, he was happy when he died. He'd tried to protest when I first told him my plan. He'd said that he didn't want anyone to die, he just wanted to reunite with his sister. It had taken a while, but thankfully he had terrible self-esteem and extreme abandonment issues – wouldn't anyone, after being separated from a mother who doted on them? – so it was easy enough to make him believe that my love for him was based on his ability to do my bidding. Sure, I know that's not great mothering. But, honestly, I've done so much worse. And besides, if he didn't do it, it wouldn't get done.

I needed it to get done.

When I first heard the news of what happened that night, when I knew Brad hadn't succeeded, when I knew Amy had picked the side of safety and social convention, I'd been disappointed. But then I set my sights elsewhere. I turned my attention to the one person who might genuinely be able to follow through with my plan, who might take real delight in punishing the woman who stole my baby and rejected my boy.

There's no way to prove my theory, of course. Only time will tell if I'm right, but I like to think I have an eye for these things. The party line is that Amy stabbed Brad in self-defence, but I'm not convinced. She's a Sanders. She finally found her brother. Why would she kill him? She wasn't willing to kill the woman who had lied to her for her whole life – so why would she kill the man who had taken care of her when she was, as she believed, sick? And, more to the point, what was a twelve-year-old girl running into danger like that for? No one would think to suspect a little kid, which is exactly why it's so perfect.

I'd like to meet her, the adoptive sister. Seems like she's got guts. We might have more in common than anyone would expect.

And that's the thing that gives me hope. You see, Amy was taken from me. She was ripped from her brother, severed from her family, and placed in a white-bread, cookie-cutter, middle-class home with a coward for a mother and God only knows about her father. She didn't stand a chance of carrying on the Sanders name.

Except she has a sister.

A pseudo-sister, born to the most normal parents in the world, destined to become another Lululemon-clad yummy mummy with a mortgage and three kids and Friday night dinner parties. But there's something in her blood. Something different. A seed of darkness that's just looking for the right soil to take root in, to flourish.

I haven't quite worked out how I'm going to take her under my wing, train her up. I do know, though, that the only way to her is through Amy. She might not realise it, might not understand the part she'll have to play, but I will make sure that, despite being scattered, the Sanders name will continue to thrive.

Amy has it in her genes. But that young lady has it running through her veins. My own blood is pulsing more quickly as I think about the possibilities. As I think about the potential that my baby girl still has in her.

If I had a rose for Amy, there's only one variety I'd choose, now that I know who she really is, and what might be achieved through her. Blush pink, innocent-looking, a climber. Destined for bigger things, always reaching.

Amy is High Hopes.

Epilogue

JEMIMA

I like to think I'm smarter than most people – ah, what am I being modest for? I *am* smarter than most people – but honestly, even I couldn't have predicted this outcome.

It's perfect. Well... almost. But even though things are not quite as they should be, soon everything will be in its rightful place. I'm working on some details, and I have full confidence in my ability to make things go my way. After all, they always have done.

If I could, I'd go back a few months and remind myself of that fact. I'd tell myself to just chill out.

Because – and despite what assumptions you've made about me, I'm not too proud to admit this – in the very beginning, when Amy first went missing, I freaked out a little bit. I didn't panic or anything; I'm not pathetic.

I was, however, furious with her for doing something so completely selfish, so totally idiotic, and which so clearly went against my instructions to always be there for me. She knew that I needed her, that I couldn't get by without her. And I thought that she was too scared to ever try anything so... reckless. So I was surprised – no, that's too mild; I was floored – when she had the guts to leave.

At that point, I had a bit of an identity crisis. You might think that twelve is too young for such a thing, but I'm no average twelve-year-old, and ultimately, my identity is more worthy of a crisis than yours.

Besides, if you'd spent your whole life carefully constructing a home in which your older sister was too scared to disobey you, and then she just ran away without even consulting you, wouldn't you start questioning if you were who you had always believed yourself to be? Don't answer that; it was obviously rhetorical.

So there I was, trying to work out where I had gone wrong, and totally uncertain of my next steps. Amy was the one who always covered for me. She was the one who would take the blame when my rage got the better of me, whether that meant laughing after I'd lashed out at her so that Mum thought we were just play-fighting, or getting suspended when I'd smashed that stupid superior smirk off Emerald's face.

Maybe, in hindsight, that was the moment when I took things slightly too far. Perhaps threatening to get her kicked off the volleyball team – which, by the way, I could have, and would have, done – tipped her over the edge, got her to a place where she was beyond fear. I mean, of all the things that would do that to her, of course it was volleyball. Of course she's that boring.

So anyway, my patsy ran away. At first, I was hoping to find a suitable replacement. Kailah could have done, at a pinch, but she's really too weak and pathetic, even for me. Amy was just too convenient a scapegoat. I also knew that Mum and Dad would never let her go, and as much as I enjoyed the freedom of their inattention, I didn't want to be forgotten forever, overshadowed by my inferior sibling. That would have been unbearable.

But mixed in with the anger and uncertainty, there was a glimmer of something else, too: desire.

Because when I stopped worrying about the things that were out of my control – and no, I won't ever be OK with things being out of my control, but there are moments when I can accept the fact that they are – I realised something important. The sister of a missing girl, grieving, confused, scared and alone . . . she could get away with murder, surely?

Turns out the answer is yes. Yes, she could.

I'd like to take the credit for creating the circumstances that allowed it, but even I wouldn't believe me. It was a stroke of luck, a gift from the universe, if you were the sort of person to believe in total nonsense like that, that led me to that shed.

There were two significant moments that made it possible.

The first was when I'd overheard Mum and Dad talking to the policemen about Satan's Ranch. I'd never heard of it before, but when those words hit my ears it was like someone had plugged my fingers into an electrical socket. My hairs stood upright, my skin prickled, my blood fizzed. I knew it was important. I'd listened hard, trying to hear past the pounding of my pulse in my ears, and I'd learned that Imogen was adopted. That Imogen was Amy.

It made a lot of sense, really. We're nothing alike, us sisters. She looks completely different to the rest of us, although she is as dull as the others, which I guess is why I'd never suspected it before that day. It was no skin off my nose; didn't actually change a lot. If anything, it just gave me more to hold over her, if she ever came back.

What I had learned about Satan's Ranch, though . . . that had changed everything.

The thing I kept coming back to was how extremely unfair it all was. Why did Amy get such a cool, twisted, incredible mother, and I had to settle for Kathryn Braidwood? I'm pretty sure the most exciting genetic gift she passed down to me is the ability to curl my tongue. Thanks, Kat. Incredibly useful, that is.

I'd become obsessed with Sally Sanders. I'd read everything I could find, trying to work her out, desperate to know her secrets. I don't think she's a psychopath, like I am. She shows too much emotion, seems to really feel love. So I'm not sure what she is, but I do know that I want to sit down with her, pick her brain, drain her of every piece of wisdom she's gathered over the years. I reckon I'd be able to, if she were my mum. But in a twist of fate so unfair that it still makes my blood boil, rule-following, emotion-driven Amy got her.

Typical.

So anyway, that was the first thing. I'd found out everything there was to know about the Sanders family by the time the second thing had happened.

I'd been sound asleep when Mum had dragged me out of bed and into the car, and I knew then that there were only two reasons she'd have done something so uncharacteristically irresponsible: either she was cheating on Dad, or it was an emergency of some description. I'm not sure which I'd have preferred at the time. Obviously now I'm happy with the outcome, but holding an affair over Mum's head – and finding out that she isn't quite as mundane as I've always known she is – would have been a pretty good consolation prize, too.

I'd pretended to go back to sleep once we'd pulled out of the driveway because I figured it would be better for Mum to believe I was oblivious. And as usual, I was right.

I was also right to call Dad when I'd given Mum a bit of time to get herself into trouble (like there was any other way that was going to go). I bet if I hadn't, if the place hadn't been crawling with cops when we stepped out, Mum and Amy would have decided to leave Brad there, go home and pretend that she'd just returned from a few days of wandering aimlessly. No one would ever have seen what I did. No one would know.

I mean, no one really knows. Not properly, apart from Mum and Amy. But whether people have the full truth or not, it doesn't change the fact that they've seen my handiwork. They've witnessed my greatest achievement. And they didn't work out that I'd done it. Is there any better feeling than that?

Well, yes. There is. It's the moment of actually killing that tops any other sensation in the world. I know it. Even now, even without experiencing all that the world has to offer, I'm certain – it's a feeling deep in my bones – that I'll never feel anything like that again. At least, not till next time.

And there will be a next time.

I don't know when. And I don't know who. But I know that Sally will help me.

She hasn't replied yet, but I have a PO Box all set up, registered using a stolen ID (people leave their stuff on the beach all the time when they go for a swim) and Dylan's credit card (he never checks the statement). I don't get a lot of free time to check it, but occasionally when Amy is at therapy with Mum I'll pretend to wait in the library, and I'll run over to the Post Office, playing the role of the sweet young daughter of Karen Demetriou.

There hasn't had a therapy session for a while, but one's coming up in a week.

I have a good feeling about that next visit to my Post Office Box. I have a good feeling about Sally. I've never wanted to be taken under anyone's wing before, but I think that's just because no one has ever been worthy.

They say you can't choose your family, and as obvious as it is, that saying is right. My own family . . . I'd never choose them. The Braidwoods exist to feed me, shelter me, provide for me. Cover for me.

If I could choose my family, I know who I'd pick. Without a doubt, I'd be a Sanders. I'd choose Sally.

And I'm just one letter away from finding out if she feels the same way about me.

Acknowledgements

Firstly, I am so grateful to my hilarious, handsome, ever-supportive husband Brendan for his constant encouragement (even if he doesn't actually read my books). Thank you . . . and I'm sorry I left you for three weeks in winter to research in the Australian sunshine.

Dad, thank you for your patience (and the constant supply of delicious food) as I edited in your living room, and for driving me through narrow dusty roads as I asked creepy questions about whether you'd hear someone screaming from there. To Tam, John, Greg and Holly, thank you for helping me track down people to talk to, for taking me to Adelaide's best food spots, and for introducing me to Adelaide Writers' Week. To Mum, thank you for your love and support, and the lovely beach walks. Thank you to the Croft family for always spreading the word about my books, and for your generous hospitality even when I don't bring Brendan along.

Maree Moore, thank you for your help in finding the right person to speak to (and for driving me there). Jeanie Lucas, your knowledge has been absolutely invaluable, and I'm so grateful for your time and willingness to help me puzzle through the intricacies of adoption processes. Thanks also to Tanya Best for meeting with me and sharing your knowledge on the subject of foster care in Australia. Thank you to the SAPOL Media Team for answering my questions so quickly.

Any inaccuracies in this book are all mine, and nothing to do with the incredible insight you all offered me.

Writing can be a solitary pursuit, but I'm so thankful to my author friends for keeping me social and sane, especially Niki Mackay and Victoria Selman, my beloved Crime Girl Gang, who I couldn't do this without. Ladykillers, thank you for your collective advice, support and hilarity, which makes me smile on a daily basis. And to my friends who aren't writers, especially Jules, Rohin, Shannon & Luke, and Jess Dante: thank you for your support and constant encouragement. I feel like I have a team of personal cheerleaders, and I couldn't be more grateful for having you in my life.

Thank you to my incredible editor, Francesca Pathak, for seeing things I can't, for continuing to champion my writing, and for always having time for a Beyoncé gif. Huge thanks also to Lucy Frederick and the entire talented team at Orion. This book is so much better for all of your hard work and enthusiasm. Thank you to Ariella Feiner, my wonderful agent, who always has my back, and to Molly Jamieson for taking such good care of me! I always know that I am in such great hands with you both, and I'm so thankful for that.

And finally, to my readers, and all of the bloggers and reviewers who have supported me along the way – I am so grateful to each and every one of you. Thank you.

Credits

Elle Croft and Orion Fiction would like to thank everyone at Orion who worked on the publication of *Like Mother, Like Daughter* in the UK.

Editorial
Francesca Pathak
Lucy Frederick

Copy editor
Jade Craddock

Proof reader
Jane Howard

Audio
Paul Stark
Amber Bates

Contracts
Anne Goddard
Paul Bulos
Jake Alderson

Design
Debbie Holmes

Joanna Ridley
Nick May

Editorial Management
Charlie Panayiotou
Jane Hughes
Alice Davis

Finance
Jasdip Nandra
Afeera Ahmed
Elizabeth Beaumont
Sue Baker

Marketing
Lucy Cameron

Production
Hannah Cox

Publicity
Alainna Hadjigeorgiou

Sales

Jen Wilson

Esther Waters

Victoria Laws

Rachael Hum

Ellie Kyrke-Smith

Frances Doyle

Georgina Cutler

Operations

Jo Jacobs

Sharon Willis

Lisa Pryde

Lucy Brem

Don't miss Elle Croft's thrilling debut psychological suspense novel...

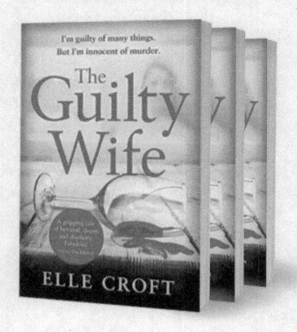

WIFE. MISTRESS. MURDERER.
If you were being framed for murder, how far would
you go to clear your name?

*'An accomplished debut with a relentless and intense pace
that kept me completely rapt and eager to find out answers.
I loved the final twist'*

K.L. Slater, international bestselling author of
Safe With Me, Blink* and *Liar

Or *The Other Sister*: a gripping, twisty novel of psychological suspense with an ending you won't see coming!

How far would you go to uncover your family's deadly secret?

'The Other Sister *is an original and thrilling page-turner with an end I didn't see coming'*

Victoria Selman, author of *Blood for Blood*